Praise for Liza Palmer

'Palm‹ ː is definitely one of my new favorite writers!' Meg Cabot

'Liza Palmer has a unique writing style' *Sun*

'A ː ɔtly sophisticated romance that outclasses most of the gɛ ːʼs other offerings . . . If it sounds chick litty, it is, but consi‹ it haute chick lit. Palmer's prose is sharp, her characters are and her narrative is laced with moments of graceful sentiment' *Publishers Weekly*

'In a word: genuine' *Herald Sun* (Australia)

'Paln likable characters and snappy dialogue make this novel stan from the crowd, and it's sure to attract fans of Jennifer W nd other authors who offer slightly imperfect heroines. Pa nages to infuse a message of self-acceptance that isn't nded or cloying. This quick-witted author is sure to develop a following' *Booklist*

'Sassy' *Star*

ing and poignant and heartbreakingly real, Liza Palmer's best friends, true love and just what size happily ever after wears is a winning conversation' Jennifer Weiner

Also by Liza Palmer

Conversations with the Fat Girl
Seeing Me Naked
A Field Guide to Burying Your Parents

More Like Her

Liza Palmer

First published in Great Britain in 2012 by Hodder & Stoughton
An Hachette UK company

1

A CIP catalogue record for this title is available from the British Library

B-format paperback ISBN 978 0 340 96217 6

Typeset in Sabon MT by Palimpsest Book Production Limited,
Falkirk, Stirlingshire

Printed and bound by Clays Ltd, St Ives plc

Hodder & Stoughton policy is to use papers that are natural, renewable and
recyclable products and made from wood grown in sustainable forests. The
logging and manufacturing processes are expected to conform to the
environmental regulations of the country of origin.

Hodder & Stoughton Ltd
338 Euston Road
London NW1 3BH

www.hodder.co.uk

For Don, Joe, Zoë and Bonnie

Acknowledgments

In past acknowledgments I've talked about holding my breath before falling asleep and challenging dogs. Rituals of gratitude and things that I'm thankful for. Writing these acknowledgments has been a practice in stopping and really seeing all that makes my life worth living. Makes me stop a minute – from the grind, from the fear, from whatever is worrisome – and see the good. Be thankful for the good. Cherish the good.

We've already clearly established that I love my mom beyond the telling of it. You have her to thank for strong moms in my books. Sitting across tables at various eating establishments as she inevitably asks, 'Noooow, what about the mom? How does she come into play here?'

I'm surrounded by love when it comes to family: Mom and Don, Alex and Joe and the girlies: Zoë and Bonnie.

To Carrie Feron and Teresa Woodward: this book is because you believed in it and me. I couldn't be more excited to join the HarperCollins family and look forward to telling stories with you in the future.

To Christy Fletcher and everyone at Fletcher and Company: as usual, you guys are . . . well, yes . . . I *will* quote Bette Midler here: 'You are the wind beneath my wings.' The wiiiiind beneath my wiiiiings.

To Isobel and everyone at Hodder: thank you for everything you do. Amazing editorial notes and deepening friendships continue to enrich this whole publishing process and me. Thank you . . .

To Araminta and her team at the LAW Agency – thank you.

To Marissa, Ben, Tim and Howie over at the United Talent Agency – thank you. And Taylor Swift says hi.

I would be a raving loon without Megan Crane, Jane Porter, Michelle Rowen and Kate Noble. That is not to say that I'm not still a raving loon, nor that you-all are not raving loons. We call it 'Book Brain,' others may call it . . . something less colorful.

To Kerri Wood-Einertson and family (Erik, Siena and Nora) – thank you for your everything. Friendships and Friday night movies cure all that ails me.

Thank you to Kim and family, Henry and Norm, Poet, Sharon, Larry and Ricca and Swanna MacNair.

One can't build little white picket fences to keep nightmares out.

ANNE SEXTON

Prologue

Operator #237: Nine-one-one, what is your emergency?

Caller: I'm a teacher at the Markham School, there's a man here with a gun. He – [shots fired in the background]

Operator #237: Ma'am? Ma'am?!

Caller: [unintelligible screaming] Oh my god. Oh my god . . . Is she dead? Oh my god . . . [unintelligible]

Operator #237: Ma'am, please—

Caller: You need to hurry . . . please. Please, god. Hurry! [unintelligible] Noooooo!!!! So much blood . . . there's so much blood!

Operator #237: Ma'am, I've sent them – the police. Now – tell me where you are in the school.

Caller: [unintelligible] The teachers' lounge. Upstairs. We're on the balc— *Just stay down! Stay down!*

Operator #237: Ma'am, please, I need you to calm down. Is the shooter still in the teachers' lounge with you?

Caller: *Calm down?* He's . . . oh my god [unintelligible] Is he dead, too?

Operator #237: Ma'am, I just want you to stay on the line with me until help gets there. How many people are in danger?

Caller: What? All of us! All of us are in danger! He's got a gun?! What do you think? *Stay down!* Oh my god! No!

Operator #237: Ma'am, is there any way you can block the door?

Caller: The doors are glass, there's no point. *No! Stay down! Frannie!?* No . . . oh my god. Oh my god . . . *Did he get her? Did he get her, too?* [unintelligible sobbing]

Operator #237: Ma'am, please. Please. Stay with me. Please. Ma'am?!

Dial tone—

Total time of call: 1:23:08

1

Lipstick and Palpable Fear

I'm not the girl men choose.

I'm the girl who's charming and funny and then drives home alone wondering what she did wrong. I'm the girl who meets someone halfway decent and then fills in the gaps in his character with my own imagination, only to be shocked when he's not the man I thought he was.

I'm the girl who hides who she really is for fear I'll fall short.

So, when Emma Dunham introduces herself to me as the new head of school, I automatically transform into the version of me who doesn't make people uncomfortable with her 'intensity,' who doesn't need any new friends and who loves being newly single and carefree. In short, the version of me that's as far away from the genuine article as is humanly possible.

'Headmistress Dunham,' she says, extending her hand. To my horror, Emma Dunham is cool, like take-me-back-to-the-fringes-of-my-seventh-grade-cafeteria cool.

'Frances Reid,' I say, extending my hand to hers. I won't slip and introduce myself as Frances *Peed*, the moniker given to me as I lurked on the fringes of my seventh-grade cafeteria.

'You're the speech therapist,' Emma says, her smile easy.

'Yes,' I say, allowing a small smile.

'It's a pleasure to finally meet you,' Emma says. I let the silence extend past what is socially acceptable. I take a sip of coffee from my mug – now stained with pink lipstick and palpable fear.

'You two have met, I see?' Jill asks. Her face has *that look,* the one that threatens to reveal all my closely held secrets. All it takes is a simple well-placed smirk from a close friend who knows exactly what you're feeling and thinks it hilarious when your carefully constructed disguise is threatened. I won't look at her.

'Jill Fleming, this is Emma Dunham. Jill is the other speech therapist here at Markham. Emma's the new head of school,' I say, averting my eyes from Jill's omniscient gaze.

'Sure. Jill and I met earlier. We're all certainly going to miss Mrs Kim,' Emma says, her white teeth momentarily blinding me.

'Kali is doing just fine, I'm sure. She finally got her dream job at Choate,' I say, rebelling slightly by not formalizing an old friend's name.

'Of course with Mrs Kim gone there will be an opening as the head of the speech therapy department,' Emma says with a smile.

'Will there?' Jill asks transparently.

Headmistress Dunham merely sniffs and tightens her mouth into a prim line.

Jill continues. 'Any thoughts you'd like to share with Ms Reid and I on your hiring process for that position would certainly be welcomed.'

'In time, Mrs Fleming. In time,' Emma says. I look past Emma's alabaster skin and beautifully tailored suit as teachers and administrators of Pasadena, California's Markham School for the Criminally Wealthy stream into the library for this year's back-to-school orientation.

'Lovely meeting you, headmistress,' I say, excusing myself from Emma Dunham and her lipstick that never smudges. She gives me what can only be described as a royal nod and quickly falls in with a pack of eager upper school faculty.

'I'm not looking at you or speaking to you for the next ten minutes,' I say to Jill as we find a seat in the back of the library. I straighten up and tell myself that my enviable posture is on par with any of Emma's myriad accomplishments.

'Why are you sitting like that? What's wrong with you? Do you have to fart?' Jill asks, her voice dipping with the word *fart*.

I immediately slouch, plummeting back to reality. Even my mimicked perfection looks like I have gas.

'No . . . no, I don't have to fart,' I say, clearing my throat.

Jill continues without missing a beat. 'She's thirty-four. Originally from Michigan, moved to San Francisco in college. Married to Jamie Dunham – she took his last name. He's a professor at UCLA. I'm humiliated I don't have a picture of him. A wedding picture would have been nice, but there just wasn't any time . . .' Jill shakes her head in frustration. 'No kids. This is her first time as headmistress.' I 'ignore' Jill – meaning I inventory every piece of information relayed to me yet act like I couldn't be bothered.

'Why does it not shock me that you're far more concerned about Emma's marital status than the head of department opening?' I ask.

'It really shouldn't,' Jill says, taking a bite of her bagel.

'Is this seat taken?' Debbie asks, motioning to the empty seat just next to mine. Debbie Manners: school librarian and self-proclaimed welcome wagon.

'Yeah, sorry,' I say, forcing myself to look apologetic. Debbie walks away in search of another empty seat, preferably next to some unsuspecting fool to whom she'll propose an innocent back-rub. A seemingly chaste request that'll ensure you never let her sit next to you again.

'What are you going to do when the orientation starts and that seat remains empty?' Jill asks. Debbie sits down next to the new lacrosse coach. He instinctively leans away from her as she whispers in his ear that he looks tense.

'Be relieved,' I say.

'I want to thank you all for being here this morning. On time and ready to work, just the kind of orientation I can get used to,' Emma Dunham says. Her delivery is relaxed and sincere. I adjust my sweater for the umpteenth time. I can't get comfortable.

Emma continues. 'I am Headmistress Dunham and am your new head of school. I am originally from Michigan and no, I'm not as young as you think I am.' The crowd laughs and nudges each other. She's funny! She's beautiful!

She's humble! She makes me feel like shit about myself! Where's the razor and warm bath?!

'Jeremy couldn't stop talking about you,' Jill whispers.

I sigh. Jeremy Hannon. Another setup. Just what every Labor Day barbecue needs: a forced blind date over corn on the cob and onion dip.

Jill continues. 'He kept mentioning that mix you made. Said he wanted a copy.'

'That was a classic rock CD I got at the grocery store for three ninety-nine.'

Jill lets out a dramatic, weary sigh.

I'm letting this golden opportunity slip through my ringless fingers! She's powerless in the face of my indifference! Her unborn godchildren are trapped in limbo and I won't burn a simple mix!

Several people give us looks of deep concern. We are not respecting the new head of school.

'I guess his cousin is also really into music. He says you remind him of her.' Jill's face is alight with excitement.

'I remind him of his cousin?'

'Yeah, isn't that great?'

'No, *Flowers in the Attic*. It is not.'

'That's a brother and a sister, and besides—'

'Shh!' It's Debbie Manners. The librarian. How predictable.

Jill continues. 'You never know how something is going to start between two people.' I shake her off, reminding her that we're in the middle of orientation. I don't want to hear about some guy's halfhearted feelings for me. Halfhearted feelings that depend on a mix of overplayed rock tunes of the 1970s. Not quite the modern-day *Romeo and Juliet* I imagined my love life would be.

Jill persists. 'I made sure Martin knew that I wasn't like other girls he was dating. He had to work.' I can't listen to Jill's 'I made him work' story again. I focus back on Emma just as she smiles, a perfect dimple punctuating her delight. I tried to have a dimple once. It consisted of me sitting on the couch with my finger in my cheek whenever I watched television as a kid. No dimple, just an Everest-size zit where my finger had been.

Jill continues. 'He tried to call on a Friday for a date th—'

'I know, but you said that you were reading a book and couldn't go,' I say, interrupting. 'I know. Except that you met up with him later at a bar, so . . .' My voice is getting louder.

'Shh!' Debbie again. This time I feel like I should thank her. I look away from Jill and try to focus back on Emma and her ongoing speech about expectations and proper behavior.

'I may have met up with him later, but . . . you know, I told him no first,' Jill says, almost to herself.

The truth is, I haven't been seriously interested in any of the legion of men Jill's tried to set me up with since Ryan dumped me. Of course, this doesn't explain why I have entranced none of them. It's much easier to rebuff willing gentlemen callers than to proclaim, '*I didn't like you anyway!*' after they say you remind them of their cousin. Although rejecting Jeremy had less to do with that than it did with his proclivity for saying *exspecially*.

I'm sure my behavior will have dire consequences. Flash forward: I'm living in some seaside cottage in my old age – possibly made entirely out of seashells. I'm clad in a faded housedress, large sunhat and Wellingtons. I make a meager living selling my seashell sculptures at the local farmer's market for tuppence a bag. The locals make up stories about me: I'm a witch, I'm crazy or talk to myself because I'm lonely or I murdered my lover when I was younger. Okay, fine. I made up that last one.

As Emma Dunham speaks, I scan the library hoping Jill will get the hint that our little conversation is over. I think she's moved on. Apparently someone's put on weight over the summer. I smile at a few familiar faces. Some stare a little too long. A knowing smile here. A rolled eye there. A nervously abbreviated glance from me to . . . *Ryan*. In the front of the library. His leg loosely crossed over his knee. Those white and red vintage Nike Dunks twitch as he struggles to focus. The worn zip-up hoodie and corduroy pants that are a bit too loose for the school's liking yet tolerated (for now) due to an impressive educational résumé that reads like a who's who of top American institutions. The early morning tangle of black hair and the coffee mug he bought in Dublin when we were there last year for his summer internship at Trinity College. I look away. Clear my throat. Sip my coffee. Try to regain my composure.

'You okay?' Jill asks, her voice soft. All evidence of the pep talk slash Spanish Inquisition is gone.

'Yeah. *Yeah*,' I say.

'He's been looking at you, too.'

'I have no response to that.'

'Maybe things are rocky with Jessica.'

'Things are never rocky with girls like Jessica.'

'Frannie—'

'Don't. Just don't.'

Jill is quiet.

I continue. 'Exspecially since it won't do either of us any good.'

'God, that was driving me crazy. I kept trying to say it correctly and he just never picked up on it.'

'Of-*ten*-times.'

'It's like nails on a chalkboard.'

'Shhh!' Debbie again.

Jill and I smile our apologies. Emma is still talking. I focus in just as I see Ryan glance back at us. I act like I don't notice. He swipes his bangs out of his eyes.

Going to be a great year.

2

The Lemon Verbena Temptress

As I wait for my apartment building's security gate to open, I realize I'm happy to be home. I breathe deep as the gate creaks along the ground and I finally pull down the narrow driveway of my apartment building. While I may be happy to be home, I'm happier to be back at work after a long, hot summer of nothing to do but plan and wait. I grab my canvas bag bursting with orientation handouts, curriculum pamphlets and binders filled with organizational fantasies of what's supposed to happen in the upcoming school year and slam the car door. I have to hurry; the new parent orientation is in less than an hour. There's just enough time to take a quick shower and chow down on some shredded wheat and fresh peaches. I've survived on shredded wheat and peaches, Greek yogurt and chocolate bars ever since Ryan left three months ago. I would probably be gaining weight if I weren't so damn regular.

I walk back down the driveway and up the outside staircase to the front door of my apartment. I fight with the front door lock for what seems like hours until it finally clicks over. I kick it open and step inside.

'I thought you'd be at dinner with Jill.'

My heart stops. I suck in my breath. There's someone in my house. Someone who knows my schedule and friends . . . *wait*.

Ryan.

'What are you doing here?' I take a deep breath and walk into the kitchen, dropping my canvas bag; its contents dump out on the floor. I'm needed in the kitchen. Immediately. It's imperative that I slit my own throat. Not to be dramatic or anything.

Ryan and I met at a friend's monthly pub quiz in San Francisco. And by 'met,' I mean we were on the same team. Then I proceeded to build an entire life around him because he knew where Erno Rubik was from (Hungary). You know . . . *met*. Month after month, pub quiz after pub quiz, I joked, answered the tough questions correctly, held trophies aloft, only to watch Ryan come and go with different women who, let's just say, *didn't* know where Erno Rubik was from. My only consolation was he never introduced them as his girlfriend. This was all the moral wiggle room I needed.

He'd mention a song he liked and I'd bring him a mix the very next month with that song as a jumping-off point. It was only coincidence, surely, that the rest of the songs had to do with unrequited love, love being right under your nose, taking a chance on true love, etc. . . . In my mind, this was foreplay. We were getting to know each other. So, when Ryan finally leaned across and kissed me late one night, I thought my prince had finally come. Someone had finally understood my subtle yet cunning signs. Someone had finally seen me as a woman and not as a friend. At long last, the fairy tale was mine.

For once, 'happily ever after' actually applied to me. When Ryan moved down to Pasadena for the position at Markham, I followed. I found temporary jobs in various school districts until a position opened up at Markham. I was perfectly comfortable leaving everything for him. Eerily comfortable.

'I had to pick up a couple of things. That I – you know – left behind.' Sadly, I don't think he's referring to me.

Ryan is holding a banker's box filled with various items. I'm mortified when I see that he's found the old Pavement T-shirt of his that I've been sleeping in. A shirt that's now being boxed up and taken to an apartment he shares with Jessica. I will myself not to dive into that box and pull that shirt out like it was my firstborn. What else is in that box? My future? My self-worth? The two years I wasted waiting for Ryan to ask me to marry him? Nope. There's just a stack of Russian novels (in the original Russian), a couple of CDs (making sure to leave behind every mix I'd ever made him) and that sad little T-shirt (of a band I never admitted to despising). Three months and this is what he came back for? A stack of items I want only because they remind me of him. He was here. We were a couple. See?

What will I point to now to show people I was once loved?

'I didn't see you at orientation,' I lie. My shoulders creep up higher. Higher still. I don't know how to be in my own apartment. Our apartment. *My* apartment. As I scan the barren living room, I regret not sprucing up the place since Ryan left. I wish I'd brought in color and light as proof of a Patti LaBelle-sized new attitude. Alas, the apartment looks just as half-lived-in as the day Ryan left.

'I was up near the front.'

'Oh.'

'The new head of school seems cool.'

'Headmistress Dunham? Yeah, I guess.' Salt, meet wound.

We stand in silence. A silence that redefines the parameters of awkward.

My toilet flushes.

Terror. A brief moment of confusion, then the stomach-dropping realization – someone else is here. I look from the phantom-flushing toilet to Ryan, who looks away. My entire body tightens – jaw clenches, arms tightly cross, fists ball up – and I ready myself. She's washing her hands. Yes, please. Take your time being hygienic; my fancy lemon verbena hand soap was definitely purchased with you in mind, petal. The bathroom door creaks open.

Jesssssica.

'I was wondering who you were talking to out here,' Jessica says, smiling.

She's not alarmed. She's not embarrassed. She's also not even that cute. I'll focus on the latter rather than the other two.

'It's just Frannie,' Ryan says, shrugging.

'Just Frannie? Is that what we're calling her now?' Jessica says, tittering and folding into Ryan.

Wow. Where to begin.

'Jessica Trapper, this is Frannie Reid,' Ryan says, shifting the box around and gesturing from Jessica to me.

'I've heard so much about you,' she says, extending her hand.

'Aren't you the woman Ryan was cheating on me with?' I ask, not taking her extended hand.

'*Frannie,*' Ryan says.

'Or was that someone else?' I ask, my voice now light as a feather. I look from Jessica to Ryan.

'No, no . . . that was me,' Jessica says, her hand dropping to her side.

'So, I imagine you would have heard a lot about me,' I say, a smile cracking its way across my face.

'Not as much as you'd think,' Jessica says, almost under her breath.

'Frannie, please,' Ryan says.

'No, we're fine now. It's all good. Jessica, right? Hey, Frannie Reid. Just Frannie,' I say, smiling and extending my hand to her.

'Hi,' she says hesitantly, her hand reaching out to me once more.

'Go fuck yourself, Jessica,' I say, dropping my hand again.

'All right, I think we should probably head out then,' Ryan says, taking Jessica's extended hand in his.

I hate that I'm blaming the other woman. Jessica certainly isn't making things better with her 'Just Frannie' bullshit and lemon-verbena-wafting newly washed hands, but it's not her fault Ryan stopped loving me. It's Ryan I should be telling off. But it's far easier, and less excruciating, to blame Jessssica. I'm not ready to blame Ryan. Hell, I'm not even ready to believe that it's over.

Two years. Ryan and I were together two years. We were the couple that the students were embarrassed to look at. Other staffers never mentioned one of us without the other. The older ladies in the front office, whom we affectionately refer to as the Coven of Front-Office Hags, ribbed him about his muss of black hair needing a cut before the wedding. They rolled their eyes and mumbled something about 'kids today' each time Ryan confessed he hadn't yet proposed. We went on double dates with Jill and her husband, Martin. We played dominoes and brought bottles of wine.

He was my plus-one.

Now I recognize I was the girl he bided his time with. The girl *before* the girl. His light blue eyes travel over me. Does he want to apologize? For moving out. For cheating. For breaking it off. For not loving me. He flips his black muss of hair out of his eyes and gives Jessica an almost imperceptible signal to evacuate the premises as quickly as possible.

'So, I'll see you tonight then . . . *Ryan*?' I ask.

Ryan adjusts his hold on the box again, letting Jessica's hand fall away. 'Jessica, can you give us a minute?' he says. She steps out of the apartment without another word, leaving Ryan and me alone. His lips are tight. Compressed. I won't inhale him as he passes. I won't close my eyes and remember what it was like to fall asleep to his quiet snoring. I raise my eyebrows and look out the open door. I think I'm smiling. I hope I'm smiling.

He says nothing. I can't help myself. Even as I take a breath for the next sentence I know I'm on the cusp of a moment I'm going to be cringingly replaying and regretting in my mind for years. Nonetheless . . .

'Why . . . why'd you bring her here? To our apartment?'

Ryan turns around. 'This is *your* apartment now and Jessica is *my* girlfriend, so—'

'Ryan, it's me. It's Frannie. Why are you talking to me like I'm some dude in Starbucks asking you to watch his shit? Come on. Think this through – maybe bringing the new girl here wasn't such a good idea,' I say, hating that my hand is reaching out for him.

'This is how it always was with you. You overthink shit, Frannie. I didn't think you'd be here. Jessica and I are together so she came with me to pick up the last of my stuff. Not everything is as complicated as you make it out to be.' My hand falls to my side. Ryan's voice isn't raised. It's worse. It's indifferent.

'No, you're right, it clearly takes two people to carry that tiny box that weighs nine ounces,' I say, motioning to the offending, flimsy container that somehow is substantial enough to carry any hope I had that Ryan would return to me – and the life we made together – out the door with him.

Ryan clears his throat and switches the box to the other side.

'Probably not a good idea to bring the girl you cheated with into your ex-girlfriend's home though, right?' The *ex* chokes in my throat.

'So intense. Always. So. Intense.' Ryan digs into his pocket and pulls out our apartment key. It's already off his key ring. He was prepared. As he presses the key into my hand, I can't stop replaying that line from *When Harry Met Sally: You're saying Mr Zero knew you were getting a divorce a week before you did*. I deflate. The key knew. The key knew it was over. We were over. I curl my fingers around it as Ryan shakes his head, mumbling something about me making things soooo difficult. He enunciates the word *difficult* with particular disdain as he turns for the door. I feel like screaming. But as he closes the door behind him what I feel most is . . . alone. Left behind. And now I just feel like crying.

I sit on the arm of the sofa. I wish I could say I collapse. I don't. I just sit. The blur of the last three months. Jill pairing me up with any man who'll take my mind off Ryan has cemented my worst fears: not only did I have someone great, but I might have been lucky to have him at all.

I remember sitting in a movie theater once. And Ryan was talking about something. Really animated. Using his hands. Passing me caramel corn in the midst of his impassioned speech. Shoving kernels in his mouth as he spoke. And I thought, holy shit. You're the one. This is it. You're perfect for me and this is it. I've found you and here you are in the flesh: my happily ever after.

I was wrong.

'Please don't tell me that you actually said, "It's all good."' Jill says. The door between our joint offices is open and we're bustling around getting ready for the parental onslaught. My dark hair is still a little damp from the shower. I took far too long sulking and eating stale shredded wheat to properly dry it. Jill has on one of her usual ensembles: a Kelly green tailored sheath. Her mane of red hair, the very embodiment of her, is caught at the nape of her neck, loosely tied with a coordinating grosgrain ribbon.

'Yep, right before I told her to go fuck herself. It was quite a lively conversation,' I say.

'What did she look like?'

'She's *that* girl. Not too cute, not too ugly. Not too fat, not too thin. She looks like everyone and no one at the same time.'

'I'm going to need something a bit more specific if I'm going to feel better about this entire situation.'

'She's utterly forgettable.'

'And yet . . .'

'Yes. Exactly. And in time I will embrace the point you're trying to make.'

'And what point is that?'

I answer in the same robotic voice that inhabits every jilted lover, 'That Ryan doesn't want a shiny penny. He wants a woman who is utterly forgettable and beige, ensuring that *he* can be "the beloved" in the relationship. I listen to the same Alanis Morissette songs that you do, dearest.' Or maybe he doesn't want someone who makes everything sooo difficult, who overthinks everything. You know, someone who is too intense. I'm just spitballing here.

'So, we're on the same page.'

'Alas, yelling along to *Jagged Little Pill* in its entirety is not quite the same thing as really digesting its message, now, is it?'

'It's a start.' Jill runs her hand down the sleeve of my

vintage sweater. She presses out a concerned smile and squeezes my hand.

'He didn't deserve you, sweetie.' Jill's voice is achingly soft and affectionate.

I nod and take a deep breath. Jill gives me a reassuring grin and a quick pat on the ass and flits back over to her desk.

It's jarring how quickly this sensation returns. The fantasy of living happily ever after was always tempered by my constant second-guessing that I would ever be, in any way, involved. Sure, happy couples exist. People walk down aisles and babies are born. Now, where do I come in again?

'Why did he even still have his key?' Jill asks as she arranges a tray of cookies, fanning them out decoratively.

'I refuse to answer that on the grounds that it makes me look desperate.'

We are quiet.

Jill finally speaks. 'You know my theory.' I look up from the stack of colorful mission statements and curricula vitae we've prepared.

She quickly adds, 'Don't kill me, but you know my theory.'

'Yes, I am aware of your theory. All of your theories, really,' I say, looking out into the quickly filling hallways of the Markham School. Families milling around, zigzagging into classroom after classroom. Polo shirts with collars turned up. Strands of real pearls. Sweaters folded just so and tied loosely over shoulders. The Markham School caters to Pasadena's elite. Our offices are located in the wing where the school psychologists, speech therapists, and counselors are housed: your one-stop mental health emporium. Parents are reluctant to look our way – like we're the red-light district of the Markham School. They peek and glance furtively at our open office doors. They're curious, but none of them can let on that they're interested in what we're selling. They think we're offering something only parents of a failed child need. And they certainly wouldn't be interested in anything like that. (Of course, that's not what it is.) That's what the handouts and cookies are for: *to lure them in.*

'Two years—'

'Jill, seriously. Not now.'

'Two years is too long to date someone. After one year, you have the marriage conversation and if he balks, dumped.'

'Which is exactly what happened,' I say.

'No, I mean—'

I cut in. 'I got dumped – wait, I got cheated on *then* dumped. And it's not because we dated for two years or didn't have the marriage conversation after the proper amount of time. I got dumped because he didn't love me. Simple, really,' I say, sitting down behind my desk. I can feel my face reddening. I can feel my anger growing. I won't start crying. I won't scream '*Why didn't he love me?!*' at the top of my lungs. I won't. I can't. Because even though Jill knows me better than anyone, I still can't show her the ugly truth of how not fine I am with this whole situation. I'm not bravely moving on. I'm not indifferent to Jeremy Hannon, the Labor Day Cousin-Loving

Suitor, and/or the battalions of uninterested douchebags who preceded him. I'm miserable and secretly naming the egion of cats I'll most certainly own by the end of the year.

'Did you copy that mix Jeremy was asking about?'

I can't help but laugh.

'I think I've made enough mixes for three lifetimes,' I say, standing up and pacing around the office. I can't sit still. I want to look professional. I want not to think about Ryan, Jessica and the apartment key that now sits on my kitchen counter like a time bomb. I look out into the hallway just in time to see Emma Dunham coming our way. Wow, that's exactly what I didn't want. I plaster a smile across my face as she approaches with a guy I peg as some moneyed donor I'll soon have to prostrate myself in front of for the good of the Markham School.

'Ms Reid, this is my husband, Jamie. Jamie, this is Frances Reid, one of Markham's two speech therapists,' Emma says. Husband? I shake hands with Jamie. His long, achingly thin fingers curl around my extended hand with an icy detachment. Jamie's beakish nose and delicate features might be considered beautiful in a sickly, Victorian poet way, but since he's not spouting esoteric verses right now it just doesn't pack the same punch.

'Nice to meet you,' I say.

'And you,' he says.

'Nice to meet you,' I say. Again.

Jamie looks pointedly at Emma, as one does when someone – a jilted speech therapist perchance – has just farted in public and a quick getaway is now past due.

'So, what is it that you do, Jamie?' I ask.

'I'm a professor at UCLA,' Jamie says.

'Go Bruins!' I say, my hand raised in a victorious fist.

Silence.

I continue. 'What is it that you teach?'

'Creative writing. The Art of the Short Story,' Jamie says.

'That sounds great,' I say, my voice overly perky.

'He's also working on a novel,' Emma adds, lacing her arm through his.

'That sounds like quite a schedule,' I say.

'I teach in UCLA's extension program,' Jamie says.

'Oh, okay,' I say.

'Online,' Jamie adds.

'Cool,' I say. What . . . what exactly is happening here?

Silence.

'It's so difficult to break into teaching at UCLA. Everyone's amazed Jamie was able to secure a position in the extension program. But it's a foot in a very prestigious door,' Emma says. His entire being has shifted from languid to tight throughout Emma's pitch.

Silence.

'UCLA has a great campus,' I say.

Jamie sighs.

'Oh, right. You're online. Great website then. User-friendly,' I say, my eyes darting, my fingers making some weird mouse-clicking motion.

I clear my throat. Has time stopped? Is it . . . is it cold in here?

Quiet. For a while. A looooong while. People mill in

the hallways. Parents who haven't seen each other all summer greet each other loudly. Teachers welcome students into their classrooms. All while our little trio drowns in discomfort.

'Jamie is as brilliant as they come. He's going to be the next Norman Mailer!' Emma says. If there were a conversational penalty-flag system similar to that of the National Football League, Emma would certainly have earned one for that. Emma Dunhamdunhamdunham, the ref's voice echoes. Personal foul for a late hit proclaiming Jamie Dunham the next Norman Mailermailermailer. Automatic first down!

Silence.

'Have you given the head of department position any thought, Ms Reid?' Emma asks.

I start to say, 'Absolutely, it would be such a—' Jamie elaborately clears his throat.

'Oh, right. *Right,*' Emma says, nervously looking from Jamie to me. He sighs. She continues. 'We'll talk about it later, Ms Reid.'

'There's a water fountain,' I say, pointing just behind Jamie. 'You know . . . for your throat?'

'What was your name again?' Jamie asks.

'Frances Reid.'

'Well, Frances Reid—'

Emma interrupts. 'We're having a mixer . . .' Jamie's eyes are fixed on me. Emma is caressing Jamie's back. 'It's for department heads and in your case prospective department heads. We'd love it if you and Mrs Fleming would attend. Since both of you are up for the position, it might be nice for the board of directors to meet their candidates in a more relaxed setting. All of the details are in your box.' The word *relaxed* echoes through the hallways. Jamie tightens his jaw as his gaze slinks over to Emma. Narrowed. Targeted.

'Sure . . . sure,' I say, noting that Jamie looked away first. I have won our unofficial staring contest.

Jill ambles out of our office. She's already in midsentence as she approaches. 'What you need to do is just hate-fuck that Jeremy Hannon guy and th—'

Aaaaand I believe introductions are in order: Online Extension Professor Jamie – or as Emma likes to call him, the next Norman Mailer – Emma, children and parents of the Markham School, meet the word *hate-fuck*. Hate-fuck? This is everybody.

'Jill Fleming, this is Jamie Dunham. Headmistress Dunham's husband,' I say.

They shake hands.

'Pleasure,' Jill says. Jamie nods. Emma's face is compressed tight. She looks around at the milling parents.

'Great turnout,' I add, following her sight line.

'Yes, it is,' Emma says.

Jill says, 'Mrs Dunham, I'm—'

'I'm sure we can talk about policies and appropriate behavior at a more fitting time, Mrs Fleming,' Emma says, her smile tight.

'I'll look forward to it,' Jill says.

'Ms Reid will give you specifics regarding the head of

department mixer, where my hope is that you will behave in a far more professional manner,' Emma says, looking from Jill to me.

'Yes, headmistress,' Jill says, her head bowed.

'Ms Reid? I believe someone wants to say hello,' Emma says, motioning to an approaching rail of a ten-year-old. I know we're not supposed to have favorite students. I know this. But . . .

'Harry!' I say. Harry Sprague trundles up to me as quickly as an awkward adolescent can while still achieving prime bored detachment. His blond hair intentionally hangs just low enough to cover his blue eyes completely.

'Ms Reid!' Harry says, patting my arm.

'Hey, sweetie! So good to see you,' I say, making a point of swiping his bangs out of his eyes.

'We're thinking about forcing him to get a haircut,' Mr Sprague says, mussing the boy's hair. Harry is not amused. Harry probably believes this more fashionable hairstyle will finally allow him to make his escape from the ranks of fellow nerds and geeks. I wish I could tell him that no hairstyle in the world can do that. Believe me, I've tried. Or should I say Frances *Peed* tried. I'd like to say that my unshakable moniker was based on some misunderstanding. A wet bench. A light rain. But no. Combine a school field trip to Magic Mountain, a terrified twelve-year-old and a roller coaster she never should have been on in the first place and you've got yourself Frannie Peed.

Mr Sprague extends his hand and gives me a powerful shake. Rolled-up shirtsleeves reveal a Patek Philippe wristwatch. Worn in. Mr Sprague's everyday wristwatch. His everyday million-dollar wristwatch.

'So good to see you, Mr Sprague,' I say, smiling. I've known the Spragues for only a short time, but I feel as though I've known them my entire life.

'We've so missed you,' Mrs Sprague says, lunging into me for a refined hug. Her perfume wafts around me like an angelic aura.

'So good to see you,' I say, breaking from our hug. Blond, headbanded hair; a butter-yellow cable-knit sweater; and a hedge fund in the billions define the family. But they love their son and will do anything for him. That trumps a popped collar every time.

I wind through introductions, lobbing Professor Jamie Dunham only a slightly rolled eye at the forced title. Jill coquettishly introduces herself. Apparently we're off the docks and back at a debutante ball. Emma and Jamie excuse themselves as Jill slinks back into our office, which is filling fast with prospective students.

I fall into easy conversation with the Spragues. As usual, the subject is Harry. Apparently his summer was chockablock with Space Camp and Comic-Con, and the Spragues constantly assure me that he hasn't forgotten everything I taught him last year.

'I'll be the judge of that,' I say, smiling. Smiling. It's hard to be sad when you're talking about kids like Harry Sprague. I take one final glance at Emma as she and Jamie walk away. Emma clasps her hands behind her back, her fingers violently gripping each other, her shoulders high and tense. Jamie whispers in her ear. Emma's head dips, chin to her chest, her pace slowing. She nods briskly. Again and again. Jamie's hand tightens around her upper arm as she flinches slightly and hurries beside him. Jesus, it's just the word *hate-fuck,* Jamie.

Certainly Norman Mailer would have approved.

3

All Balls

Later that night, I take out my contact lenses, put my glasses on, grab my dental night guard and switch off the bathroom light. The first week after Ryan left, I blamed the dental night guard and the glasses for his cheating and our subsequent breakup. I think of Harry Sprague and his hopeful non-nerd hairstyle.

We (your tired, your poor, your huddled misfits yearning to breathe free) all fervently hope that we'll be loved and cherished someday. But that far-off dream hangs in the balance as we struggle to figure out what we can change about ourselves to make it happen. Different hairstyle? Contact lenses instead of glasses? Dental night guards tossed away? I'm sure my mom would – and has – sermonized that it's not about me at all. *Those* people aren't worth my time, anyway, she'd say, teacup in hand. If *they* can't love me for who I am, then I don't want *them,* she'd add as she offered a piece of pie and an unendingly available shoulder to cry on. Yet, I'm haunted by this ever-present feeling that it's not about the hairstyle, glasses, body image, or overpriced makeup that promises to 'look natural' at all. As I get older, I'm afraid it must be me, *all of me,* that is so chronically repellent.

I tuck into my bed; the kitchen light streams down the hallway. It makes me feel like someone else is moving around this little apartment. Ryan's not here in bed with me, but maybe he's in the living room watching television. He'll come to bed soon. I toss and turn, tucking the pillow into the crook of my arm. I've gone from loving bedtime to dreading it. It used to be a time when, no matter what went on during the day, Ryan and I could check in with each other. The world stopped. The grind faded away. It was just us, tucked tightly under blankets and duvets. We whispered, giggled and loved. Now I have Jeremy. A guy who wants me to make him a copy of a classic rock mix I bought at the grocery store for $3.99 as a joke. I hit the pillow again, tucking and tucking it. I can't get comfortable. It's ten P.M. and I'm in bed. Why does it surprise me that I'm not tired?

As my mind races through that last run-in with Ryan and the nine-ounce box that took two people to carry, I understand – on some level – that I'm relying on selective memory when it comes to my relationship with him. The pictures on our walls, the screen savers on our computers, the stories we told were all from the first year we were together. It was as if the memory of those times kept us going. Then the ennui set in like a low fog.

Then came the deals. When we get married, I won't feel like this. When we get married, something magical will happen and we'll fall in love all over again. If he would just propose, everything would be fine. We'd be back on track. A marriage proposal means Ryan chose me. Officially. I could write off Frannie Reid – or Frannie

Peed – forever. I'd finally be someone else. Mr and Mrs Ryan Ferrell. I'd be Frannie Ferrell. And Frannie Ferrell was the girl who was chosen. Frannie Ferrell was loved. Frannie Ferrell is now just another alliterative pipe dream.

It's fine. I'm fine.

As I feel myself drifting toward sleep, I'm proud of myself. Despite a few bumps in the road, I'm taking this whole thing remarkably well. It doesn't bother me. It really doesn't. Ryan did us a favor. Ryan did me a favor. And with Jill and her revolving door of available men, I'll be dating in no time flat. Yeah. He did me a favor.

The silence.

The kitchen light streaming down the hallway.

My breathing quickens. I can't catch my breath.

This pillow won't behave.

Yeah . . . *really* proud.

I roll over onto my back and stare up into the darkness. Ghost dots flicker and fade in front of me. I've never been more wide awake. Proud. *Proud.* Next, I'm going to be telling myself that these aren't the droids I'm looking for. More darkness. More silence. *You gotta know when to hold 'em, know when to fold 'em.* Great. Now I've got Kenny Rogers stuck in my head. Alone. Cold. Dumped. And humming Kenny Rogers.

I whip my covers off and walk over to my computer. I scroll through old e-mails, finding the one from Jill that I'm looking for.

Frannie: Okay, so just in case – here's all of Jeremy Hannon's information. I can see it now: an outdoor wedding with dragonflies and strings of lights. Maybe that one song can be the first song you dance to? The one he was talking about on that mix? Talk soon . . .

Writing down Jeremy's e-mail and cell number, I have to laugh. I seriously doubt my wedding song is going to be by Lynyrd Skynyrd, Jill.

To e-mail or to call, that is the question. It's a bit late to call. And an e-mail – I don't know. It seems a bit formal. I'll split the difference. I'll text. It's what all the crazy kids are doing these days, right? As I take my iPhone off the nightstand, unplugging it from its charger, I am fully aware that I am taking the chicken's way out. Texting is for booty calls and . . . *wait*. Am I making a booty call right now? No. Seriously, no. I'm making a late-night request for . . . I believe I'm making a booty call with no booty. I just want someone to talk to. Someone who'll keep me from singing Kenny Rogers. Ugh, that's even worse.

I hold my iPhone in my hand and curl my legs underneath me. Summer is waning and a slight chill has found its way into my apartment.

I type in Jeremy's phone number and then begin the tedious process of crafting the perfect text. This could take days. It has to be one part breezy, one part sexy and once again, as far from the real me as is humanly possible. I finally come up with:

Hey there! Frannie here from the BBQ at Jill and Martin's . . . Jill had mentioned you wanted a copy of that mix I brought?

Then what? Do I ask him what his mailing address is? It's a wonder I've gotten one date *ever*. My fingers hover over the keypad. Minutes pass.

Let me know!

Before I can think better of it I hit send. And then I wait. I start to tidy up a bit. Clothes in the hamper. Do a couple of dishes, mostly bowls due to my obsession with shredded wheat. I walk through my apartment absently dusting shelves lined with framed family photos: cross-country road trips in wood-paneled station wagons, Christmas mornings with pink bicycles (I held on to a belief in Santa Claus way past what is customary). School plays where my role as 'Chorus member' won parental rave reviews, splashing around in swimming pools with zinc oxide spread generously on my nose. I study the photos closely as I try to ignore the silence of my dormant iPhone. I see my childhood through my parents' eyes. To them, I was a happy baby, a rambunctious child and a scholarly adolescent. My phases, not unlike the moon's, melted and dissolved seamlessly into one another.

The childhood I remember, strangely not depicted in these framed photographs, is a bit bumpier. As my coltish enthusiasm became an annoyance to teachers, my need for their approval reached epic proportions. I began swallowing that enthusiasm – now defined as 'hyperactivity' or, in Ryan's words, 'intensity' – and replaced it with a zeal for schoolwork akin to an obsessive-compulsive's need to open and shut a door three times before exiting. Not surprisingly, the other kids didn't applaud my new role as teacher's pet. The adolescent art of apathy eluded me. I was labeled an oddity and given a nickname that haunts me to this day: the Notorious Frannie Peed. I've done everything I can to leave Frannie Peed in the past, but she's a worthy opponent. Shaking her is the gauntlet I have to run daily: instinctual nerdisms I don't say and the second-by-second reminder to myself to 'act cool.'

I run the dust cloth over the empty place where a framed photo of Ryan and me in happier times used to be. It was the one of us with my mom and dad that time we all hiked into Muir Woods in Marin County, which was right by my parents' house. He was laughing with my Dad, shoulder to shoulder. I was telling him to look at the camera while Mom motioned for the stranger taking the picture to wait. We needed to collect ourselves. It was my favorite picture ever . . . and the last one to be taken down after Ryan left. As I wipe down the rest of the kitchen counter, I hear the ting-ting of my iPhone in the other room. A text. I run down the hall. It's from Jeremy.

Hey, who is this?

I calmly close out of the texting screen – the adorable green and white text bubbles making a mockery of me – and then violently hurl the phone across the room. It careens against the red wingback chair in the corner and bounces off onto the hardwood floor. I take a long deep breath and walk into the bathroom in search of the bottle of Excedrin PM. I dump two little blue pills into my hand.

My mind is on hold. Are we going to spiral into depression or anger? There's a tiny possibility that I could just laugh it off and look forward to telling Jill that I was right. I walk to where I threw the iPhone and am relieved to find that it still works. It lives to send embarrassing texts another day. Huzzah. I plug it back into its charger, climb into bed and tuck in tight. Tomorrow. Tomorrow. Tomorrow.

Despite an Excedrin PM hangover, I arrive at the first day of school wide eyed and excited. Just like every other first day of school since I can remember. Kids getting dropped off, buses taking up way too much space in tiny parking lots, and teachers barking orders as they hold on to clipboards filled with lists and classroom numbers. I pick my way through the crush, coffee in hand, and make my way to our little mental health stalag. I've got a solid hour before I pull Harry Sprague out of his second-period English class for his first speech therapy session. I plan on filling up this coffee mug as many times as I can between then and now.

No Jill in sight as I set my canvas bag down in our office. She's probably foraging in the teachers' lounge. It *is* the first day of school. The amount of delicious goodness that is teeming in that lounge right now is mind-boggling. Bagels? Danish? Bins filled with Red Vines? I could go on and on. My mouth waters as I walk down the hallway, out the double doors and toward the teachers' lounge. It's far enough away that teachers can let their hair down but close enough that a cup of coffee (or a handful of Red Vines) is mere steps away at any given time.

I excitedly push open the door, already tasting that cream cheese, bagel and fresh cup of coffee.

'Hey, Frannie.' Ryan. *Ugh*. Ryan. It's as if someone has thrown a bucket of cold water on my face and I'm frozen in the doorway, mascara trailing down my cheeks. It takes milliseconds to gather myself, an undertaking that's barely visible to the naked eye: masks are pulled, shoulders are cocked back, chins lifted.

'Hey,' I say, my eyes scanning the room. Jill. On the balcony.

'Hey . . . I wanted to—'

I cut in. 'Ah, there's Jill! Have a great first day!' I escape from Ryan's shrugging apologies and bob and weave past several sad looks, pitying smiles, and 'you go, girl' raised eyebrows. I march past the obstacle course of feigned sympathy and walk out onto the balcony.

'What the hell? You leave me in there with Ryan and the Coven of Front-Office Hags?' I say, trying to look as happy as possible.

'Leave you? What are you talking about?' Jill asks, talking to another woman. Who I don't know. *Great*. I extend my hand in greeting. She quickly takes it with a firm grip.

'Frances Reid. I'm sorry, I don't usually . . . he's my ex and now he's dating Jessica and I'm . . . I'm just . . . I have to act like it doesn't bother me and it's—'

'Lisa Campanari,' she says, cigarette dangling out of her mouth. Her New Jersey accent is thick. I like her immediately.

'She's in the upper school science department,' Jill says with just the slightest hint of a Jersey accent by osmosis.

'So, what room are you in?' I ask, knowing Lisa will be most affected by the construction of the new science building and tech center expansion.

'Some makeshift annex. Whatever. The new building looks like it's going to be worth waiting for,' Lisa says, putting out her cigarette. I'm not staring into the lounge. I swear I'm not. Ryan sips his coffee . . . not sweet enough. More sugar. I clear my throat and focus back on Jill and Lisa.

'Best money can buy,' Jill says.

'Oh yeah?' Lisa asks.

'My husband works for the architectural firm that's doing the expansion,' Jill says.

'Nice gig if you can get it,' Lisa says.

'He's with an international architectural firm, so everything was aboveboard,' Jill says.

'I doubt you working here as a speech therapist would have anything to do with whether or not an international architectural firm was hired,' Lisa says, popping a breath mint.

'Well, it didn't,' Jill says, almost to herself.

'Jill?' Lisa asks, focusing.

'Hm?' Jill answers, her voice hesitant.

'Get over yourself,' Lisa says, smiling.

'I like you,' Jill says, pointing directly at Lisa. Lisa laughs – open, assured and booming.

'Hey, gals.' Debbie Manners peeks out the door to the balcony. A) Anyone who says 'gals' should be drawn and quartered. B) It's too early in the morning – and the school year, for that matter – for Debbie to be saying anything to us.

'What's up, Debbie?' I ask, shark eyes in full effect.

'Just wanted to have you guys sign the birthday card we've got going around for Headmistress Dunham,' Debbie says, passing me a file folder that apparently conceals the key to the lost-wax process if you judge by how carefully she's handing it off to me.

'It's the first day of school, Manners. Come on,' Jill says.

'It'll just be a dash,' Debbie says, moving farther out onto the balcony.

'We don't have a pen,' I say, hands in the air.

'Here you go,' Debbie says, fanning an entire pastel spectrum of Sharpies in front of me. I choose the least-offensive light blue. Debbie is disappointed and resolves, surely, to take that color out for future signees.

As I sign the card Debbie continues. 'We're doing cake and ice cream in the teachers' lounge next Wednesday after school. We're asking everyone for a donation to help with the present.' I pass the card and the pen to Jill.

'Debbie, right? That's a full week and a half away and we just want to get through this first day,' Lisa says.

'If you could just sign the card,' Debbie says, growing ever more panicked.

We are quiet.

Debbie continues. 'We're getting her a Waterford apple for her desk and any donation will do, but we're hoping you'll be generous.' Debbie snatches the blue pen away before Jill passes it to Lisa. She quickly replaces it with a bright pink one. Lisa looks none too pleased as she passes Debbie back the card along with the bright pink Sharpie.

'So stop by the library anytime with the money,' Debbie

says. She heads back into the teachers' lounge, thrusting the card and request for a generous donation at another group of unsuspecting teachers. '*We'd really appreciate it,*' I hear from the balcony.

'Great. We have Emma's birthday thing on Wednesday and then that whole fund-raising fair that Friday? That's a whole lot of extracurricular activities we're sure not getting paid for,' Lisa says, putting this new information into her calendar.

'Try saying that ten times fast. Friday's fund-raising fair, Friday's fund-raising fair . . . can't do it,' I say, sipping my coffee.

'And we have that head of department mixer thing tomorrow night,' Jill says, eyeing me.

'I'm the one who told you about it, weirdo,' I say, scanning the teachers' lounge once more. Jill looks from me to Lisa.

'You told me about us going to the head of department mixer tomorrow night?' Jill says again.

'Head of department mixer?' Lisa asks, standing. She's wearing capri pants and a pastel sweater set. Her figure is an hourglass – feminine. I can see her tugging on her sweater set, trying to conceal this obvious capital crime. Shaped like a woman? In Los Angeles? I don't think so, missy. I'm sure some good Samaritan has a nice glass of lemon juice, cayenne pepper and honey with your name on it. Whether you like it or not.

'Hm?' Jill asks.

'The head of department mixer?' Lisa asks again.

'Oh, that. No big deal,' Jill says, a yawn at the ready. I roll my eyes.

Lisa continues. 'You guys want to grab a beer after?'

'Absolutely,' Jill and I say in unison, standing.

Lisa starts for the balcony door. Jill is panicking.

'I don't think we know which bar,' I say. Jill narrows her eyes at me.

'Lucky Baldwin's,' Lisa says, opening the door.

'Perfect,' I say.

'I knew that,' Jill mutters. Lisa stands in the open balcony door. Debbie is cornering Ryan with the birthday card for Emma. Her approach with him seems much more . . . affectionate.

'He's cute. Ferrell. He's your ex, right? He's cute,' Lisa says, looking back. I balk.

'Yeah,' I say. Ouch. Ryan thanks Debbie and quickly exits the teachers' lounge, away from her and her offer of a first day back rub. Debbie gloomily moves on to another group of teachers. They are wary.

'Tiny penis though, right?' Lisa says, door wide open. Full lounge.

Silence.

Lisa asks again, 'Right?'

I am quiet. My words. My knowledge. All caught in my throat.

Jill and Lisa wait. Jill looks like she's about to explode.

'Frannie?' Jill finally yelps.

'Yeah,' I say, looking away.

'What?' Jill looks shocked.

'You can tell,' Lisa says.

'How?' Jill blurts. The teachers in the lounge are busy acting like they're not eavesdropping. On one hand, I feel fiercely loyal to Ryan. It doesn't feel right airing his dirty, albeit tiny, laundry. I focus back in on Jill and Lisa's conversation regarding my ex-boyfriend's endowments already in progress.

'I checked his package. He had a little something, but it's all balls, right? It's all balls,' Lisa says, letting us into the lounge first. Lisa's Jersey accent combined with the word *balls* causes an atmospheric concussion within the four walls of the teachers' lounge. It seems to reverberate like Big Ben at noon – ear-piercing and unrelenting. Balls. Balls. Balls.

I cut in. 'Yes. It's all balls.'

'That's what I thought. Better off without him then, right?' Lisa says.

'Hm,' I mutter, and give a quick nod. I stride past the Coven of Front-Office Hags, who have done nothing except offer me either the contact information for the local sperm bank with a Post-it note saying, *Don't waste any more time!* or the phone number for the local suicide hotline. Lisa hardly gives them a second glance.

'I'll come get you guys after school,' Lisa says. And she's gone. The door closes behind her.

'Ladies,' Pamela says, oozing over to us. Pamela Jackson: the school psychologist and recently promoted lower master. Last year's lower master quit once he found out he was being passed over for the head of school position. For a woman, no less. Big scandal at the Markham School.

'Hey, Pamela. Congratulations on the big promotion,' we say in unison. Pamela's cocoa skin is dewy, wrinkle free and made up to look natural. Her expensive clothes are just deconstructed enough to convey that she's naturally spontaneous.

'Oh, thank you. It was a huge honor,' Pamela says, clutching at the strand of pearls around her neck.

We are quiet.

'You've met Lisa Campanari, I see,' Pamela says.

'She's amazing,' Jill says.

Pamela is quiet . . . in that way that people are quiet when they want their silence to talk shit for them.

'Well, we'd better head on out,' I say, only after I'm sure Pamela's silence suggested I'm going to die alone. She allows a quick nod as we walk away from her and her judgmental silences.

'I texted that Jeremy person the other night,' I say, continuing out into the breezeway.

'And?'

'He had no idea who I was.'

'Wait, what?' Jill stops me just before we walk back inside the school hallways.

'He had no idea who I was,' I repeat.

'What exactly did he say?'

'*Hey, who is this?*' I say, doing my best Jeff Spicoli impersonation.

'You know my theory and he doesn't sound like that.'

'I know your theory and he *does* sound like that.'

Jill continues. 'You shouldn't text. Texting doesn't count.'

'You're right. I knew I was being chicken, but in the end we can both agree that it was actually the smart thing to do. Had I called it would have been way worse.'

'You'd think you would have learned your lesson about the dangers of texting after the whole Ryan debacle,' Jill adds just for good measure. I wonder if by 'the whole Ryan debacle' Jill means just the chucking via text or the entire two-year relationship.

Jill shrugs as if my texting faux pas has prevented us from ever knowing the majesty of an outdoor wedding – complete with dragonflies, strings of lights and a couple of thirtysomethings who've settled for one another as they dance to Lynyrd Skynyrd.

As I'm about to launch into yet another speech about how thirty-six years old plus newly single doesn't equal Threat Level Midnight in Datingland, a knot of men and women in rolled-up shirtsleeves, wearing hard hats and carrying roll upon roll of blueprints, hurry down the breezeway just outside the teachers' lounge. Jill pulls at her dress and tucks her hair quickly and neatly behind her ear. I see her do a quick once-over of her reflection in the windows of the HR department. They seem to approve, but it's clear that Jill is not pleased with what she sees. She shakes it off and greets her husband, who is front and center, as if none of the past few seconds has occurred. Martin Fleming: a man perfectly comfortable being Mr Jill Fleming.

'Hey, sweetie,' Martin says, bringing the clutch of suited workers to a halt.

'Martin!' Jill trills, her entire demeanor changing. I like to think that Jill's transformation is because Martin makes her so blissfully happy, but sometimes I'm afraid Jill's chameleonic personality is due to much darker reasons.

'Hiya, Frannie.' Martin pulls me in for a quick hug.

'Great to see you,' I say as the brush of the stubble forming on his jawline tickles my cheek.

'Introductions are in order, I suppose,' Martin says, turning to present the now inconvenienced yet overly pert group of architects hovering just behind their fearless leader. Martin goes around the circle quickly. Names. Hands held aloft as if answering 'Present' on a new day at school. Polite smiles. I'll remember no one and no one will remember me, yet we all act like we're clearly thrilled meeting each other. Martin looks around the group of now old friends with a gleam in his eye.

'We're all meeting at the bar tonight. You guys should come!' Jill looks from Martin to me to the group of architects, or more specifically, from Martin to the few single men among the group of architects.

'The bar?' Martin asks.

'You know. Lucky Baldwin's?' Jill's voice is sure. *Knowing.*

'Sure, Lucky's. We'll walk over after work,' Martin says, looking at the slowly nodding architects.

'Great!' Jill says, now eyeing those few single men in the group as a lioness eyes the few straggling wildebeests.

Martin waves one last time and hurries down the corridor and into the depths of the school.

'Cute,' Jill says, downright beaming.

'Yes, Martin is very cute,' I say, certain she's not referring to her own husband.

'You know who I mean,' Jill says as we nod at a couple of lower school teachers who are rushing into the lounge for a last-minute cup of coffee.

'I didn't even notice,' I say, telling the truth. Which is kind of sad in its own right.

'Help me help you, Frannie. *Help me help you,*' Jill says, her hands clutching at her chest.

I give her a quick wink as we walk into the bustling hallways of the first day of school.

4

J. T. and Kermit the Frog

Lucky Baldwin's is as advertised: a local Pasadena pub that's been allowed to stay just as it is for years. Red vinyl booths and wobbly wooden tables that serve as a background for a crowded maze of regulars. The oddly beguiling aroma of greasy fish and chips and spilled beer wafts over the revelers. The same faces appear night after night. Muted football games play on the various TV screens while the jukebox blares Led Zeppelin, ZZ Top and Al Green.

Jill takes my arm and pulls me past a blur of architects who, I gather, are either in a couple already, female and/or deemed undatable. She squares me off in front of two men. Single, I'm gathering by Jill's viselike grip on my arm.

'Frances Reid, this is Grady Davis and Sam Earley. They're originally from Memphis. Martin is working with the Earley Group, *Sam's firm,* on making the school's expansion more sustainable,' Jill says, her voice quivering with excitement.

'We order yet?' Lisa asks, appearing after her first smoke break.

'Not yet,' I say.

'Lisa Campanari, this is Grady Davis,' Jill says, pulling Lisa over to the two men. I take this opportunity to really look at Grady. Black hair with piercing blue eyes. Bright orange tie. He looks like the guy you send for the keg, the guy who bails you out of jail no questions asked or the guy who urges you to 'drink! Drink! Drink!'

'Pleasure's all mine, darlin',' Grady says. Lisa's entire body is now a puddle on the floor. Wow. She gets *darlin'* and I get *ma'am*. If this night goes really well, maybe Grady and Sam will help me across the street later so I can get my weekly blue rinse at the beauty parlor. I'm going to need a lot more beer.

'And Sam Earley.' White-blond hair. Tall and lanky. And waaaay out of my league. I give Jill a quick melty smile in these seconds. Amid all of her more shallow inclinations and superficial dress-downs of other women, Jill has always seen me as beautiful. Beautiful in a way I have yet to see myself. Beautiful in way I don't even think she sees herself as, despite all evidence to the contrary. The night Ryan left I sobbed to Jill that my brown hair was too drab. It's mysterious, she said. I think I should take off a few pounds. You've got great tits, she said in a particularly uncomfortable moment. I have no style. Let's face it, I wailed, it boils down to me wearing a lot of beaded cardigans. You're rocking a hearth-wear-meets-vintage thing! It's effortlessly perfect, she said. I may believe I'm not up to snuff, but Jill? Jill thinks I can date the Great Gatsby.

'Nice to meet you,' Sam says.

'Nice to meet you, too,' Lisa says, still eyeing Grady.

'They're not from here,' Jill trills. The other nameless architects tuck into the table with pitchers of beer and empty cups. Let's face it: they might as well just go home.

'We kind of got that when you said they were from Memphis,' I say.

'The accents don't help, I expect,' Grady says.

'I expect!' Jill swoons. My face flushes. Jesus. These are two grown men, not adorable, southern-accented golden retriever puppies in a cardboard box.

'Men from here aren't as chivalrous.' Jill giggles, motioning to the random riffraff (which includes her husband) already drinking and in deep conversation, as if that simple action is akin to their soiling themselves in public.

I cut in. 'What are we drinking?'

'No, please. Allow us,' Grady says.

'First round's on me, boys. Relax,' Lisa says, and she's off. Grady and Sam stand awkwardly as they watch their southern hospitality get trumped by a Jersey girl who wants her drink without ceremony. I follow Lisa on her beer run.

Lisa orders a couple of pitchers and hands the bartender her credit card.

'Here, let me get part of it,' I say, digging in my purse for some cash.

'Nah, I said the first round's on me,' Lisa says, brushing me off. As the silence grows between Lisa and me, I realize I'm intimidated by her.

'What about them Lakers?' I ask, startled that the words have actually escaped from my mouth.

'What?' Lisa asks.

'The Lakers. They play basketball,' I say, clearing my throat.

Lisa rolls her eyes and continues. 'So, Grady's kind of

cute, right? Built like a brick shithouse.' She signs her name to the credit card receipt and passes it back to the bartender.

'He looks kind of old-fashioned to me . . . you know, shithouse aside,' I say.

'I like 'em old-fashioned,' Lisa says, smiling.

'Is that why you insisted on paying for your own beer . . . and theirs?'

'Oh . . . *right*.'

'Dirty feminist,' I say.

'I'll just grab his crank later,' Lisa says, lifting the pitchers one-handed and motioning for me to grab the glasses.

As Lisa steps away from the bar, I start to make a joke about checking packages, but my tongue gets tangled up as I try to be offhandedly hilarious. I'm left standing there alone with six empty pint glasses as an older gentleman in an ascot stares at my boobs, the word *crank* hanging in the air between us. Moving on.

'So, you teach with Jill?' Grady asks Lisa as I slide into the booth with the glasses.

'Jill and Frannie are speech therapists. I teach upper school science,' Lisa answers, pouring herself a glass of beer from one of the two pitchers. She passes the pitcher to Grady, who pours himself a glass. Sam takes the other pitcher and pours me a glass, then one for himself. I nod a quick thank-you. He offers a tight 'You're welcome' back.

I let myself linger on Sam just long enough to really see him. I realize how rarely I allow myself to truly take people in. Somewhere down the line (read: junior high school) I learned that taking notice of people yielded more unwanted attention than I was comfortable with. I've yet to loosen my grip on the PTSD terror level of a junior high school hallway.

'You teach people how to give speeches?' Grady asks. Sam takes a pull on his beer. He quickly licks his lips, ridding them of a tiny mustache.

'No,' I say, and smile.

'Oh, right. *Right*,' Grady says, his eyes darting around the room. I take a deep breath. Why don't I, at least for once, try not to be so intense?

'Teaching science doesn't take any explanation at all,' Lisa says, nudging Grady.

I press out what I hope is an easy smile and continue. 'We help kids who have trouble with speech, voice and language.' The waitress takes our orders: different variations on fish and chips. Sam calls the waitress 'darlin'.' I'm not sure if this is awesome or misogynistic. Jill is going back and forth between her matchmaking candidates sporting a wide grin.

When the waitress leaves so does our conversation. And then it's quiet. For a long time. I sip my beer. Sam sips his. I almost down mine. This is going great. The jukebox plays: 'Summer of '69.' Lisa and Grady suggestively pat and 'hit' one another.

With Grady and Lisa off in their own world of Uncomfortable-for-Others Public Displays of Affection, it's down to just Sam and me. And we're quiet. Tight smiles. I sip my beer and act like I'm ridiculously interested in the football game on the TV, the posters of various beers, the ant moving across the sticky floor. I stop scanning the bar and smile at Sam again. I think he's smiling back. Fine.

'So, you're an architect?' I ask, motioning to the other people as if 'so you're an architect' wasn't clear enough.

'Yes, and I do the—'

'Green.'

'"Doing the green" seems a bit suggestive,' Sam says.

'Maybe a new tagline for your consulting firm.'

A brief silence.

Sam cuts in. 'You're thinking of—'

'Kermit. Yes . . . with *Kermit*.'

'Thank god.' Sam laughs. He eases back against the booth. I hear the sounds of years and years of old vinyl shifting under his weight. The smile lingers across his face as he lets the joke roll over him again.

'You could have totally left me hanging, been all "I have no idea what you're talking about, Girl I've Barely Met,"' I say.

'Can you imagine? Just met me and I'm already the biggest dick.'

Jill almost falls out of her chair.

I continue. 'You calmly excuse yourself with a rolled eye and a heavy sigh.'

'Maybe a muttered, "This girl wants to do it with Kermit! Jim Henson's little angel!" as my pace quickens,' Sam says. His eyes crinkle as he lets his head dip back. Another laugh.

We lean toward one another across the sticky, wobbly table. Our beers slosh out of their pint glasses as our sentences overlap. I'm not thinking about anything before I speak. No Frannie Peed gauntlet in the forefront of everything I do and say.

I quickly continue, not wanting to halt the momentum. 'How do you like L.A.?'

'I've been here for a few years now. Went to school at University of Tennessee—'

'Go Vols!' Grady says, cutting in. Sam smiles. A cracking smile right across his face. Beautiful.

Sam continues. 'And then went to Cal for my master's and London for a few years. At that time, Europe was far and away . . . never mind. This is not interesting at all. I have a tenden— ugh, never mind again . . . needless to say, I fell in love with California a while ago. Knew I wanted to end up here.' Sam gives me a sheepish grin and takes another sip of his beer.

'I'm from the Bay Area originally,' I say, shocked by how easily I followed every hairpin turn of that last monologue.

'Really?' Sam says, sipping his beer.

'Mill Valley,' I say.

'Gorgeous town.'

'I know,' I say, leaning back into the booth as the waitress puts my plate of fish and chips in front of me. Sam thanks the waitress and flips his paper napkin onto his lap.

'You were born in Memphis?'

'No, ma'am. I'm from Shelby Forest, Tennessee.' *Ma'am*. I catch myself. So stupid. I'm getting too comfortable with him. I'm not Daisy Buchanan. Never forget that, Frannie. I straighten up and remember who I am.

'It sounds lovely.' I take a long, deep breath as Sam scans the filling bar.

'Justin Timberlake is from there,' Sam says, clearing his throat.

'Hm?'

'Justin Timberlake is from there,' Sam repeats, shifting in his chair.

'Where?' I ask.

'Shelby Forest.'

'Oh, yeah?'

'Yes.'

'Hm.'

'That's usually a big piece of trivia for most people.'

Quiet.

'*I'm bringing sexy back*,' I sing.

'I'm sorry?' Sam asks.

'A little J. T. for you,' I say, popping a French fry in my mouth. A French fry that, from the temperature of it, was apparently fried in oil plumbed from hellfire. I exhale, trying to cool down my mouth. Anything. Am I . . . am I going to have to spit this out?

'J. T.? We're calling him J. T. now?' Sam asks.

I mumble through the cinders of my mouth, 'J. T. is short for—'

'Justin Timberlake,' Sam says, cutting in. 'Yes. I got that.' I swallow. Hard. My eyes are watering. Great. Now Sam thinks talk of Justin Timberlake has brought me to tears.

'It's what the kids call him. The cool kids.'

'Do they?'

'Clearly,' I say, motioning to myself. As if I would know. As if I am a cool kid.

'I'll have to make a note of that,' Sam says. His accent is relaxing.

'So you don't embarrass yourself in the future.'

'Yes, because to use his full name would be—'

'Social suicide,' I say, finishing his sentence.

'Ha!' Sam laughs. Wrinkled eyes, open mouth, head tilted back. I want . . . him. This. Us. Already, Frannie? How . . . how am I being so possessive of him so quickly? I haven't the right to be this enchanted. I barely know the man. This is clearly a rebound thing. Choose the least-available man to safely take my mind off Ryan. But . . .

I can't help myself.

My mind flashes forward to one year down the line. Sam and I are sitting in front of the television; he's resting his hand on my knee and wearing his pajama bottoms and a University of Tennessee T-shirt (one that I'll soon sleep in). I'm drinking a cup of tea and wearing my glasses. Maybe someone just farted. We think it's hilarious. I sexily reach for my dental night guard just as he suggests we turn in for the evening.

And like an excited little kid, I decide I have to go to the bathroom. And trust me, I've learned my lesson on this one.

'Excuse me,' I say.

'Oh, sure . . . sure,' Sam says. He stands as I slide out of the booth.

'Bathroom?' Lisa asks, looking up from her prey, I mean Grady.

'Uh, yeah,' I answer, my face reddening as I take a quick glance at Sam.

'I'll go with you,' Lisa says, standing.

Lisa and I wind through the bar with excuse-me's, hands on backs and apologetic smiles – trying to politely move the clusters of people talking and drinking.

We push open the door to the bathroom. There's a line, as usual.

'It's fun, right?' Lisa says. I smile at the girl coming out of the stall and scoot forward in line. Another girl peels off the line and goes into one of the two stalls.

'Fun . . . hm,' I say, laughing.

'Grady asked if I wanted to go to dinner tomorrow night.' A toilet flushes and another girl appears from the stall with a polite smile. The line moves.

'You guys seem to be hitting it off,' I say, deflating. See? It happens. People get asked out on dates. Unbelievable.

'It's that southern accent. Drives me crazy,' Lisa says, bending over and pulling her boob up in her black, lacy bra. Same with the other side. Her now-lifted breasts accost me as she stands up straight once more. The entire bathroom stands in awe.

'Definitely a plus,' I say.

'Sam seems nice. Super cute,' Lisa says, swiping her lipstick and looking at herself in the mirror on the far wall.

'Yeah, I guess.'

'You guess?'

'I just don't think we have a lot in common.' Distancing from him just a bit.

'I see what you're getting at. But, straight up – these are men, at the very least, worth getting to know,' Lisa says, her voice booming through the small echo chamber of a bathroom. The girl next to me smiles, indicating she thinks I should give Sam a shot, too.

'I don't know,' I say.

'You do what you want, but you guys seem to be having a good time. Why not see where it goes?' Lisa asks, looking away. Do I let her in on the crazy now? Is it too early in our budding friendship?

'It might be the whole Ryan thing, as well,' I say, deciding to save face a bit.

'I get that. But the best way to get over a man—'

'Is to get under another one, I know. I actually don't think that works.'

'Yeah?'

'Because the rebound guy then becomes some kind of *Penthouse Forum* anecdote you share with your girlfriends over cosmopolitans. When, in actuality, you've done one of two things: sabotaged a relationship by sleeping with a man too quickly or slept with someone you don't even like, and you feel even shittier about yourself.'

'You think too much.'

'I get that a lot.'

'Why don't you just let this shit ride?' Lisa finally suggests.

Hm.

'You mean not—'

'Throw it over a cliff just yet,' Lisa says, cutting in.

'Do you know me well enough to say such things?' I ask, my face reddening as I look to the girl behind me in line. Another toilet flush. Another girl scuttles out. Lisa walks toward the now open stall.

'Am I right though?' Lisa says, turning around.

I am quiet. Ahem.

Lisa closes the door behind her. 'Then it seems I know you well enough.' Her words echo. An apologetic smile from the girl behind me. The stall door is locked. Quiet.

Lisa and I make our way back through the crowded bar, acquiring two more pitchers of beer in the process, Lisa with her boobs aloft and me hopped up on super-cool theories about 'letting shit ride.'

I slide back into the booth next to Sam. The table is more convivial during the second half of the night. It's one of those nights. I'd like to believe it isn't just my imagination, but I think I catch Sam staring at me a few times. It's clear that we get along. We actually get along great. I'm happy and glad I came. I doubt there will be a classic rock mix in the offing any time soon.

'We'd better be heading out,' Jill says.

'It *is* a school night,' Lisa says, standing. Grady immediately stands and pulls her chair out just that much more. She smiles at him, grabbing his belt buckle and pulling him toward her. It's freeing, however creepy it is to think of one's friends in that context, to see someone so in touch with her own sexuality. Of course, I'm looking at this from a completely sociological standpoint, because I can't fathom ever being comfortable pulling some dude closer via his belt buckle. It's not that I'm a prude, I just couldn't keep a straight face. The good-byes drag on as I watch Sam move through the crowd, shaking hands and patting backs. His southern drawl is now heavy with the late hour.

'It was nice meeting you, Frannie,' Sam says, finally

making his way over to me. Is he going home to someone right now? Is there someone he's going to call on his way home just so he can talk about his day? Is he in love with someone else?

'You too,' I say.

Sam gives another quick wave and a crooked little smile and is gone.

Gone.

The civil war inside my head starts as the night retracts into a blur around me.

You said yourself that maybe you weren't ready for Sam.

Right. But that shouldn't have stopped him from asking.

You barely met the man.

Is it too much to ask that someone make the effort to see me again?

You're a beautiful woman and he could tell you weren't quite sure.

But don't all the books and movies out there tell you that the most desirable women are the plucky heroines who play hard to get?

Right, but one could argue that people who aren't fictional need a bit more encouragement.

Encouragement?

Letting someone know you're interested might help him make a move.

I'M SHY.

Has it ever occurred to you that Sam might be shy, as well?

Not shy enough to just walk into the night without so

much as a mention of a coffee date. An e-mail address. Something.

That's kind of the epitome of shy.

Is this where my subconscious tries to convince me that Sam, a perfect stranger, left because he loved me too much to ask me out?

Fine, but you can't say that he left because you were so repellent.

NO, THAT IS EXACTLY WHY HE LEFT.

Long. Weary. Sigh.

We all walk out through the patio and into the alleyway that serves as the entrance to the pub. Grady and Lisa split off from the crowd quickly. Martin and Jill kiss good-bye and say they'll see each other back home. I wave a warm farewell to Martin as he walks back to where his car awaits.

'Sam was totally into you,' Jill says, her smile faltering just slightly.

'Hm,' I say, checking my watch. Eleven thirty P.M. I'm exhausted and ready to go home.

'He was probably in a rush to get home. It was all so courtly.'

'A mannerly dismissal. That makes it so much better.'

'Frannie—'

I interrupt. 'It's cool. It really is. I don't know how . . . It wasn't like I was that attracted to him in the first place. That's a lie. Total lie. He's inconveniently remarkable. I just don't think I can get my hopes up, you know?' I say.

'We should plan something. The four of us.'

'I think I'll pass.'

'I just want you to be happy.' Jill is growing frustrated.

I am quiet. She takes my silence as an opportunity to press her luck. 'Why don't I plan a casual dinner? Me and Martin and you and Sam?'

'I don't want someone to be with me because I'm handy,' I say, trying to find the words.

'Like . . .' Jill is now miming giving someone a hand job in the middle of Old Town Pasadena. I bat her hand down.

'No, no! Jesus. Like, *around.* I don't want someone to date me because I'm convenient,' I say, waving off a curious gentleman.

'Because handies shouldn't even enter into the equation until the fourth, maybe fifth date,' Jill says, as if quoting gospel.

I continue. 'I don't want to be the corner store where you can buy your loaf of bread, container of milk and a stick of butter.'

'That's from *Sesame Street,*' Jill says.

'I couldn't help myself,' I say, lacing my arm in hers as we walk down the alleyway to Fair Oaks Avenue. 'I want to be the place you plan a whole trip around. Remember that store in Summerland we went to? That had that candle? We gassed up the car, made a playlist, got road food. Planned the whole day around it.'

'I love that store,' Jill muses.

'I want to be that store. A store that's not on the way. I want to be inconvenient . . . for once,' I say. Jill's face twitches in frustration.

'You know, we could have just gotten that damn candle online,' Jill says, giving me an affectionate tug closer to her.

5

Sprague v. Stone

'Headmistress Dunham wants to see you in her office,' Jill says as I walk in from a session.

'What? Why?' I ask, setting down my canvas bag filled with my tools of the trade. I'm tired. It's not even lunchtime and I'm dragging. I couldn't sleep last night. And it's embarrassing. I paced, fantasized and delivered a monologue – not necessarily in that order – about Sam all night. He affected me more than I'd like to admit and far more than I am comfortable with. Trying to sift through the topography of my psyche was exhausting and more than a little discouraging. What percentage of this fascination has to do with Sam versus rebounding from Ryan? (Unknown at this time.) The Frannie Peed gauntlet was ever-present with Ryan. Every word, every action, every . . . thing had to be weighed and measured by the critical jury in my head urging me to 'act cool.' With Sam, words tumbled out of my mouth as my body bent close to him without a thought of crowding. I felt emancipated. But if Sam is the genuine article, what does that make Ryan? What does that make what we had together? If one of us was a fake, how can what we had be real? As the dawn broke through it came down to the simplest yet most complicated of questions: Am I real enough to have genuine feelings for Sam?

'Emma didn't say why she wanted to see you,' Jill says, gathering up her stuff and heading out. Is this about the head of department position? Ugh. While I know I want the position, it would make things a lot easier knowing Jill *doesn't* want it. But why would someone not want a promotion? I bite the bullet.

'Do we need to talk about the head of department position before the mixer tonight? You and I?'

'I know, right?'

'It's going to suck. We both want it, one of us is going to get it and one of us is going to have to be the boss of the other.'

'Well, when you put it like that . . .'

'Look, we've both done the footwork. We turned in our applications and now we'll just have to wait and see how the chips fall,' I say.

'I like that.'

'Because it won't matter who the boss is, we're still us. Right?'

'Right.'

'You're thinking about Tony Danza right now, aren't you?'

'Maybe.' Jill pauses, then continues. 'I need to be . . . I think you're going to get it.'

'Oh yeah?' I ask, trying to act like I don't know for sure that I should get the promotion.

'I've got other stuff going on, so . . .'

My eyes narrow.

Jill continues. 'You know, so . . .'

'It's villainously ingenious how you can say so much while saying so little,' I say, stepping closer.

'What?'

'You're trying to insinuate that all I have is this job.'

'I am not.'

'Are too.'

'Am not.'

'Cut it out.'

'Well, maybe I'm . . .' Jill deflates in her chair.

'You better start talking. And this time with actual words, not just silent unfinished statements.'

'Fine.'

I wait. She starts and stops a million sentences. Jill is the queen of the trail-off. She begins innumerable offensive sentences and trails off just as she's about to really hurt someone's feelings. She always makes sure it's the listener who fills in the blanks. Therefore the listener is the catty bitch . . . and never Jill.

'Jill?' I urge her on.

'Why doesn't she like me? You know? There's no way I'm getting this job and we both know it. Everyone likes you better,' Jill says.

'Oh, so I'm getting the job because Emma *likes* me more than you?'

'Well, that's part of it.'

'So I'm the gutsy spinster who dolefully climbs the corporate ladder because she has no other options?'

'Of course not,' Jill says, looking up at me.

I am quiet . . . and growing angry. Hurt.

'I'm having a hard time not being jealous,' Jill finally says in a whisper.

'Is that the right word?' I ask.

'Jealous?'

'No, *being*. Yes, *jealous*.'

'Really? Now? You're going to do that now?'

'What word did you think I meant?'

'Well, how is that not the right word?'

'I think it's more complicated than just jealousy. Not for nothing, but this is a terrible situation. We're best friends. You feel badly that you want the job because you think you should sacrifice your own ambitions and want your best friend to get it. And you'd actually be happy if she did. But you want it yourself. And on and on in a vicious cycle. Is that jealousy? Or is this just a really complicated set of circumstances?' I say.

Jill makes a face. Like she's trying to figure out a crossword puzzle.

I continue. 'Am I right?'

'Yeah, I guess.'

'So, it's actually not about jealousy at all. It's just complex,' I say.

Jill pulls me in for a big hug and says, 'I like that. Love you, smarty.' She squeezes tighter.

'I love you, too, weirdo.'

'Let's make out.' And she breaks out into hysterics.

'Unbelievable. And now I only have like ten minutes before I have to pull Harry Sprague. Hopefully this little meeting with Emma won't take too long.'

'It's about Harry,' Jill says, taking a sip of her coffee.

'You said she didn't say what it was about.'

'Right, but she did say *who* it's about.'

'Why does she want to see me about this?'

'Probably because you're the Harry Sprague expert.' Although Harry has had several different teachers over the years, as his speech therapist, I'm the one constant in his school life. I like that Emma has recognized this and is calling me in for my opinion. It's a good sign. Jill closes the office door behind us and continues down the hall with me.

'So, we on for dinner this Sunday? Martin just got that new smoker monstrosity. He's all keyed up to smoke something called a Boston butt. Don't ask,' Jill says.

'Sure, I'm excited . . . not specifically about Boston butt, but about eating something other than shredded wheat and peaches,' I say.

'It'll be a group of us – people from Martin's office, neighbors. I'm going to feel Lisa out and see how things went with Grady. See if he'll be there . . .' Jill says, her voice trailing.

Jill is quiet. Too quiet.

'Jill?'

'Hm?'

'I want it on the record that I am asking you – point-blank – not to invite any potential suitors.'

'You can't ask me to do that.' Jill's voice is strained.

'What? Why can't I?'

'I simply cannot be expected to do that!' Jill takes on the demeanor of a hostage, bound and tied to a wooden chair, as she's asked where the weapons of mass destruction are hidden.

'You . . . you're honestly—'

'Mrs Fweming?' A little blond girl approaches Jill hesitantly.

'Try it again, Kaylee. Fleming. Get that l,' Jill says, giving me a quick wink.

'*Fleming*. Mrs *Fleming*,' Kaylee says, victorious. Jill gives her a quick high five. She's nothing if not good at her job. Whether it's speech therapist or matchmaker.

'This isn't over,' I say as I head down the hall feeling like a freedom fighter defying an iron-fisted despot. Jill and Kaylee disappear innocently around a corner. Unbelievable. Maybe I'll burn a copy of that classic rock mix after all. Just in case. I continue down the stairs toward Emma Dunham and her summons.

'I'm here to see Headmistress Dunham,' I say to the receptionist, a tight, overdressed seventysomething woman called Dolores.

'I'll see if she's ready for you,' Dolores says, looking down her nose at me. I smile brightly and find a seat in one of the leather club chairs in the luxurious anteroom. Gilt-framed oil paintings of past heads of school line the wood-paneled walls: all old, white men. While Emma's the first female I remember being head of school, I hadn't really put it together that Emma is the first female head of school ever. The lower master – an older white gentleman whose painting would have fit perfectly with the others in this anteroom – leaving his post in a huff now makes a lot more sense. I grab a *New Yorker* off one of the mahogany coffee tables and flip through as I wait. After several minutes, Dolores picks up her phone.

'Yes, ma'am? Fine,' Dolores says into the phone. Then to me she says, 'Headmistress Dunham will see you now.'

'Thank you.' I open the door to Emma's office with as much confidence as I can muster.

Emma picks up the phone behind a massive wooden desk. 'Headmistress Dunham, I know you're on a call, but Ms Reid is here.' Dolores is quiet as she awaits instruction. She gives me the signal to hold on and keep it quiet. I think I can manage that. I close the door behind me and proceed toward one of the two tufted leather wingback chairs. Harry Sprague is sitting – gangly legs dangling – in the chair farthest from the door. He is sporting a very sizable black eye. I lunge toward him.

'You okay? What happened? Harry?' I whisper, swiping his bangs out of his eyes, taking in the black eye as close as I can.

'I'm fine, Ms Reid. I'm fine,' Harry says, his eyes darting from Emma to me and back to Emma.

I try to hold my temper. Hold. I stand quickly and walk out of Emma's office. She's still on the phone; she holds her hand over the receiver as I walk out of the office.

'Ms Reid?' Emma whispers. I ignore her and continue to walk out of the office, past Dolores – whom I shall now refer to as Cerberus the Three-headed Hound of Hell. By the time I'm out in the hallway, I'm at a full-out run. I hop the steps two by two and continue down the hallway, through the double doors, out onto the breezeway and into the teachers' lounge. I don't acknowledge the huddling group of lower school English teachers as I whip open the freezer. Ice. I pull open one of the drawers, get a freezer bag and fill it with ice. Fasten it closed, slam both freezer and drawer – hard. I rip off a paper towel and wrap it around the bag as quickly as I can.

'Everything okay?' one of the teachers asks. I disregard her and I'm back out onto the breezeway, through the double doors, down the stairs, through the anteroom, past Cerberus and back into Emma's office. I kneel down in front of Harry, short of breath and red faced.

'Here, sweetie. Put this—' Harry winces as the cold hits his swelling eye. I pull the leather wingback chair close to Harry, holding the bag on the ever-swelling eye myself. I settle in. Look at Emma. Still on the phone and pissed. Well, that makes two of us, lady.

Harry's blue blazer with Markham's seal is buttoned and loose on his rail of a body. His white oxford-cloth shirt is ironed and his blue tie is tight and businesslike. Little crimson droplets of blood dot the perfectly ironed oxford-cloth shirt. I can't imagine what Mrs Sprague will think about this. She's going to lose her mind. I look down to see Harry's one act of rebellion: a pair of scuffed, unlaced skateboarding shoes. I give Harry a smile as we both try not to listen to Emma's phone call.

I scan Emma's office while we wait, my hand numbing from the bag of ice, despite the paper towel, that rests on Harry's eye. Three long, thin vases anchor her pristine desk, each holding a single orange gerbera daisy. The water is sparkling and the flowers laze to one side. The vases are exactly the same distance apart from one another. She has one expensive-looking artisanal basket on her desk filled with a few files.

My eyes focus on the altar of photos arranged on the mahogany credenza on her far wall. Photos of Emma and Jamie in every imaginable part of the world. Great Wall of China. Houses of Parliament. Sydney Opera House.

Harry is sitting stock-still, only his hands are a tangle of nerves. I give him an easy smile. He quickly looks away behind the freezer bag filled with ice. If I act like I'm bored, he'll just think this is business as usual. I can't let him see I'm nervous, too.

Just as Emma is winding down her conversation, my eyes fall on her wedding photo. Jamie and Emma. Once again, I'm reminded of what a mismatched couple they are. I recognize the backdrop immediately as Mount Tamalpais in Mill Valley, a tiny suburb just outside of San Francisco, more commonly known as my hometown. Emma Dunham got married in my hometown? I thought she was from Michigan . . . wait, Jill did say she was in the Bay Area for a time. I store that piece of information in my memory bank for future conversation starters – conversations that will inexplicably wend their way right into the head of department position. A head of department position I am on the cusp of throwing away because of how angry I'm growing by the second. Emma signs off, hangs up the phone and jots down a couple of lines in an opened file.

'Thank you for coming, Ms Reid,' she says.

'What can I do for you, headmistress?' I ask.

'It seems Mr Sprague got into a fight with Mr Sean Stone,' Emma says.

'The lacrosse player? He did this?' I ask. Sean Stone is

at least six foot three with the IQ of someone just wealthy enough to buy his way into any school he wants.

'Yes,' Emma answers.

'Then I'm not following,' I say. Having Harry here makes it difficult to point out the obvious holes in Emma Dunham's theory without hurting his feelings.

'What's there to follow?' Emma asks. I inch forward in my chair.

'Harry has a black eye, headmistress. Clearly it wasn't . . . where is Mr Stone now?' I ask, deciding to start with the obvious.

'In class,' Emma answers.

'Why is he not present at this disciplinary meeting?' I ask.

'He's being dealt with another way.'

'Another way?'

'Yes, Ms Reid. Another way.'

'Harry, can you excuse us for a second?' I ask, turning to the terrified ten-year-old.

'Yes, Ms Reid,' he mumbles, situating the ice bag on his eye as he shuffles out of the office. I wait. My face is unruffled as he looks back in fear. Emma smiles, too. The door closes.

'Ms Reid, I certainly do not appreciate you asking Mr Sprague to leave after I've summoned him.'

'Surely you couldn't expect an honest conversation with him present.'

'I expected you to help discipline him.'

'Why would I discipline him when I don't understand the situation completely?'

'Mr Sprague got into a fight with Mr Stone. He attacked him in English class.'

'Harry is one hundred pounds soaking wet and goes to panels on how to learn the Vulcan language. Sean is a two-hundred-and-fifty-pound brute who slams soda cans into his forehead for fun. I assure you, this "fight" has way more to it than you're acknowledging.'

'No matter.'

'You're going to have to walk me through how Harry having a black eye is "no matter." '

'From what I've inferred Mr Sprague provoked Mr Stone, which then caused Mr Sprague's injuries,' Emma says, slipping on her glasses briefly to read the scribbled notes on an accident report.

'Provoked?' I ask, inching ever closer to the edge of my seat. Emma refers once again to her notes.

'When Mr Stone threatened to throw Mr Sprague's backpack in the trash, Mr Sprague ran to get Mr Stone's backpack from his workstation. Mr Sprague then dropped Mr Stone's backpack out of the classroom window, saying, "How do you like that, you *effing penis-faced ape*?" ' It takes everything I have to keep a straight face. I love that kid. Effing. Penis-faced. Ape. Emma takes her glasses off and looks up at me as if she's just proven her case in court beyond a reasonable doubt. I breathe deep. Collect myself.

'What you're describing is someone finally standing up to a renowned bully and then getting penalized for doing so.' Penalized. I can't help myself.

'You're arguing that his actions should be applauded?'

'Of course not, I'm not condoning violence, but it's

confusing to me why the reasons for the fight haven't been discussed or looked into by you.'

'Mr Sprague should not have provoked him.'

'I hope you're not insinuating that Harry, in any way, asked for this beating.'

'In my opinion, and more importantly the opinion of the Markham School, Harry Sprague is to blame for this altercation.'

'I disagree. It's well known that Sean Stone hits people. He's just too Machiavellian to ever get caught. So, by your logic, and more importantly the logic of the Markham School, the inexperienced kids who finally stand up to their tormenters are the ones who deserve discipline?'

Emma is quiet. I'm beyond angry but more mystified. How could Emma's take on this situation be so skewed? Bullying and pecking orders: middle school's own lovely brand of Darwinism.

'Mr Sprague shall be given a warning,' Emma finally says.

'Verbal only. This will not go into his record,' I say, scooting to the end of my chair.

'Fine.'

'And I'd like to request that we revisit Sean Stone's ongoing behavioral issues at a later date,' I say.

'I'll get back to you on that, Ms Reid.'

'Thank you, headmistress.'

'You're welcome.' Ha! I didn't really mean it.

'Will there be anything else?'

'No, Ms Reid.'

We are quiet.

Emma continues. 'The board looks forward to meeting

you and Mrs Fleming at tonight's head of department mixer.'

'Yes, ma'am,' I say, my eyes to the floor. Great.

'You don't need to call me *ma'am,* Ms Reid,' Emma says. She looks drained.

'Thank you, headmistress. I'll take Mr Sprague with me when I go, if this meets with your approval?' I ask. Standing. Straightening my skirt. Holding my temper. I will not scratch your eyes out, Emma Dunham. I will not blast 'We Are the Champions' as I proclaim, 'No one is ever going to be free until nerd persecution ends!' No. I will hold it together. For Harry. For the bullied. For nerds everywhere.

'Yes, that will be fine.' Emma lifts one of the files from her in-box and puts her glasses on once again. I look like a 'before' picture in mine and she looks like one of the women in Van Halen's 'Hot for Teacher' video. Awesome.

'Good day, headmistress.'

'Please close the door behind you, Ms Reid,' Emma says, not looking up. I walk the ever-elongating expanse to Emma's door, becoming more and more upset. I can feel it building in my shoulders. My throat. I . . . I have to say something about this conversation to show that I am an effective leader in even the most pressing circumstances. To prove that I am the perfect person for the head of department job, not that I'm an insolent debater who overthinks everything. Before I go out the door, I whip around and find Emma, head in hands, hunched over at her desk. Her fingers are raking through her hair. Violent. Aggressive. Brutal.

I catch my breath and reach back for the door, hoping she hasn't noticed me.

Emma lifts up her head. And I see a demon. A possessed woman. A deeply furrowed brow bordering on satanic, laser red-rimmed eyes and a mouth set in a hard line. Within a millisecond it flashes from recognition to pain to cool and collected. I give her a quick nod and let myself out, closing the door behind me.

'Is . . . uh . . . is everything good?' Harry asks.

'Absolutely,' I say, donning an easy smile and choosing not to correct his grammar.

'Oh . . . uh . . .' Harry says, looking around the office.

'Come on, sweetie,' I say, motioning for him to exit this hellish vortex of an office before Emma thinks better of it. Harry doesn't question me as he quickly stands and shuffles out of the anteroom.

'Thank you for your hospitality,' I say to Dolores. Dolores doesn't acknowledge or look up at me. The door shuts behind us as we walk down the hallway and toward the stairs. Harry trundles along, his hand holding the now dripping plastic bag of ice.

'Sweetie, you've got to keep the ice on your eye. It'll start to swell,' I say, stopping and reapplying the bag to his delicate face. 'Do you want to talk about it?' I ask, nonchalant. Easy. No big deal. Sharing your feelings is, you know . . . whatever, dude.

'Not really. Is that okay?' Harry asks, looking up at me through the overgrown brush of his blond bangs.

'It's more than okay,' I say, having a hard time not getting emotional.

We are quiet.

I continue. 'So, Sean Stone, huh?' I say, walking down the hallway. A smile curls across Harry's pale face.

'*Kling akhlami buhfik,* Ms Reid,' Harry says in perfect Vulcan.

'No, you're right, Harry. Nobody is perfect,' I say at the base of the stairs.

'Frannie?' I look up. The sun streams in through the double glass doors at the end of the hall. The hard hat held loosely in one hand and the scrolls of blueprints in the other.

Sam.

'Hiya,' I say, my mouth going dry. Harry looks past his plastic bag filled with now melting ice from Sam to me. I see Sam inventory Harry's eye. Sam offers a warm smile, tucks the blueprints tight under his arm and extends his hand to Harry. In the millisecond Sam's eyes flick to me, I see the tiniest of imperceptible acknowledgments that Harry's eye will be handled with diplomacy.

'Sam Earley,' he says, shaking the boy's noodle arm with vigor.

'Harry Sprague,' he says behind his plastic bag.

'Nice to meet you, Harry,' Sam says, letting go of the boy's tiny hand.

'Sam, this is my star pupil, Master Harry Sprague,' I say. Harry and I have been working on introductions and how to greet people for years.

'Nice to meet you, Harry,' Sam says.

'Where are you from?' Harry asks . . . *blurts* really.

'Tennessee,' Sam says, smiling.

'You talk funny,' Harry says.

'I know,' Sam says, looking from Harry to me. Smiling.

'*Harry,*' I say gently.

'Don't you worry, Frannie,' Sam says with a quick wink to Harry.

'The correct way to say it is "You *speak* funny,"' I say.

'Ha!' Sam laughs.

'I'm quite fond of Mr Earley's accent,' I say, flushing immediately.

Sam looks at me. A smile. Flipping wildly through my slide show of Sam Earley smiles, I realize this is one I had yet to see.

I say to Harry, 'Come on, sweetie. We've got work to do. Say good-bye to Mr Earley.'

'Bye, Sam,' Harry says, resituating the plastic bag filled with ice. I lay my hand on Harry's shoulder and guide him over to the stairs. Harry begins up the stairs.

'You'll tell me later about the eye?' Sam asks, his hand reaching out just a bit.

'It's a long story that ends in me tilting at windmills,' I say, trying to joke about a situation about which I'm still equal parts confused and enraged.

'That's my girl,' Sam says, scanning the hallway.

Um, what?

'Yeah, well,' I say, looking from Sam to a very curious Harry. I motion to Harry with an apologetic smile and a wave.

Sam waves back. Standing where he was. Unmoving. I look back and give him a smile. A little wave.

He raises his hand, the hard hat held aloft.

Ouuuuuuuch.

6

I Was Pretty Good, Too

'"That's my girl"? What's that supposed to mean?' Jill asks.

'I have no idea,' I answer. Truthfully. So begins the exhausting analysis of the cavalcade of unknowable smiles and cryptic sentences uttered by someone you're newly interested in. When everything boils down to a succession of enigmatic moments. Moments played and replayed from the perspective you attribute to your lover-to-be, but that are actually from the part of you that's sure you're far too flawed to be loved. Every action, every word, every inch of one's body is judged. Life's normal fluidity melts away and is obliterated by the roller-coaster-like ups and downs of a really bad electrocardiogram.

Jill and I walk quickly up the long driveway to Emma's house that night for the head of department mixer. We stop short of the house and take it in. Jill pulls out her phone and takes a quick picture. Emma and Jamie's house is a midcentury modern. Two stories, lots of windows and clean lines. You can see the entire interior of the house from the driveway. No privacy at all. The minimalist staircase leading upstairs and the orange lacquered credenza and pair of Barcelona chairs that grace the main entryway are all clearly visible from the driveway.

'There better be wine,' Jill whispers just as the front door opens. I shoot her the first of many disapproving glances of the evening.

It's Jamie.

'Hi, it's so good seeing you again,' I say, extending one hand to Jamie as I'm holding a ridiculously expensive bottle of red wine with a name I can't pronounce in the other.

'Jamie Dunham,' he says, his icy fingers curling around mine.

'Yes, I know. We've met,' I say, passing him the bottle of wine.

'I know,' he says.

'Good,' I say, looking into the living room.

'Jill Fleming,' Jill says, passing Jamie a hostess gift: a basket containing far too many decorative soaps, bath salts and lotions.

'Jamie Dunham,' he says, opening the door just enough to let us both walk in. He sets Jill's basket in the hallway and takes my red wine over to the bartender.

As usual, everyone is milling around the living room and not eating a thing. The bow-tied waiters thread through cliques of people with full trays from which no one partakes. A perfectly catered fete and no one is touching the beautiful food. Welcome to L.A. But, of course, everyone's wineglasses are constantly being topped off. That's something we certainly don't skimp on. Carbs – sure. Wine – *never.*

'Sam might have a woman back in Tennessee,' Jill says, taking a crab cake off a full tray.

'You think I haven't thought of that?' I say, waving off the waiter.

Jill nods. An apologetic smile and a quick shoulder squeeze. She's deftly treading water between giving me a pep talk and keeping my emotions in check just in case this whole Sam thing goes south. She has to prepare for the possibility of both outcomes this early on.

I continue. 'It's such a catch-22. I have to allow myself to be vulnerable in order to be open to something, but being vulnerable to him opens me up to getting hurt.' Tears sting my eyes. You're at the head of department mixer, Frannie. Lock it up.

Jill can't contain herself. 'Maybe I can ask if Martin has some—'

'Are you kidding me?'

'What?'

'How can you stand there and talk about other setups?' I ask.

'I'm not understanding,' Jill says.

'You talking about other setups makes me think that you think that this whole thing with Sam is over. That I'm—'

Jill interrupts. 'Makes you think that I think . . . what are you talking about right now? I want you to be happy. If another dude makes you happy, then Sam can take a long walk off a short pier is all I'm saying.' Jill's voice is quiet and intense. She's serious. For once in her life. And I should be listening. I get it. I'm the queen of putting all my eggs in one basket. I always had the fear of only having one batch of eggs and one basket. Everything's more precious when you think there's no hope of more. Saved voice mails. Treasured notes scrawled on the backs of envelopes. Always being on hand for fear that I wouldn't be there on the day he decided to proclaim his undying love for me. I'm afraid everything about me is fleeting.

Jill continues. 'So, we'll just play the whole setup thing by ear then?' She squeezes me close.

'That's Jill Code,' I say, waving down the waiter again. I better eat something if I'm going to continue drinking like this.

'For lining up a rebound fuck, yes. Most assuredly—'

'Ms Reid? Mrs Fleming.' Emma Dunham.

'Oh, for crissakes,' Jill says under her breath. We straighten up.

'Yes, Headmistress Dunham,' I say, shoulders back, head high.

'Headmistress, I'm—' Jill starts.

'Mrs Fleming, I don't need an explanation. It seems you're catching on however – at least you're not in a public hallway during Back-to-School Night. One has to acknowledge the little victories,' Emma says, giving the smallest of smiles. She is beyond dazzling. Her blond hair is sleek and falls in a Veronica Lake-style wave down the right side of her perfectly sculpted face. She has more makeup on than usual, but it only amplifies her already glorious features. She's wearing a simple light pink, sleeveless shift dress and a pair of silver Grecian sandals. Effortless, stunning and completely beyond anything I'd ever consider wearing.

'That's right!' Jill says, guffawing.

'Thank you so much for having us. Such a lovely home,' I say, shaking her hand.

'Thank you. The board is anxious to speak with you two. We're all so happy to have you,' Emma says, her eyes flitting from group to group, from Jill to me, from Jamie to the kitchen. She's in complete control. Emma pulls over a well-heeled couple. 'Jill Fleming, this is Mr and Mrs Murphy. Please.' Emma puts them together like an awkward pair of teenagers at a Sadie Hawkins dance. They fall into conversation easily. Weather. Markham. The usual.

'I want to thank you again for the invitation and the opportunity to be considered for the head of the speech therapy department,' I say.

'Frannie, you earned it, you don't have to keep thanking me,' Emma says.

'I guess it's about you believing in me then. It means a lot,' I say.

'You're funny,' Emma says, smiling. Her smile is beautiful . . . and rare.

'How am I funny?' I feel like Joe Pesci.

'It's just . . . your résumé is impressive, your educational background and work ethic are just as stellar, of course you're in the running,' Emma says, taking a sip of her white wine.

'Did you always want to work in school administration?'

'Of course not.' Emma laughs. Another drink of her wine. I believe Emma Dunham is getting a bit tipsy. Jill and her duo of board members cackle with laughter. Jill is telling one of her stories. They're riveted. The job is as good as hers anyway, so why not just wow the board while you're at it? Not that I'm jealous. It's just complex, right?

Emma continues. 'I wanted to be a painter. I was pretty good, too.'

'Why didn't you?'

Emma takes another drink and scans the house quickly. Efficiently. 'It just wasn't in the cards.'

I am quiet. Emma senses my trepidation. She continues. 'My parents had a very clear plan for me. Rebellion was my sister's full-time occupation, not mine.'

'That tends to be the case.'

'You have sisters?'

'No.'

'So, hypothetically speaking?'

'Yeah . . . um, yes, hypothetically speaking.'

'Clara, my sister, is the artist of the family. That's quite enough for my parents.'

'What does Jamie think of your painting?'

'He wants what's best for me. What challenges me. Academia offered me a respectable future and a very real career as well as . . . No, Clara paints. She's happy and . . .' Emma laughs the tiniest, most intimate little giggle and continues. 'She was always the one who questioned our parents. She questioned everything . . . she was so . . . wild. So strong willed. I loved her for that. She was always the stronger of the two of us.' Another drink and a little sway.

'I imagine it took a certain degree of strength to become the first female head of school at Markham. I don't think they're handing that title out to many weaklings.'

'True.'

'Have you ever thought about getting back into it? Taking some art classes?'

'Every day.' Emma doesn't hesitate.

We are quiet.

Emma continues. 'I simply don't have the time. And I love my job at Markham, don't get me wrong.'

'Well, at least you can live somewhat vicariously through Clara,' I say, offering the worst argument in the history of arguments.

'Clara and I haven't spoken in quite some time, I'm afraid.'

Shit.

'That's too bad,' I say.

'It really is.' Emma is suddenly distant.

Shit.

I scan the photos along the mantel as the awkward silence expands between us.

'And is this your dog?' I ask, pointing at a candid photo of an elegant, poised Weimaraner with a red collar, ice-blue eyes and floppy ears.

Emma's face lights up; she grabs the silver frame in such a way that I wouldn't be at all surprised if she clutched the photo to her chest and spun about the room.

'John Henry. He's . . . he's our baby. *My* baby.' Emma sighs, her entire face changing. Softness, dropping any and all professional airs.

'Must be hard to walk with that hammer in his paw.'

'I'm sorry?'

'John Henry? The folk hero? Challenged the steam hammer?'

'Oh, of course. Jamie named him. He always loved the symbolism: working class, dying with your hammer in your hand after conquering the establishment. Of course, now I don't even think about the folktale. John Henry is just my baby now.'

'He's beautiful,' I say.

'Thank you,' Emma says, setting the frame back down on the mantel.

'Where is he now?' I ask.

'We put him in his crate for the evening. All the guests. Jamie thought it'd be best,' Emma says, looking pained.

'That makes sense,' I say.

'I hate that he's not here. He's my . . . he's my everything. Embarrassing, right?' Emma blushes slightly. A small smile.

'No way. Are you kidding? At least you have a dog. I've always been too scared. I just . . . I just know I'll outlive them and I . . . ugh . . .'

'Well, that's not going to be a problem for me,' Emma says.

'Oh, well—'

Emma cuts in with a conspiratorial whisper. 'John Henry is immortal, so . . .'

'Ha!' I say, laughing, caught off guard by Emma's wry humor.

The laughter subsides. Silence. Again.

'May I use your restroom?' I ask.

'Sure, up the staircase and to the left,' Emma says, pointing me in the right direction. She lays her hand on my shoulder as I pass. Gentle. Affectionate. I give her a quick smile. I motion to Jill that I'm heading upstairs. She gives me a nod of understanding and falls back into conversation with the now large group of board members who are hanging on her every word. Great.

I walk up the stairs and to the left, just as directed. Emma watches me as I climb. I look down and realize that if someone were standing beneath the staircase they would be able to see directly up my skirt. I grab the bottom of my skirt and hurry up the stairs.

'In a hurry?'

'What?'

Ryan.

'What are you doing here?'

'I'm the head of the history department. Remember?' Ryan says, taking a long swig of his beer.

'Are you already drunk?' I ask, eyeing the bathroom.

'Maybe.'

'I don't think that's the best idea in the world.'

'Shocking. You're thinking about something.'

'Okay, well. This has been nice, but—'

'I'm sorry, okay. I'm sorry,' Ryan says, grabbing my arm.

'What are you doing?' I ask, looking from his hand and back to him. He quickly lets go.

'I'm sorry . . . I'm sorry. It's just . . . I don't want you to be mad at me,' Ryan says, slurring just slightly.

'I don't want me to be mad at you either,' I say honestly.

'Then don't.'

'Okay. Noted. Good talk,' I say, patting his shoulder and taking a few steps toward the bathroom.

'You're making this way more complicated than it has to be, you know? We can just move on. Be happy with other people and just . . . go back to the way it was before we started dating. Friends. Can't we do that?' *Friend*. How can such a seemingly lovely word also be one of the most reviled? At times I've thought that I would rather have someone hate me than 'just want to be friends.'

'You mean go backward?'

'No, forward.'

'You just said that you wanted it to be the way that it was, meaning that it was a time in the past. You're the head of the history department; surely you understand that concept. Do you see where I'm going with this?'

'Ugh. Just . . . never mind,' Ryan says, steadying himself on the banister.

'Why don't you go find Jessica and maybe a cup of coffee,' I say. I can't make out what Ryan says in reply, but I know it's mean. I can hear the bile beneath the slurred words. Tears spring up before I even know what's happening. I notice Jill watching us from the ground floor. I see her zero in on Ryan just as he gets to the bottom of the stairs. She excuses herself from the group of board members and pulls Ryan aside. Her gesticulations are violent and her words are hushed yet passionate. Ryan is nodding; she grabs his arm, tugging him closer. I need to get somewhere private and fast.

My throat is choking closed and I'm thankful for my proximity to the bathroom. Once inside, I close and lock the door. The sounds of the party just downstairs are muffled and far away. And in the solace of this bathroom I allow myself to cry.

We can just move on. Ryan's words echo as I try to

regain some kind of composure. I thought I'd have some post-breakup epiphany where I'd all of a sudden be this whole other person. Strong. Sure. Secure. But that's not what this is. I feel cold and confused.

I splash cold water on my face over and over again. Wake up, Frannie. Wake up. I dry my face with a monogrammed guest towel and begin the long process of reapplying the mascara that is apparently going to be my plus-one for the evening.

When I finally exit the bathroom, I take a quick scan of the upstairs. I take out my iPhone, snap another quick photo of the general splendor and text it to Jill just downstairs. I notice there's already a text from her waiting for me.

'Had nice chat with Ryan. We now understand each other. While you're up there, take a picture of the master bedroom and any marital aids you find, if you get my meaning.' I immediately look up, as if the text itself were all the evidence necessary to condemn me for my misdeeds. Jill is staring at me from the bottom of the stairs. She flicks her hand as if to say, 'g'head.' We then have the most silent fight on record. Curt nods. Flicked, urgent gazes. Elaborate eye rolls. Shrugged shoulders and pointed fingers.

The deal is struck. My body deflates. Jill has worn me down, as usual. I'll go. I'll go. He'll keep calling me . . . he'll keep calling me . . . Great. I've devolved into impersonations of Cameron Frye from *Ferris Bueller's Day Off*. I give her the most polite middle finger I can. She blows me a kiss.

The master bedroom is right off the bathroom and no

one else is anywhere around. I take another scan. The mixer rages on downstairs. Look, if I'm caught I'll just say I was looking for the bathroom. Time to start pushing the envelope a bit, Frannie.

I'm going in.

The Dunham master bedroom is . . . clean. White. Sterile. It looks like an operating room. A tightly made, all-white platform bed anchors the large room. I bet I could bounce a quarter on it. It's the one room with no large windows. Absolute privacy. Well, that's something. I pad around the room as quietly as possible and find the en suite. I flip on the light. I open up a few drawers to find the usual: hairbrushes, toothbrushes and deodorant. Nothing spectacular. I take a quick picture. Proof of my expedition. I lean down to the lowest drawer and open it up to reveal stacked towels. Perfectly stacked white towels.

'That's something you'd never find in my house,' I say, taking a quick picture of the over-the-top perfection for Jill. I'm just about to close the drawer when I hear something shift beneath the towels. I reach under and find a silver framed photo. A family. Emma's family. They're standing by Emma, who, it looks like, is graduating from college. She's young. Beautiful. Her parents are exactly how I'd picture them, like they stepped right out of a yachting magazine or something. And . . . the sister. Clara. The spitting image of Emma, but . . . edgier. She hasn't gone all black sheep yet but is definitely rocking a seriously pissed-off expression. She's clearly separate from the rest of the family unit. But as I look closer . . . they're all separate. They may be standing together in the picture, but each looks like they're completely unaware that anyone else is standing close by.

I focus in on Emma's diploma: Emma Jane Stanforth. Hm. I tuck the picture back under the towels and ease the drawer closed, sure to keep everything just as I found it.

'You looking for something in particular?' Jamie. In the doorway. And thank god I just peed or else I would have most certainly wet myself. They don't call me Frannie Peed for nothing.

'Oh my god, you scared me,' I say, lurching up, my heart in my throat.

'*I* scared *you*?'

'Yes,' I say.

'You mean I scared you as you were rifling through our personal belongings?' Jamie says, stepping closer. Too close.

'I'm sorry. I was embarrassed. I was . . . I was looking for a tampon,' I say. *Score! Huzzah! Score!* Jill would be *so* proud of me right now.

'Oh,' Jamie says, not backing away.

'Yeah,' I say, leaning back as Jamie takes another step forward. What exactly is going on here?

I continue. 'And I didn't really want to announce it but figured Emma might have some stowed away, you know, back here,' I say, attempting a smile.

Jamie is quiet.

'So . . .'

'So . . .' Jamie is inches away from me now. His beakish face is too close and his pale skin glimmers in the bright fluorescents of the bathroom. He's been drinking.

'We cool?' I ask, apparently channeling Ice-T.

'I will be once you get out of my private bathroom,' Jamie says, moving just enough so I can ease by him but not enough so that it's not . . . well, *weird*.

'Then let's make that happen as soon as possible,' I say, taking another step out of the bathroom.

'I won't tell Emma about this,' Jamie says as I finally pass him.

'I don't care if you do; it would actually help if you did,' I say, apparently now believing my own lies and need for a tampon.

'I won't,' Jamie says, not looking at me.

'You can if you want to,' I say, turning around and facing him.

Jamie is quiet.

I've always been tall. I've never been particularly fond of being tall until right this very moment. I don't know what comes over me in these seconds, but I hold my ground. I stare Jamie down. Tilt my head just a bit and swear that if he does or says anything, I don't know how or why, but I'm pretty sure the next words out of my mouth will be, 'You want a piece of this?' I turn around to walk out of the ever-shrinking bathroom.

Jamie is quiet.

I continue as I stride. 'Next time you want privacy, maybe don't throw a party.' Out of the corner of my eye I see it in the mirror: Jamie reaching up as if to grab my hair. The swipe of his hand is as chilling as hot breath on my neck. I can feel him – slowed down and threatening – in the deepest, most basic part of me. I'm in danger. In that same way you know to pick up your pace in a darkened parking lot or keep walking past a particularly ominous alleyway. Jamie is that darkened alley. I turn quick. My eyes dart from his still swiping hand to his crazed sunken dark eyes.

'What do you think you're doing?' I ask, my voice low and powerful.

'Closing the door behind you,' Jamie says, his hand falling clumsily on the door handle.

'I won't tell Emma about this,' I say, staring right at him. He says nothing, but his entire body is seething. And I walk out of that bathroom. Quickly. I need to get out of here. I walk. And keep walking. Out of the master bedroom, down the hallway and down the stairs quickly. My heart is racing. Jamie is right behind me. I see Jill see me . . . then Jamie. Her face is cartoonish as she sees both of us. I try to act like I didn't just get caught going through the Dunhams' personal belongings. I try to act like the person who caught me – and then threatened me – isn't behind me right now. What exactly just happened?

I finally reach the first floor and go over to stand next to Jill. Quiet. I can feel her entire body buzzing just beside me. As I speak, Jill tries to stop me at every pause, trying to jump in as I relay my crimes and misdemeanors.

'I was caught, Jill. After All-Balls Ferrell jacked me on the staircase, I then got caught rifling through the personal belongings of Ichabod Crane and his comely wife. I need you to really take this in, Jill. I need you to really take this in,' I say, taking a genteel sip of a water I grab from a passing waiter's tray.

'All-Balls Ferrell.' Jill crumbles into a fit of hysterics.

I smile. And then laugh. And laugh. All of the adrenaline from my run-in with Jamie bubbles up into uncontrollable laughter. I spot Jamie as he walks into the kitchen with Emma. Great. Now the job is really Jill's. He's probably retelling the story now. As I scan the room, I see Ryan. He's swaying and slurring his way through what looks to be quite the involved story. As usual, his audience is riveted. I don't have the time or energy to go into what that was about on the staircase. Actually, it doesn't take time or energy. Despite my inability to see him clearly, Ryan has always been transparent. He wants me to do the heavy lifting of a friend, but without all the muss and responsibility of a real relationship. I believe this is what one would call having one's cake and eating Jessica, too.

'Why is Emma married to that guy?' I ask as Jill and I catch our breath.

'Money?' Jill suggests quickly.

'I think she genuinely loves him, but he gives me the creeps,' I say.

'Why?'

'I think he took a swipe at me. Up in the bathroom. You know, after he caught me going through their stuff?' I hear myself say it. After he caught me going through their stuff.

I continue as Jill opens her mouth. 'I know. I just heard it. Totally.' Jill nods in agreement as she tries to control her laughter.

'Ladies.' Pamela, the lower master and school psychologist. Perfect. I take a deep breath and try to collect myself.

Jill's sniggering takes on a life of its own. The partially suppressed bursts of laughter. The convulsing shoulders.

'Pamela, so good to see you,' I say, shaking her hand.

'Pamela,' Jill squeaks out, motioning to the bartender that yes, she'd like a glass of wine. *Stat.*

'Pretty amazing house, right?' Pamela says, gazing up high into the rafters.

'Yes, definitely,' Jill and I say. I look into the sleek kitchen, complete with Carrara marble countertops and an oversized island in the middle. The entire back of the house is French doors leading out to the backyard that is lit with Japanese lanterns and colored lights floating in the dark blue pool.

'You met the crypt keeper, I see,' Pamela whispers.

'What?' I am taken aback. Is the school psychologist talking shit right now?

'Emma's husband, Jamie? Gives me the creeps,' she says, taking another sip of wine.

'Yeah, what's up with that?' Jill asks.

'Definitely an intense guy. I mean, I get it, my husband wouldn't be all that thrilled if I invited half the school over for dinner,' Pamela says, tugging a tall gentleman in a tweed coat in close. 'Frances Reid, Jill Fleming, this is my husband, Paul.' We shake hands with Paul. He seems delightful. Wide smile, beautiful cocoa skin and salt-and-pepper hair. I'm tempted to check his blazer for elbow patches.

'It's a pleasure,' I say as we finish shaking hands. He pulls Pamela close and they melt into each other.

'I didn't know this mixer was for significant others,' Jill says.

'Oh, sure. It's the only thing that makes it bearable,' Pamela says, looking up at Paul. A slight gasp from Jill as she succumbs again to All-Balls Ferrell. Pamela pats her back, thinking she's choking on her wine. Jill smiles. Embarrassed.

'For you. It's the only thing that makes it bearable for you, dear,' Paul says, giving me a quick wink. I didn't know Pamela was married. And I certainly didn't know that Pamela was married to the nicest guy in the world and that they were ridiculously cute and so clearly still in love.

'Pamela, Paul, will you please excuse us?' I say, tugging a still gasping Jill aside.

'Oh, sure. Poor thing. Went down the wrong pipe. Maybe you can use it as an excuse to leave early,' Pamela says, curling into her husband. I feel as though I've misjudged everyone. Pamela Jackson couldn't be lovelier. Emma Dunham wanted to be a painter and loves her immortal dog beyond the telling of it. Ryan is clearly not the man I thought he was. Jamie, not for nothing, is just as vile as I remember and thought, so that's at least one in my column.

As Jill and I say our good-byes, I come back to the idea of really noticing people. Maybe I spend so much time and energy hiding behind walls I never realized that people will stop looking after a while.

Is it too late to change my mind?

7

Prelude to a Restraining Order

'Don't be mad,' Jill says, opening her front door for our big Boston butt smoke-a-thon.

'Are you going to slam the door in my face?' I ask, holding a bag of peanut M&M's and a bottle of wine.

'No,' Jill says, laughing.

'Then why would I be mad?' I ask, stepping inside her house.

'No reason,' Jill says, closing the door behind me. I walk inside Jill and Martin's house, shaking my bag of peanut M&M's like a tambourine.

'Now, who wants some Boston buuuuuuutt?!' I announce, doing what can only be described as a shoulder-twitching come-hither dance worthy of a 1980s music video. Like I'm lamenting that love is a battlefield.

Sam.

'You remember Sam Earley?' Jill asks. He stands, wipes his hands on his jeans and approaches me.

'Nice to see you again,' I say, clearing my throat and shaking his hand.

'Ms Reid,' Sam says. He's as inconveniently remarkable as ever.

'Please. It's Frannie,' I say.

'Frannie, then,' Sam says.

'Honey, can you help me in the kitchen for a quick sec?' Jill asks, motioning for me to follow her.

'Good seeing you again,' I say to him as I follow Jill into the kitchen. Sam smiles and sits back down on Jill and Martin's large sectional with a group of Martin's colleagues.

'Where's Martin?' I ask.

'Out by that damn smoker.' We make our way through the smattering of guests who have already arrived. Jill quickly introduces me to a few neighbors (all married), an old friend from college (he's gay) and a trio of women Jill knows from various other places (they're desperate and looking).

'That little one has been eyeing Sam,' Jill says, just out of earshot. I crane my neck to take in 'that little one.' Brown, stringy hair and a long flowing skirt that hangs low enough so we can all count ourselves lucky to see her bronzed abs. She's, of course, wearing a flimsy vintage Foreigner concert tee. If I tried to re-create this outfit, I'd be picked up for a seventy-two-hour hold. On her it looks accidentally sexy. It's not that I don't think I'm beautiful. Maybe it's that I don't think I'm pretty. *Beautiful* implies there's more going on than looks or that your looks are deeper than the features themselves. Girls like That Little One are pretty. Simple, undeniable; walk into an online date and that first hurdle is always cleared. Me? Not so much.

Following That Little One's gaze – sure enough, there's Sam. He's lounging back on the sectional, one leg extended fully, perfectly comfortable taking up as much space as he needs. Gray crewneck sweater over a plaid collared shirt, worn-in jeans and dress shoes. His white-blond hair is mussed just that much in the front to make me think he actually took some time on it. He's got more stubble than he did previously.

None of this is helping me push away my curiosity about Sam. I've replayed that night at Lucky Baldwin's, as well as that day in the hallway, more times than I'm comfortable with. Now that I've come face-to-face with him once more, I have to laugh; for all of the yarns I've spun, I don't know Sam at all. If I sat down next to him right now, I wouldn't have anything to say to him. Maybe just to sit down next to him and get to know him better should be the first step. I know this is elementary (dear Watson) to most people, but for me the art of flirtation usually looks a bit more . . . unhurried. So far, my tried and true method is I befriend someone for years while they date other women and then I'm completely shocked when they finally condescend to date me. Obviously, you'd have to put in some time, but the benefits are pretty clear. You too could find yourself in a two-year relationship with someone who doesn't know or satisfy you in any way. Win-win!

'Peanut M&M's?' Martin asks, beer in hand, as he takes a quick break from the Boston butt.

'More protein,' I say, handing him the bag.

'Yes, that's what we're in dire need of. More protein,' he says, giving me a quick hug.

'That's why they're better for you than plain,' I say, on tiptoes.

'I tried to tell her not to,' Martin whispers.

'It's adorable that you thought you could stop her from inviting Sam,' I say.

'Sam?' Martin says, pulling out of the hug.

'Yeah, I—'

'You remember Jeremy Hannon, my friend from college?' Martin asks. I'm stunned. It's actually stunning. I've said countless times before now 'I'm stunned' and now I know that that was all hyperbole. Because right now . . . this? This is stunned.

'Nice to meet you,' Jeremy says, extending his hand.

'We've actually met,' I say through gritted teeth.

'Oh, yeah?' Jeremy asks.

Oh. My. God.

I continue. 'Yes, at Martin and Jill's Labor Day barbecue?' I hear Jill scuttle around the kitchen. A kitchen replete with knives with which I will gut Jill and smoke her in Martin's ridiculous new contraption. I can hear Lisa and Grady arriving in the other room. Loud, boisterous greetings.

'Oh, sure – you were playing that great music.' Jeremy nods. As Jeremy and Martin reacquaint themselves with the Labor Day barbecue, introducing the two of us *again*, I sneak a quick glance at Sam as That Little One approaches him. She asks if someone is sitting next to him on the couch. No, he says. She squeezes her body in next to him, thanking god, she exclaims, that she's so tiny, otherwise there clearly wouldn't have been enough space. Yes, Alex Trebek: I'll have Things I'd Never Say for $500. I look away. I can't watch.

I refocus back on Martin and Jeremy as their relaxed Southern California drawls erode into just saying, 'Dude,' over and over again. Jeremy could be the poster child for Southern California. Sun-streaked blond hair, tanned skin, blinding white teeth and ice-blue eyes always at half-mast. His easy, gravelly speech and the deep, pensive nods he affects as he follows various conversations seem to connote a depth of character. The fact is, he's probably thinking about some Grateful Dead lyric right now. Of course, he has that apathetic detachment thing down pat. Maybe it's more the marijuana than genuine apathy.

'What was that . . . that one great band . . . with the song?' Jeremy searches his memory banks. This won't take long.

'Lynyrd Skynyrd,' I say.

'*Dude,*' Jeremy says, nodding and smiling.

'Indeed,' I say.

'Lynyrd Skynyrd,' Jeremy repeats.

'Which song?' Sam asks, inserting himself into our little circle of awkwardness.

'What?' I ask. *Stunned*. Who would've thought *stunned* would be a word I'd use so much tonight? I thought I was just being invited to dinner.

'Which Lynyrd Skynyrd song were you playing?' Sam says.

'I believe it was "Sweet Home Alabama,"' I confess.

'Oh,' Sam says, clearly disappointed.

'I'm more of a fan of "Simple Man" myself,' I add truthfully.

'Me too.' Sam smiles and nods. Crinkly-eyed, face-changing smile.

Jill is watching intently as she puts together her famous

guacamole. She leaves the pit in. It's the custom and keeps the guacamole from turning a less desirable brown, as she has informed me.

'Gotta love that "Sweet Home Alabama" though, right? Jeremy Hannon, man,' Jeremy says, extending his hand to Sam.

'Sam Earley.'

'You from there? Alabama? The accent,' Jeremy asks, clarifying why he's asked the question as if we hadn't already put it together.

'No, sir,' Sam answers.

'Oh, ha! I get it,' Jeremy says.

We all act like we understand what Jeremy is talking about.

'I'd better get back out to the smoker,' Martin says, swigging the last of his beer.

'How long you been at it, man?' Jeremy asks, pulling two new ice-cold beers from a red bucket and handing Martin one.

'For like . . . I don't know . . . three or four hours now,' Martin says, exhausted.

'You've only been smoking for three or four hours?' Sam asks, clearly concerned.

'Yeah, why?' Martin asks, taking a swig of his beer. Jeremy is now checking out the group of women that originally included That Little One.

Martin asks again, 'Why?' Sam clears his throat and looks around at the house filled to the brim with guests waiting for some smoked Boston butt.

'I hate to tell you this . . .' Sam trails off.

'Dude, spit it out!' Martin says.

'Have you ever heard the saying "low and slow"?'

'Sure,' Martin answers, getting more and more anxious.

'Okay. Good. Well, a smoker runs at about two hundred and twenty degrees,' Sam says gently.

Quiet.

Sam continues. 'I'm from Tennessee, we take our barbecue very seriously.'

'I thought you were from Alabama,' Jeremy says. Sam ignores him. Jill approaches our group with the fresh guacamole in one hand and a bowl of corn chips in the other. So, if I'm following where Sam is going with this, those chips will be our dinner this evening.

'Who's from Alabama?' Jill asks. We all ignore her.

'That meat needs to smoke for at least eight hours. It'd be best if it went to twelve, truth be told.' Sam crosses his arms across his chest and waits. He gives me a look. Like a little shared glance of 'I had to tell him, right?' I secretly think this means he loves me. Martin is quiet. Stunned. Again with the stunned.

'Wait, what?' Jill asks, her voice cracking.

'I'm sorry, Martin. I really am, but serving that meat before that is just downright unsafe, not to mention . . . it would taste terrible,' Sam says, and clears his throat.

'Serving what meat? Is this conversation hypothetical? Please tell me this conversation is hypothetical!' Jill blurts, slamming the guacamole and chips down on the large buffet table. Over the din of the crowd plus the music only a few select guests hear Jill's little outburst. She doesn't seem to care. Lisa and Grady approach.

'Is everything okay?' Lisa asks, a bottle of beer perched in her front jeans pocket and Grady's arm laced around her waist. From the look of it, things are apparently cruising along with Lisa and Grady. Cruising along with no questions about either of their intentions. They're together now. This is what that looks like. I sneak a quick glance at Sam.

'He's only smoked the meat for three or four hours,' Sam says to Grady.

'What now?!' Grady asks, horrified.

'I know,' Sam says. Martin is growing more and more fidgety. He's doing the math. It's seven P.M. That Boston butt will be ready for consumption right around three A.M.

'It needs to go to twelve hours, son,' Grady drawls.

'I told him maybe eight,' Sam says.

'Eight?' Grady winces. Sam shoots him a very pointed look.

'Martin, what are we going to do?' Jill asks, motioning to the crowd of guests.

'Pizza Joe's is open,' I say.

'Pizza Joe's?' Jill says.

'It's right on Lake Avenue. I'll go pick it up. People won't care,' I say, choosing not to tell her that this is most assuredly her karmic punishment for inviting Jeremy Hannon to tonight's doomed festivities.

'People won't care? That's our best-case scenario?' Jill is distraught.

'People just want to hang out. It'll be a funny story. We'll do the smoker thing another time,' I say, looking from Jill to Martin, hoping I'm not overstepping my bounds.

'Go for it,' Lisa says, swigging her beer.

'I can't believe I did that. I bought this great rub and everything,' Martin says, shaking his head.

'*Bought* a rub?!' Sam and Grady say in unison.

'Yeah,' Martin says.

Sam and Grady share a look of deep, deep concern.

'Let's definitely do the pizza, chief,' Grady says, patting Martin on the back.

'And maybe Grady and I will take over next time?' Sam asks, shaking his head. Martin looks panic-stricken.

Jill huffs into the kitchen in search of the phone. Lisa and I follow, leaving the men to discuss the wonders of barbecue.

'You know my theory,' I say as Jill pulls out a phone book from under the kitchen sink. She takes a long pull from her bottle of sparkling water as she violently flips through the pages.

'Don't you even say it,' Jill says.

'That if you invite douchebags like Jeremy Hannon to parties where they don't belong your entire meal will be ruined,' I say, smiling at Lisa, who barks out a laugh.

'That's who that dude is? He's the texting guy?' Lisa asks.

'In the flesh,' I say.

'Cute,' Lisa says, checking Jeremy out.

'Didn't remember me,' I say.

'How do you know?' Jill asks, scanning the phone book.

'He said, "Nice to meet you,"' I say.

'So?' Jill says.

'Tonight. He said that tonight,' I say.

'That'd be the first clue,' Lisa says.

'Not for nothing, but I was playing the odds. And you? We haven't seen or heard from you in days,' Jill says to Lisa as she dials the phone.

Lisa just smiles.

Jill doesn't miss a beat. 'I need details, pictures if you've got them, video would be better. Let's just . . . you know what? I'm just going to, I need you to show me on this cucumber – oh, hello? Yes, I'd like to order some pizzas?'

'A part of me intentionally kept it from her just to see her squirm,' Lisa says, taking another swig from her beer. I smile.

'You can go fuck yourself – oh, no, not you, sir, I mean, no, you're lovely, I was talking to my friend,' Jill says into the phone.

'He's the best man I've ever known,' Lisa says, gazing at Grady. I smile; shit, I'm almost teary eyed. Lisa continues. 'I honestly never thought I'd be this happy.'

'I love that,' I say with a wide smile. Once again, I'm moderately intimidated by Lisa and what I want to do is ooze all over her, hugging her and cuddling her up against my face like a puppy on Christmas morning. I imagine that would result in my getting shivved, so I decide on the breezy 'I love that.'

'No, no delivery. We'll come pick them up,' Jill says, motioning to me to ask if that's still okay. I nod. It'll be good to get out of this haunted house of my failed betrothals. Jill signs off with the man I'll have to apologize profusely to later regarding the 'go fuck yourself' incident. She gets right down to business.

'So you guys are dating?!' Jill asks Lisa.

'He's great – you know, good in the sack, good job—'

'Good in the sack? You've slept with him?' Jill asks, horrified.

'Yeah, sure,' Lisa says.

Jill is silent.

Judging.

I crane my neck to see where everyone is. 'Everyone' meaning Sam. And kinda Grady. I imagine the next few minutes are going to get a tad messy. They're both out by the smoker. From the looks of them, their mannerisms going back and forth between stifled laughter, arms tightly crossed across chests and conciliatory pats on Martin's back, they're quite involved in what they're doing. Involved enough not to hear or be a part of what is sure to be a revealing conversation . . . if Jill has anything to do with it.

Jill blurts, 'Grady is a southern gentleman! How could you sleep with him so quickly? You're now the . . . you're now the girl he—'

'A southern gentleman? Jesus, he is actually from this century,' I say, trying to lighten the mood. I pop a grape in my mouth from a platter yet to be set out.

'They do things differently down there. It's very clear who they . . . you just shouldn't have—'

Lisa cuts in. 'He wasn't a southern gentleman when we had sex in the alleyway right outside of Lucky Baldwin's.'

'Had sex? Are you—'

'You're so busy defending his honor that you've forgotten it takes two,' Lisa says, opening the fridge for another beer.

'Yeah, but he's not . . . he doesn't . . .'

'*Jill* . . .' I say.

'But now you're just the girl he has sex with rather than the girl he marries,' Jill says, stepping closer to Lisa. To implore Lisa, beg Lisa. *Pray. For. Lisa.*

I fear for Jill's safety in these milliseconds.

'Whether I want to be the girl Grady has sex with or the girl he marries is a choice I get to make, not him. Or do you not know that?' Lisa says, opening up her beer with a bottle opener on her key ring.

'Wait, what?' Jill asks.

'I get to choose what happens next.'

Jill is quiet, her mouth opening and closing like a dying fish's. She shakes her head every once in a while, with a little huffing sound. Another grape. Another swigged beer. Jill is stuck in a blustery continuum. As I swallow the last bits of the grape, I wait for Lisa's simple words to stop floating around in my head and make sense to me.

I get to choose what happens next.

Why this is as revolutionary as man's first flight is a debate for another day, a day that will hopefully involve a lot of bourbon. Women make proclamations about how amazing they are in the privacy of girls' nights out across the globe. '*The best thing that ever happened to him!*' But most of us believe men are somehow doing us a favor when they choose us. That we are something to be borne, tolerated, changed and asked to stay quiet and slim down. There's this set of rules we must abide by in order to be worthy of love. A love that's based on a persona as far away from our real selves as possible. The secret you. Was

I a partner in my relationship with Ryan or was I constantly amazed that he deigned to date me for as long as he did? As Lisa reaches across and pops a grape in her mouth, I close my eyes.

Did Ryan ever even know the real me?

Lisa offers me a grape.

'No,' I say, almost in a whisper.

She pops one in her mouth and goes back to waiting for Jill's pending reply.

I continue. 'No, I mean . . . yes. I'd like a grape.'

'Then why'd you say no?' Lisa asks, extending the platter.

'Because I just asked myself a question and the answer is no,' I say, putting the grape in my mouth. I breathe in the cold sweetness.

'What was the question?' Lisa asks.

'Did Ryan ever know the real me.' Another quick glance outside. The men are crowded around the smoker. Sam bends all the way back, shaking with laughter, as Martin finally comes around to how funny this all is. The confused guests milling around them, however, are less than thrilled about the night's food prospects.

Lisa's mouth tightens and she nods. She doesn't say anything.

'Oh, sweetie,' Jill says, reaching over to me. I take her hand. I choke back a surprisingly strong wave of emotion.

Jill senses this and cradles my hand even tighter in hers. Lisa just looks like she wants to kill someone. I'll give her Ryan's address later.

I continue in a whisper. 'He hadn't touched me in

months – closer to a year. Okay, he hadn't touched me in over a year. Said something about me being too clingy. Of course, I thought it was my fault and made the usual leap to me being repulsive and untouchable.'

'As you do,' Jill says, trying to get as close to me as possible.

'Of course it couldn't have anything to do with his tiny-ass dick,' Lisa says, shaking her head, her mouth tight. I crack a smile and act momentarily offended.

'We were all thinking it, sweetie,' Jill says, soothing me and urging me to continue.

'I always tried to be so cool, so indifferent, you know? Like my entire life was no biggie—'

'No pun intended,' Jill says, interrupting.

I continue. 'Because he always told me how intense I was. And I just thought, I'm not intense, I just . . . I just care. It became more and more clear that he didn't,' I say, my voice climbing several octaves, soon to be heard only by whatever dogs are unlucky enough to be in the vicinity.

'Oh, sweetie,' Jill says, now squeezing my shoulder, pulling me closer.

'And I can't even . . . I can't even begin to tell you how exhausting it was,' I say for the first time.

'*Was* being the key word here,' Lisa says.

'What did I think . . . what *do* I think is so wrong with me?' I ask, tears streaming down my face.

'That he's right. That you are too intense. Whoaaaaaa,' Lisa says, miming someone turning down the volume on a stereo. A pack of guests walk into the kitchen. Jill gives them a warm greeting, tells them food is on its way and that booze is in the red buckets. So good to see you, she oozes. Lisa blocks me, and my streaming tears, from the pack of guests. I love her for that. My dad used to say that there were only a chosen few he'd 'go in the jungle with' – referring to his time in Vietnam. While I love Jill dearly, in any 'going in the jungle' scenario she'd be disastrous. But Lisa? Lisa I'd go in the jungle with.

As I gather myself, I feel lighter. But at the same time, I'm somehow burdened by this new knowledge. Maybe I don't have to be someone else for someone to love me. I can be me. But I went underground for a reason. That nerdy kid with the hyperactivity problem was a tough sell.

'So, what's up with you and Sam then?' Lisa asks.

'Who knows?' I say, blowing my nose.

Jill and Lisa are quiet.

'You think I should go over there and grab his crank?' I say, laughing.

Lisa looks like that's exactly what she thinks I should be doing. I stop laughing. People are still arriving. This is an official party now. The wafting smells of the smoker tantalize the guests with meat they'll never have. That and the fact that apparently there's a lucky man in attendance who is fixing to get his crank grabbed by a panicked brunette with something to prove.

'You guys are ridiculous,' I say, my face flushing.

Jill and Lisa are quiet.

'What?'

They look at each other.

I ask again, '*What?*'

'I don't know. You were just talking about how Ryan

never knew the real you, you know? And how, I don't know, I'm going to go out on a limb and hazard a guess that there was no crank grabbing in that relationship,' Lisa says.

'There was no crank to grab,' Jill says, unable to help herself.

'I can't believe we're having this conversation,' I say, completely embarrassed.

Jill says, 'We're not saying you do anything you're not comfortable with—'

Lisa interrupts. 'And I think we're kind of using *grabbing his crank* as a euphemism at this point.'

'A euphemism?' I ask.

'Yeah,' Lisa says.

'A euphemism is supposed to be less offensive,' I say.

'You want me to say *cock*?' Lisa says, the word *cock* ringing throughout Jill's house like the bells announcing Paul Revere's fateful midnight ride.

'Fine. *Crank,*' I say, checking to see where Sam is. Out of earshot, I pray. I can't . . . I can't find him. Okay. Good.

'Like I said, I think we're using *grab his crank* as a euphemism for maybe doing something a little outside of your comfort zone,' Lisa says.

'And maybe a little naughty,' Jill says, her voice literally quivering with excitement.

'Naughty? Really?' I say, shaking my head. I don't . . . I don't know why I'm so against this. It's actually kind of hot. I'd like to fancy myself as someone spontaneous and a little risqué. I've never given this a second thought since I'm so positive I'll be rejected as an asexual female friend who's clearly misread the signs. I'm afraid of my own sexuality. When I dipped my toe into what I thought was the Real Me, Ryan told me to back off. Even worse, he seemed more annoyed than turned on. And it was just a toe. It was a flirty nightie and a dog-eared page in Jill's *Kama Sutra*. It was me playacting at what I thought a vixen would do. And even then I was rejected.

But it worked for that relationship. If I never let loose, I never really gave over. Of course, it's not about crank grabbing at all. It's about intimacy. I always held some piece of me apart like it was something to be ashamed of. Something to be embarrassed by. Something to perfect. Now I know what I was holding back, what I'm embarrassed by . . . is my love. I fear that my defenseless heart and my unconditional love is a burden no one wants.

So, it sits. Behind a wall. Safe and waiting. For someone who keeps looking and doesn't ever give up.

'You guys need any help?' Grady says, sliding his hand back around Lisa's waist. She places her hand over his and gives him a quick kiss.

'No, thank you,' Jill says.

'I'll head over to pick up the pizzas in a few minutes,' I say, my face flushing as I sense the heat between Lisa and Grady.

'How many did y'all order?' Grady asks.

'I thought one pizza for every three people?' Jill replies.

'So, thirteen?' Sam says, sidling over and leaning against the shining granite countertop in Jill's galley-style kitchen. I can't help but look at his crotch. I fear I just may lunge at it, unable to stop myself. I dig my hands into my jeans pockets.

'Yes. Thirteen,' Jill says, smiling coquettishly.

'It's a parlor trick. I've been waiting for someone to have a math-related problem all night,' Sam says.

'Ha!' I laugh. Loud. There is a rippling shift in the physics of the room. Time jumps, then stops. People freeze. Yet somehow my barking laughter echoes and echoes and echoes throughout the room. Sam's stare is fixed. Maybe there's a line of spittle from the bottom of my lip to the top. Perchance I have a smattering of grape still on my tongue. I don't know. I've clearly gone insane.

Sensing this, Jill and Lisa jump in with loud laughter meant to drown out my single blurt of hysterics. Sam smiles and watches me. Pointedly.

'I'd better be heading out to Pizza Joe's,' I say, sighing out of my fit of laughter.

'Have Martin give you some money on the way out,' Jill says, pouring herself a glass of wine.

'Got it,' I say, smiling and slinking past Lisa and Grady in the forever narrowing kitchen. Then Sam. As I inch past him, I place a hand on his waist. The ribbed base of his gray sweater is woolly and soft; the slippery hardness of his leather belt slides just underneath. The tips of my fingers rest and then press into . . . him. His torso. His skin. His body. It only took milliseconds, but I feel like I've crossed the Rubicon. My hand falls away as I continue out into Jill and Martin's living room. I don't look back. I don't check to see if Sam is wiping away my cooties. As I look for Martin I keep telling myself that what I did was hot. That Sam might have even been turned on. That this fledgling attraction I'm feeling is reciprocated. Even as I'm becoming exhausted by my mantras, I vow not to allow my fears and insecurity to get the better of me.

I find Martin in the living room, he gives me the money and as he winds through how embarrassed he is about the smoker, I look out into the driveway.

'Oh, wait. I'm blocked in. Do you know who . . . who drives a, it looks like a Datsun 280ZX or something.' I crane my neck so I can see the car better. It's an old, low-slung, bluish sports car. I can't quite make it out. Martin walks out onto the porch, takes a closer look, walks past me with a disapproving look and back into the living room.

'Hey! Who's driving the old Ferrari?'

Ferrari? I whip my head back around. Now I can just make out the slightest hint of the bright yellow hood ornament.

'That's mine,' Sam says, looking past us to see what the problem is.

'Frannie's got to get the pizzas, can you move your car so she can get out?' Martin says. Sam drives a vintage Ferrari. No, this is fine. I can . . . I can handle this.

'Sure,' Sam says, patting his pockets and pulling out a set of keys. I'm watching him. Studying him. Remembering what his body felt like beneath my touch.

Sam walks past me and out into the driveway. I follow him as Martin closes the door behind us. The cold weather hits me and I can see my breath in little hyperventilating puffs.

'Thanks for doing this,' I say, pulling the keys from the depths of my purse. I beep my car unlocked. I can take or leave you, Sam Earley. You and your vintage Ferrari and knowledge of Lynyrd Skynyrd's 'Simple Man.' It's fine. He's totally out of my league yet kind of perfect for me. Lisa's words ring in my head. It's my choice how this night goes. I decide. Maybe he's just as nervous as I am. Ever think of that? I throw my purse onto the passenger seat and take another look at Sam as he ambles down the driveway: a successful architect, way over six feet tall, blond and walking toward a Ferrari. Right. And he's lovely and smart and has a southern accent.

No, nope. This dude is seriously out of my league. Audrey Hepburn circa *Breakfast at Tiffany's* would have to look long and hard into a mirror to wonder if even she was worthy of this guy. Nope. Maybe Jeremy can get me stoned later and make a move on me. I'll woo him into submission with 'Sweet Home Alabama.' I'm just about to get into my car when—

'Frannie?' Sam calls from down the driveway. I stop midlaunch. I'm off balance and awkward as I turn to face Sam.

'Yeah?'

'It's right around the corner, right? Why don't I just drive?' Sam asks, holding the passenger-side door open for me. I'm holding on to my open driver's-side door.

In a fugue state, I pry my fingers away, grab my purse and slam the door. I beep my car locked. I blink and try to loosen up. Force my eyebrows down. Breathe. Smile, for crissakes. He's asked if he could help me pick up some pizza, not take me from behind as the entire group of thwarted non-Boston butt-eating partygoers looks on.

It's okay to let him know that I want his company.

Accepting Sam's invitation to allow him to drive doesn't have to be a prelude to a restraining order. Conversations about cranks and pod people who do things I would never do swirl in my brain for the briefest of seconds.

'Frannie? I said I could drive?' Sam says. The drawl of his voice licking over my name sends shivers up my spine and tingles to previously unknown parts throughout my body. I gulp.

'That would be lovely,' I say.

8

In the Air Tonight

As I walk past Sam and slide into the low Ferrari, I feel like I'm living someone else's life – someone who gets to ride in Ferraris with southern gentlemen who hold the door open for them. As the door slams behind me and Sam walks around to his side, I have just enough time to check out my body – how did I look from that angle? Was my shirt down and my jeans up? Do I look like I should be in a Ferra— Sam opens the driver's-side door. My internal dialogue must wait. I'm still unable to say anything. He starts the car. I can feel the purr of the engine inside my body, holding on to the aortic valve of my heart and tightening. I shift in the biscuit-colored seat and take in the antiquated dashboard. The stereo emits a low muffled song. I strain to hear it. I can't quite make it out.

'What is this?' I ask, my finger pointing at the stereo.

'It's a stereo,' Sam says, smiling. He cranks the steering wheel hard as he reverses down the driveway, his arm easily resting on the back of my seat.

'You're funny,' I say, nodding and laughing.

'For a speech therapist you should really try to be more specific,' Sam says.

I nod and laugh, my mind racing through a Rolodex of jokes: too cheesy, too mean, too obscure.

Sam continues. 'It's David Gray.'

'I love David Gray,' I say. Quiet. Sam quietly sings along with the music. Barely audible.

I continue. 'It's just on Lake Avenue, so back down Hill Avenue and right on New York Drive,' I say, pointing in the direction we should be going and trying to break my gaze away from Sam's quietly moving lips.

'Sounds good,' Sam says, cranking the steering wheel again, putting the car in gear. Soon we're humming down Jill and Martin's street, the Ferrari's engine still holding my heart tightly.

'So, power steering wasn't really part of the design then?' I ask.

'Uh, no. I'm afraid not,' Sam says, smiling. We turn down Hill Avenue.

As the silence permeates the space, I realize that it's that terrifying point right after you've met someone when you wish you could talk to them for days. There's so much you want to learn about them. But you have to hold yourself back from asking questions you simply don't have the right to know the answers to yet. You are acutely aware that you barely know him.

We drive in silence with just the hum of the Ferrari's engine and David Gray in the background. It comes to me that the person I really want to know about is me. If I focus on Sam, I won't have to understand the new things I've started unearthing about myself. It's really win-win. Set up a completely unavailable guy as an obsession, spend years swooning over him . . . and you get to hold the painful realization that you don't know who you are at bay. Of course, the shell cottage and legion of feral cats loom large . . . alas, it's not a perfect plan. The scarier alternative: somehow during the last three months I've excavated enough about myself to understand that the kind of man I want is Sam. The kind of man I need is Sam. That this is no rebound.

'You're going to have to tell me about the car,' I say, summoning the courage from somewhere deep. Acting like this is just another guy, in just another car. And Angelina Jolie will play the part of Frances Reid in this evening's performance. I turn down the stereo and wait.

'It's a 1973 Ferrari Daytona,' Sam says as we wait at the light on Hill Avenue and New York Drive. The stream of cars speeding down New York Drive keeps us from turning right just yet.

'It's beautiful,' I say, taking it in.

Sam smiles to himself, his head shaking just a bit.

'What?' I blurt before thinking.

'It really is a beautiful car,' he says.

'But that wasn't what you were just thinking.'

'No.'

'You're going to have to tell me now. Them's the rules.'

'Oh, really?'

'Clearly.'

'Here's the thing. My level of . . . suaveness right now is pretty high. Right?'

'The car pretty much ensures a high score, although the use of the word *suave* will have to be a deduction.'

'Ah, yes.'

'But continue.'

'I got this car because of Sonny Crockett.' Sam finally makes the right on New York Drive and the Ferrari's engine is humming again.

'I'm sorry, what?'

'Sonny Crockett. From *Miami Vice*?'

'Sonny Crockett as in Don Johnson, Crockett and Tubbs? Sonny Crockett?'

'The one and only.'

'And how did the power of Sonny Crockett draw you to the 1973 Ferrari Daytona?'

'He drove one. It was black and a convertible, but in the first three seasons of *Miami Vice* he drove this very car,' Sam says, trying desperately not to smile.

'So, you were a *Miami Vice* fan, I take it?'

'It was instrumental in making the man you see before you today, darlin'.'

Deep breath. Darlin'. Okay . . . just file it away. Can't deal with that right now. 'That would be easier to believe if you were wearing a pastel blazer with no socks and Italian loafers. A 1973 Ferrari Daytona does not a *Miami Vice* fan make,' I say.

'Left or right?' Sam asks as we approach the stoplight at Lake Avenue.

'Right, sorry. You'll have to excuse me. I'm a bit taken aback. You can't just spring that kind of information on a girl and expect her to be able to do something as pedestrian as giving you directions to Pizza Joe's.'

'My apologies,' Sam says, smiling and wrenching the old car to the right.

We're quiet for a few seconds. I'm smiling and kind of shaking my head. Sam Earley is a *Miami Vice* fan who thought my knowing this would change my opinion of him.

'There's nothing that can really top that,' I finally say.

'Ha!' Sam laughs, his head whipping back as he shifts the Ferrari into a higher gear. His long fingers curl around the gearshift. It's such a raw moment – a private moment. In the tiny humming cockpit of a 1973 Ferrari Daytona that was inspired by a horrible 1980s pastel cheese-fest.

Life just doesn't get much better than this.

'It's right . . . right there? See it?' I say, pointing to Pizza Joe's.

'Yeah, I see it.'

'Are you going to need a soundtrack by Jan Hammer in order to get there?'

'Ha!'

'A speedboat and an impending cocaine bust?'

Sam is still laughing as we park in front of Pizza Joe's.

'I don't think Philip Michael Thomas is doing much these days. We could give him a call and get the old team back together.'

'Is there a statute of limitations on jokes about nerdy pursuits?'

'I'm afraid not.'

'I didn't think so,' Sam says, turning the car off.

'Now I understand your hesitation about sharing that information.'

'No longer cool enough, I expect?'

'Cool enough?' I say, my smile wide but confused.

'For you.' My brain whirls. A catalog of possibilities of what he means spins by.

Sam opens his door and climbs out, his lanky frame curling gracefully out of the low sports car. I start to follow his lead just as he's slamming his door. I've been problem-solving this Ferrari dismount since I got in the car and realized it's basically sitting just inches off the ground. It's going to take every bit of leg muscle I've got, as well as a burst of adrenaline, not to look like a pregnant woman getting out of a hammock. I creak open the large Ferrari door and begin to heave myself out, only to find Sam standing over me with his hand extended.

'I might be the poor man's Sonny Crockett, but at least I'm well mannered,' Sam says, pulling my car door the rest of the way open and offering me his hand again.

'A definite plus,' I say, my voice catching in pure terror. I curl my fingers around his hand and swing my legs out and into the gutter. It's either that or step up onto the sidewalk and risk looking like a pole-vaulter midleap. Sam's hand envelops mine, and in the time it takes me to panic about how this whole thing is going to work and and *and*, he has me out onto the sidewalk in one swift, nimble motion. The door is slamming behind me and his hand is resting on the small of my back as we ease towards Pizza Joe's.

'I'm sure my mother has spies put here to make sure California hasn't eroded my proper southern upbringing away,' Sam says. What just happened? How . . . I mean, how did I get out of that car so easily?

'A very real concern,' I say, hitching my purse over my

shoulder as I wonder what other freakish mutant powers this man is hiding.

Sam and I head into Pizza Joe's. He holds the door for me as I hurry embarrassedly in front of him.

Pizza Joe's is a local mom-and-pop establishment in Altadena. Its no-frills exterior belies the majesty within. Red plastic booths and a man behind the counter flipping pies high into the air. Four types of pizza to choose from and red checked boxes for takeout. The real deal.

After fumbling through the pizza guy's uncomfortable realization that we are the people picking up the 'go fuck yourself' order, we begin the process of taking the pizzas to the car.

'I've got it,' Sam says, taking the top four pizzas and backing out of the restaurant. The pizzas are dense and heavy. I take the next two and follow him out to the car. He has the trunk open and is shifting items around as he balances the four pizzas in one hand. He sets the pizzas down and looks over to me.

'This is going to be a tight fit,' I say, handing him the two pizzas I have. Sam takes the pizzas and stacks them in the trunk. I begin to walk back into Pizza Joe's for the rest. Sam reaches out and takes my arm, sliding down to my hand and then quickly letting go. I pull my hand back. Instinctively.

'I'm sorry,' I say quickly. Can I grab his hand back? Why? What did I just do?

'No, I'm sorry . . . I wanted to get your attention and it seemed absurd to call your name when I'm standing a foot away from you,' Sam says, stepping up onto the curb. So tall. I look up at him. I gulp. *I literally gulp.*

'Oh, not a . . . not a problem,' I say, turning around again.

'Frannie?' Sam says. I turn back around. 'I was going to do the hand thing again, but then I thought we had the whole conversation about it . . .'

'Maybe I should just stop running away,' I say. He has no idea how globally I mean this.

'Nice inadvertent segue.'

'I'm queen of the inadvertent segue,' I say, apropos of nothing.

'I wanted to apologize for the way I left things the other night,' Sam says, stepping ever closer. My breath catches. My brain freezes.

'Oh?' I say, my voice crackly and quivering.

'I shouldn't have left so quickly.'

'It was the Justin Timberlake sing-along, wasn't it?'

'It most certainly was not.'

'Please, it wasn't even a—' I lay a peacemaking hand on his arm. And I'm struck dumb. Sam watches as my hand travels from his arm to his chest.

'I . . . uh . . .' My hand is now resting on Sam's chest, his soft gray sweater just underneath, the crisp collared plaid shirt crackling and pressed just below.

I pull my hand back. Quickly. Urgently. I feel like I've just been pushed out of an airplane and I'm frantically checking to see if there's a parachute or an anvil strapped to my back.

'It won't happen again,' Sam says, looking me in the eye.

'See that it doesn't,' I say.

Sam leans in. And down. He turns his head and watches me. Watches me watching him. Do I want this? he's asking himself. I have no idea what I look like right now. I'm not ready for any of this. I'm not ready to be here with this man. Not ready to handle what's standing in front of me. How can this be happening to me? Men like Sam don't happen to me. Men like *Ryan* happen to me.

Well, fuck that.

I reach up and touch the side of his face. Warm. Warmer than I thought he'd be. His skin is stubbly and soft at the same time. His jawline right under my palm. His eyes locked on mine. Light brown. Spoked and outlined with cinnamon. And before I know what I'm doing I've laced my hand through his hair and I'm pulling him toward me. It's as if I've been wandering the desert and what he's offering me is the first drink of water I've had in my life.

And then I can't get enough. I'm clutching fistfuls of gray sweater as we're thrust against the Ferrari; Sam's mouth is warm and wet. There's no thought except the desire to have him closer. There's no fear except that I won't be able to get enough. There's no doubt that what's happening is terrifyingly free and new. Sam wraps his arms all the way around me and is pulling me close – pulling my entire body close – because, except for my lips, my body is arched outward at a safe distance. His hands are on either side of my waist, dangerously close to my ass, and he pulls me in. Up and close. Everything, every part of us pressed against one another. He brings one hand up and laces it through my hair, closer . . . closer . . . closer. His fingers long and determined. He makes the slightest noise as I arch into him, letting my body take over. My face flushes as I realize it's a good noise . . . an intimate noise.

'Sir?' The pizza guy clears his throat from the now opened door of the pizza joint. I wrench my face away out of a sudden sense of propriety. Sam's lips are millimeters from mine. He doesn't turn around and I can feel his warm breath on my face. He dips down and gives me one more kiss. Long. Sweet. Unhurried. As he pulls away slowly I realize that my hand is curled around his belt. Pulling him.

'You don't want those pizzas to get cold, sir,' the pizza guy says again before letting the door swing closed. Sam looks from me to my hand at his belt. A raised eyebrow. I don't move. I pull him closer. Sam smiles. His lips are red, his face flushed.

'I'm going to need that back, darlin',' he drawls.

'For now,' I say, letting him go. I take a deep breath as if I've been underwater. The world comes back into focus. The cars on the street. The chill in the air. All of it. Sam watches me as I tune back in. My face flushes, because as the hum of the traffic returns, so does my own personal mythology. I'm not the girl who makes out with men like Sam on street corners pressed up against Ferraris. I'm not the girl who pulls men closer by their belt buckles.

I'm not the girl men choose.

'Wait here. Be right back,' Sam says, kissing me once more. As he goes back into Pizza Joe's, I feel my smile slowly wane. My brow furrows as Sam's absence yields a far more heightened emptiness than I've ever felt before. An emptiness that quickly begets questions: Was I too wanton? Was I pawing at him? Was he as invested as I was? Did I just make a prize idiot of myself? For those fleeting moments there was no inner monologue. I wasn't even cognizant enough to be proud that I was 'in the moment.' It was just Sam and me. Sam is watching me from inside Pizza Joe's. He looks distracted as he takes the remainder of the pizzas. He lifts them easily and makes his way out to the car once more. I stand next to the open trunk, the smell of fresh pizza wafting, and watch Sam as he shuffles the pizzas around in the shrinking Ferrari trunk like a real-life version of Pizza Tetris. Sam finally gets the pizzas set and slams the trunk.

He pauses. It takes me a second to realize as I focus back in on him. He looks . . . torn.

'What is it?' I ask, my heart thumping out of my body, my own mythology screaming inside my brain.

'Nothing . . . nothing, darlin'. We'd better get these pizzas back,' Sam says, smiling. He leans in for another kiss and it's already different. No longer wild and swirling, the kiss is measured and . . . considered. Something has already changed. I hate that my knee-jerk reaction is to think it's something I've done.

Sam takes my hand and leads me around to the passenger side, opens my door and deposits me safely inside. The door slams behind me. In the span of fifteen minutes my entire life has been altered in a way that is so . . . cruel.

There is more.

That middling life I thought I was destined to live – with its all-balls love and half-assed requests for classic rock mixes – is a crock of shit.

There is more.

There are people out there who have X-ray vision. They can see through my walls, armor and scrims and filters right down to the Real Me. And the saddest thing in the world? I haven't forgotten who that person is. She's in there and waiting. Like Sleeping Beauty locked high in a tower, she's been patient and aware of the coma I've been in all these years. As Sam folds into the Ferrari and starts the beautiful hum of the car once more, I realize the one hitch in someone having X-ray glasses is that I'm utterly exposed to him. It's one thing to want someone to keep looking, to swim over moats and dodge flaming arrows to find you. It's quite another when you ask yourself, really ask yourself, if you're finally ready to come out into the open. No matter what.

Sam and I drive down Lake Avenue in silence that stretches itself over us like a fog. And then a poisonous gas. Sitting in the passenger seat, my brain is in overdrive. The sad reality is I really don't know Sam, and I certainly don't know how to ask what exactly happened back there. As we turn left on New York Drive, I decide it's because I acted outside of the norm. I went outside of my comfort zone. If I want to know what's going on, why don't I just . . .

'Sooooo, this isn't awkward or anything,' I say, looking over at Sam. He smiles. Immediately.

'No, not at all,' Sam says, his voice gravelly and low.

'Is it . . . is it, uh . . . hot in here?' I ask, tugging cartoonishly at my collar.

'Ha!' Sam laughs, cranking the steering wheel left on Hill Avenue and continuing on to Jill and Martin's house.

'You wanted me to get specific,' I say, smiling.

'That I did, darlin'. That I did,' Sam says.

'The wafting smell of pizza really does make it that much more dramatic,' I say, my hands in tight fists. Breathe.

'It certainly adds an upmarket air.'

We are silent. Both smiling to ourselves. Not sharing what exactly we find funny. It could be very different things. I might have to go back to a life without Sam. He might just have gas. How can I know at this point?

Sam continues. 'I finally felt like Sonny Crockett.'

'What?' I blurt, laughing.

'That was very *Miami Vice* of us,' Sam says, pulling into Jill and Martin's driveway.

'I swear I heard the opening chords of "In the Air Tonight." '

'You've finally fulfilled my schoolboy fantasy.' Sam turns off the car, pulls the key from the ignition and rests it on his lap.

'Ha . . . I'm glad to have been of service,' I say, smiling. Sam opens his door and climbs out; he bends back in just as I'm about to open my door.

'Nope. Wait. Hold on,' Sam says, slamming his door. He jogs around the front of the car and back toward my door. I watch him. And watch him. And watch him. And wait for any of this to feel real at all. Maybe I should stop questioning and start enjoying myself. Not that I could wipe the smile off my face if I tried, or the look of terror that takes its place when I fear I've gotten in way too deep way too fast. Sam creaks open my door and extends his hand.

'Thank you, good sir,' I say, taking his hand and

marveling once again at how quickly and smoothly Sam extricates me from the car with just one swift motion. This time, though, he doesn't move as I stand. He holds on to my hand. So tall. Looming and focused. The world falls away once more. My breath quickens, puffs of chilled air nearly fogging the space between us. Sam wets his lips.

'Fiiinallllly!' Jill says from the porch. Sam turns to look, the muscle in his neck tightening and stretching down below his collared shirt, tucking warmly underneath that gray sweater. I look from Sam to Jill. We're too close for her not to suspect something.

'Martin, honey? Come help bring the pizzas in!' Jill says, trotting down the front steps. She approaches us quickly as we've both taken a step away from each other. Sam slams the passenger door and opens up the trunk. The pizzas are full to bursting and the smell immediately drifts out into the ether.

'We'll talk later,' Jill rasps as she passes me on the way to Sam with a quick wink and pat on the ass.

'I—'

'Don't even try to deny it,' she whispers.

I am quiet.

Martin hops down the front steps and approaches quickly. Lisa and Grady are just behind him.

'These smell amazing. Thanks for picking them up, man,' Martin says, lifting out another stack and handing them to Grady. Grady passes his beer to Lisa and takes the pizzas. Sam and Grady head inside, pizzas in hand.

I stand next to the Ferrari. Jill and Lisa are quiet. I feel like I'm out behind the handball courts with the tough girls and they're about to shake me down for my algebra homework.

'You'd better start talking,' Jill says, stepping closer.

'We were loading the pizzas into the trunk and he wanted to apologize for how he left things the other night. Then he reached out to me and I just . . . it all came down on me. Everything we talked about. And then he stepped up onto the curb. He was so tall and . . . I—' I'm reliving it. My heart begins to race once more.

Jill interrupts. 'Oh my god . . . did you grab his crank?' She skips slightly, as a little kid would upon hearing she was going to Disneyland.

'No, I didn't grab his crank, for crissakes,' I say, flushing.

'Let her finish, perv,' Lisa says, shoving Jill slightly. She giggles, giddy and happy. Jill cranes her neck to see inside her full house. Martin is announcing there is pizza; there are cheers and clapping. She rolls her eyes.

'I can't believe we had to order pizza,' Jill says with a sigh.

'Go on,' Lisa says.

'And it was like I couldn't speak anymore, couldn't stop touching him. So, I just gave over,' I say.

'Are you kidding me?' Jill says.

'I know!' I say, letting my voice drop.

'Good for you,' Lisa says, smiling.

'We should get in there before he knows exactly what's happening out here,' I say, starting to walk into the house.

'I'm so proud of you,' Jill says, draping an arm around me.

'It's scary though, you know?'

'Yeah . . .' Jill and Lisa say in unison.

'What am I supposed to do . . . what am I supposed to do with this? With the knowledge that someone like him exists?' I plead.

'You let that shit ride,' Lisa says. Repeats, really, from the Lucky Baldwin's bathroom.

'Yeah, I guess,' I say as we climb the steps into Jill's house. Jill stops and turns to me. Serious.

'You choose. You know? *You* choose where this goes,' Jill says, looking me in the eye. She looks from me to Lisa. Lisa nods. And nods.

'I choose,' I repeat.

'Where this goes is your choice,' Lisa says.

'I want him to go everywhere,' I say.

'Damn right, you do,' Lisa says, and we walk inside.

'Just don't blow him on your first date,' Jill says, and closes the door behind us.

The night wears on. We eat our pizza, the conversation moves quickly and we're all laughing and having a good time. Lisa and Grady join in, Grady ribbing Martin for the earlier barbecue faux pas. Martin is a good sport. It's the six of us. A utopian sextet of happy couples. Martin and Jill: married and settled. Lisa and Grady: constantly touching, smiling from ear to ear, excited about what the future holds.

Then there's me and Sam: veterans of myriad match-making schemes. And with age comes the knowledge that *everyone* has baggage, but you can hope that when you encounter someone else's, it'll match your own. The complicated algorithms of the pre-relationship: 1 mix tape + 2(accidental run-ins in the hallways – serious ex-girlfriends/possible fiancée(?)) + 1 set of in-laws + X(number of sexual partners – one night stands) will = eternal bliss.

But the truth is that when it's right – when it's *really* right – that algorithm fades away and the equation simply becomes 1 + 1 = 2.

'I think I'm going to head home,' I say as the party winds down. The simplicity of just doing what I want is freeing yet completely terrifying at the same time.

I've tried the other way. I've been the girl who waited around until the end of the party in hopes of being chosen. And as most economists will attest, if there's too much supply, the demand dwindles.

'I'll walk you out,' Sam says, putting his glass in the sink. Jill relaxes a bit. This is acceptable, not the best-case scenario (i.e., a spontaneous backyard wedding), but this *will* do.

'Thank you for a lovely evening,' I say, gathering my purse.

'So, see you guys tomorrow then,' Jill says, quickly lumping Sam and me together. This is her way. Being friends with Jill is sometimes similar to being a victim of Stockholm syndrome.

'Thank you for the dinner,' Sam says, shaking hands with Martin and then giving Jill a quick hug. She gets flushed and giddy as he pulls away.

'So gentlemanly,' Jill trills. I roll my eyes and can't help but smile.

'Ready?' Sam asks, and I nod.

'Byeeeee,' Jill says as we finally leave.

The door closes behind us. As I walk down the stone steps, I'm aware of Sam every inch of the way. His Ferrari still sits just behind my car. What happens now? Do we go back to his place? Do people still say that? Even if there's no hot tub and Asti Spumante? I can't breathe.

I beep my car unlocked and open the driver's-side door. Somewhere in all my newfangled thinking, I've decided not to try to manipulate this entire night. I want – no, need – to find out what it's like to just be me and have someone like and choose that. Choose the Real Me. Respond to that. I morphed into a whole other person for Ryan and he cheated on and chucked me for Jessica, the vacant-eyed vet's assistant.

And that wasn't the first time.

Every relationship I've had has involved some form of dismantling: the midwesterner who I put down California with, the Beatles fan I listened to hidden piano-bench creaks in 'A Day in the Life' with, the beat poet I went on the road with. Just as I shouldn't blame Jessica for Ryan's indiscretion, I can't blame these men for what I allowed to happen to me. I was never my own champion. I never sat a man down and talked about how much I love Jane Austen or why a good drive up the coast is as good as therapy sometimes (especially if you don't insist on talking) and why it's always okay to cry during the Olympics when someone gets a gold medal. It's time to try something different. You know, in theory. In practice? We'll see.

'Thanks for walking me out, I hear this neighborhood gets really rough past ten P.M.,' I say, throwing my purse on the passenger seat and turning back around to face Sam. He's stepped in closer. There's something he's not telling me. Girlfriend back home? Wants to tell me that I've clearly gotten the wrong idea? Wrongfully accused of murder and searching for a one-armed man?

'Thank you,' Sam finally says, pulling just inches back. Inches . . . miles . . . same difference.

'For what?' I ask, my voice instantly icy and cold.

'A great night,' Sam says, his brow furrowed, his smile tight and layered.

'My pleasure,' I say, clearing my throat and looking at my car.

'Okay, so . . .' Sam says, hand on my driver's-side door.

'See you later, then,' I say, shutting down completely. Sam's body reacts like he wants to pounce, but then . . . stops. He swallows and looks away. I nod. I understand. Tonight was a mistake. Over and out. I smile, as much as one can while on the brink of sobbing, and get into my car. I reach over my shoulder for the seat belt, thankful that my arm is acting as some kind of barrier between us. Maybe he won't be able to see the tears welling up in my eyes. The frustration builds in my shoulders. I'm thankful I'm a titleholder in the blood sport of 'I'm going to reject you before you reject me.'

'See you later,' Sam says, watching as I latch my seat belt. He gives a small nod when it clicks. Sam is unmoving, buzzing and muted. I put my key in the ignition and start up my car.

'I'd better get going,' I say, my hand on the gearshift. I put the car in reverse, my foot on the brake pedal.

'Sure,' Sam says, stepping back and looking at the white lights reflect off the hood of his Ferrari just behind mine.

He continues. 'Oh, right. I have to move my car.'

I nod and attempt a smile. Sam pulls his keys from his jeans pocket, steps back again and takes one final second. Motionless and muted. I lock eyes with him. The spoked, cinnamon-brown eyes that were so passionate earlier are now darting and urgent. As he finally slams my door and walks to his car, I let my entire body deflate. Feel the weight of what I've lost. Try not to feel ridiculous for being overly dramatic. It was one kiss, for crissakes. One night. Why do I feel so . . . altered?

As Sam's headlights light up in my rearview mirror, I hate that tomorrow, instead of tales of a night of passionate sex and cooing whispers of newfound love, I'm going to have to tell Jill and Lisa that tonight ended the same way all the others have: driving home alone. Wondering what I did wrong. Sam's headlights dim and fade as he pulls out of Jill and Martin's driveway and out into the night. He's gone. And I'm here. And there's never been anything more unfair in the entire history of the world.

As I drive home, I have that old sinking feeling. I've been overly available, sickeningly sweet and forever enabling all in the name of being 'liked.' I've compromised myself. I've suffered fools, idiots and dullards. I've gone on far too many dates with men because I felt guilty that they liked me more than I liked them. I've fallen deeply and madly in love with men I've never met just because I thought they looked 'deep.' I've built whole futures with men I hardly knew; I've planned weddings and named invisible children based on a side glance.

I've made chemistry where there was none. I've forced intimacy while building even higher walls. I've been alone in a two-year relationship. I've faked more orgasms than I can count while being comfortable with no affection at all. I wouldn't know the first thing about my own pleasure.

As I drive down Lake Avenue in a haze, I realize I have to make a decision right here and now. Do I go back to the sliver of a person I was before or do I, despite whatever bullshit happened tonight, hold on to this . . . this authenticity? If I go back to the way I was before tonight, I'll have to compromise myself, follow rules with men who have none, hold my tongue, be quiet and laugh at shitty jokes. I have to never be challenged, yet be called challenging when I have an opinion or, really, speak at all. I'll never be touched by someone and get goose bumps again. I'll never be outside of myself. I'll never let go. I'll never lose myself. I'll never know what real love is – both for someone else and for me. I'll look back on this life and wish I could do it all over again.

As I sit at the red light at Orange Grove, gnawing on my fingernails and unable to focus on anything, I finally see the consequences of that life.

The path more traveled only led to someone else's life: an idealized, saturated world of white picket fences and gingham tablecloths. A life where the Real Me is locked away in an oubliette with nothing but bread and water in which to live. Sure, I had a plus-one and a warm body in my bed, but at what price?

No. No matter how awkward and painful this gets, I can't go back.

The light turns green.

9
The Catalyst

My apartment feels even colder as I toss and turn in bed that night. I get up in the middle of the night and slip some wool socks on, hoping they will stem the frigid tide. Nothing. The sheets feel like an ice floe and my skin just can't get warm. I'm exhausted and inexplicably smell of pizza and abandonment. I flip onto my other side and thank god the upcoming week is a busy one. I just won't think about it. Him. I won't think about him. Sam. Nope.

I don't stop at the breezeway and ogle Sam the next day. Or the day after that. I can't hear another pep talk from Jill and/or Lisa. And I certainly won't think about the promotion I probably didn't get based on my snooping and then getting into a slight altercation among the headmistress's toiletries. No, this week is all about smoke and mirrors. Authentic smoke and mirrors, but smoke and mirrors nonetheless. It's now Wednesday.

Jill barrels through the door of our office. She's already pissed and midsentence. 'That hag in the front office? You know the one . . . with the hair? I was eating a bag of trail mix and she stops everything and says, "Oooh, I wish I could eat like you!" clearly insinuating that I'm so fat that

I no longer care about watching what I eat.' Jill slumps into her office chair and rests her hands on her nonexistent belly. Just rests them there.

'Or that you eat really healthy and she doesn't,' I say.

'Unlikely!' Jill yells. She heaves a big sigh and continues. 'So, are we fudge packing tonight after the party?' Jill asks.

I just hang my head.

Jill clarifies. 'You know, making fudge for Friday? For the booth?'

'Oh, I know what you meant.'

'Well?'

'Sure, that sounds good. At your place?'

'Yeah, totally.' Jill is now standing and looking at herself in the full-length mirror on the back of our shared office door. From the side. From the front. From the side. She is smoothing her Lilly Pulitzer shift dress down and down and down. A rolled eye. A look of disgust and she finally slumps back down into her office chair.

She opens her desk drawer and pulls out a sandwich bag filled with trail mix. She offers the now-open bag to me. Jill swirls her chair around – obstructing the full-length mirror and the offending reflection.

'Can we start walking around the Rose Bowl? Like . . . this Sunday?' Jill says as I take a handful of trail mix from her. The Rose Bowl is not only a world-class stadium, but for locals it and the surrounding roads serve as a gathering place for recreational activities of all kinds. The bike path covers a distance of three miles from Seco Street up to Washington Boulevard with the actual Rose Bowl Stadium at its center. It'd almost give us enough time to catch up on the happenings of the week.

'Sure, that sounds good,' I say, trying not to play into whatever emergency Jill thinks is happening with her body.

We are quiet.

I continue on the thinnest of ice. 'You okay?'

'I'm fine. Fiiiiine,' Jill says, her teeth grinding.

'Yeah, you sound fine,' I say.

'I'm just . . . I want to get this stupid day over with, get through this lame-ass birthday party and then we'll fudge-pack tonight. I'm just really looking forward to fudge packing,' Jill says, shoving another handful of trail mix in her mouth.

'You would literally do anything just to keep saying *fudge packing*,' I say, heading out for a full day.

'Damn skippy,' Jill says as I step into the hallway.

'Coffee?'

'Yes, ma'am,' Jill says, joining me.

Jill and I walk toward the teachers' lounge and, in so doing, bring my streak of 'no breezeway ogling of Sam' to a very abrupt halt. I 'innocently' look out from the breezeway and take in the construction site just to the left of the school's parking lot. A dirt lot alive and humming with different trucks I recognize only from their Tonka counterparts. Caution tape, red webbing and building supplies form a makeshift obstacle course at the dirt lot's fringes. Men wearing hard hats swarm around with tool belts and shoulders heavy with stacks of wood. At its center is Sam. He's wearing a hard hat and pointing at the large dirt expanse, surrounded by a group of construction workers. His shirtsleeves are rolled up, exposing the blond wheat field of hair and tan skin I had yet to see until now. A scroll of blueprints is tucked tight under his other arm. His white-blond hair is ruffling in the early morning wind. Ouchhhhh.

'Stop staring,' Jill says.

'It's just not fair,' I say, tearing my gaze away.

The group of construction workers gathers around Sam. He pulls the blueprints from under his arm and smooths them on the ground at his feet. He squats down. They quickly follow. One last look down at the construction site just as Sam nods at the group of construction workers and begins rolling up the blueprints.

'Come on. Coffee,' Jill says.

I continue on down the hall. I won't look down at the construction site again. I won't. My head turns of its own volition. Sam is standing in the same position; this time, however, he's turned around – his hand over his eyes shielding them from the sun – staring right at me. He raises his hand, his eyes squinting into the sun. It's not a wave, really. It's more of an . . . acknowledgment. I put up my hand. And we stand there, hands raised. Jill stands by helplessly, able only to watch in horror as I, with my hand aloft, look like I'm protesting oppression at the 1968 Mexico Olympics.

'You need to walk away, Frannie. Frannie? You need to walk away,' Jill says, her mouth not moving, like she's a ventriloquist.

'Okay . . . okay . . .' I say, my hand lowering.

'Leave him wanting more,' Jill says, giving Sam a wave

and smile. Sam takes a few steps toward the school, but once I continue on toward the teachers' lounge I can see that he's stopped. His shoulders lower. Someone calls his name. He turns. It's over. Jill gives me a sympathetic smile as the doors close behind me. I've seen him since that night by the Ferrari. It's over. And I survived. I didn't hurl myself over the breezeway railing. I held it together and now I'm here. *Know when to hold 'em, know when to fold 'em.*

All the bravado in the world won't mask the haunting feeling that while Sam may have been important, he might be just a catalyst. Someone who made me see how I was living my life but who won't be a part of the life he had a hand in creating. I don't think I get to keep him. He's the adorable puppy you find roaming the streets, only to have to pass him on to a pigtailed child later as proof that you understand the real power of love.

I know I'm desperate when I start using words like *catalyst.*

The morning fades away in a blur and surviving the day becomes my singular focus. I've shifted into high gear, pulling students, talking and laughing with Jill, sitting in on a lengthy Individualized Education Program meeting – or an IEP to the cool kids. And after a full day, I knock on Jill's door and peek my head in. It's almost time for Emma's birthday cake and ice cream in the teachers' lounge. I figure if we get there early, we can leave early and I'll have made it through the longest day ever. One that's been heavy with epiphanies and rebellions. Kaylee and Jill look up from the desk where they've been busy at work.

'It's almost time,' I say as the last bell of the day sounds.

'Yep,' Jill says, giving Kaylee a quick nod. Kaylee begins to pack up her stuff.

'Do you want me just to meet you over there?' I ask, giving the little girl's white-blond hair a tousle as she squeezes past me in the doorway. She giggles and skips down the hall.

'I can't believe we have to go to this thing,' Jill says, packing away all of her supplies.

'I know,' I say, stepping inside.

'Martin and the rest of the architects are going to be there. Thought it would look good in front of staff. Wanted to warn you,' Jill says.

'Why are you talking like a telegram? "Sam might be in vicinity. Stop. Hold yourself together, spinster. Stop." '

'Stop doing that. Stop.'

'That wasn't really the correct usage of that. Stop.'

Jill just sighs. A long, weary sigh.

'Fine,' I finally say.

'Remember, we're—'

'I know,' I say, cutting her off.

'We're fudge packing after,' Jill says, finishing with a flourish. She picks up the phone and continues. 'Let me make a quick call first.'

'Who are you going to call?' I ask.

'Ghostbusters.'

'Nice. But really.'

'I'll tell you later on tonight . . . you know, when we're fud—'

'Yes, yes, I know. Fine, I'll save you a section of the wall,' I say, closing the door. Kids straggle out of classrooms and run through halls like little bats out of hell, late for buses and parents. They'd probably think that cliché is quite accurate given the circumstances. I tell kids to slow down, I'll see them tomorrow, and to make sure to check their homework online. I get nary a reply – well, not counting eye rolls.

'Frannie? Frannie?' Emma glides across the hallway as if on a cloud. Her body is elegantly poured into matching black separates with pops of tasteful gold jewelry glistening under the neon lights. Lights that make me look like Edward Munch's *The Scream*. She is, once again, wearing impossibly high-heeled stilettos that would be more at home on a catwalk than the crowded hallways of a private school.

'Would you mind taking a second before the festivities?' Emma asks, motioning for us to stop and chat among the buzz of the quickly emptying hallways.

'Not at all,' I say, my stomach dropping. I want to blurt out that I needed a tampon that night in her bathroom but reconsider. That might not be where this conversation is going, so it's maybe not the best idea to lead with that.

'I wanted to have a quick follow-up regarding Mr Sprague,' Emma says.

'Oh?' I ask.

'I've asked around and have found that your evaluation of Mr Stone was correct. He is quite the bully.'

'I know.'

'I understand that it looks like I was being mulish and not seeing the boys in a clear light. Clearly Mr Stone is much bigger than Harry, but in my experience bullies come in all shapes and sizes.' Emma is calm and collected. And way cool apparently.

'I love that you look at every child on a case-by-case basis,' I say truthfully.

We are quiet.

Emma continues. 'There have been significant studies done on bullying in the last few years and I have decided to focus on the needs of the victim here at Markham. It's a method that began in Scandinavia – I'm sure you don't want to know all the boring details, but it basically boils down to a switch in what, or rather whom, we focus on. While it is usually the case that staff focuses on the why of a bully – why does he/she feel the need to victimize – it is my feeling that while we're offering a kind ear to the bully, the victim's needs go unmet. Mr Stone knows the difference between right and wrong without a discussion with me about whatever deficiency might have caused such chronic lapses in judgment. I feel the concern needs to be for Mr Stone's victims. I've extended the use of Pamela Jackson's psychology services to any and all students who come forward – privately, of course – as victims of Mr Stone or, for that matter, anyone's bullying.'

I am speechless.

Emma continues. 'I defer to you as to Harry.'

'In what capacity?'

'Do you think he needs to speak with Pamela regarding bullying?'

'I honestly don't know. I could ask him about it,' I say.

'That would be lovely.'

'He's kind of a quiet kid.'

'A bully wouldn't pick on someone who spoke up, now, would they, Ms Reid?'

'I suppose not.'

'That's what needs to change.'

'I agree.'

We are quiet.

I say, 'Thank you.'

'For?'

'You've really done some serious research. It's going to make a huge impact on a lot of lives. A lot of little lives. I wish someone had been so thoughtful when I was in school.'

I am quiet. Emma waves hello to an excited throng of teachers on their way to the lounge. She lets them know she'll be there in a second. Happy birthday, they say. She thanks them.

'Well, you're welcome, Ms Reid,' she finally says, her voice quiet and touched. 'I have also taken disciplinary action against Mr Stone. Probation from the lacrosse squad, weekly assessments, etc. . . .'

'Thank you.'

'I would hope that you would pass along my apologies to Harry.'

'Apologies are certainly not necessary. He used violence to solve a problem and you were correct to bring him in.'

'Most assuredly, but I was incorrect in my assessment that it was, in any way, his fault.'

'I agree.'

'What time is it?' Emma asks, picking up her pace.

'You can't be that late if you're the birthday girl, right?' I say.

'I got caught on a phone call. My husband's going to be a bit late,' Emma says as we bob and weave through the crowded breezeway. Must be an emergency on the Internet where he works. Extension student in need of an emergency comma consult? Short-story idea that just can't wait? Thwart another party guest snooping in his en-suite bathroom? The mind reels.

I am quiet. Nodding.

Emma continues. 'One more thing, Ms Reid. This may not be the best time, but I've decided to give the head of department position to you rather than Mrs Fleming. You were the obvious choice in not only my eyes but the board's, as well as the other heads of department. It was unanimous.' Emma extends her hand. She is smiling. She's excited. She was looking forward to telling me this.

'I'm stunned,' I say. The job is mine. *The job is mine.* But if the job is mine that means that it is not Jill's.

'Thank you, Emma,' I say, extending my hand to her.

'You've earned it,' Emma says, giving my arm a squeeze. Can I hug her? Do we hug? Is . . . I lean in – maybe it's a lunge, I can't think about that now – and give Emma a tight hug. The gathering teachers in the hallway smile, gawk and sneer depending on their place in the pecking order. Emma hugs me back.

'Thank you . . . This means more to me then you'll ever know,' I say, unable to stop saying thank you.

'You're quite welcome. I've notified human resources of the promotion; they'll be expecting you tomorrow morning to go over the promotion paperwork,' Emma says, breaking from the hug.

'Thank you again,' I say, almost to myself.

'You're the right person for the job, Frannie,' Emma says, waving to a group of teachers. They wave back.

'And happy birthday,' I say, beaming. Smiling. From ear to ear. I can't wait to tell . . . well, my parents. Lisa. Less Jill, but I'll cross that bridge when I get to it. Sam. Shit, I can't wait to tell Sam.

'Thank you,' she says. Emma and I catch up to the rest of the teachers who are gathering for her birthday. Debbie and her minions are making everyone wait outside the teachers' lounge in the breezeway. The room isn't ready yet, apparently. Isn't ready yet? Put a cake on the table, sing happy birthday, how hard can it be? As I stand there craning down the hall to see if Jill is on her way and where Lisa is, and trying to act like I'm not looking for Sam, I eavesdrop on the teachers as they oozingly wish Emma a happy birthday. She's lovely and polite in reply. I actually don't mind being here to celebrate Emma's birthday now.

We're finally allowed to go into the teachers' lounge. As we all stream in, I notice that round tables and chairs have been set up in the now-cramped lounge. Emma looks from me to a free table in the front of the lounge. The tables are set for dinner. Breadbaskets, linen napkins and the promise of a very long night. She raises her eyebrows and motions for me to nab it. I oblige. I grab three seats right across from Grady, who's also saving two seats. I find myself seated next to Emma and an empty seat her creepy husband will eventually occupy. Jill whips open the door to the teachers' lounge and I can read her lips from here: 'What the—' She scans the room and we lock eyes. I'm pinned behind Emma and next to an empty chair.

'Grady? Who are you saving for?' I ask, leaning across the table.

'Hey, darlin',' Grady says, his body languidly melting over his folding chair.

'Hey,' I say quickly.

'I'm saving one for my baby and then that one's for Sam,' Grady says, pointing at the chair directly next to me. Grady gives me a quick wink. Great. My face drains of color. Jill scans the room again and motions for me to look. Martin's saving a seat for her at another table. I don't need to worry, she mouths. She walks over and plops down next to him. Martin wraps his arm around the back of her chair. I settle in and freeze a smile on my face. It's going to be a long night. Emma is thanking Debbie for the amazing party. Debbie looks like she's about to cry or try to make out with Emma. It's a toss-up.

In an attempt to avoid being ensnared in Debbie's inappropriate Emma fantasy, I try to insinuate my way into various conversations around the table. I stare furtively at Grady until he catches my eye. He gives me a big smile and a wink and then falls back into conversation with a couple of the architects who are seated a table over. Close enough for conversation with Grady but not with me. I resituate my napkin on my lap, recross my legs under the table and ponder whether to try the same tactic on someone else. I find Ryan at a table way in the back sitting next to that teacher who glared at me earlier in the breezeway.

They're laughing and talking, passing around the bread, pouring wine. A veritable party. I heave a long . . . *long* . . . weary sigh.

'I don't know how you do it. Living alone just seems . . . I mean, all those different windows people could break into. Jamie told me that you and Ryan split. That you live alone. He and Ryan really hit it off at the mixer, apparently,' Emma muses. What is happening here? Jamie hit it off with Ryan? What . . . how did this evening go from totally cool one minute to completely, surreally terrible the next?

'I live in a pretty safe neighborhood,' I say, trying to put a stop to an internal dialogue that'll surely end with me rocking back and forth in some dimly lit corner of my apartment, clutching a flashlight and a kitchen knife.

'Still. Jamie was excited to hear you'd gotten the promotion. Said that women like you are perfect for advancement,' Emma says.

'Women like me?' I ask, not wanting to know the answer. Soooo not wanting to know the answer.

'Yeah, you know. Unmarried, no family,' Emma says, matter-of-fact. What happened to the Emma I was just talking to? The door to the teachers' lounge opens and I know before he turns the corner that it's Sam. We need to stop talking about this right now. *Right. Now.* Grady waves him over to our table and points to the chair next to mine. Sam's face is . . . unreadable. I act like I don't notice he's walking over. It's a proud moment. A mature moment. A moment women like me are quite familiar with, to be sure.

As Sam sits down, Grady goes around the table for drink

orders, motioning to the bar Debbie has set up on the far wall. I want to kiss him full on the lips for saving me, if just for a moment. I say I'd just like sparkling water, Sam asks for a beer – whatever they've got is fine. Emma says she'd like sparkling water for herself and a glass of red wine for Jamie.

'He loves the Spanish reds,' Emma says, giving Grady a coy smile.

'I don't know about a Spanish red, but it looks like they've got some Two-Buck Chuck back there,' Grady says, smiling.

'That'll be fine, Mr Davis. That'll be fine,' Emma says, laughing. Lisa rushes into the lounge and scans the room, finds Grady, and they smile.

'Beer, baby?' Grady asks, motioning to the bar.

'You know it,' Lisa says, and walks over to our table. I have yet to acknowledge that Sam is sitting next to me.

'Hey,' I finally say.

'Hey,' he says.

'Tight squeeze,' I say, motioning to the chairs and tables that have filled the teachers' lounge to bursting.

'Definitely,' Sam says, smiling.

'What?'

'Tight squeeze just sounds wrong,' Sam says, laughing.

'It does, doesn't it?' I say, smiling.

'I mean . . . that's what you open with?' Sam says, laughing more.

'I just . . . I'm just making conversation.'

'Tight squeeze,' Sam repeats, tilting his head back and closing his eyes. Laughing.

'All right. Enough already,' I say, touching his arm. Warm. So warm.

'Tight squeeze. Didn't you say that about those pizzas, too?' Sam sighs, bending forward now, eyes open. I take my hand off his arm, my fingers now resting inches from him. I smile at Emma as she settles into her seat. I hear her take a breath. Before she continues her out-of-the-blue one-woman jihad against my imagined musty life of spinster solitude, I turn to face her head-on.

'Emma Dunham, have you met Sam Earley? He owns the Earley Group. They're working with the architects to make the school expansion project more sustainable,' I say.

'I don't believe we've met formally, no,' Emma says, extending her hand in front of me and to Sam.

'Nice to meet you, ma'am,' Sam says, taking her hand.

'Oh, please. It's Emma,' she says, blushing slightly.

'Emma is the head of school,' I say.

'Oh, wow,' Sam says, nodding, taking his beer from Grady as he hands it across the table. Sam sets the beer down and then takes my sparkling water from Grady and sets it down on the left side of my plate rather than the more convenient and far more proper right side.

Sam continues. 'Here you go, darlin'.' He knows I'm left-handed. It's a bizarre detail to remember. When would he have seen that?

'Thank you,' I say, lifting the glass to my lips and drinking.

'Jamie is late,' Emma says, looking apologetically at the empty chair.

'Traffic, I'm sure,' I say. *On the Internet*.

'He . . . we had a fight. On the phone. You know . . . earlier?' Emma says, looking back down at her lap. Sam politely excuses himself from our conversation and falls in with Grady and Lisa.

'Oh?' I ask, treading lightly.

'It was actually about what we were talking about the other night,' Emma says, still not looking at me. My stomach drops.

'Oh?' I repeat. Is this where I blurt that I was just looking for a tampon? I'll have to do it quietly with Sam right here—

'Clara, mostly. That I missed her. I was talking about looking her up. Her art, you know? Her painting. All that? She's so close, just right over the hill in Los Feliz. We should be seeing each other,' Emma says, her eyes finally locking on mine. Now this – *this* is the Emma I've come to know.

'Sure,' I say, wanting her to continue.

'I told him I wanted to start painting again,' Emma says, her shoulders back, her smile wide.

'Yeah?' I ask, smiling myself.

'He thinks it'll just be a distraction.'

'And?'

'And I'm going to look into it anyway. I basically told Jamie as much.'

'That's amazing,' I say.

'Yeah, it really is,' she says.

'And Clara?'

'I called her. We talked. It was . . . she's just the same,' Emma says, unable to keep from smiling.

'Really? That sounds great,' I say, still smiling. Smiling. Smiling.

'I told her all about you, isn't that weird? Well, she asked why I'd called, I think that's why I brought you up. But . . . we're going to meet for brunch on Sunday at eleven. Some place in Silver Lake. Probably serves just edible flowers or something.' Emma laughs. Her entire demeanor has changed. She's not the same person she was two minutes ago when she was spouting Jamie-isms. It's absolutely beautiful.

'How long has it been since you guys have talked?'

'Her oldest is eight. So, almost that long. She's got three now. I knew that, but . . . the littlest one—' Emma breaks off.

I wait. Sam looks over. Checking in. I give him a quick wink and he smiles. Maybe I'll invite him to Jill's after this? *No*. Wait. I'm going to go to Jill's and he can ask me what I'm doing. Yes. That's it.

Emma continues. 'She named the littlest one Emma.' She is beaming.

'I just . . . that's beautiful. Congratulations. Seriously,' I say.

'I never thought of myself that way. Someone you would name your baby after,' Emma says, her voice hushed.

'Well, you should certainly start to,' I say, smiling.

'Yes, maybe I will,' Emma says, smiling from ear to ear. I smile back. Her joy is contagious. This is turning out to be a pretty decent night after all. Bit of a rough patch there, but we seem to be back on track now.

Emma continues. 'So, Sam, where are you from originally? The accent . . .'

Sam looks up. 'I'm originally from Shelby Forest, Tennessee,' Sam says. I'm watching him talk and just smiling.

'Shelby Forest . . . isn't . . . weren't you saying earlier that Justin Timberlake was from there?' I ask. I immediately blush.

'You mean J. T.,' Sam says, correcting me.

I laugh. '*Ha!*'

'Oh, is that what people call him?' Emma asks.

'Yes, ma'am. He's from there,' Sam says.

'I educated Sam earlier about calling Justin Timberlake "J. T.,"' I say, trying to explain. Sam laughs.

'Oh, you two know each other?' Emma asks. Sam and I stop. Like two errant kids caught laughing in church.

'We do,' Sam answers.

'Oh,' Emma says, nodding.

'Yes, ma'am,' Sam says, giving me a quick sidelong glance.

'Everyone? Everyone, can I have your attention?' Debbie announces, lifting her glass of champagne. 'I wanted to thank everyone for attending tonight's little gathering in honor of Emma's birth—'

'Oh, can we wait?' Emma asks, interrupting. 'Jamie – Jamie's my husband – he's still on his way. He'd hate to miss the toast!' Emma pleads, laughing nervously.

'Oh . . . of course. That would be . . . I'm so sorry for rushing into it!' Debbie says, now considering performing hara-kiri on herself right there. Sam asks me to pass the bread. I oblige, making eye contact with him a bit longer than either of us is comfortable with.

'Butter, too?' I ask him.

'That's customary,' Sam answers, his hand outstretched, his drawl making me feel somehow naughty.

'You could have asked for . . .' I trail off, searching the table for other condiments.

'You're in too deep, Reid. One could say . . . a tight squeeze,' Sam says, buttering his bread, his mouth an impossible smirk.

'Ha!' I say, letting my head fall back, my hand resting on his arm. I'm unable to keep myself from touching him. He's within touching distance; he shall be touched. He's lucky I'm not grabbing his crank right now. The night is young.

'You're oh-so-predictable,' Sam says, laying his hand on top of mine. It's as if we're choosing who's going to be first up at bat, for crissakes.

'Here's Jamie! I want him to meet you two,' Emma says, urging Sam and me to stand and shake hands, once again, with the mythical Jamie Dunham, the future Norman Mailer. I begrudgingly take my hand from beneath Sam's as we all stand. I look at Sam in confusion. Why has Emma singled us out for this auspicious introduction? He just smiles and shoos me along. The entire teachers' lounge swoons and beams at the happy couple.

Jamie is wearing a striped shirt under a heavy blazer that hangs on his tiny frame. The weather is cool, but certainly not cool enough to warrant so heavy a coat. I imagine it's because he has zero fat on his bones. Probably gets cold a lot. Or it's just his demeanor incarnate. Jamie's dark hair is 'accidentally' tousled to perfection. His pale skin is delicate and transparent. He resembles a brittle dauphin from somewhere back in the annals of French history. He's carrying a bouquet of flowers and a little pink gift bag that probably contains the Hope Diamond. Jamie approaches the table as Emma, Sam and I stand. Emma smiles at me and Sam and then back over at Jamie. She's glowing and animated. We return Emma's smile and I extend my hand to Jamie, fake smile in full effect. I hate that I have to shake this weirdo's hand and smile. It's one night. *Fine*. Sam stands just behind me, waiting for his turn to meet the petit dauphin.

Jamie ignores me completely and brings up the little pink gift bag. I lower my hand and will myself not to look around at my colleagues who've just witnessed Little King Jamie completely disregarding me. Great. So, we're going to keep up with the whole pissed-because-of-the-snooping-through-the-bathroom thing. I take a tiny step back just in time to see a black handgun emerge from the little pink bag. And before it registers – *crack*. Blood. On me. On the wall. Emma is lifted off her feet and lands like a sack of potatoes a few feet back. My ears are ringing. I can't stop saying Emma's name over and over again. My voice is far away and muffled in the aftermath of the deafening gunshot.

Chaos.

Slow-motion chaos. Teachers running out of the lounge, out onto the balcony, diving under the tables. Barely audible screams and gasps of horror seem far away as the bouquet of flowers drops to the ground. Ryan sits frozen in his chair. I can see Jill reaching out for me, reaching and being pulled under the table by Martin. She's crying. Sobbing. Someone's grabbing me from behind, pulling me back and tugging my arm. Sam. He's saying something, telling me to do something. He's covered in blood. All over his face, his shirt. It's everywhere. I pull away from him and kneel down next to Emma. Her beautiful blond hair is matted and bloody in my hands. Her blue eyes are glassy. Her lips, lined and glossed, are still curled into a haunting smile. A red oozing hole in her forehead. Lifeless. Dead. Sam's hands are around me again, pulling me away.

Jamie points the gun at us. I turn away from Emma to look straight down the barrel of Jamie's gun. Recognition. I'm the Girl from the Bathroom. The one who stood over him and asked him what he was doing. Jamie narrows his eyes at me. Aiming. I can't . . . I try to cover Emma with my body. I'll be damned if he puts another bullet into her. Grady charges Jamie like a lineman blitzing a quarterback. *Crack*. Grady is whirled around and slams into the ground. Blood. I see Lisa clutching Grady and howling primally. His eyes are alert. She drags Grady under the table.

'Emma? Emma?! Please . . . please . . . please wake up. Emma!' I scream, my bloodied hands cradling her face. I try to find somewhere to stop the bleeding. She'll be okay. Stop the bleeding. The back of Emma's head is slick and sticky . . . there's nothing to . . . there's nothing *back* here. More muffled screams and turned-over tables and chairs.

'You want to ask me what I'm doing now?' Jamie growls, stepping toward me. Time stops. I hear the click of the gun. The creak of the floor beneath Jamie's feet. And then, I'm being scooped up. Sam. He turns his back toward Jamie and that big, black gun and blocks me from any further gunfire. Lisa lunges at Jamie from under the table. Knocking him off balance. The gun skitters toward us. I look up. Jamie knocks Lisa away and her own fierce momentum crashes her forward into a bank of cupboards in the lounge. She is dazed as Jamie pulls another gun from that heavy blazer pocket. His pockets are loaded down. There are more? How many guns does he have?

Crack.

Another shot. The coffeemaker inches from Lisa's head shatters and broken glass is everywhere. Lisa covers her head with her arms, tucking her entire body into the fetal position. Through the shrieks and sobs I can hear her muttering, 'I just want to go home . . . I just want to go home.' More shrieks. People are sobbing. Calling for help, their mothers, anyone. I reach for Lisa. One hand on the back of what was once Emma's head and another lunging for Lisa.

'Stay down. She's gone. I'll go. I'll go,' Sam growls, his arms tight around me, his full weight on top of me. *She's gone.*

'No! No! Sam!' It's all in slow motion. Sam's eyes are focused. Fixed. On me. Calm yourself, he nods. Calm yourself. Wait. Wait for me. Here. I nod, even though no words were spoken. I understand. I understand.

Sam stands. Another crack. Another group of sobbing teachers shield themselves.

Jamie's first gun lies inches from Sam. Jamie focuses in

on us. Emma – what was once Emma – me and now Sam. And then the gun. The gun. Jamie tries to act fast. He aims. He aims. His face is monstrous, not even human. Empty. With flashes of anger. Flashes of annoyance.

Sam dives for the loose gun, his lanky frame stretching out, his fingers curling around the gun. *Crack*. Into the wall behind Sam. Sam ducks. Refocuses. Jamie can't aim at a moving target. So, he turns. To me.

Jamie. The gun. The barrel. I'm next.

I close my eyes. And wait.

So, this is how it ends.

When I was little, my parents took me horseback riding in the beautiful lush mountains surrounding Mill Valley. My parents. No. *No*. I feel the tears stream down my cheeks. And as we trotted down this dirt path, I began to fall. Off the saddle. Off the horse. And I thought, Well, this isn't that bad. I'm going to fall. It's not as bad as I thought.

It's not as bad as I thought.

Crack. Crack. Crack. Crack.

10

I Didn't Consider Him a Threat

Nothing. All I can feel are my eyes tight . . . so tightly shut that my entire face closes around them like a black hole. My hands are uncontrollably shaking as I try to steady them: one on Emma's heart, the other behind her head. But it's as if my entire being stands on those three points like a barstool. The rest of me is vapor. I find myself unable to connect to the ground. I will myself, with whatever I have that remains, to just . . . be brave. Wake up. Look.

I open my eyes. Just as Jamie falls. His tiny body falling like a crackling autumn leaf just as the seasons change. He's even insignificant in death. I blink. And turn.

Sam. Lying on his side, his face steely and focused, his arm outstretched and the gun – Jamie's gun – smoking, aimed and ready for another round if need be. Jamie. Unmoving as the pool of blood spreads from his lifeless body.

All she wanted to do was start painting again.

'Ms Reid? Do you want me to repeat the question?' the detective asks. His name is Detective Samuelson and he looks about nineteen years old. It's been almost an hour since Emma was murdered and I'm sitting on a bench outside the school with a blanket around my shoulders. My clothes will be evidence. When I finally had the chance to go to the ladies' room, what I saw in the mirror was horrifying. Even after the techs had been all over me, blood and other more gruesome bits of Emma were still splattered across my face, crimson droplets glistening eerily in my dark hair, my pale skin a road map of Jamie's crime. My dark eyes were as haunted and glassy as Emma's.

I have yet to really fuse the two identities back together – the person I knew myself to be and that specter looking back at me in the mirror. I would like nothing better than to forget what happened this afternoon. But whoever that is in the mirror won't forget it. *Can't* forget it. Can't stop hearing those gunshots. Can't unhear the sobs of my colleagues who thought they'd never see their loved ones again. Can't unfeel the weight of Emma's lifeless body in my arms.

The red, blue and white police lights flash and swirl against the outside of the school. Every emergency vehicle in Pasadena is in this parking lot. The Markham staff and administrators dart around the school and parking lot with two agendas: make sure everyone's safe and see that this is handled in the most delicate way possible. The human resources department has already issued a press release to the gathering media: This was an after-hours shooting due to a preexisting domestic abuse issue. There were two fatalities and one minor injury. No students were on campus at the time of the shooting. The Markham School will take tomorrow off in remembrance but will resume classes on Friday. They will also be offering grief counseling to those who need it. Pamela Jackson, the acting headmistress and former school psychologist, has already been called in and all staff will be expected to conduct an exit interview with her before we leave the crime scene.

'Yes, please,' I say, shivering. Jill and Martin were under a table during the shooting. Ryan slipped away before emergency services arrived. The rumor was that he had wet himself. Grady was taken to the hospital with a gunshot wound to his right shoulder. Lisa went with him in the ambulance after physically threatening the EMT who told her, 'You can follow the ambulance in your car if you want.' That's *not* what Lisa wanted and instead she told the EMT that she was either getting in that ambulance or snatching the EMT's hair from her head. The EMT wisely chose the former. From Lisa's updates, we know that Grady is still in surgery. He should be fine, the doctors are telling her. He'll have some muscle trauma, but the bullet didn't hit any bone, which is apparently very lucky. Jill and Martin are there with them now. From what I've gleaned, the guns (all four of them) that Jamie used were .45s. I don't know a whole lot about them, but I can tell you exactly what a gun like that will do to a person. I'm not comfortable knowing any of this new information.

'Here you go,' Sam says, giving me a Styrofoam cup filled with tea and settling in next to me. The steam from the hot tea wafts up and into the cold night air. We were supposed to be at Jill's by now. We were looking forward to just another Wednesday night. I don't understand what happened. I have to know why. I have to know why a room filled with people became extras in Jamie and Emma's tragic and bloody demise. How Grady Davis is in the hospital, Emma is dead and Sam was made to shoot someone because . . . what? Because Jamie didn't want Emma to start painting again? Because she had the audacity to call her sister? *Why?* So senseless. How did this happen?

'Thank you,' I say, taking the cup in one hand and holding on to Sam with the other. I'm still shaking. I can't stop shaking. Sam spent most of the last hour being questioned about the shooting. Everyone is assuring him that he did what he had to do. That Jamie had been planning this and had every intention of killing everyone in that room had Sam not stepped in. Sam did what he had to do, they keep saying.

He's a hero.

'How many shots were there?' Detective Samuelson asks, his notepad out, his eyes eager. I close my eyes. The deafening sounds of the gunshots. The slide show of images that will be forever burned in my brain. *Crack. Crack. Crack. Crack. Crack . . . Crack.*

'Nine,' I say, reliving each shot.

'Nine,' Detective Samuelson repeats.

'One at Emma, one at Grady, one at Lisa, one at the other teachers, one at Sam and then . . .' I say, my voice robotic.

'Then?'

'My four,' Sam says. I look at him. Take him in. His jaw is tense, the muscles tightening, his teeth clenched. This is what I look at. Not his focused eyes or his mouth that keeps telling everyone he's fine. Yes, you're welcome.

Thank you, he doesn't feel like a hero. Yes, it was terrible. It's his jaw. His jaw is telling the truth.

He continues. 'Mine were six through nine.'

'You're a real hero, Mr Earley. You saved everyone in there,' Detective Samuelson says, still writing in his book.

'Thank you,' Sam says, pulling me close. His gaze is fixed, his jaw tight.

'And where were you, Ms Reid?'

'I was stupid enough to throw myself over Emma. So stupid . . . I could have gotten . . . I could have been killed, gotten you killed, Grady . . . Lisa . . .' I say, trailing off, looking at Sam. He pulls me closer.

I know, even though I dread the knowing, that my life is going to be divided into the time before Emma's murder and the time after. It's not that I suddenly feel like making a Bucket List or shaving my head and trekking to India in search of the meaning of life. But I understand I've been sucker punched and I won't know what the impact is until the bruise forms.

But there's nothing for me to do. Emma's dead. She's gone. I was just getting to know her and now I realize I had no idea who she was at all.

'A violent crime such as this one isn't something you can necessarily prepare for, Ms Reid. You did what you thought was right,' Detective Samuelson says.

'You're clearly new to the force,' I say, looking him dead in the eye.

'Yes.' He nods.

'Thought so. My dad's a cop and will be none too pleased with my behavior,' I say.

'He'll understand it, though. Right?' Detective Samuelson asks.

'He might,' I say.

'Did anyone else get hurt?' Sam asks.

'Besides Mr Davis and the two fatalities?' Detective Samuelson says, reading from his notepad.

'Yeah,' Sam says, his breath catching.

'There were some bumps and bruises, but that was mostly from the commotion,' Detective Samuelson says, waving over a CSI.

'The commotion,' I repeat.

'Would have been a lot more if Mr Earley here hadn't stepped in,' Detective Samuelson says.

'Stepped in,' Sam repeats, a haunted curl of a smile quivering on his lips. I don't know what to say. I wrap my arm around his waist and pull. Curling my fingers around him. Trying to curl my entire body around him. He shakes his head and looks down. At me. Calm yourself, he says. I'll be fine. I pull tighter and take a deep breath.

'We're going to need your clothes, I'm afraid,' Detective Samuelson says to me.

'I think I've got some extras in my car. I was preparing for the dunk tank on Friday,' Sam says, standing.

'We're going to need yours, too,' Detective Samuelson says to Sam. Sam looks down at himself as if for the first time. His light-blue collared shirt is covered in blood – down the sleeves, the collar. It's everywhere.

'Right. I have enough for both of us,' Sam says. I stand, gripping my tea with one hand, whipping the blanket off my shoulders with the other.

Sam continues. 'May I go out to my car, detective?' The detective nods, telling him to be quick. Sam gives me a look – furrowed brow, tight lips. I try to smile. It feels creepy and misplaced. I'm okay. I'm alive and okay. And something about this piece of information makes me feel crushingly guilty. Sam takes off down the street at a run, his lanky frame disappearing quickly into the dark night.

'I can't stop shaking,' I say to Detective Samuelson.

'That's normal,' he says.

'So stupid,' I say.

'So, your father was a cop?'

'San Francisco PD.'

'Wow.'

'Just retired.'

'And how did you know the victim?' Detective Samuelson is buttering me up with talk of my dad. We're back on point.

'Emma was the head of school. The headmistress,' I say, snapping back into witness mode.

'And that was the extent of your relationship?'

'We might have been becoming friends.'

'Might have?'

'She talked about wanting to paint again. Reconnecting with her family.'

'Was this new?'

'Yes.'

'Anything else?

'Initially, we had gone back and forth about one of my speech therapy kids . . . Harry Sprague. We went back and forth about Harry being bullied.'

'Back and forth?'

'Harry was being bullied and, uh . . . she . . .' I trail off. I'm sick to my stomach. All the pieces. All the clues. I knew. I knew something was wrong and I—

'What is it, Ms Reid?'

'In the beginning she sided with the bully, said Harry was asking for it. Provoked it. Deserved it, even.'

'Harry?'

'My student.'

'Go on.'

'Right before her party she took me aside and told me she'd changed her mind. Said that when we focus on the bully, the victim's needs go unmet. She had clearly had a change of heart.'

'Did you know anything about the domestic abuse?'

'What domestic abuse?'

'So, that's a no.'

'He was creepy, but I never thought . . .'

'You never noticed anything?'

Sick. Sick to my stomach.

'Ms Reid, if you know something or saw something . . .' Detective Samuelson says urgently.

'I was at this party at their house last week and he caught me snooping in their bathroom cabinets,' I say, embarrassed. Sam reappears over my shoulder with a duffel bag and some clothes tucked under his arm.

'And?'

I hesitate. Sam listens. 'I could have sworn that as I was walking out of the bathroom, he tried to snatch me back. By my hair,' I say.

'What?' Sam asks.

'We fought. I didn't consider him a threat; he was small, you know?'

'Why didn't you say something?' Sam asks.

'I convinced myself it wasn't what I thought it was. I was snooping and he said he was just trying to close the door behind me. How was I . . . How was I supposed to know?' I say, the emotion choking in my throat. Sam pulls me in close. Closer.

Detective Samuelson starts to say, 'How did—'

I cut him off. 'Emma was perfect and fancy. I can't express that to you more. Her clothes were impeccable, her demeanor. Everything. She was lovely. Just . . . lovely. There wasn't a hair out of place. In my mind, a woman like that lives on a puffy cloud with little cherubs and violins,' I say, my eyes wild.

'Well, that didn't seem to be the case here.'

'No, I guess not.'

'It was all a fantasy, Ms Reid.'

'Wait. No, there was a . . . there was a dog!'

'A what?' Detective Samuelson flinches slightly at my yelp.

'A dog. Did you get the dog?' I say, panicked.

'I don't know.' Detective Samuelson looks to the CSI. She shrugs her shoulders like she doesn't know.

'Do you have a crew at their house?' I ask.

'Yes,' Detective Samuelson says.

'Can you ask them if they found a dog? It's a Weimaraner. Super-trained, nothing to fear. Name is John Henry,' I say.

'John Henry?' Detective Samuelson says.

'Yeah, like the guy with the hammer,' I say, watching.

They stare at me.

I continue. 'It's not made-up – well, the folktale has sketchy origins, but the dog is real. It's not a fantasy dog. I saw it. I saw him. Well, I saw a picture of him. But he's real. And he's probably terrified right now. Can we see if the dog is okay?' Detective Samuelson pulls out his cell phone and dials. The look on his face is annoyed; the dog's not a priority to him.

'Hey, Jay – yeah, it's Mark over at the school. Can you tell me – is there a dog? At the Dunham house? A Weimaraner? Yeah, it's one of those gray—' He is cut off. He's nodding. Nodding. He continues. 'Right. Okay. Thanks, man.' Detective Samuelson hangs up.

'Well?' I ask.

'The dog was in his crate. Animal control took him to the pound,' he says.

'The pound?' I ask.

'Yes, that's procedure,' Detective Samuelson says.

'Isn't there something we can do?' Sam asks, handing me a stack of clothes. I take them.

'Emma loves that dog. She *loved* it; now I know that it was the only thing . . . he's at the pound. They took him to the pound,' I say, my voice rising as I clutch at Sam. Make him understand.

'Okay,' Sam says.

I continue. 'Detective Samuelson, that dog shouldn't be at the pound. Emma had family. Clara. Her sister is here in Southern California. She should know . . . that . . . she should have the . . . the dog should be with them!'

I am using the newly acquired stack of clothes to make my point.

'That's not our job, Ms Reid. Now, if you could get out of those clothes and give them to Ms Reyes here, I'd much appreciate it,' Detective Samuelson says, motioning to the CSI.

'Frannie,' Sam says, taking my arm and guiding me away from Detective Samuelson. Ms Reyes leads us through the school hallways and points to the student bathrooms like she knows these halls better than we do. A little boy and a little girl in blue circles adorn the doors.

'Please,' she says, and opens the girls' bathroom door for me. Sam steps inside the boys' bathroom after one final look at me and a quick nod. He locks the door behind him.

Ms Reyes continues. 'You can go down to the pound first thing in the morning. Fill out the paperwork necessary to adopt the dog and then take him to her sister. If you want.' She looks away. Clearing her throat. She wasn't supposed to tell me that. She's not supposed to care about shooting victims and their dogs. But she does.

'Thank you. I'll do that. I'll do that,' I say, tears welling up.

'Okay, now. Okay,' she says, guiding me into the girls' bathroom. The door shuts behind me and the neon light is cruel and bright. I don't look in the mirror. I don't focus on anything except getting these bloody clothes off. I flip off my ballet flats, now soaked in blood, and let them rest under the sink. I peel my vintage beaded sweater off, the blood soaked through and dark red. I lay it on the sink.

I undo the buttons of my blouse, my hands shaking uncontrollably. I breathe. Deeply. Focus. One button. The next. The next. I lay it on top of the sweater. Do I . . . do I take off my bra?

'Ms Reyes?' I call out through the door.

'Yes?'

'Do you need my bra, too?' I ask.

'Is there blood on it?'

'Yes.'

'Then we need it.'

I am quiet.

'Frannie?' Ms Reyes calls in.

'Yeah?' I ask, taking off my bra.

'Same rule goes for anything else,' she says, her voice insinuating.

'Like my panties?' I ask, sliding out of my skirt.

'Yes, Frannie. Like your panties,' she says.

'Okay . . . got it.' I fold up my skirt, lay it on my other clothes on the sink. I look at my panties and sure enough, they're soaked through. The waistband, all along my left hip. Blood. Emma's blood. I slide them off and stack them. I'm naked. I finally look at myself in the mirror. There are hints of dark stains all over my pale body. On my torso mostly. My hands are still sticky and can't be washed enough. My hair is a tangle and I refuse to run my hands through it before I shower. I just don't know what I'll find. I reach down and pick up the stack of clothes Sam gave me off the floor. A pair of Adidas sweats and a University of Tennessee hoodie.

How in hell did we get here?

I pull on Sam's sweats, cinching the drawstring tightly as they pool around my bare feet. I thread my arms through his bright orange hoodie and zip it up tight. I'm swimming in it and yet . . . it's comforting. His smell. The warmth of it. Of him. I sit on the toilet and pull on a pair of white tube socks, pick up my stack of bloodied clothes (now evidence in a homicide) and unlock the door.

'Put them in here,' Ms Reyes says, holding open a plastic evidence bag. I oblige.

'I'll never see them again, right?' I ask as she seals the bag.

'I'm afraid not,' she says.

Sam unlocks the boys' bathroom door and comes out in a pair of swim trunks and a white T-shirt, clearly part of his preparations for the fund-raiser's dunk tank. He's holding a peacoat in his other hand. He's obviously freezing.

'In here, Mr Earley,' Ms Reyes says, holding open another plastic bag.

'Yes, ma'am,' he says, obliging her. She seals the bag as Sam looks over at me. She labels the bags, gives us a quick thank-you and heads back out into the parking lot.

'You warm enough?' Sam asks, holding out the peacoat.

'You need to put that coat on right now,' I say, pushing the coat back to him.

'Are you warm enough?' he asks again.

'Yes, I am. Now put it on,' I say.

'You're shaking,' he says, stepping forward.

'It's not because I'm cold,' I say, taking the coat from him. I hold it out and motion for him to put it on. He turns around and I thread the coat onto his now-extended arms. One and then the other. He turns back around.

We are quiet.

'Thank you,' I say, stepping closer to him.

Sam is quiet.

'You saved my life,' I say, the words on one hand so clear and true, and on the other so unbelievable and dreamlike.

Sam is quiet, his jaw tightening, his eyes focused on me. He pulls me in close, his arms wrapping around me. He's situating and resituating, bringing me in tighter . . . closer. I wrap my arms around his waist and let my head fall onto his chest, tucking into the folds of the peacoat and settling in next to the thin white T-shirt just beneath.

'I didn't save your life,' Sam says, his voice a growl in his chest. I pull back and look up at him.

'Yes, you did,' I say, my brow furrowed.

'Fran—'

'You need to let me thank you. You need to let me be thankful for you,' I say, emotion rising in my throat. Vast, endless emotion that scares me. My body is shaking. My voice is quivering. My mind is a chaotic mess of images and scenarios I don't have any idea what to do with. I have to start with something I know and work from there. I have to feel something I can label and maybe that will give me some foundation for how to take on the rest of this. I am outside of my body right now, floating and terrifyingly untethered to anything familiar.

'Okay,' Sam says, his face still twisted.

'Okay,' I repeat, letting my head rest once again on his

chest. He wraps his arms around me once more. He breathes. Deep.

'You're welcome,' Sam says, his voice quiet and wandering.

'Thank you,' I say again. He tightens his arms around me.

I am quiet. The red, blue and white lights of the police cars still playing off the halls of the school. The not-so-distant sound of walkie-talkies and urgent calls to action. As Sam and I walk back outside and hopefully away from all this, I can't help but think about all the things we leave unsaid. All the things we hide, keep secret and are ashamed of.

We're only as sick as our secrets.

Emma's secret? She'd rather have died than tell the truth about her marriage.

'Frances, can we have a minute?' Pamela Jackson emerges from Emma's office. Sam and I both stop.

'Pamela, I've had kind of a rough couple of hours,' I say, motioning to my outfit, the police cars . . . the blood still threaded through my hair.

'I know that, Frances. I would like to do a quick check-in before you leave. I've been informed by Detective Samuelson that he's done questioning you, so if we could just have a few minutes,' Pamela says, her voice calm.

'I'll be right outside, maybe see if I can get in touch with Lisa, ask if Grady's out of surgery yet. See if they need anything,' Sam says, pulling his cell phone out of his swim trunk pockets. I nod.

'Come on in,' Pamela says, leading me into Emma's office. A chill. My body convulses as the surroundings impact me. The pictures. The wingback chairs. The perfect flowers lolling to one side in exactly measured vases. A woman so at odds with herself, and yet . . . lovely. A leader in the making. Human. Flawed.

Dead.

I look away and focus on the seat of the wingback chair. Just sit. Pamela motions for me to sit in the chair I'm maniacally staring at. I oblige. She sits in the other. I like that she's not sitting at Emma's desk. I twist my body to face her, my leg inching up onto the seat of the wingback.

Pamela starts. 'How are you doing?' She leans back in the chair.

'Fine.' Numb. Foreign in my own skin.

We are quiet.

Pamela continues. 'I know you want to get home. I really thank you for taking the time to speak with me.'

'It's fine.'

'It doesn't have to be fine.'

I am quiet. My mouth contorts and twists as I try to swallow everything. It's burning my throat.

Pamela continues. 'We thought it might be a good idea to check in with the staff who were in attendance tonight. Just get a quick vibe, if you'll pardon the hippie speak,' Pamela says, her face serene, her voice calm. Flashes of Jamie's face. I blink it away.

'You okay?' Pamela asks.

'Fine.'

'You had a moment there.'

'It's fine.' *Crack*. The loudest noise I've ever heard.

Quiet. Chewing the inside of my mouth. The ringing in my ears is an unnerving and constant reminder of what's happened. I'm swallowing. Swallowing the emotion. The leather is cold and slick under my clammy palms. Pamela waits. I focus on my feet. Little white tube socks. Where am I? What the . . . how did I get here?

'From what I've gleaned from the detectives who worked the scene, you were standing next to Emma?'

'Yes.' The blood. So much blood.

'Emma Dunham was in an abusive marriage. One that ended tragically, but sadly somewhat inevitably. Do you get that?'

I am quiet.

'Frannie, I need you to acknowledge that you're hearing me.'

'I hear you,' I say.

'Good. If you could, I'd like for you to come and talk to me early next week. Monday. Do you think you can do that?'

'Yeah.'

'Frannie, what you've been through is going to affect you in ways you're not going to see coming. I want you to talk to people. Tonight. Keep talking. Let stuff out that feels . . . it's going to feel like a lot. But I need you to let it flow. I know that sounds touchy-feely, but I need you to do that. Will you do that for me?' Pamela says, taking my hands.

I nod.

'I don't want you to put any judgments on yourself in the coming days. It's going to be scary and confusing, but I just want you to feel whatever it is that you're feeling. I know that sounds like psychobabble, but you've survived something traumatic. And your brain isn't equipped to handle things like this. You're going to feel a little lost. I need you to know that.'

I nod.

'Feel. It's okay. Cry. Scream. Laugh. Hug. Talk. But don't judge. Can you do that?'

I nod.

'Okay,' Pamela says, guiding me out of Emma's office. 'Monday, we'll talk again.' She passes me her business card. 'This is my card. My cell phone number is on the back. I want you to call me anytime. You don't need a reason. And please, if . . . if Sam needs me, please have him call. I'm here.' I take her business card and slip it into the deep pockets of Sam's Adidas sweats.

'Thank you,' I say. And stop. I turn to Pamela. 'You're really good at your job,' I say, tears streaming down my face.

'Thank you. And thank god for Condoleezza Rice and Oprah, otherwise these Markham people wouldn't know what to do with me,' Pamela says with a wide smile and a quick wink.

I smile. And my face crumples. Pamela smooths her hand over my shoulders and back. As we walk through the anteroom, she says, 'Take care of yourself tonight, Frannie. Please.'

I nod.

'You survived, Frannie. You don't need to feel guilty about that. Got it?' Pamela says, opening the door to the hallway. As the door creaks open, Sam looks up.

I nod.

'We'll talk Monday,' Pamela says. She gives me a warm smile and steps back into the anteroom. The door closes behind her.

'Grady's out of surgery. He's doing well. He's out for the night. Sedated. Lisa's with him. She says we can see him in the morning,' Sam says as we pass through the double doors and back out into the parking lot. The crime scene. Still packed with emergency vehicles and police and firefighters.

'Okay . . . that's . . . that's good,' I say, breathing. Not judging, just breathing. I begin to meander to my car. Not saying good-bye to Sam. Not really doing or thinking about anything but a hot shower.

'Do you need a – let me follow you home. Frannie?' Sam asks, taking my hand. My fingers curl around his as the red, blue and white police lights play against the school's exterior.

'Sure. Thanks,' I say.

Pamela says I'm going to feel lost. Lost.

Going to?

11

In

'Thank you for making sure I got home,' I say, closing my front door behind us. I spent my entire ride home on the phone with Jill. By the time we spoke, she and Martin were already safely tucked in bed. The only time she perked up was when I told her I was with Sam. That's my girl.

We're all going to meet at the hospital first thing in the morning; Grady should be alert by that time. Well, second thing in the morning. I have a dog to adopt first thing. Friday we have to attend and work the most morbid, sullen and tragic fund-raiser in the history of fund-raisers. I hope it will be healing and not just plain awkward and shitty. I hope. I've also decided not to call my parents just yet. My dad will question me like a suspect and my mom will just worry. I can't handle either of those things right now. I'll call them tomorrow. I'll need errands tomorrow. I'll want something to do on our official day of remembrance, a day when the last thing I want to do is remember.

I've been floating through these last few hours like someone who's whistling past a graveyard in an effort to keep the ghosts and flashes of blood at arm's length. Arm's length, football field length, *China* . . . pick one. I've held other things at bay for a lot longer. Rejecting my true self for decades is good training to keep me in denial about how horrific tonight's events were. I've turned into a single-celled amoeba who wants only two things: a long hot soak in a tub and a warm bed. That's it. I can't handle anything else. And yet, I feel this buzzing inside that has me worried. I'm either going to fall asleep or explode. Or vomit. I'm hoping it's the former. I need this day to be like an Etch A Sketch: one shake and it's a clean slate. I need a do-over. We all need a do-over.

Emma.

'We both need showers and we need something to eat,' Sam says, walking through my apartment. I wish I'd cleaned it up a little. My apartment is always relatively clean, but I didn't know I was going to have company. I didn't know a lot of things about today. It's a good sign that I'm worried about something as trivial as dirty panties on the bathroom floor at a time like this. Although in a moment of rebellion against everything Emma died for, I kind of wish there *were* dirty panties on the ground. I'm not perfect, Sam Earley. What do you think of that? Oh god, I'm going to be sick to my stomach. I lunge into the bathroom.

'I'm in agreement so far,' I say, scanning the bathroom floor. Nothing. We're clear.

'We could order a pizza,' Sam says. I decide that I'm going to wait and see if he brings *it* up. The *it*. The shooting. His shooting. The four shots that stopped the madman and saved us all. Except Sam. We were saved and he became a killer.

'Ah, pizza,' I say, checking his jaw. Tense. Still grinding. In time.

'We have good luck with getting pizza,' Sam says, slurring slightly. We're both exhausted.

'Pizza and baths!' I say, unable to censor what I really want or have any decorum about inviting Sam into my apartment.

'Sounds like a plan,' he says, walking through my apartment, the hardwood floors creaking beneath him. He picks up the phone, finds a pizza-place magnet on my fridge and begins dialing. The biggest comfort I have tonight is that Sam understands. He shares that same glassy-eyed, single-cell-amoeba look. We want the same things. We've gone through the same things tonight. Is he . . . as in denial as I am? A scary wave of fear grips me. Will I even know how this night has affected me? Is this where I just . . . *become* different?

I walk into my bathroom, shuffling along in the too-long Adidas sweats, fidgeting with the zipper to Sam's University of Tennessee sweatshirt. The old-timey porcelain tiles on my bathroom floor are cold underfoot; my 'good' towels are all rolled up and displayed in a wicker basket. Totally unused. My favorite towel hangs on a hook on the back of my bathroom door. Bleach-stained and holey, it has yet to be surpassed. On my counter is a toothbrush, my perfume and a few products left out from my morning regimen. God, this morning seems like a lifetime ago. I sit on the rim of the large bathtub (one of the reasons I rented this place was because it had a huge soaking tub separate from the shower. It was a luxury I couldn't pass up), insert the stopper and turn on the water. Hot. Too hot. More cold. Just right. I run my hand underneath the stream of water. It feels . . . *heavenly*. Sam walks into the bathroom with the cordless phone tucked into the crook of his neck. He's still wearing the white T-shirt and swim trunks.

'What kind of pizza do you want?'

'It doesn't matter.'

'You've got to have some – oh, hi, yes, ma'am, I'd like to orderrr . . .' Sam trails off, looking at me. In this millisecond I wonder why this whole 'Sam in my apartment' thing isn't having more of an epic impact on me. But the armor has been lifted. From me. From him. From in between us. If only for tonight, I'm done with the bullshit. I'm not sure what will happen come morning, but I'm going to take Pamela's advice and go with the flow. I'm perfectly comfortable with Sam being in my apartment, on my phone, and me with nary an undergarment on, telling him what kind of pizza I want. How's that for not overthinking shit, Ryan? Ryan. I'll deal with him tomorrow.

'Cheese? Pepperoni?' I mouth.

'Let's do pepperoni,' he says. I didn't think he would go for just cheese; there would have to be some kind of meat. The water pours into the slowly filling bathtub. Sam walks back out into the living room. I close my eyes again. Tired. Quiet. *Crack*. *Crack*. *Crack*. *Crack*. Emma being lifted off the ground. Jamie's blank stare. I blink my eyes open. Nope. We're not doing that right now. I walk out into the living room just as Sam is hanging up.

'Okay, let me hop in the shower before you get in the tub,' Sam says, pulling the white T-shirt off over his head. It's a shockingly intimate gesture.

He stammers, 'I don't know . . . I don't know why I just

did that, forgot where I was,' he says, holding the T-shirt out.

'Well, you're inside someone's apartment. I've almost taken my shirt off in a Laundromat before. Like came thiiiis close. And then I caught myself. I didn't even have an excuse,' I say, perching on the arm of my couch.

'I'll hurry,' Sam says.

'You don't have to,' I say, looking off into the distance, Sam's naked torso completely lost on me. Lost.

'Make yourself comfortable,' Sam says. And then catches himself. A small embarrassed smile. A nod at my bloody, matted hair and tight mouth, and then the bathroom door is closed. A second later the shower turns on.

I perch on my couch and don't move. Time is irrelevant and in what feels like seconds, Sam peeks his head out of the now-steamy bathroom.

'Do you have anything I could wear? Anything warm?' Sam asks, his hair slicked back, his face blotchy and red.

'Let me check,' I say, walking past the bathroom and into my bedroom. I scan my wardrobe for something big enough to fit Sam. I realize I'm wearing the best option. I walk back to the bathroom.

'If you can hang for a second, let me get rinsed off and you can have your clothes back,' I say.

'You're right,' Sam says, opening the bathroom door all the way. My favorite towel is wrapped around Sam's waist, his upper torso bare. 'I turned off the bath. You're all ready to go. My suggestion would be to hop in the shower for a quick . . . you know, rinse,' Sam says, motioning to my hair.

'Yeah, I thought of that,' I say.

'I'll be out here. Waiting for the pizza,' Sam says.

'Just wait right there,' I say, noticing he's shivering. I close the bathroom door and strip off Sam's Adidas sweats and UT hoodie. Creak the door open and pass them through. 'Here you go,' I say, keeping my body out of sight.

'Thank you,' Sam says, taking them. I close the door. The steam is still thick, the mirror fogged over. The bathtub is full; a layer of bubbles sits atop the warm water. I smile. I walk over to the shower and turn on the water. Hot . . . too hot. Cold. More hot. There. Just right. I step into the shower. Immediately. Red. Everywhere. There was already a red ring around the drain from Sam's shower before I got in.

I step under the hot water and close my eyes. *Crack*. *Crack*. Emma lifting off . . . nope. Open. Open the eyes. Got it. The water falls over my face and I finally run my hands through my hair. It's matted and tangled and takes some doing to navigate. Red drains in a swirl as in an Alfred Hitchcock film. If only everyone wore their crazy like Norman Bates did. But no. Murderers don't dress up in their mother's clothes and victimize pretty blondes in showers. I pour out some shampoo and lather up. No, sometimes murderers are little priggish weaklings who've realized the jig is up. The emperor has no clothes. Their control is waning. *Crack*. Grady whirling around. I shake my head. Nope. I let my head fall back under the hot water, rinsing my hair and body. I turn off the shower. Ready for the tub. Ready to go underwater and hear nothing. See if this ringing in my ears will finally subside.

I carefully step onto the bath mat and pad over to the bathtub. Clean. I don't look back. I won't. I refuse to look at the red ring around the drain. Tomorrow. I'll take that on tomorrow. I step into the bathtub; the warmth shoots through me at once. I sink in. Dipping my shoulders below the bubbles, my face tickled by their froth. Quiet. Safe.

After another unknowable stretch of time, I hear the doorbell and voices. The pizza's here. I perk up. I start to straighten and sit up. A knock on the bathroom door.

'Pizza's here,' Sam says.

'Bring it in,' I say, my shoulders just over the top of the bubbles.

'What?'

'Bring it in. We can eat in here,' I say.

'In the bathroom? Didn't your mother ever tell you that you can't eat in the bathroom?'

'Yes. Yes, she did.'

'Are you still in the tub?'

'Yes.'

Sam is quiet.

I continue. 'The bubbles are providing the necessary camouflage, don't worry.'

'Yes, *that* was my concern,' Sam says. I can tell he's smiling.

I am quiet.

He continues. 'Let me get some plates.'

'In the kitchen, upper right. By the sink,' I say, motioning with my arm, as well.

'You keep dishes in the kitchen?' Sam says, already out into the living room. I smile. I look down at myself. I fluff the bubbles closer to me. Sam stops at the bathroom door again.

'What's going on over there?' I ask, sinking lower into the bathtub.

'I'm just . . . I don't know,' he says, creaking the bathroom door open slowly. I'm watching him.

'It's like you've never eaten pizza in the bathroom with someone in the tub before,' I say. Sam smiles, laughing a little – as much as one could after the day's events. Every laugh is heavy with meaning. I'm laughing . . . after today. I'm smiling . . . after today. I'm alive . . . after today. Should I be doing any of this? Should I be feeling any of this? How does one behave after a day like today?

'Yes, imagine that,' Sam says, arranging a towel on the cold tiled floor and sitting down. He balances the pizza in one hand and two plates with paper towels on the other. He sits in the middle of the bathroom floor and pulls two bottles of beer from his Adidas's pockets with a flourish. He twists them open, one after the other. Hands me mine as I sit up a bit straighter in the tub, the bubbles hanging on to my skin just as they should. My hair is slick and wet to my back. Sam holds his beer high.

'To Emma,' he says, his face serious.

'To Emma,' I say, her name getting caught in my throat. We clink beer bottles and drink. For a long time. Quiet. For Emma. *Crack*. Her ice-blue eyes glassy and . . . I shake my head. Out. Get out. Sam opens up the pizza box, puts a slice on a plate and hands it over to me.

'Thank you,' I say.

'You're welcome,' he says, serving himself up one.

'See? It gets easier,' I say, taking a big bite of my pizza. I'm starving.

'Ha,' Sam says, smiling. And then taking a big bite of his slice as well.

We are quiet. Eating pizza as the water laps against the walls of the bathtub, the random drips of water from the spigot. Sam's hoodie lists open, his naked chest just underneath. I take covert glances at it.

'So, why Pasadena?' I ask, navigating between the bathtub, the pizza, Sam's exposed chest and the bottle of beer quite well.

'I'm sorry?' Sam asks, his mouth slightly full.

'It's a long ways from Shelby Forest, pardner.'

'That's Texan.'

'Is that . . . *what*?'

'Or was that John Wayne?'

'It might have been . . . I don't know exactly . . . just answer the question.'

Sam is quiet for a second. He takes a swig of his beer and pulls one of his legs up, balancing his pizza plate on his knee.

'I'm the third of four brothers.'

'That's a lot of . . . brothers.'

'And being the third meant by the time I did anything in my hometown, some other Earley had done it better, worse, the same, with natural talent or with malicious intent.'

'And your parents?'

Sam is quiet.

'You don't have to—'

'No, it's okay. Especially today. My daddy and I have a complicated relationship,' Sam says.

'With all of the boys or . . .'

'Just me.'

'Oh.'

'I don't know why I'm telling you this.'

'Pamela said we were going to experience weird stuff, but that we should just go with the flow,' I say, motioning that I'd like another piece of pizza, please. Sam obliges.

'Go with the flow?'

'You're in California. People say things like that. And not ironically either.' I take a big bite of my pizza. Sam serves himself up another piece. We eat in silence. Beers clanking against tiled floors. Sam helps himself to another piece and swigs the last of his beer.

'We're going to need more beer.'

'I imagine Grady's got some pretty good drugs right now.'

'The good stuff.'

'He's not feeling a thing.'

'Jealous?'

'A little.'

Sam begins to stand.

I blurt, 'What part do you keep seeing?'

'Part?' He sits back down.

'From tonight?'

Quiet. Water droplets fall into the bathwater. The apartment settles around us. Bubbles pop and froth crackles.

I wait and watch as Sam goes through a series of emotions – wanting to get out of this answer, probably something from tonight flashing through and then . . . resolution.

'We used to shoot watermelons back home. My daddy was a Ranger and then Steven after him, the oldest. Ranger as in the Army. The .45 was standard issue back in the day. That's the gun Jamie was using. The one I used . . . used on him,' Sam says, crossing his arms across his chest.

'Oh,' I say.

'Yeah, so James and I – Billy was always too young and Steven was never around – so James and I would go out back and line up these watermelons. Daddy would kinda be watching us, but in retrospect it probably wasn't the safest summer activity.'

'James is . . .'

'My brother – he's two years older. He was wounded in Iraq, came home early. Steven is the oldest, still in the army, and Billy is ten years younger – just thirty. He's over in Afghanistan.'

'So, the army is the family business?'

'Yes, ma'am.'

'But you're an architect?'

'Yes, ma'am.'

'That probably didn't go over well.'

'My mom loves it – all she does is worry about Steven and Billy, especially after what happened to James. But Daddy saw it as an insult. To him. To country. He never quite . . . never quite saw me as a man. A real man, anyway.'

'Does he still feel that way?'

'Yes, ma'am.'

Quiet. 'And James?'

'James is in construction now; he's actually the one who got me into architecture in the first place.'

I smile. 'So you and James are the closest?'

'He probably, looking back, had the biggest hand in raising me.'

'He's back in Shelby Forest?'

'Yes, ma'am.'

'Kids?'

'Four.' Sam's face lights up.

'Must be hard being away from them.'

'At times.'

'So, James and you . . .'

'Right. We'd go out back and shoot these watermelons with Daddy's .45. We were outside, so the gunshot wasn't ever as loud as it was tonight, but I remember one of Daddy's friends from Vietnam came out back one time and told us that the watermelons were what—'

Sam stops. He shakes his head and looks away. He's struggling. His mouth twists and contorts as he tries to keep in control. His eyes are panicked and uneasy. He finally continues, his speech halting and stilted. 'He said those watermelons were what it looked like when someone gets shot in the head. And I thought that was so cool, you know?' He stops again. He clears his throat and continues. 'Turns out it's not so cool.' I am quiet. Sam sets his plate down, hops up and quickly exits the bathroom.

I lean over and set my plate and beer on the tiled floor of the bathroom and drain out a bit of the now lukewarm water. Anything but thinking about watermelons and . . . the gurgling moan of the draining water echoes through the bathroom. I realize now that I didn't factor in how quickly the bubbles would recede. I can hear the water running in the kitchen. I plug the drain once more, lean forward quickly and turn on the hot water. Scalding. The fridge door slams. Cold. Colder. Hothothot. Wait. There. Just right. The water pours in, warming me once more. Sam walks through the bathroom door with an entire six-pack of beer. He looks at the low tide happening in the bathtub, the receding bubbles, and stands unmoving. I don't look down at my body. I know what's showing. My heart races. Races in a way as if I've freed a caged animal. Let a greyhound off its leash and given it a meadow all its own. I lean forward and turn off the water.

'I apologize,' Sam says, averting his gaze. He looks back over at me. I lock eyes with him. Those cinnamon-brown-spoked eyes. I sit up straight, the bubbles receding to my waist, and extend my hand toward him. He takes it. I guide his hand to my heart; his fingers curl around my shoulder, his palm resting on my naked breast. His attention now on what is just below his hand. What he can feel.

'Don't apologize,' I finally say, bringing my knee up. Sam looks into my eyes. He gives me a quick nod, as if to ask for his hand back. I oblige, feeling just a pinch of unease. Sam takes a few steps away from the tub and from the corner of my eye, I see him unzip his UT hoodie and let it fall to the floor. He quickly slips off his Adidas sweats, bending over in a futile attempt to hide his now uncovered body.

'Scoot forward,' he says. I look up at him. His gaze is unwavering. His eyes are calm for the first time tonight.

I scoot my body forward, the squeak of the bathtub under my body momentarily causing me to blush. I pull my knees in tight, encircling them with my arms, and watch as Sam tucks in behind me. Feel him tuck in behind me. One leg, then the other sliding around me. The water laps at the walls of the bathtub and even lightly splashes over onto the floor, wetting the bath mat below. I hug my knees close.

'Lean back,' Sam says, his arms on either side of the bathtub. I let my shoulders drop, my back curves and I sigh into Sam. The warmth envelops me in a way that I never thought possible. I close my eyes and let my head list to one side, his chest just underneath my cheek.

'You will go to any lengths not to talk about yourself,' I say, my voice an exhausted rasp.

'What about you? What was I supposed to do? I was blameless. Walk back in and . . . I was powerless,' Sam says, smoothing my hair to one side.

'Yes, I am truly a femme fatale.'

'Quite the temptress.'

'That's actually hilarious.'

'Why is it hilarious?'

'Because I'm *so* not.'

'Says the woman who wanted to eat pizza naked in the bathtub.'

'I know! That is so not me.' I have to laugh. Lisa and Jill would be so proud of me. Guilty. I feel guilty for . . . let's face it, I feel guilty for getting out of that teachers' lounge alive. Feel guilty for what Sam had to do. Guilty about not knowing what was going on in Emma's life. All of it. Trivial musings about my burgeoning sexuality feel inappropriate and trite.

‘How is that not you? You did it. Pass me that sponge. Up there, around the tap.’ Sam extends his long arm, pointing. I lean forward; Sam slides his hand down my spine. Goose bumps. Everywhere. I unhook the sponge from around the spigot and pass it to him. He lays his hand against my back. He wants me to stay forward. I obey.

‘I’ve just never seen myself like that in the past. Like a temptress.’ Sam runs the sponge down my back, lathering my body. Washing me clean. My skin is a raw nerve. Goose bumps and shivers follow wherever the sponge goes. I close my eyes. The sound of the gunshots is gone . . . for now. A twinge of guilt remains. Wash that away too, Sam. Wash that away, too.

‘In the past?’

‘With . . . other relationships, I mean.’ My voice is tentative. Self-conscious.

‘How many are we talking?’ His hand hitches.

‘Are you honestly asking me my number right now?’ I look over my shoulder. Sam’s not looking at me, but the smirk. The smirk tells me he is hearing me just fine.

‘Pamela said we should just go with the flow.’

‘Oh, so now you’re comfortable with the whole “go with the flow” thing?’ I ask, my voice nervous and . . . eager. Excited. Invigorated.

‘You’re evading.’

‘You never told me why you relocated to Pasadena.’ Sam rolls his eyes, moving the sponge up and down each one of my arms.

'I thought I could start fresh. Not be Buck's kid, or Steven or James or Billy's brother, or "that poor Tilly's boy." Thought I could . . .'

'Run.'

'Yes, ma'am.'

'Did it work?'

'It seems to be working out pretty well, actually. I've only had to kill one man in the process.' I can feel Sam's entire being deflate behind me. Before I know better I whip my body around, water spilling out, the bathtub squeaking under my body and knees. I take extra-special care not to knee anything important and settle in between Sam's legs. I take his face in my hands. Make him listen.

'You saved us all. You saved us all. I know . . . I know you're the only one that . . . that can't really experience that saving, but you're a good man. And I know this is going to affect you, but you did what a hero would do. You did what . . . you did what had to be done. And I love that. I love . . .' I smooth white-blond strands of hair that don't need to be smoothed. I watch his cinnamon-brown eyes well with tears. I watch him watching me. Listening. Wanting to believe me. He eases his hands around my waist.

'I want to believe you,' he whispers, his head bowed. I pull his face up, the strong jaw, the stubbled skin beneath my hands.

'It wasn't our faults. Jamie walked in there with a gun. We are all victims. We have nothing to feel guilty about,' I say, searching his eyes. Searching him for some understanding.

'I keep replaying it. It was so fast, but then it wasn't. The bullet. The bullets. How he got knocked back and then . . .' Sam trails off, his eyes closing.

'Don't,' I say, knowing what happens every time we close our eyes like that. *Crack. Crack.* I continue. 'Don't.' His eyes are fixed on mine as I kneel before him utterly naked in every way, our bodies a tangle of comfort and sorrow. He licks his bottom lip. I smile. There it is. His tell. There's my boy. 'I love when you do that,' I say.

'Do what?' Sam asks, his arms pulling me closer.

'You lick your bottom lip right before you're about to kiss me,' I say, brushing his bottom lip with my thumb.

'Do I?' he asks, leaning into my touch.

'Yes, you do,' I say. He smiles. A crinkly-eyed smile. A smile of someone I pray is starting to heal. I lean the few inches in and give Sam the sweetest, purest kiss. I hold nothing back. His mouth is warm and sweet and the entire day rushes away. He tightens his grip around my waist as he pulls me closer. I stop and lean back from him with a smile.

I continue. 'I . . . it's . . .' My voice catches on my quick intakes of breath as Sam lights up another part of me that was kept in the dark. My entire body is calling out for him. Screaming, really. A feeling . . . a feeling of completion I've never had before. That utter terror of knowing that it might be too much and I might flame out.

Without a word Sam scoots me forward in the tub. The water laps and splashes as he steps out of the bath and onto the now-damp bath mat. He offers his hand. I take it. Stand. Utterly naked. I step out of the bath and into his arms.

'Thank you,' he says, stepping even closer.

'For what?'

'Tonight could have been really bad,' Sam says, nodding slightly.

'I know.'

'And you've . . .'

'It seems kind of silly that the same two words are used for such different actions,' I say, my voice impossibly quiet.

'My thank-you is just as heartfelt, I assure you,' Sam says. He grips me tightly.

'Most people believe the people in their life will take a bullet for them. I *know* you would,' I say, my voice now a whisper.

Sam's eyes are fixed on mine. He licks his bottom lip . . . and catches himself.

'It's sad to think that I'll never be able to surprise you with a kiss again,' Sam says, smiling.

I run my hands up his still-wet torso. He focuses in on me. Zeroes in. His hand curling around my naked waist. A completely spontaneous and uninhibited display. It starts something. As if a match is held to a trail of gunpowder. All we have to do is light it. The explosion is imminent.

And I plan on lighting the shit out of it.

I hold on to Sam, my grip determined, my intent clear. I feel him watching me, his breath steady yet deepening. My hands tremble as they drop lower, playing with the proximity, knowing how close I am. His breath is coming faster as he grips my hand, pulling me into my own bedroom.

And before I know what's happened, Sam has lifted me up, his arms strong and powerful, and I'm under him on my own bed. Just like he got me out of that low-slung Ferrari in one move.

'How long did you think I was going to let that go on, darlin'?' Sam says, now levered over me, his eyes heavy. He licks his bottom lip as it curls into a reckless taunt. I smile, joy bursting up through my throat as I throw my head back and laugh. I blink open my eyes and see for the first time the way Sam looks at me. Who he sees. In the past, I was someone who was told to tone it down, slim it down or just sit down and be quiet. But right here and right now, I see who I really am. To Sam, I'm someone to be treasured and adored. Protected and kept safe. He swallows hard and in that moment I know, with his face flushed and his eyes fixed, that he's not as in control as he'd like me to believe. I envision the match falling in slow motion, the trail of gunpowder waiting to be set ablaze.

1 + 1 = 2.

I pull Sam down and let him . . . let him set me on fire. Let him affect me. Let him in.

And in. And in. And in.

12

Nothing Wrong with a Little Intensity

The dream goes like this: I'm searching in this dusty campsite for the group. They're leaving. They're leaving and I'm about to get left behind. The rickety staircases and old dirt roads are confusing. My suitcase is heavy and I question why I brought it. *Crack. Crack.* It's coming. It's coming. Drag the suitcase faster. Run. Catch up. Get them. *Crack.* But they're behind me. I'm not . . . I'm not running to something, I'm running away from something. *Crack. Crack.* My hand is curled around the suitcase's handle. Slippery. Sticky. Let go. I bring up my hands. *Crack. Crack.* Blood. Everywhere.

'No!' I jolt awake. Sam stirs.

'You okay?' Sam asks, his eyes still closed. My hand is gripping his.

'Nightmare,' I say, leaning forward. Sam opens his eyes.

'Do you remember anything?' I flip onto my back, still holding on to him.

'Your hand was a suitcase handle,' I say, smoothing it. The ridges and lines of his knuckles and fingers are now visible as the morning sun streams in through my bedroom windows.

'A suitcase handle?' he says, now on his side.

'Yeah,' I say, trying to steady my breathing.

'I was baggage,' Sam says, smiling.

'Merely a prop.'

'Something to drag behind you,' he says, flipping the covers off and walking out of the bedroom. I hear the bathroom door close behind him.

In the quiet of the morning, the reality sets in. I had three seconds. Three blissful seconds where I got to be relieved that my dream wasn't real before I remembered the real nightmare – not the allegorical dusty campsite version, but the reality that sometimes life can be just as terrifying as the monsters we think are under our beds.

I whip the covers off my still-aching body. In our desperation to not feel anything, it seems Sam and I opened ourselves up to feeling everything. Or, at least, I did. My body and mind came together in ways I never dreamed possible. To feel that much actually hurt at times. I was cracked open. I allowed him to touch me in places not even I ventured. And with the heat of him, I felt myself break through the soil and bloom with the exquisite pain of pleasure.

I pad over to my closet, pull on a T-shirt and pajama bottoms and head out into the kitchen. I hear the bathroom door creak open and Sam creak his way across the hardwood floors.

'Coffee?' I ask, pulling a coffee filter down from the cabinet.

'I think I'd better get going. I want to get a shower and some other clothes on before heading over to the hospital,'

Sam says. I turn toward the freezer, tears welling in my eyes, and grab the bag of coffee beans.

'Oh, sure. Okay,' I say, pouring the beans into the grinder.

'Frannie, I—'

I turn on the grinder. Sam's eyes are fixed on me as the beans whirr into a powder. Maybe I can put my heart in there next? I stop the grinder.

'I'll see you at the hospital then,' I say, pouring the coffee into the awaiting filter. Sam's face is creased, his brow furrowed; he's starting and stopping a thousand sentences. I turn away from him, milliseconds away from becoming hysterical, and turn on the tap, sliding the coffee decanter underneath the silken water. I sniff. I can hear the quickening ticking of the bomb that is my composure about to blow.

'Okay . . . at the hospital,' Sam says, stepping toward me. I turn around with the filled decanter, pouring the water into the top of the coffeemaker. I press out a tight smile and make my body as unwelcoming to him as possible. I've walled myself up again. He luxuriated in me and now wants to retreat. It's definitely something I can understand, being as uncomfortable with my own vulnerability as I am, but . . . I thought Sam was different. Apparently, last night was just 'going with the flow' after all.

For him.

'I don't want this to come off . . .' Sam trails off. He steps closer, closer . . . I look up at him. My entire body tenses. I turn the coffeemaker on.

'What?' I ask, my voice catching.

'I need to know you're okay.'

'I'll be sure to lock the door after you leave,' I say. The smell of the coffee wafts throughout the apartment. A new day.

'That's not . . . I . . .' Sam's entire body is buzzing.

'You'd better run along,' I say, hitting the word *run* with a pain that cuts me in half.

Sam nods; his eyes fall to the floor. He rakes his hands through his mussed hair.

I lean against my kitchen counter, my chin high, my heart dismantled and somewhere in my throat. Sam turns and walks out; the door closes behind him.

Yes, this is much better. Showing Sam the Real Me worked really well. Because instead of standing here, coffee percolating in the background, my entire body still aching from him, I can be certain that it wasn't one of my many put-on masks or apathetic guises that Sam walked away from this morning.

Nope, Sam saw – *and walked away from* – the Real Me.

'The dog would have been brought in last night. By animal control?'

I am first in line at the Pasadena Humane Society. I've filled out the paperwork. I've called my landlord to make sure I can have the dog, even temporarily. I am sitting in a tiny cubicle just off the main office. I am busying my mind. I am not thinking about . . . *Crack. Crack.* Nope. I'm not thinking about . . . Sam's hands all over my body.

Nope. I shake my head. In the present. We're just going to practice staying in the present, Frannie.

I focus in on my surroundings. The steady traffic is heartening. Families excited about adopting animals in need, kids barely able to contain themselves. As I watch a little boy light up as a mutt comes barreling out of the kennels with nothing but kisses and nuzzles for his new owner, I think, There's more good than bad out there. There's more good than bad. It's a choice I have to make: feed one or the other. Notice one more than the other. Reward one more than the other.

'You said he would have come in last night?' the girl asks, searching her clipboard and various sheets of paper. She's got a short pixie cut with a tiny bejeweled barrette placed just so. Her ASPCA polo shirt is tucked into a pair of faded skinny jeans and her entire demeanor is one of . . . protective condescension. I must prove myself worthy of this dog or this girl is not going to let me get near him. Once again, there's more good than bad.

'His owners were involved in a shooting. Over at the Markham School? His name is John Henry and he's a big male Weimaraner. Three years old?' I say, inching toward the end of my chair.

'Oh, okay. Here he is,' the girl says, pulling a sheet of paper from a file. She sits down behind her desk and I can't help but notice that she's way younger than me . . . by far.

'So, I want to adopt him. I want to have him,' I say, unable to sound anything but determined.

'He has to stay here until Saturday. We check for

diseases, anything at all. Make sure he's healthy and adoptable,' the girl says, clearly working off a script.

'He won't have any of that, I'm sure he's got all of his . . . everything,' I say, inching forward again in my chair. I'm going to be squatting on the ground just in front of it at this rate.

'Okay, well, we'll check him out anyway. You have to pay the fees listed on your intake sheet and then you can pick him up on Saturday,' she says, writing some notes on the sheet of paper.

'Oh . . . okay. Can I see him?' I ask.

'See him?' the girl asks, looking up from her desk.

'I just want to see if he's okay. It was . . . rough. What happened,' I say.

'Was he there during the shooting?' the girl asks, her voice dropping.

'No, but I was,' I say.

'Oh my god,' the girl says.

'Yeah,' I say, emotion rising.

'I'm so sorry.'

'It's okay . . . can I see him?' I ask again. I plan to mark this day of remembrance by trying not to remember anything about last night.

'Let me . . . see where he is right now,' the girl says, and excuses herself.

'I just need to see him,' I say to myself, looking around the office to make sure no one heard. My energy is off the charts; I feel like I've just pounded a Red Bull laced with cocaine. Either I'm all over the place or I'm only able to deal with minutiae. No gray area. No middle ground. Even with my to-do list. I nod to myself and wait and bite the inside of my cheek, then my fingernails . . . maybe I'll start gnawing on the girl's desk next. The girl reemerges from the back. I perk up.

'Okay, we've got him in one of our privacy rooms. So, if you'll follow me,' the girl says. I feel like I'm about to see some kind of X-rated dog peep show. I stand and follow her through the office and back into the maze of the Humane Society. I can hear the distant barking of the dogs, but we're not anywhere near the kennels. I'm glad; I honestly don't know if I'm up to seeing a kennel filled with stray dogs right now. I just . . . I would probably break into sobs and howl at the injustice of it all. And then adopt every last one of them. No, best to stay the course and follow the Littlest Humane Society Worker into whatever this privacy room is. She stops and opens a door just to my right. She walks in first. John Henry is still in his crate, cowering in the back. He is terrified. The tears spring up immediately. Instantaneous and uncontrollable. I choke them back, clapping my hand over my mouth. The Little Humane Society Worker's gaze is fixed on me. I nod. I'm okay . . . I'm okay.

'He's terrified,' I say, tears streaming down my face.

'For now,' she says, looking me in the eye. Making me look her in the eye. 'For now,' she says again gently.

'It's just been a rough couple of days,' I say, trying to smile.

The girl nods and gets down to business. 'He's clearly high-strung. A little intense,' the girl says, setting her clipboard on a shelf.

'Nothing wrong with a little intensity,' I say.

The girl ignores me as she approaches John Henry's crate. He skitters back. She continues speaking, but now her voice is light and kind and friendly. 'Hi, sweetheart. Hi, sweet boy . . . do you want to come out?' The girl pulls a treat from her pocket as she unlatches his crate. She urges him out. He's terrified but simply unable not to follow orders.

'Good boy,' I say quietly. To myself. John Henry is low to the ground and his melty blue eyes are darting around the room. I try to get low, too. I don't know why. I don't want to look big and mean. John Henry nervously sits for the girl and she gives him the treat.

'We want to get him to drink something,' the girl says, filling up a stainless steel bowl with water. John Henry approaches me, smelling my jeans and pulling back. I do nothing, don't look at him, don't move . . . I stay still but relaxed. I sit down as slowly and smoothly as I can. John Henry lurches back.

'It's okay, sweet boy. It's okay,' I say, my hand out. Low and open. He walks over to me, nervous and darting. He smells my jeans, my shoes, my hand again. I make no attempt to pet him. The girl sets down the stainless steel bowl. John Henry immediately goes over and drinks, loudly lapping up the water for minutes.

'So, his owners. They're dead?' the girl asks as John Henry drinks.

'Yeah,' I say.

'Did you know them?'

'One of them,' I say.

'What happened?'

'I have no idea,' I say, not wanting to talk about it, not wanting to relive it. For this girl, this story could be a juicy bit of gossip. For me? It's a recurring nightmare I can't seem to wake from.

'You said you were there,' the girl says.

'So, the dog?' I say, motioning to John Henry.

'Oh,' the girl says.

'What happens now? With John Henry?' I ask, standing. John Henry lurches a bit, but then does his low walk over to me again. I keep my hands still as John Henry smells them. As the girl motions me toward the door, John Henry happily goes back into his crate with a treat. Maybe I would have gotten more time with John Henry if I'd been more forthcoming about his owners. She's clearly better with animals than she is with people. The girl walks me back through the maze of hallways with assurances that John Henry will be well cared for.

Do I even know where Emma's family lives besides maybe in the Bay Area? Clara being an artist residing somewhere in Los Feliz isn't really a lot to go on. I wonder if human resources would have that kind of information. I was so cavalier about this plan and now . . . how . . . how is this going to actually work?

'Am I being weird about the dog?' I say on the phone to Jill as I drive to Huntington Memorial Hospital later that morning. This morning's to-do list has kept me busy. All so . . . normal. That's the most astonishing thing about all of this. The sun came up this morning like any other day.

'I don't even know what's weird anymore, to be honest,' Jill replies, her voice crackling through the cell phone.

'True. Where are you?' I ask.

'Stopping for coffee and doughnuts before heading over.'

'Oh good – I'm starved,' I say, turning onto California Boulevard.

'So—'

I cut her off. 'It's a long story and I just . . . I can't tell it right now.'

'Unacceptable!'

'It's going to have to be, young lady. And no weirdo looks or . . . just, can you hold it together? I swear I'll tell you everything,' I say, pleading with her.

'I want this to go on my permanent friend record,' Jill says. There are the unmistakable sounds of a bustling doughnut place behind her. Talk of maple bars, doughnut holes . . . my mouth waters.

'Can you get me a maple bar?' I ask.

'Yes, you terrible friend you,' Jill says.

Quiet.

'Go ahead,' I say.

'Did you see Sam's maple bar?'

'Feel better?'

'A little.'

'See you in a few.' I hang up just I pull up to the valet at Huntington Memorial. Yes. A valet. At a hospital. I stop in the gift shop on the way in. I don't know what to bring Grady. While I may have a deep connection to him based on our shared experience, I actually don't know Grady at all. I decide on a nice, tasteful vase of flowers. I walk over to the information desk with my purchases.

'Patient name?' the woman behind the information desk asks.

'Davis,' I answer.

'What would he or she be here for?' the woman asks, her Halloween pin blinking *Boo . . . Boo . . . Boo* over and over again. Jesus. Halloween isn't for another month, lady.

'He would be here for a gunshot wound,' Sam says from just behind me, a plastic convenience-store bag in his hand as well. *Annnd* back to reality.

'Hey,' I say, trying not to stare.

'Hey,' he says back.

'What did you . . .' I ask, pointing to his plastic bag and wanting to move things along. Don't dwell. Don't linger on the fact that we woke up in the same bed – my bed – this morning. That I made coffee like my life depended on it as Sam politely bolted. Sam opens up the plastic bag to reveal a *Playboy* magazine, a handful of Slim Jims and a six-pack of Cactus Cooler. I can't help but smile. Now those are the purchases of someone who really knows Grady.

'Grady Davis. Gunshot wound,' the woman reads, flipping through a stack of papers. It hits me that I've only been to hospitals for the births of friends' babies. I've never . . . Grady is here for a gunshot wound. Grady was shot. By Jamie Dunham. Jamie Dunham. Who Sam killed. *Yesterday*. Wow.

'Yes, ma'am,' Sam says. The woman takes a map of the

hospital off the top of a stack and, using a yellow highlighter, draws us a path to find Grady's room. Sam and I thank the woman and walk to the elevators. Sam pushes the call button.

'I can't believe it's almost October,' I say, unable to deal with the quiet. I'd gotten so used to his face. So used to him.

'I know,' Sam says as the elevator dings open.

'This year is flying by.'

'Are you trying to make small talk?' Sam asks, a smile breaking across his face.

'Am I?' I ask as the elevator dings open on another floor. A couple of doctors get on. We all smile politely.

'You're trying to make calendar-related small talk,' Sam says. One of the doctors looks back at us.

'So what if I am?' I say, blushing.

'Why don't you just say that this elevator is a tight squeeze?' Sam says, his eyes crinkling. We laugh. And then . . . it fades. I clear my throat and step just a bit away from him. Is there ever going to be enough distance?

The elevator dings open on our floor and Sam motions for me to step out first. The doctors give us a quick smile and then are back to business. Sam and I search for Grady's room number. This way and that. Back through . . . no, wait . . . over here. The squeak of our shoes on the sterile floor, my vase bobbing with my every step, Sam's plastic grocery bags crinkling and swaying with his long strides.

'Here, here it is,' I say. The door is closed. I wait, then ask, 'Do we?' Sam knocks lightly on the door, feeling the same trepidation I do. Lisa flings open the door.

'What are you guys doing with that pussy-ass knock!?' Lisa yells, opening the door wide. She takes my vase immediately, setting it down on Grady's bedside table. And she pulls me in. Close. Tight. Her shoulders convulsing one second and then tighter. I hug back. I pull her in.

'You saved me,' I whisper in her ear.

'That madman almost took everything I had,' Lisa says, pulling away from me, taking my face in her hands.

'Thank you,' I say, tears streaming down my face. Again. Again with the tears.

'We need to thank him,' Lisa says, her eyes welling up with tears as she looks at Sam. Sam's smile is meant to reassure Lisa.

Lisa continues as she lunges into Sam. 'You . . . you did what I shoulda done. Grady . . . he hit my Grady. You finished what I started is what you did. Thank god for you. We owe you. I owe you.' Lisa is clutching at Sam. I can see bits and pieces of her monologue getting through to him. He softens as she whispers Grady's name, but I see him tense at the mention of god. Sam hugs Lisa back and just keeps saying 'You're welcome, ma'am . . . you're welcome, ma'am . . .' over and over again. They finally break apart. Sam settles back in next to me. He takes a long, deep breath and continues to listen to Lisa rant. This hospital room is too tiny. We're practically standing on top of each other. Great.

Lisa continues. 'I wasn't going to let him do it. With all the blood on you and Earley, I didn't know for sure whether he had . . . had . . . and then when he got Grady . . .' She steps aside and I finally allow myself to take in our fallen hero. Lisa wipes at her eyes, her mouth contorted in a twist of emotion. Grady and . . . Jamie's handiwork. Grady's entire right shoulder is bandaged and in a tight sling.

'It's not as bad as it looks,' Grady says with a wide smile, his other hand held high.

'How you doin', son?' Sam says, stepping in and shaking Grady's free hand. His accent is thick and casual and yet, Sam is tentative and overly gentle. He doesn't know what to do, how to handle this version of Grady. I can see Sam start and stop, so used to barreling into his old friend knowing he could take whatever Sam dished out.

'That was a close one . . . I . . . uh . . . I'm glad you were there, Earley. For . . . for all of us,' Grady says, patting and clapping Sam on his shoulders. They're awkward in their greetings, in their happiness, in their concern and mostly in their gratitude. Lisa has yet to let go of me; her arm is tight around my waist. She's watching Grady. Beaming. Tears pooling in her eyes, her head tilted in awe. I see her breathe . . . exhale. Calm herself. She nods. He's fine. He's alive and fine. We're all okay.

Sam turns away from Grady and for a brief second I see a haunted look flash across his face. He wasn't ready to be affected that much; he was caught off guard by Grady's appreciation. Sam walks over to Lisa and gives her another hug. They're speaking to each other . . . each so glad the other's okay, thank-yous . . . we all made it. We're all fine. I look from Grady to Sam and Lisa. Smiling. And then I hear Lisa speak in Sam's ear. Quiet. Barely a whisper. *Thanks for saving us*. Lisa claps him on the back and the tears stream down her face as he repeats *you're welcome* over and over again. I look away from Sam and Lisa and over at Grady. He's smiling and happy . . . or as happy as someone could be with a newly acquired gunshot wound. Maybe it's the drugs. Sam and Lisa finally break apart. Sam grabs his grocery bags and brings them over to Grady.

'I brought you the necessities, G,' Sam says, putting the bag on Grady's bed.

'Awww, man – Cactus Cooler! This is . . . and some Slim Jims. Earley, you shouldn't have,' Grady says, holding up the *Playboy* magazine. Lisa laughs. A barking laugh that seems to split something open, burst it into the room: joy. Life. Goodness.

'Knock-knock,' Jill says, creaking open Grady's door. Martin is standing behind her with a pink box filled with doughnuts and a to-go decanter of coffee with all the fixings. Jill carries nothing. And with their entrance, it all starts again.

'Heeeey,' I say, pulling Jill in for a tight hug. Images flash. Jill sobbing and reaching out to me. The sound of her screaming. And now she's here and she's fine. She's laughing and crying and wearing a ridiculous harvest-orange shift dress with matching grosgrain ribbon.

'See? See how good I'm being?' Jill whispers in my ear. I smile and wrap my arms tighter around her as Martin makes the rounds. Clapping hands on shoulders, uncomfortable spikes of emotion as he realizes he was worried, he was . . . waiting to exhale, as all of us were. He gives Sam a hearty handshake and an even more heartfelt thanks. Sam is uncomfortable but polite in his reply.

'I thought I lost you. I thought . . . I can't . . . I'm never setting you up on another blind date, I swear,' Jill says, her voice crumbling into laughter and then eroding into tears.

'Empty promises,' I say in her ear.

'I'm going to need those details *stat,*' Jill says, and pushes me back to take a look at me. She tilts her head and just lets the tears fall. She lays her hand on my cheek and tells me that she's glad I'm okay. All the blood, she keeps saying. I know. I know about 'all the blood.'

'Get your skinny ass over here,' Lisa says, pulling Jill over. Hugging. Crying. Muttering and sobbing. Martin walks over and just . . . envelops me. No words, just . . . a need to hold on. To make sure. To reacquaint with the living.

As Lisa and Jill hug and sob, Jill motions to Grady, saying she's sorry and sorry and sorry. Lisa keeps telling her everything is fine, we're all fine . . . we all made it. See? See? She keeps saying. Jill is nodding, her face buried in the crook of Lisa's neck. Lisa and Jill break from each other. Jill walks over to Sam and through childlike sobbing we all kind of make out that she was worried and that he was so strong and such a . . . hero, and then it's just dolphin-speak from then on in. Sam, despite not being able to understand a single word Jill is saying, keeps telling her he appreciates that, ma'am, it's fine, darlin' . . . you're welcome, you're welcome . . .

And then we're all just standing there. The six of us. The living. The survivors. The heroes and the saved. Sam walks back over and settles in next to me. Jill is watching us like a hawk. It's killllling her.

'So, the shoulder?' Martin asks Grady finally.

'Yeah, no bone damage, which is a miracle, and it just has to be immobilized for a long-ass time,' Grady says.

'And how long do you have to stay in the hospital?' Jill asks.

'Around ten days depending on how well I heal,' Grady says, handing Lisa one of the Slim Jims. She tears it open and passes it back to him. He takes a giant bite. Bliss. Lisa cracks open a Cactus Cooler, holding it at the ready.

'Anyone . . . anyone hear anything?' Martin asks, looking around the room.

'Nothing,' I say.

'No,' Jill says.

'Nope,' Lisa says.

'The EMT said that both Jamie and Emma died at the scene,' Grady says, taking another bite of the Slim Jim. Sam shifts his weight.

'And do we know *why* this happened?' Martin asks.

'The detective was asking me if I knew anything about domestic abuse,' I say.

'Domestic abuse?' Lisa asks.

'I know. I said I didn't.'

'Domestic abuse,' Lisa says again.

'That would explain a lot,' I say.

'The Harry Sprague thing,' Jill says, pointing at me.

'I know,' I say, not wanting to talk about that angle right now, because I secretly think I got Emma killed.

'Would have never known,' Jill says.

'So, I say we plan an Out of the Hospital barbecue,' Martin says, clapping his hands together. Sam and Grady wince.

'Oh, honey,' Jill says, lacing her arm through his.

'I think . . . I think we might have something else to celebrate,' Lisa says, walking over to Grady. They look at each other. Grady smiles and smiles. Lisa smooths his muss of black hair out of his face and flips his hospital gown collar right-side up.

'This morning I asked Lisa to marry me,' Grady says, his voice crackling and excited.

'*What?!*' we all say in unison. Or maybe it's just Jill. Jill claps her hands together and rushes Lisa, hugging her and congratulating her.

'The key here is to ask whether or not she said yes,' Sam says, giving Grady a wink.

'I said yes!' Lisa says.

'Oh, sweetie, that's just the best news . . . it's . . . it's lovely,' I say, hugging her again.

'I just . . . something about yesterday, you know? Made shit real,' Grady says, as the romantic he is. We're all nodding. Indeed. We quiet down. Watching the new couple. The new fiancés.

'When I saw him go down—' Lisa's voice catches and she can't finish. Grady pulls her in close. Comforting her. Telling her it's okay. I let my head drop to my chest and close my eyes. I hear Jill sniffling.

'Come on, now,' Sam whispers to me. I look up at him. Calm yourself. Calm yourself.

'Life's too short, you know?' Grady says, finishing Lisa's sentence as she tries to regain herself.

'Do you guys know when . . . or where?' Jill blurts, getting down to business.

'My folks are coming into town. I called 'em last night and they were worried. That's kinda when I got the idea. I get out of here in ten days and I don't want to waste any more time,' Grady says, gazing at Lisa. She just exhales and tries to smile. Tears.

'Man oh man,' Lisa says, slamming her fist in frustration. 'I can't stop crying.' She rolls her eyes and pulls a tissue from the box on Grady's bedside table.

'Wait, so you're saying you want to get married in like . . .' Jill trails off, getting her facts straight.

'Right around Halloween,' Lisa says.

'Something like that,' Grady says, looking at Lisa. She nods in agreement.

'*We could do it at our house!*' Jill yelps, clapping her hands and giving the tiniest of leaps. Martin looks at her. Pointedly.

'You could barbecue,' Sam adds.

'Oh man, that'd be perfect, Earley. My daddy would love to do that,' Grady says, looking at his old friend. I look up at Sam. He's finally smiling again.

'A backyard barbecue is exactly . . . that's exactly what I want,' Lisa says.

'Are you telling me that I get to plan a backyard barbecue wedding?' Jill asks, her voice barely contained.

'Well, it is my wedding, but—'

'*So you* ARE *telling me that I get to plan a backyard barbecue wedding!*' Jill yells.

'Yes, sweetie, I believe that's what we're telling you,' Lisa says, looking from Jill to Grady.

13

The Girl Who Cried Epiphany

I head back to my apartment later that night after picking up something at the grocery store for dinner. A little remembrance-night dinner of macaroni and cheese with little bits of bacon and three different kinds of cheeses. I also bought the makings for chocolate chip cookies. Comfort food much?

I pull into my parking lot and wait for the gate to close behind me. The gate slowly creaks across the pavement and rolls its way across the threshold of the driveway. *Crack. Crack. Crack. Crack.* In the quiet of my car, I replay the conversations Emma and I had about her marriage and wonder . . . was it *all* a lie? If it was, that's pathological.

No. Maybe. Not pathological. Just sad. Tragic, really.

The gate finally creaks closed behind me and I ease into my parking space. The only light that remains is my car's automatic headlamps on the wall. The darkness surrounds me as they slowly dim. My heart races. All of a sudden I can't get out of my car and into my apartment building fast enough. I'm positive something is nipping at my heels. I grab my purse and the grocery bags and run up the stairs and into my apartment. I fling open the front door and slam it behind me. I immediately feel ridiculous and happy no one was there to witness what just happened. What *did* just happen? There was nothing lurking in the darkness of my garage. Nothing was 'after me.' What's happening to me? I lean down and hold on to the arm of the sofa, trying to steady myself, catch my breath and get my heart rate down from around a billion beats a second. I take a deep breath, gather my bags and continue into the kitchen. Dinner. Think about dinner.

The dream goes like this: I'm searching this dusty campsite for the group. They're leaving. They're leaving and I'm about to get left behind. The rickety staircases and old dirt roads are confusing. My suitcase is heavy and I question why I brought it. *Crack*. *Crack*. It's coming. It's coming. Drag the suitcase faster. Run. Catch up. Get them. *Crack*. But they're behind me. I'm not . . . I'm not running to something, I'm running from something. *Crack*. *Crack*. My hand is curled around the suitcase's handle. Slippery. Sticky. Let go. I bring up my hands. *Crack*. *Crack*. Blood. Everywhere.

'No!' I jolt awake.

My bedroom. My bed. No Sam. I haven't heard from him since last night. No explanation for what happened or why he left. I get it, though. After such a trauma, we just wanted to feel something good. Feel alive. Whatever newfound flirtation was developing between us took a tragic Icarus-like turn and now lies in pieces among its melted wax wings. We just didn't know each other well enough to handle that level of intimacy that quickly. We flamed out.

My apartment is quiet. Too quiet.

Flamed out.

So why do I feel abandoned? My hero finally found me in that too-high tower, rescued me from its cold walls, set me down among free men and bolted.

Freedom, with all its possibilities, just feels cold and lonely. I want to go back to my tower. I need those walls. I need the protection.

The walls were always my true plus-one.

Teachers gather their classes and stream out of the auditorium the next morning after the acting headmistress, Pamela Jackson, finishes with the assembly. Jill and I stand in the back, arms crossed, a slightly glazed look in our eyes. Trying to explain to a school filled with kids what happened on Wednesday is like . . . well, trying to make sense of it myself. Pamela talked about bullying and solving problems with violence. She also talked about how this was something that happened but that it's not going to happen again. She wanted to make sure the kids felt safe. Her voice was calm and soothing and . . . the more I traverse this minefield, the more I realize how wrong I was about people. Emma. Pamela. Even me.

Everyone who wasn't there on Wednesday is maintaining an odd, encircling – yet conspicuously detached – orbit around those of us who were. No one wants to ask what happened, so the rumors are swirling. A few teachers are talking about it, a few teachers are trading on it, and then there's us. Shared glances and knowing smiles. The teachers' lounge is boarded up, remnants of police tape here and there. When we arrived this morning, Pamela Jackson redirected all of us to an annex just off the main school for our gathering and coffee needs. There were bagels, coffee and fresh flowers. She'd thought of everything. It still felt . . . cold. Very few gathered, even fewer ate. People did pour themselves coffee – I mean, let's not get crazy. Jill mentions that Markham's board of directors and Headmistress Jackson approached Martin about rebuilding the old teachers' lounge along with the ongoing school expansion. He agreed to it right away. I remember I haven't even told Jill that I got the promotion. It was probably the last piece of business Emma handled. Once on the balcony – makeshift, but it'll do – Jill lasers in.

'Spill,' she says, sipping her tea.

'I'm tired,' I say.

Jill is quiet. Fine.

'He drove me home. We ordered pizza. We took a bath together then had sex. It was mind-blowing and I actually can't talk about it without . . . then he left the next morning and I have yet to hear from him.' My voice is robotic and detached.

Jill is quiet. Quiet. Her eyes are wild. This is worse than I thought.

For the first time in her life Jill Fleming is speechless.

'I knew I'd find you two up here.' Lisa. She looks exhausted. Lisa sits and takes a long inhale of her coffee. No cigarette.

'How's Grady?' I ask. Jill is still stunned. Lisa takes notice. She's wary.

'He's doing better every day,' Lisa says.

'*I don't understand one thing you just said!*' Jill yells, her finger one inch from my face, her tea spilling out of her tasteful toile-patterned mug.

'Did I miss something?' Lisa asks, a smirk cracking across her depleted face. Jill slams down her mug, mumbling to herself as she paces around the tiny balcony.

'Go ahead, Frannie. Just say it again. Maybe I'll get it this time!' Jill says, gesticulating wildly.

'Sam drove me home after . . . well, after the . . . whatever. We ordered pizza. We took a bath together then had sex. It was mind-blowing and I actually can't talk about it without . . . and then he left the next morning and I have yet to hear from him,' I say again. Wow. It hurts just as much the second time.

'*Bullshit!*' Jill yells.

'You okay?' Lisa asks, reaching across and taking my hand.

'I'm as far from okay as a person can get, I think,' I say, my voice quiet. Jill flops down in the nearest chair. Lisa looks from her to me. We share the tiniest of smiles. Jill is gobsmacked.

'Aren't we all,' Lisa says.

'Seriously,' I say.

'How do you . . . *How do you?!*' Jill stammers.

'It makes sense. You know it does. It's the whole Icarus thing,' I say.

'Frannie, I need you to speak normally. I can't wade through all of your theories and "epiphanies" and analogies that don't make any sense. I don't know how you're using Icarus, sweetie. You turn mythologies into just single words and I need you to just . . . can you just speak normally? For once?' Jill asks, her voice imploring.

'No! I can't!' I snap. Tears. Rolling down my cheeks. I close my eyes and continue. 'It helps, okay?! It helps to talk about things like Icarus so I don't have to . . . so I can compartmentalize Sam leaving, making it into something that's poetic instead of the saddest thing in the entire world. I've never . . . I've never been like that with someone, do you get that?! I didn't know sex like that was possible. I really didn't. And I hate that I'm making it sound like it was just the sex or whatever. It wasn't. I didn't know I could be like that! That a man could be like that! That I could be like that with anyone, much less a man! It was just . . . god, it was beyond anything . . . beyond anything I'd ever dreamed. And now he's gone? How terrible am I?' I sob. Lisa squeezes my hand tighter.

'You're not terrible!' Jill says, kneeling down in front of me.

'Well, he's not terrible! You know he's not! So, what made him leave?' I cry.

Silence permeates the little balcony. We're all thinking it. And I feel like a whiny teenager who doesn't know how selfish she sounds.

I continue. 'I know. I can't know what he's going through right now.'

'No,' Lisa and Jill say in unison.

'I am so trifling,' I say, taking a tissue from Lisa.

'You're not trifling. Jesus, who would blame you for wanting to think about what happened with Sam instead of . . . I went so far as to get engaged,' Lisa says, laughing.

'Yeah, can we talk about *that* for a minute?' Jill asks, shifting in her chair so she's facing Lisa.

'It was the easiest decision in the world. All of those years spent trying to become some other woman, when all I had to do was wait for the one man who was looking for me. And then to watch him . . . well, I was done wasting time,' Lisa says.

'Clearly we're going to have to set up a schedule. Wedding planning,' Jill says, patting Lisa's knee.

'Clearly,' Lisa says, giving me a quick wink.

'We'd better get going,' I say, noticing the time. Pamela Jackson believed today should feel just as routine as the ones before the shooting. We're on a half-day anyway, due to the Fiesta Fund-raiser, so we'd better get a move on.

'Did you fudge-pack at all?' Jill asks as we open the door into the teachers' lounge.

'Yes, I did. I made real fudge, Jill. And no matter how easy that recipe is, I'm vowing right here and now that I'm never making it again,' I say.

'Meet you back in the office. We'll talk about about . . .' Jill raises and lowers her eyebrows. I nod. I know exactly what and who she's talking about, sadly. Jill and Lisa head out as I pour another cup of much-needed coffee. The door pushes open. Ryan. I haven't seen him since the shooting.

'Hey,' I say as he ambles toward the coffee. He looks up.

'Oh, hey . . . oh my god, Frannie,' he says, slamming his empty mug down on the counter and lunging into me with a hug. His black hair is combed and moderately kempt, and his Puma jacket is loosely zipped, exposing the collared shirt and tie just underneath.

'I know . . . I know . . .' I say, hugging him back. So comfortable with soothing him. We break from the hug and tears are streaming down his face.

We are quiet. There's nothing to say.

'How are your students taking all this?' I ask, pouring coffee into my mug and turning my back to Ryan and the shampoo I can smell from here.

'As well as can be expected,' Ryan says, smoothing his tie.

'Is this fancy outfit here for the fund-raiser later?' I ask, trying to change the subject.

'Thought I'd dress up for the parents,' Ryan says.

'Kiss-ass,' I say, pouring in cream and sugar.

'What are you gonna do?' We're happy to change the subject and never speak of Wednesday again.

'Make fun of you to your face and then behind your back.'

'Ha!'

We're quiet.

Ryan continues. 'It's good seeing you.'

'You see me all the time, weirdo.'

'I mean . . . you know what I mean.'

'No, I actually don't.'

'Talking to you. It's good talking to you.'

'Do you mean sober?'

'Ah yes. A proud moment. You know I . . .' Ryan stops. His face pales. He looks away as he continues. 'I talked to that guy for over an hour at that mixer. He . . . uh . . . he seemed like an okay dude.' Ryan walks over to the coffeemaker and pours himself a cup. I notice his hands are shaking. He sets down the mug with its now-spilling contents and balls his hands into fists. 'They keep doing that. I can't stop them from shaking.' He looks away. Embarrassed.

'I imagine we're all suffering from some form of post-traumatic stress. Have you talked to Pamela?'

'Yeah. We're talking again next week,' Ryan says.

'You should tell her about the shaking,' I say, briefly touching his hand.

'Right.' Ryan is smiling. The light blue eyes, the pinkish lips curling into a smirk.

'Well, godspeed, John Glenn,' I say, throwing the stir stick into the trash.

'I broke up with Jessica,' Ryan says, not looking at me.

'What?'

'I broke up with Jessica.'

'I have no response to that.'

'You're quoting *Joe Versus the Volcano*?'

'Yes . . . *and* stating my feelings.'

'By quoting *Joe Versus the Volcano*?'

'Why are you telling me this?'

'After what happened, I just . . . being with someone to . . . I just had to get out of there. I had to find you.'

I am quiet. A flash of what it would be like to be with Ryan again as the Real Me. Is that . . . is that even an option? If Sam was some sort of catalyst, is this the destination? To try again with Ryan as the Real Me? Maybe not think so much and just let shit ride?

'Why would you want to find me?' I ask loudly. Inappropriately loudly. Like I don't understand volume or inside voices. Ryan steps just that much closer. The shampoo. The aftershave. The laundry detergent. It's eau de Ryan. And it's doing the same thing to me it always did.

The door creaks open. I jump back. I can't have the Coven of Front-Office Hags thinking anything is happening between Ryan and me. Wait . . . *wait*. What *is* happening between Ryan and me? He broke up with Jessica and I have no one – thought I had someone for a minute, but . . . What about Sam? Is it over? Are we done?

'I have to go. I have to go,' I say, my hand on Ryan's chest. Pushing him away. Or am I keeping myself away?

'Frannie,' Ryan says, his voice breathy. His hands are no longer shaking. He holds them up for me to see. Steady. 'See? I need you, Frannie,' he says.

'Okay, good. Good talk,' I say. Nodding. Nodding. I can't look at him as I race out of the teachers' lounge. I hear Ryan calling after me but don't turn around.

After a hazy morning of filing, report writing and generally trying to keep busy, I head back up to our office to prepare for the Fiesta Fund-raiser. The saddest fund-raiser in the history of fund-raisers. I've spent the entire day avoiding the crime scene, searching for Sam, letting everybody know that I'm fine, putting on a brave face for the kids, pushing Ryan's 'offer' into a dark corner of my psyche, while the entire time I'm slowly unraveling. My hands won't stop shaking either. I find myself on the brink of tears for no apparent reason. And I'm scared. All the time. I can't close my eyes. *Crack*. *Crack*. I'm positive something is lurking in the shadows and I can't stop mourning a woman I was just getting to know. I walk into our office, barely functioning. Jill is already bustling about.

'They should have canceled this,' I say, slumping in my desk chair.

'It'll be good. People need to be together in times like these,' Jill says. Her speech is clipped and agitated.

'I had a whole thing last night. A whole . . . whole *thing*,' I say.

'With Sam? What . . . like anal?'

'You're just . . . it's all just . . .' I say, not able to really pinpoint the majesty of Jill. She looks like she doesn't understand. You mean, that *wasn't* what I was talking about?

'After yesterday I went back to my apartment and I got all freaked out in the parking lot and I just . . . I panicked,' I say. Jill looks at me impatiently. I stand. We gather colorful banners, speech therapy handouts and container after container of the fudge I made and chocolate chip cookies. Jill scoops up the handouts. She points to a folded banner in a corner of our office and I pick it up. I load it and our cookies and fudge in a little red wagon and pull it behind me. We exit the office and head toward the elevator in our secret corner of the school.

'I'm not used to this,' I say, my hand moving between us.

'What?'

'Yeah, I mean . . . I never really had . . . real friends,' I say, admitting it finally. While Jill and I have only known each other for a short time, it feels like forever. We became fast friends and never looked back. It's times like these when I feel the most tentative. When I'm exposing more of my crazy than I'm comfortable with.

'Not even in school? Like when you were younger?'

'I had a Sony Walkman, a Depeche Mode tape and a pair of roller skates.'

'Can we just get this stuff down to the fund-raiser?' she asks, her voice short.

'What's going on over there?' I ask, opening the door for her. She wheels the wagon out into the hallway.

'You know, not everyone likes to sit around and talk about . . . all this,' Jill says, motioning around the hallway.

'Okay . . .'

'A lot changed that day, but apparently one thing that didn't was you blathering on about your feelings,' Jill says, her finger on the elevator call button.

'So I'm a blatherer now,' I say, nodding my head.

'Yes. You. Are.'

'Jill . . .' We wait for the elevator to sloowwwwwlllly climb the one floor.

'Oh, let me guess . . . you want to taaaalk about it,' Jill says.

I am quiet. The door dings open and we shuffle inside. I pull the wagon in and tuck it between us. Jill pushes the button for the first floor and the doors ding closed. We are quiet as the elevator moans its descent.

'Jill, I—'

'I don't want to talk about it, Frannie! Ever!' Jill yells, not looking at me. She opens her mouth, then closes it. Then she looks directly at me; her eyes soften and tears well up in them. The elevator wheezes to a stop. The doors ding open. The halls are alive and chaotic.

'Sweetie, you're going to have to talk about it. If not with me, then with Pamela. Or Martin?' I say, looking around at the bustling teachers and administrators as they get the main parking lot ready for the big tragic fund-raiser. White tents and cotton candy kiosks have appeared in the parking lot that contained every emergency vehicle in Pasadena just two days ago. Teachers and students are milling around putting up signs and decorating booths for this afternoon's upcoming festivities where once there were body bags. People should be arriving within the hour where just days before a group of people ran for their lives. And I have fudge.

'I can't talk about it with Martin,' Jill says.

'Why wouldn't you be able to talk about it with Martin?' Jill is quiet. We walk in silence and finally reach our bare booth. It's ready for banners and colorful handouts. Jill ducks underneath the table.

'You guys look like you're in the middle of something,' Lisa says, her arms heavy with costumes, hats and masks.

'Shock of all shocks, Frannie wants to taaaaalk about her feelings,' Jill says, setting out the fudge and cookies.

'Shame on me,' I say.

'And you don't?' Lisa asks.

'What? No,' Jill says.

'Sweetie, we're your friends,' I say, handing her the platters from the wagon.

'You're a bunch of assholes is what you are.' Jill's voice is hushed as she makes sure no kids are around. 'If you don't talk about it then enough time will pass and it'll just go away.' Tears well in Jill's eyes once again. I know where Jill's rage is coming from, but why now?

'It doesn't go away,' Lisa says.

'It has to,' Jill says.

'Oh, sweetie,' I say.

'I've never seen anything like that . . . I've never seen anything like that,' Jill says, angrily swiping at her tears.

'None of us have,' Lisa says, stepping closer.

'I'm having nightmares,' Jill says, her voice barely audible.

'Me too,' I say.

'Me too,' Lisa says.

'Headaches,' Jill says.

'Me too,' Lisa says.

'I don't have that one,' I say.

'I just keep seeing it. Her. All that bl— . . . all that blood,' Jill says, still setting out fudge and chocolate chip cookies.

Lisa and I just keep nodding. Everything Jill is saying is right on point. We're all being haunted by the same ghost.

'At least you didn't get dumped in the same night. I'm sorry – I mean, the next morning,' I say, trying to lighten the mood. Jill pounces.

'Sam loves you,' Jill says.

I am quiet. Can love even be possible? In all this?

Lisa continues. 'This is a good thing, Frannie.'

'Doesn't feel too good,' I say.

'Even if nothing comes of this thing with Sam, and I

highly doubt that, it's still better than anything you would have had with Ryan,' Jill says, her whole demeanor calming down. She becomes oddly quiet.

Lisa and I turn to her.

'What?' Jill asks, looking up.

'Why are you so quiet?' I ask.

'I'm just . . . I can't believe Lisa and Grady are getting married. I . . .' Jill trails off.

'What?' Lisa asks.

Lisa and I finally notice. We both look at her.

'I can't believe it worked, you know? Crank grabbing and . . . now you're getting married,' Jill says, mumbling to herself.

'What do you mean?' Lisa asks. I say nothing. Thank god everyone is busy and distracted in this parking lot. This conversation could get ugly. Uglier, I mean.

'I had these inalienable rights, you know? Pursuit of happiness, perfect husband and kids, tablescapes . . . the gamut,' Jill says.

'I'm not sure that's quite what Jefferson had in mind, but continue,' I say.

'I've been on a diet for thirty years. I've brought hostess gifts to bitches I'm sure made a play for my husband and it . . . it's all for nothing. Clearly,' Jill says, motioning at Lisa.

I clap my hand over my mouth. It's instantaneous and instinctual. Jill looks mortified. With herself. Lisa looks hurt.

I start to speak. 'Jill, you'd bet—'

Jill blurts, 'I don't mean to say anything about your

body. I mean . . . You know what I mean, right? You know what I mean. That there needs to be a certain layering of one's personality when you meet the man you think is the One and apparently . . . apparently I was wrong.'

Lisa is quiet.

'Is that what you were saying about not being able to talk to Martin about the shooting?' I ask.

'I guess,' Jill says.

'So, your marriage is built on what, exactly?' I ask, treading lightly.

'When Martin came along he had everything I knew I wanted in a husband, so I followed the rules,' Jill says, her voice detached and teacherly.

'You're not answering my question,' I say.

'You've got to be kidding me with this,' Lisa says.

'That's why we're now married and I'm not just another notch on his bedpost,' Jill says, reaching back down for another container of cookies.

'You realize that you're saying that you not only hid who you really are from the man you later married, but that you are still hiding who you are,' Lisa says.

'I didn't hide anything,' Jill says.

'That's what you just said,' Lisa says.

'I layer.'

'You're using fancy speech bullshit to evade the question.'

'I am not.'

'Are too.'

'Enough,' I say, cutting in.

'I'm saying that there are parts of my personality that I

believe to be more attractive than others and that it's just good business to put one's best foot forward,' Jill says.

'Good business?' I ask.

'You see your relationship with Martin as a business transaction?' Lisa asks.

'In some ways, yes.'

'It's clearly a compliment that you can't comprehend my relationship with Grady,' Lisa says, somewhat relieved.

'A compliment?' Jill asks.

'Silly me, I thought you were just calling me fat,' Lisa says.

'I would never—'

'Oh, I know that now. Your insanity goes faaaar deeper than just being shallow. Which is rather ironic, don't you think?' Lisa says, her face reddening.

'I've been up-front with both my insanity and shallowness from the beginning,' Jill says, wanting to win one part of this fight.

Lisa and I laugh. And laugh.

'You're the wind beneath our wings, Jill Fleming,' I say in between hysterics. 'And what were the parts of your personality you believed were your best?'

'I'd heard that his ex-girlfriend was this bookish girl who didn't really like sex, so . . .' Jill trails off with a flourish.

'You what?' I ask.

'I became this sex goddess. I knew it was the one thing I had that she didn't. That, and I was way cuter,' Jill says.

'What are you talking about right now? I am never taking advice from you ever again,' I say, looking around at the growing crowd of people gathering in the parking lot.

'Those actually aren't parts of your personality. You know that, right?' Lisa asks.

'They . . . what?'

'Dialing up your sexuality and your appearance is not why someone marries someone or stays married to someone,' Lisa says.

'Men are visual,' Jill says.

'So, you masked a lot of who you really are to snag your man,' I say.

'This is going to come out in a way that I mean as a compliment but clearly you're going to think is not. Honey, that's not why Martin married you,' Lisa says.

'It's the first reason,' Jill says.

'The first reason?' Lisa asks.

'You get that all these rules about keeping up appearances and hiding who you really are . . . You know who the queen of that was, right?' I ask. Jill beams as if this is a compliment and that I'm about to crown her. I continue. 'Emma.' Jill looks shaken. Lisa nods. We wait.

'It's not . . . it's just . . .' Jill stutters.

'It's a dangerous lie you're perpetuating here, Jill. More dangerous than you ever imagined,' I say.

'Oh, okay, Ms Sam Only Slept with Me Because He's Duty-Bound!' Jill says.

'That's not the same thing! I'm just incredibly insecure! I'm not hiding who I am!' I say.

'That's exactly what you've been doing! Hellllloooo!?' Jill says.

Quiet. Stunned.

'They're not . . . they're not dangerous rules,' Jill mumbles.

'Keep telling yourself that,' I say.

'Headmistress Jackson is going to be coming around to make sure we're all on the same page, so if you guys could tidy up and do any last-minute readying . . . that'd be great,' Debbie says. She's eyeing Lisa, whose arms are filled with costumes, hats and masks that clearly need to be deposited somewhere else. Apparently our spiraled cookies and platters filled with fudge pass muster with Debbie.

'We'll be ready,' I say, raising a victorious fist aloft. Debbie smiles and moves on to the next booth. I narrow my eyes at Jill as she sticks her tongue out at me.

'We'll talk later,' Lisa says, giving us a quick nod and walking off into the growing crowd.

'Very mature,' I say to Jill. I scan the parking lot. Ryan and his fifty tiny glass bowls filled with water are set up at the far end of the parking lot.

I look over to the left and see the dunk tank. Martin is holding a hose connected to a spigot at the side of the school and is almost done filling up the tank with water. I see one of the other architects holding his hand beneath the steady stream of water and making a face. It's freezing. He shakes his head as Sam approaches them. The minute I see Sam, I feel like I am made a fool. Whatever lies I tried to tell myself about his being a duty-bound saint or some other crazy bullshit I'm trying to sell, my body isn't buying. It reacts to him as purely as it should. Clammy hands, racing heart and a flushed face reveal my true feelings for him. He affected me. He affects me. I want him to continue to affect me. And not in a conceptual detached kind of way. It's a good thing. It's a good thing . . . right?

Sam is wearing a pair of swim trunks and that same bright orange University of Tennessee hoodie from that night. My stomach flips.

I see Sam and the rest of the architects huddled around the dunk tank. They're doing rock, paper, scissors. The crowd reacts. Sam throws his head back and then just shakes it. Shakes it, closing his eyes and raking his fingers through his hair. He throws up his hands and I can hear him saying, 'Fine! Fine!' over and over again.

The parents begin arriving. Everyone is hesitant and . . . cautious. As if they're expecting another gunman to appear. There might as well be eggshells spread out on the cement. The kids don't really understand and it's better that they don't. That is one thing on which all of us can agree.

'Ms Reid!' Harry Sprague and his parents.

'Hey there!' I say, melting just a bit. I duck under the table and extend my hand to the Spragues. Harry, tears welling in his ice-blue eyes, pounces on me. His arms wrap around my body, his hands tugging at my sweater.

I hug him back, pulling my arm around his lanky body and cradling his head in the other. Tears choke in my throat. I kneel down. 'Sweetie, I'm okay. See? I'm okay. Harry?' I wipe away the tears streaming down his blotchy face. He's nodding, nodding, nodding. I look up at the Spragues. Not a dry eye in the house.

'He was so worried,' Mrs Sprague says, pulling a handkerchief out of her Hermès bag.

'We all were,' Mr Sprague says, pushing his sunglasses up a bit more.

'I thought that man got you,' Harry finally squeaks out.

'No, baby. He didn't,' I say, pulling him in for another hug.

'He didn't,' Harry repeats.

'No, baby. He didn't,' I say again, tears now streaming down my cheeks as well.

'Oh, for crissakes,' Jill says, blowing her nose into a napkin reserved for fudge and chocolate chip cookies.

We all laugh. A much-needed laugh. As I bring Harry in for another hug I turn. Sam. Watching. Smiling.

'I told my parents you were making your famous fudge,' Harry says, gathering himself.

'Five-minute fudge, easiest recipe ever,' I say, passing all three of them napkins filled with treats and trying to get back on a professional footing even as my heart melts right there and then.

'You guys want more fudge?' Jill blurts through tears.

Harry's parents and I have a good laugh as Jill swipes her wet cheeks and offers Harry a handful of fudge. She won't take no for an answer. He accepts it.

'We'll leave you to it,' Mr Sprague says, taking his wife's hand.

'Thank you again, Frannie. We just don't know what we'd do without you,' Mrs Sprague says.

'He's such a good boy. I'm the lucky one,' I say. Barely.

The Spragues walk hand in hand through the fiesta.

'Are you kidding me?' Jill says, pulling the roll of paper towels from the wagon. She takes one and starts dabbing at her eyes.

'That kid. I swear. I try not to play favorites, but that kid gets me every time,' I say, ducking under the table and starting to take the tickets from the newly formed line of kids. I place the tickets inside a large jar. We give them each a napkin with one cookie and one piece of fudge on it. They shove the treats into their mouths and run off to the next activity. The Fiesta Fund-raiser, which is not a fiesta at all, has officially begun.

'Wouldn't the kids be more excited about dunking teachers and not architects?' I ask Jill.

'Teachers were probably smart enough to steer clear of something as embarrassing as a dunk tank. I'm not complaining, though. We've got quite the view,' Jill says, handing out more treats to another group of kids. She motions to the dunk tank. Or more specifically, she motions to Sam. I breathe in. As the line of kids rabid to dunk an adult becomes more and more crazed, Sam unzips his University of Tennessee hoodie and hangs it over a folding chair. A plain white T-shirt is just underneath. Of course it is. It's the same outfit from that night. Sam looks over and gives me a wave. I smile and give a thumbs-up back. He just shakes his head.

As Martin hands a softball to a little girl at the front of the line, Sam climbs the ladder to the dunk tank like a man approaching the hangman's noose.

'You're next,' Sam yells to Martin as he navigates the slippery transition from ladder to sitting just above a tank of freezing hose water. Another group of kids, another set of treats. I replenish our platters and unload more containers of goodies from the wagon. I am quick to get back to the business at hand. I watch as Sam settles his big body on the tiny, perilous crossbar. His face contorts in an annoyed tangle. He can't stop shaking his head in disbelief.

'This most certainly was not in the job description,' Sam yells, finally settling in. Martin and the other architects howl with laughter. A little girl steps up and cocks her arm back, the softball almost as big as she is.

'Come on, darlin'. Let me have it,' Sam says, gripping the crossbar and forcing a smile. The little girl throws; Sam watches the ball soar through the air and fall short of the target. The crowd reacts. The little girl deflates slightly. Martin quickly hands her another softball, giving her a quick lesson in throwing. He models the throw for her, his hand pointing at the target. Sam's face just looks . . . amused. Martin nods. The little girl stands a bit taller. I take a quick peek over at Jill. She's watching, too. Martin with the little girl is swoon-worthy. This is definitely a moment for Jill's pantheon – although, knowing Jill, I have no idea which moments she values and which she pays no mind at all. I always thought she wanted kids, but that's contrasted with her seeming not to have one maternal bone in her body. In the past, when Jill's talked about kids it's always been about what she should do. What's expected of her. The next chapter. I wonder if Jill has ever thought about whether or not she actually wants kids.

'Okay, darlin'. This is the one!' Sam cheers, clapping his hands. He's still shaking his head and pursing his lips, probably due to the impending hypothermia.

'This is like Chinese water torture,' Jill says, watching the action at the dunk tank.

'I know. Poor thing,' I say, watching as the little girl throws another shot and misses. One more opportunity.

'No, I mean we want him to get dunked, right? That white T-shirt is going to be completely see-through once it's wet. Although, who am I talking to? You've already seen everything,' Jill says, bending down to pick up another container of fudge out of the wagon.

'Yes, I have,' I say, sighing, my body being pulled toward him.

'Okay, sweetheart – here's the one. This is the one!' Sam says. Martin hands the little girl another softball and tells her, once more, to keep her eyes on the prize. He points at the target. I look at Sam. Eyes on the prize indeed.

The little girl throws the softball and hits the target, wrenching it back just millimeters. I can hear the sound of the target moaning as it causes a creaking reaction in the tiny crossbar that's just under Sam. And then time stands still. Sam looks from the target to the little girl, across to me and then . . . down. He plunges into the water below. The waves splash over the sides as the crowd roars. Sam is a swirling mass of lanky limbs and navy blue swim trunks in the clear water. I see him set his feet on the bottom of the tank and then he bursts through the surface. His silken blond hair is swept back from his face, the white T-shirt transparent, revealing everything for all to see.

'I told you,' Jill says, slapping me on my shoulder. She's nodding her approval. I just nod.

'I don't have the right to him. I don't get to sit here and act like he's anything to me,' I say, almost to myself. For once, Jill is quiet. Her newfound discretion is not appreciated.

Sam rests his hands on the side of the dunk tank and smiles at the little girl. She hops up and down and gives him a high five. The tiny crossbar has been flipped back in place. Sam pulls himself up, whips around and sits on it once more. His face is flushed. I can't take my eyes off him. The outline of his chest, the T-shirt sleeve hitched up and caught on the rangy muscles in his arms, the glistening skin. It's too much. Catalyst, my ass. I don't want him to be a stepping stone in my life. However terrifying this is, what's even more terrifying is the idea of not having him in my life at all.

Sam tucks a leg underneath him and stands, navigating off the crossbar and down the ladder. Martin offers him a huge beach towel as he touches down. Sam pulls it around himself tightly, teeth chattering, his lips a nice soft shade of blue. The crowd gives him a round of applause; he raises his hand high and bows low.

'Ms Reid. Mrs Fleming,' Pamela says, standing front and center at our booth.

Jill and I immediately respond – I'm jolted out of my reverie, and Jill's probably just stunned she wasn't caught saying something X-rated this time. A fresh start with a new headmistress. It just . . . it just doesn't feel right. I see Sam walk into the school with a duffel bag, the beach towel hanging across his broad shoulders.

'Headmistress Jackson,' we say in unison.

'You remember my husband, Paul?' Pamela says, presenting her husband. A huge roar from the crowd. Martin has been dunked. He bursts through the surface with a splash, not unlike Shamu, and drenches the first three rows of bystanders. The kids laugh and shriek. Their parents? Not so much. Jill claps wildly and gives him an enthusiastic thumbs-up. Sam has yet to reappear and Ryan has been staring at me all afternoon.

'Sure, good to see you again,' we say. Paul partakes in some of our fudge and cookies.

'Frannie, have you been up to see HR yet?' Pamela asks.

Oh, shit.

'Uh, no,' I say, my face draining of color. Pamela picks up on it immediately.

'That's fine then. Why don't you come see me after the fund-raiser?' Pamela says, giving me a quick smile before moving on to the next booth. Another group of kids. More fudge and cookies. More tickets in jars.

'What was that about?'

I'm unable to stop myself from licking a napkin and wiping the face of David, one of my students. That and I'm stalling. Poorly. Jill watches my every move.

I tell David, 'You've got chocolate everywhere, sweetie.'

'Ms Reeeeeeeeeeid,' David says. Jill. Still watching. Intent.

'Just a second,' I say, leaning over the counter that separates me from the little towheaded boy. He's holding cotton candy in one hand and a goldfish swimming around in a plastic bag in the other.

'Groooooooossssss,' David mews just as I'm finishing.

'Go on,' I say, mussing his hair and sending him on his way. Jill tucks the napkin filled with cookies and fudge into his cotton-candy-laden hand.

'Frannie?' Jill says again.

Just rip the Band-Aid off, Frances.

I clear my throat.

'I got the job. The head of department,' I blurt.

'What?'

'I got the job. Emma told me I got the job right before . . .' I say.

'That's amazing!' Jill lunges into me for a hug. And it's genuine; she's not trying to stab me or anything.

'Really?'

'Really,' Jill repeats, squeezing tighter.

'I thought you'd be mad,' I say as she pulls out of the hug.

'Why would I be mad? Would you have been mad if I got the job?'

'Yes.'

'Right, because you're a competitive little shit, but not me. So see? The best man won,' Jill says, ducking below the table to pull out another container of fudge.

'You really aren't mad, are you?'

'No, I said I wouldn't be.'

'Wow, you are officially a better person than I am.'

'Right.'

'Right.'

I look up as Sam walks over to our booth. My heart races. My face flushes. My hands get clammy.

Jill continues. 'I'd better go see if the . . . uh, those other napkins are available. Hey, Sam.' Jill ducks under the table and trots off. Sam's wet white T-shirt isn't the only thing that's transparent.

'Fudge and cookie?' I ask, holding up a little pink napkin filled with homemade treats.

'I would love it,' he says, taking the napkin. His cold fingers brush against mine.

'You look freezing,' I say.

'I am freezing,' he says.

'How much longer do you have to stick around?'

'Just for another half hour,' Sam says, checking his watch – a stainless steel diving watch that's as big as my head and was on my bedside table not forty-eight hours ago.

'Good.'

Sam pops the piece of fudge into his mouth. 'This is amazing,' he says once his mouth is no longer full.

'Easiest recipe in the world.' My entire body aches. A gasping ache that reinvents the word *yearn*.

'Really good.' Sam bites into Jill's chocolate chip cookie. Then finishes it. 'Your fudge is better,' he says.

'I expect you have to say that.'

'You expect?'

'Yeah, I—'

'You trying to talk like me now?'

'No, I—'

'I'm only kidding.'

'You're funny.'

We are quiet. Sam is looking around. As am I. I clear

my throat. He folds up his napkin into a billion little fractional parts.

'I'd better be heading out,' Sam finally says.

'Good seeing you,' I say.

'You too.' He reaches across the table with what I think is going to be an awkward handshake; I extend my hand. Oh, how the mighty have fallen. An earth-shattering night has been downgraded to an uninspired handshake across a card table at a fair.

'Oh, are we doing a handshake now?'

'No, I . . . uh . . .' Sam drops the little balled-up napkin into my hand.

Oh my god.

'Oh, right,' I say, curling my fingers around it.

'I just—'

'Nope. I got it,' I say, throwing the little napkin into the trash with all the vim and vigor of the scorned woman that I am. Of course, it floats effortlessly in the wind. Downright graceful.

'Okay, well . . .'

'You'd better be going!' I yelp as a couple of teenagers approach the booth. I motion to them to step forward and yell '*Customers!*' just as Sam is walking away. The kids get their fudge and cookies and back cautiously away from me.

'That went really well,' I say to myself, shoving three pieces of fudge into my mouth.

Later that day after cleaning up, I make my way to Pamela's office to talk about the promotion. I didn't see Sam again. I avoided Ryan. I didn't fight with Lisa or Jill again. And I ate my weight in fudge. All in all an okay day, considering.

'Hello, Dolores. I'm here to see Headmistress Jackson?' I say, resting my hand on her desk. She eyes it. I don't move it. I raise my eyebrows. I'm broken inside, Dolores. My hand shall stay put!

'I'll let her know,' Dolores says, her eyes boring into my rebellious hand. I take a step back and slowly peeeeeel my hand away with a flourish.

'Ms Reid here to see you? Yes, ma'am,' Dolores says, hanging up the phone. She motions for me to head in. 'Motions' meaning looks at me, looks at Pamela's door, then sniffs.

'Thank you, Dolores,' I say with a huge smile. I open the wooden door and step inside Emma's old office. Pamela's things are in boxes, canvas bags and wicker baskets on the floor. The office is already warmer. A decorative throw here, a picture of a smiling family there. So many clues.

'Ms Reid, thank you for agreeing to see me on such short notice,' Pamela says, motioning for me to have a seat. I oblige. I approach the wingback chairs and once again I see there's a stranger in our midst. A woman this time. I vow that if I ever plan on creeping up on someone, a must-have prop will most certainly be a wingback chair.

'Frances Reid, I'd like you to meet Clara Grey. Mrs Grey is Emma's sister,' Pamela says. My stomach drops.

'Nice to meet you, Mrs Grey,' I say, extending my hand to the woman. Judging by her appearance, she's no longer playing the role of black sheep. She's tall and lithe, wearing a linen tunic that on someone less fashionable would look like a tablecloth. Her hair is a golden blond and cut stylishly, hanging to her shoulders. Her blue eyes are . . . well, Emma's. I'm staring at her. I'm now actively staring at her.

'I know. We look a lot alike,' Clara says.

'I'm so sorry,' I say, breathless. I tear my gaze away from her and look to Pamela. 'How can I . . . I'm confused.' I look from Pamela to Clara and back to Pamela.

'I hadn't spoken to Emma in around eight years and then all of a sudden she calls me three days ago out of the blue. And now she's dead. You'll have to excuse the straightforward nature of this, but . . . I want answers. I want to know what happened. She mentioned you, Frannie. Talked about you. I thought maybe . . . maybe you could tell me something about my sister. I just . . . I just need to know what happened,' Clara says, choking through tears.

I am struck dumb. Quieted. Clara. The woman I heard about in passing is sitting here now asking me about her sister. Her dead sister. As if I know Emma. As if I have answers. As if . . .

'Clara, you'll excuse us, but we're all still dealing with what happened. And piecing together information without tapping into the trauma of the event might be a bit difficult for Frannie,' Pamela says, her voice calm.

'I understand,' Clara says, sniffling. 'Thank you for your time.' She bends down and gathers the leather straps of her purse in one hand.

'She said she thought you were strong. She admired that in you,' I say. Clara crumples back down into her chair, her breath ragged, her sobs instantaneous. I continue. 'We were brought together because one of my kids was being bullied. He'd stood up for himself and Emma took the side of the bully at first. Said that my boy had provoked it. Deserved it. Deserved no safe harbor. And I fought her. I thought she was a bitch who just didn't understand what it was like to be bullied, you know? She was so perfect. So perfect. How could she understand?' The tears are streaming down my face now. Pamela offers me a tissue.

'She was always perfect, you know? Even when she was little,' Clara says, smiling.

'There was this mixer at her house for the heads of department and the board of directors. I went and of course her house was lovely and she was lovely. And I think that was where we started to become friends. You know? She talked about you. She was beaming. God, she loved you,' I say, reaching out for Clara. She clutches my hand, unable to look at me. I can't look at her. I hear Pamela sniffle in the distance.

'I thought I embarrassed her,' Clara says, her voice a whisper.

'No, no way. She admired you. She talked about painting and choosing academia. I could tell she regretted it, choosing academia,' I say, finally looking up.

'She got me into painting in the first place. She painted in oils – skill, patience . . . she had it. I have some of her paintings at home if you want . . . if you want to see them,' Clara says, coming alive.

'I'd like that,' I say.

We're quiet as the weight of *it* hangs around us like a poisonous gas. We've celebrated Emma. Her life. Her loves. It's time . . .

'Had you met Jamie?' Clara asks, her voice ice cold.

'Yeah,' I say, my eyes set elsewhere.

'Before that night?' Clara asks.

'I met him at Back-to-School Night and then again at that mixer,' I say, becoming detached.

'And?' Clara's voice is loud, catches Pamela and me off guard.

'And he was exactly what you think he would be. A mincing, beak-nosed weakling,' I say, my mouth curling in disgust.

Clara is quiet yet buzzing with anger.

'Mr Dunham was the worst among men,' Pamela adds, her chin held high.

We are quiet.

'Emma has a dog,' I say, my voice soft.

'What?' Clara asks, confused.

'Had. Emma had a dog. I'm sorry,' I say, feeling stupid.

'What . . . why are you telling me this?' Clara asks, edging closer.

'Because he was the love of her life and I'm sure she would love it if you could give him a proper home. With the girls,' I say.

'I don't . . . I . . .' Clara starts and stops, tears rolling down her cheeks.

'His name is John Henry and he's beautiful. And he's lost without her. Please,' I say. 'Please,' I say again.

'You . . . I . . . I have to think about it. I can't . . . she . . . I have to think about it,' Clara says, tugging on her purse straps once again. She stands. Pamela and I stand.

'Here, please. I know it's a lot all at once, but take my

phone number. And . . . just think about it. I'd love to see Emma's paintings and . . . well, just think about John Henry. Please?' I ask, scribbling my phone number on some Markham card stock on Pamela's desk. Clara takes my phone number and nods. And nods. And nods. She sniffles and wipes the tears from her cheeks.

'If you need anything, please don't hesitate to call,' Pamela says, passing Clara her business card. Clara takes it. She stacks it in her fingers next to mine.

'Here's the memorial service announcement. It's in Mill Valley. This weekend. I haven't decided whether or not I'm going, but you're welcome to. I'm sure it's just going to be some ridiculous farce put on by my parents. It'd be nice to have someone there that Emma actually liked,' Clara says with a sheepish smile. Then she lunges into me for a hug. It catches me off guard at first, but then I wrap my arms tightly around her. She whispers, 'Thank you. Thank you.' She breaks from me violently and races out of Pamela's office, her sobs urgent as she closes the door behind her.

I look at the memorial service invite.

> *Emma Jane Dunham passed away on September 14 at the age of 35. Emma was a loving daughter, a devoted aunt and patient sister. She will be greatly missed by all of her family and friends. A celebration in her memory will take place on Saturday, September 24, at the Marin County Country Club's Crystal Ballroom at 10 A.M.*
>
> *Nigel and Jane Stanforth*
> *Floral tributes may be sent*

Passed away? *Passed away?*

'I'm so sorry to spring that on you. She showed up here asking about you and . . .' Pamela speaks quickly, motioning for me to take a seat. I stuff the invite in my pocket.

'I thought I was coming in here to talk about my promotion,' I say, dazed.

'I know. I walked in and she was waiting in the anteroom. Dolores just . . . sat there,' Pamela says.

'Did I make things worse?' I ask.

'I doubt things can get worse than they are, Frannie,' Pamela says, pulling two candy bars from one of the desk drawers. She offers me one. I take it. We both tear our candy bars open and take a bite. Breathe.

We sit in silence for another fifteen minutes.

14

The Roast

Again: I'm searching in this dusty campsite for the group. They're leaving. They're leaving and I'm about to get left behind. The rickety staircases and old dirt roads are confusing. My suitcase is heavy and I question why I brought it. *Crack. Crack.* It's coming. It's coming. Drag the suitcase faster. Run. Catch up. Get them. *Crack.* But they're behind me. I'm not . . . I'm not running to something, I'm running away from something. *Crack. Crack.* My hand is curled around the suitcase's handle. Slippery. Sticky. Let go. I bring up my hands. *Crack. Crack.* Blood. Everywhere.

'No!' I jolt awake. Saturday morning. Another terrible sleep. Another morning where I cherish those three seconds between realizing the dream wasn't real and that reality is sometimes worse than we can ever imagine. I get dressed quickly. After I visit Grady and Lisa at the hospital, I get to finally pick up John Henry at the pound. I haven't heard from Clara, but I still have hope. I have no idea why . . . but I still have hope.

I walk over to my laptop, set my cup of coffee down next to it. I plop down into my desk chair and wait for the computer to come on.

Once the computer buzzes to life, I click on the web browser icon and navigate myself to one of those review sites where people leave their opinions on everything – from restaurants and hotels to the best neighborhood hardware store and beyond. I type in *doggie day care* and watch as an entire world opens up to me. I click and read, click and read, and then, finding one that sounds exactly like what I'm looking for, I pick up the phone and dial.

'Southern Comfort, this is Jenny,' a woman's voice answers. I couldn't help myself.

'Hi, I'm adopting a dog today and wonder if you have any space available for him?'

'Well, we have a few spaces, but we'd have to meet him and see how he gets on with the other dogs and all that. What are you guys doing later on today?' Jenny asks. Her accent is deeper and twangier than Sam's.

'Today?' I ask.

'We're slow on the weekends. This would be a great time to meet him. We have just a few dogs here.'

'I'm picking him up later on this morning. I could be there by noon,' I say.

'You said you're getting him today?'

'Yes, it's, uh . . . it's complicated,' I say.

'I like complicated.'

I smile. 'Then you'll love this.'

'You're funny!' Jenny laughs. I am really going to hate to bring the room down, but . . .

'I work at a private school over in Pasadena. We had a shooting here on Friday,' I say, starting in.

'Oh my god! I saw that on the news! You were there?!'

'Yeah.'

'I just thought what a shame that was, what an utter shame that was, when I was watching it. Shouldn't be like that, you know? Shouldn't be like that.'

'Yeah.' *Crack. Crack. Crack. Crack*..

'I'm sorry, I don't mean to go on. I just can't believe you were there.'

'Me either.'

'Got that right.'

'So, the woman who was killed . . . he was her dog,' I say, barely getting it out before the emotion of it strangles me. I exhale. Focus.

'Oh my god,' Jenny says, breathy.

'He's a good boy. Three-year-old Weimaraner. His name is John Henry and he's sweet and . . . I just . . . I don't know how he'll be around other dogs. The husband had him on quite a tight leash. Had everyone on a tight leash, it seems,' I say, my voice icy and clipped.

'The husband, *hm*,' Jenny says, clucking.

'Yeah,' I say, my voice dead.

'Well, you can bring 'im on by and we'll see how he does.' I can hear Jenny tuck the phone into the crook of her neck.

'The thing is – I think it's only going to be for a few days. Hopefully,' I say.

'Why would it only be for a few days?'

'I want to take him back to her family. Her sister lives in Los Feliz and she's got three little girls. It's a home, you know? A proper home. I just . . .' Choking. Tears.

'No, I get it. I get it,' Jenny says, her voice quiet. Finally. Someone. Someone gets it.

'So, noon?' I ask.

'Sounds good,' Jenny says, giving me quick directions to her house. We sign off with hope that John Henry will fit in. I feel myself keeping him at arm's length. The last thing I want to do is get attached to this dog.

As I'm walking into the hospital, my cell phone rings. It's my mom. I stop and sit on a bench just outside of Grady's hospital room.

'Hello?'

'Frannie?'

'Hey, Mom.'

'What's wrong, sweetie?' I can see my Mom now, sitting at the kitchen table wearing her usual khaki cropped pants with loafers, a cable-knit sweater in a soothing pastel. The last time I trekked up to Mill Valley was just a little over a month ago and while she looked essentially the same, I was caught off guard by the realization that she's getting older. A little more hunched over, her hair a bit more gray, it takes a bit longer for her to stand. Needless to say, these realizations are unwelcome.

'How do you know something is wrong?'

'Sweetie?'

'I don't want you to get worried, okay?'

'Frannie, you tell me right this instant what is going on.'

'There was a shooting. At the school. The headmistress was killed by her husband,' I say, my voice calm.

'Was she a friend of yours?' Mom asks. The cell phone

crackles as I finally break the news to my parents about Wednesday. I'll start with Mom and work my nerve up for Dad.

'No, but I didn't think she was a complete stranger either,' I say, watching people bustle about the hospital. Worried looks, bouquets of flowers. What a gamut of emotions and situations.

'Does she have family?' Mom asks.

'Yeah, here's the weird part. They live in the Bay Area apparently.' I can hear Mom moving around the kitchen now, the kitchen they just renovated. I told them – go media room! Pool! Cabana! Sunken fire pit! Nope. A breakfast bar and more cabinet space in the kitchen. They even kept their old kitchen appliances. They're proud of the fact that they still have the same furniture they had when they moved to Mill Valley from the Bronx in 1972.

'What's their last name?'

'Her maiden name was Stanforth, but her married name is Dunham.'

'I don't know any Stanforths or Dunhams off the top of my head. I'll ask around though.'

'The memorial service is at the Marin County Country Club this weekend.'

'So, you're coming to Mill Valley?'

'It looks like it.'

'Not the best of circumstances, but a nice surprise just the same.'

Crack. Crack. Crack. Crack. Shake it off. Shake it away.

We fall quiet.

This is not a good thing.

'Frances?'

'Yeah, I'm here.'

'You okay?'

'Sure.'

'It sounds like you've gone through a lot.' Shake it away. I ball my hands in fists. The blood. So much blood.

'Yep.'

Quiet.

'You remember Jackie? She lived on the corner, right here on Miller?' Mom asks.

'Yeah, she had those super-high heels,' I say, remembering a woman who was so fancy I thought she was a movie star.

'When she committed suicide, I couldn't help but think I could have done something. But I couldn't have done anything, sweetie. Unfortunately, some people are past saving before you even meet them. Do you get that?' Mom says.

'Not yet,' I say honestly.

'In time,' she says.

'She lied about everything,' I say.

'It looks like that's the case.'

'Why? Why lie about that kind of stuff?' I ask.

'It's easier to lie than face the truth. Isn't it?'

'I suppose.'

'Women are competitive, Frannie.'

'I know that.'

'And it seems that Emma was playing to win no matter the cost.'

I think of Jill. 'Or the reality,' I say.

'There was no reality.'

'Oh, it got real. It got really ugly, really fast.'

'That's usually the case. These kinds of scenarios never end well, honey.' *Crack*. Nope. *Nope*.

'I know.'

We are quiet.

'You couldn't do anything,' Mom says.

I nod and nod and nod.

'Frannie?'

'I know.'

'Okay, sweetie . . . your father wants to talk to you about what happened,' Mom says. My dad. The retired police officer can figure out something is wrong from just one half of a conversation.

'Okay.'

'I'll go finish the roast then,' Mom says.

'Thanks, Mom. I'll let you know about the trip up there. When it's happening. All that.'

'Okay, sweetie. You take care, okay? Take care?'

'I will.'

'I love you, my sweet girl.'

'LoveyoutooMom,' I squeeze out before a torrent of tears rumbles out in its place. A security guard looks over. A narrowed eye. I smile . . . *ish*. I mouth that I'm fine. A raised eyebrow. A pause.

'Frannie, honey? Is that you?' Dad says, getting on the phone. Then the sound of a referee's whistle and my dad's reaction (not a good one) to the call.

'Hey, Dad,' I say.

'Hey, sweetie,' Dad says. I always thought there'd be a

time when my dad wasn't a giant, like how you go back to your elementary school and realize it's actually tiny. But my father has remained larger than life. For all of Mom's apple stencils and home-baked cookies, Dad's all guns, tools and bringing home the bacon. Hank Reid, resident tough guy.

'So, what happened?' Dad asks, muting the television.

'There was a shooting.'

'Where?'

'The school.'

'Lay it out for me.'

'Suspect walks in, unloads one into the victim, wings another, couple more into the wall before getting taken down,' I say, getting down to business.

'What kind of gun was it?'

'Guns,' I say, hitting the *s*.

'Jesus.'

'He had four forty-fives.'

'He meant business.'

'Yes.'

'And where were you?'

'Standing next to the victim.'

'She went down with the first shot?'

'It was a head shot.'

'Someone got winged?'

'Yes.'

'They okay?'

'He's good. It was a through-and-through, didn't touch the bone.'

'A forty-five will definitely do some damage.'

'I know.' Blinking back the images. The damage.

'And the other ones went into the wall?'

'Yes.'

'And you were standing next to the victim?'

'Yes.'

'So, one of the shots that went into the wall, it was actually aimed at you?'

I am quiet.

'Frannie . . .'

'I got really possessive of her. It was weird.'

'That can happen.'

'I know. You've said stuff about it before. I always thought those people were idiots.'

'Well, now you know.'

'That I'm an idiot?'

'No, sweetie.'

We are quiet.

Dad continues. 'How did he finally get taken down?'

I think of Sam. 'Someone stepped in. Saved us.'

'Frannie . . .'

'I know.'

'You can never tell your mother about this.'

'I know.'

'Dinner's ready!' I hear Mom call in the distance.

'Not a word,' Dad says. Final.

'Okay.'

'Sweetie . . . I . . . I don't know what we'd do if we lost you,' Dad says, his voice heavy with worry.

'I couldn't let him put another bullet into her, Dad,' I say, the tears welling up finally.

'She was dead, honey.'

'I know.'

'She was a friend of yours?' Dad asks.

'No. No, she wasn't.'

'Funny way to act about someone who wasn't even a friend.'

'I know. I know.'

'Okay, sweetie. Your . . . what is it, Polly?' I hear muffled conversation and my dad gets back on the phone. 'Polly says you're coming up here?' More muffled voices. Dad continues. 'For a memorial service? Who? Polly, I just . . . The victim? The girl who got shot?'

'Yeah, Dad.'

'Then . . . sweetie, I don't understand.'

'I was telling Mom that I was going to be coming up there this weekend for Emma's memorial service. Emma, that's the girl that got . . . that got . . .'

'You don't have to say it, sweetie,' Dad says.

'Thanks, Dad.'

'I love you, Frannie.'

'I love you, too, Dad.'

I hang up. And sit. On the bench. The phone clutched in my hand. My palm sweaty. I breathe. Deep. The only thing that gets me off that bench is that I'm going to see my parents. And that there's a Starbucks in this hospital.

I walk into Grady's room with two coffees just a few minutes later. I've gathered myself enough so that I won't be a sobbing mess when I see him again. I walk in to find the patient sleeping soundly and Lisa curled up in a chair reading a novel. She looks up. A smile. Beautiful. I walk over to her and give her a quick hug, the tray of coffees perched in my hand. I give her the large mocha with an extra shot. She thanks me.

'How's he doing?' I whisper, settling into a smaller chair next to her with my coffee.

'Better every day,' Lisa says, gazing over at him.

'I just talked to my parents. About what happened,' I say.

'Not fun.' Lisa sighs.

'I'm glad they know. Have you told your parents?'

'About what?'

'About all of it, I guess.'

Lisa is quiet.

'So, no?' I ask.

'No.'

'The shooting?'

'No.'

'The wedding?'

'No.'

I am quiet.

'Yeah, I know. I'm going to have to tell them,' Lisa says, motioning to the very injured Grady.

'I don't understand,' I say.

'My mom is a bit of a drama queen. Everything is a huge deal. Me moving to California was enough for her to call for her smelling salts – and yes, she still calls for smelling salts.'

'Oh, dear.'

'Exactly. She wanted to be an actress. Never made it out of Jersey, though,' Lisa says, dog-earring her novel and setting it on Grady's bedside table.

'So, she's just—'

'Dramatic in her everyday life, yes. No, if I want this wedding to be about Grady and me at all, I have to figure out a way to tell her about this so she can't turn it into the Cleopatra Campanari show.'

'Your mom's name is Cleopatra?'

'Of course it is.'

'Dude.'

'People try to shorten it to Cleo, but Mom corrects them every time. Plus, it's just weird to talk about it. Explain what happened. It sounds so . . . gruesome.'

'It was gruesome.'

'Yeah . . . yeah, I guess it was,' Lisa says, checking on Grady. His breathing is deep and slow. Such a strong man. Taken down. Like that.

'I get what you're saying. It doesn't feel real. Like you know you're going to make it out, whereas if you're hearing someone you love tell that story it would be terrifying.'

'Exactly.'

We're quiet.

Lisa continues. 'But seeing Grady . . . that bullet hit him in the right shoulder. If you really . . . *really* think about what could have happened with that . . .' Lisa trails off, shaking her head. The scene plays again. Always ready to be relived. Easy to pull it up. Easy to let it play. Jamie shoots the gun with his right hand at a charging Grady. Hits him in the right shoulder and he whirls around, hitting the floor. Slow it down. Back it up. My face drops and the color drains. Slow motion. Jamie fires and the bullet travels across the space between him and Grady. If Grady were one hundredth of a second faster, if Jamie were one hundredth of a faster shot, that bullet would have hit Grady square in the temple. Lisa watches the realization unfold.

She nods. 'See what I'm saying?'

'I never even—'

'Grady played defensive end at UT. Watching him get put down like that . . .' Lisa trails off again, not looking at me.

I am quiet. There's nothing I can say. She has to feel this, no matter how much I don't want her to. No matter how much I want to make this better, the only thing I can do right now is listen. Be here. Like she was for me.

'I know,' I say, almost in a whisper.

'I know you do.'

We are quiet. Sitting in it. The grainy Super 8 footage of that day. Rewinding and playing. From different angles. Playing the what-if game. Moving the different players around like chess pieces. How did we survive? There's no reason we should be sitting here. Jamie had every intention of killing everyone in that lounge. The only time I saw any emotion move across his face, other than resolution and demonic detachment, it was annoyance. It bothered him that we were fighting back. Our will to survive was something he hadn't factored in. He was a coward. He had been so used to people being intimidated by him – dogs sitting when he told them to, women walking on eggshells. The idea of a group of human beings stopping him from dictating how the scene would play out simply never occurred to him. He lost his cool when Grady came at him, but Lisa threw him for the biggest loop. A woman.

A woman who wouldn't let him dominate her. He simply didn't know how to process that. And in the end, when challenged, like the bully he was, he became the great Oz. A tiny man behind a big curtain.

'He was a paper tiger,' I finally say.

'A paper tiger with a gun and nothin' to lose.'

'That's usually how it works.'

'True.' We are quiet again.

'Are we still doing the Rose Bowl this weekend?' Lisa asks.

'Yeah, I'm sure it's so Jill can get all the details out of you,' I say.

Lisa smiles. 'You're adorable if you think your night with Sam isn't on her agenda, as well.'

'Ah yes,' I say. Ouchhhhhh. 'I'm taking John Henry to the doggy day care lady today at noon. If that doesn't go so well, I might have John Henry with me tomorrow. But, you know – he might actually like that walk, so I might just bring him regardless.' Lisa nods.

Quiet.

'Do you want to know what I think?' Lisa asks.

'About John Henry?'

'No, I think what you're doing with that dog is amazing.'

I smile.

Lisa continues. 'I mean about Sam.'

'Oh. That,' I say, my entire body deflating.

'I don't think you should throw the baby out with the bathwater. I think there's something there. Just . . . give him time,' Lisa says.

'I choose how this ends?'

'Something like that.'

After hanging around for another hour or so, I say my good-byes to Lisa and pass along well wishes to the still sleeping Grady. I close the door behind me and . . .

'Hey.'

Sam.

'Jesus, you scared the shit out of me,' I say, clutching my chest.

'I'll try to walk down a hospital hallway more—'

'You don't get to be funny,' I say, the words coming from nowhere.

'I'm sorry?'

'You don't get to be funny. You don't get to act like that night didn't happen anymore,' I say, the words coming fast. I've wanted to say them since that morning.

'Frannie, I—'

'You ran. It's what you do. You ran to California. You ran out of my apartment that morning without so much as an explanation and now you're here trying to make jokey small talk?'

'I know.'

'Do you?'

'Yes, ma'am.'

'Don't "ma'am" me. Your southern bullshit charm doesn't play anymore, Earley.'

'Okay, then.'

I wait.

Sam is confused.

'Emma's sister came by the school yesterday after the fund-raiser. I got that promotion. I adopted Emma's dog.

I finally told my parents about the shooting. There's a memorial service in Mill Valley this weekend for Emma. I'm still having nightmares,' I blurt.

'Okay.'

'I just thought you should know.'

'That's a lot.'

'I know.'

'How are you doing with all this?'

'Wouldn't you like to know?!'

'I would actually.'

'I'm not okay, Sam. I've been crying a lot.'

'I'm sorry.'

'I imagine you are.'

We are quiet. The hurt bubbles back up where the bravado was. My shoulders slump as my chin lowers.

'How are you?' I ask, my voice just that much louder than it should be.

'Not good.'

'I'm sorry.' My voice is softer now.

Sam nods. His jaw is tight. Still.

'You know, you could talk about it. You should talk about it.'

'No one wants to hear what I have to say.'

'I do.'

Sam is quiet. Shaking his head no. Shaking his head no. He looks down. At the ground.

'People deal with things differently, Frannie.' Sam's voice is cold.

'I know that.'

'I know you do,' Sam says, softening immediately.

Silence. For a long time.

'I'd better get going,' I say. Please ask me what I'm doing later. Please don't let me be alone again tonight.

Sam nods. Nothing. Tense jaw. Pursed mouth. Hands in fists.

I continue. 'Grady's sleeping so be quiet when you go in. Take care, Sam.' And I walk down the hallway waiting to hear my name. Waiting to be stopped. Waiting for my explanation.

Nothing.

'I'm here to pick up a dog . . . *my* dog? The Weimaraner,' I say, looking at the girl behind the counter later that morning.

'Oh, sure. John Henry,' she says, picking up the phone. The woman looks brokenhearted that he's leaving. She tells someone that the person who's adopting John Henry is here. She nods, says, 'I knooooow,' as if the person on the other end of the phone is just as crestfallen as she is. She gives me a quick sneer and hangs up. 'She'll be right out.'

'She'll? John Henry is a boy.'

'She'll – the girl who's handling your case,' the woman says. She motions for me to have a seat. I oblige her. I sit stock-still and focus on the comings and goings of the pound – always busy, always buzzing. I stopped at a local pet store on my way home from work last night and got an embarrassing amount of dog paraphernalia: beds, collars, chew toys, food, treats, leashes . . . the gamut.

'Frances Reid?' The hipster girl from the other day. She

motions for me to come into her office. I am seated in the same chair I was in on Thursday. I can't believe it's only been two days. I hold tightly to the leash I bought last night. I knew John Henry had a red leather collar from before, so I bought him a red leather leash to match. The leather squeaks and crinkles as I nervously bend and twist it. I try to quiet my hands.

The girl continues. 'The good news is that John Henry has a chip, so we called his vet, the Small Animal Hospital over in Arcadia, and they faxed over proof of all of his shots.' She hands me a packet of papers. I scan through them and see . . . this dog was cared for. Everything is up-to-date. I'm thankful I can have access to his medical history, especially since I'm sure proof of his shots will be needed with Jenny later on this morning.

'Is there bad news?' I ask, looking up from the papers.

'I'm sorry?'

'Bad news? You said, "The good news is . . ."' I trail off.

'No, no bad news,' she says, threading her fingers together on her desk.

'Oh, good,' I say, relaxing.

The girl stands and begins to walk out of her office. 'So, I'll bring him on out and . . .' She picks up the phone and dials. 'Can someone help me with John Henry's crate?' She waits, thanks someone and hangs up.

I stand and meander out into the main office. My hands are sweaty; my knuckles whiten as I grip the leash. I clear my throat. Again. Smile at the front-office girl. She gives me a polite smile. I look out one of the windows, biting my nails. My heart is racing. I don't know why. This is a dog. A dog. He'll . . .

The hipster girl bursts through the side door with a low-walking John Henry at her side. He is watching her, staying behind her, not pulling on his leash. Always the little soldier. He has a makeshift leash around his neck and as I watch the pound tech load the crate into the back of my SUV in the parking lot, the hipster girl motions for me to clip my leash to his collar. The changing of the guard. I lurch forward, uneasy and nervous. John Henry skitters away, cowering behind the hipster girl. I'm immediately embarrassed and recoil.

'It's okay, you're doing great,' the hipster girl says to me, taking the leash from my hands and clipping it to John Henry's collar herself. I nod and thank her as she hands me the looped handle to the leash. No longer twisted and bent in my hands, the leash is connected to Emma's legacy. I inhale sharply. John Henry sits. Waiting. His melty blue eyes darting around the buzzing front office, his floppy ears twitching and turning.

'Hi, sweet boy,' I say, bending down. John Henry gives me a quick glance, then looks at the desk, back at me, up to the hipster girl, out the door, back at me . . . it's dizzying.

'You should be fine,' the hipster girl says, giving me a sage nod.

'Thank you,' I say, looking from her to the girl behind the front desk.

I walk out of the office, John Henry at my side. He keeps pace with me, never moving in front of me, always watching me, his gait stilted and truncated. The pound tech, a young kid of about seventeen clearly interning on the weekends, waits by my car, his arm resting on the open hatch.

'He walks like a Lipizzaner,' I say.

'A Lipizzaner Weimaraner?'

I narrow my eyes at the tech as we get closer. A huge smile. He thinks he's hilarious.

'We're doing it,' I say, motioning to me holding John Henry's leash.

'Yes, congratulations, you can walk a dog,' the tech says, taking the leash from me and motioning to John Henry to hop up into the hatch of my SUV.

'You're funny, kid,' I say, pulling my keys out of my purse. John Henry hops up into the back of the SUV and the tech gives him a quick pat as a reward. John Henry wags his tail and happily gets in his crate for the ride over to Jenny's. The tech latches the crate and closes the hatch.

'Good luck. Seriously, he's a special dog,' the tech says, coming around to my window.

I hear John Henry situating himself in the crate.

'I know,' I say. The tech taps my open window with a nod. I've passed muster.

'Good boy,' I coo, craning around and seeing how he's doing. It looks like John Henry is settling in. I want him to feel like he's not just being driven around for driving's sake. I wonder if . . . did he like his home? I mean, I know Jamie was a tool, but did John Henry know that? Of course, he knew. Did Emma make up for it? As I pull out onto Raymond Avenue, I can't believe I'm deliberating about the inner workings of a dog's brain.

As John Henry and I wind through Pasadena on our way to Jenny's, I feel like I've gotten myself all entangled into some fool's errand. I haven't thought it through. Sure, while delivering John Henry to Emma's grieving sister might be cleansing for me, what's it going to be like for her? Is it going to open a wound that I've no right to rip open? I grab my iPhone and dial Jill on speakerphone. The ringing of the phone is heard throughout the car.

'Am I being selfish?' I blurt as Jill answers the phone.

'Because you won't tell me how big Sam's dick was? Yes. Incredibly,' Jill says.

'Remind me never to call you when I have anyone else in the car.'

'What are you talking about then?' she asks.

'Am I being selfish?' I repeat.

'In what regard?'

'Are there so many occasions that I have to specify?'

'Wow. Really?'

'Fine.'

'Are we talking about John Henry?'

'Yes.'

'No, I don't think so,' she says, her voice crackling through the car.

'It feels messy, you know?'

'Yeah, I get that,' she says as I move through an intersection.

'Right? It's like, get the dog, take the dog to the grieving sister, who knows what kind of relationship they have and drive up to San Francisco for the memorial service,' I say.

'I think I want to go,' Jill says.

'Really?'

'Yeah.'

'Let me guess, you don't want to talk about it.'

'Oh, and let me guess, all you want to do is taaaalk about it?'

'If you do go I've got six to seven hours with you in an enclosed vehicle. I have a whole theory based on the hydra that I want to run past you.'

'Let me guess: you've had an epiphany about it. I bet we could get Lisa to go,' Jill says as I make the turn into Jenny's driveway.

'Okay, I'm here at the doggy day care. We'll talk tomorrow around the Rose Bowl,' I say.

'Definitely. Lot K. Nine A.M.,' Jill says.

'Deal. See you then,' I say, signing off. I turn off the car and hop out. John Henry low-walks out of his crate and hops down out of the SUV, waiting for guidance. I take his leash and we hike up Jenny's steps to her house. I can hear barking and yipping as I walk up. John Henry can too. I see his floppy ears perk up and his eyes dart around as he tries to acquaint himself with his surroundings.

'Good boy,' I say, looking down. He looks up. The melty blue eyes. The silver-gray fur that looks like silk. I'm in way over my head with this dog. He's the sweetest animal I've ever known.

'Welcome!' Jenny says, standing at her open front door. She's exactly as I'd pictured her: friendly, confident, with that beautiful femininity that defies all rules. She's someone who'd bandage a knee, give you a glass of milk and be positive that her kiss would make it all better.

'Hey!' I say, extending my hand to her. 'Jenny, this is John Henry.'

'Hey there, John Henry,' Jenny says, looking down at the dog. I follow Jenny's lead to come inside her house. John Henry keeps pace with me.

I clear my throat and look out into Jenny's backyard. A pack of dogs. Some playing, some lying in the grass, others just sitting at the gate, watching the world go by. They look happy and content.

'So, Mr John Henry,' Jenny says, looking at the dog. He snaps to attention.

'He forgot his hammer at home,' I say with a wide, shit-eating grin. Jenny just shakes her head. I clear my throat.

'He's beautiful,' Jenny says, letting him smell her.

'Thank you,' I say, happily moving on.

'Yes, you are. You're a pretty boy,' Jenny says as John Henry easily lets her pet him. He's leaning into her as she scratches behind those floppy ears, around his neck and down his back. I watch and feel . . . lots of things: relief that he looks happy and then this undercurrent of sadness. Emma would have loved Jenny, would have loved seeing John Henry here. Would have loved . . . to have loved. I clear my throat again. Jenny looks over and does a quick double take as she realizes that I'm getting emotional. I try to muster a smile.

'So stupid,' I say, wiping away a traitorous tear.

'It's not stupid,' Jenny says, still petting John Henry, who has completely forgotten about us.

'Thanks,' I say, rolling my eyes at my behavior.

'They just get to you. They're these little beings whose only purpose on this earth is to unconditionally love us. And it's our job to ferry them through this life as best we can. Isn't that right, John Henry?' Jenny says, taking his face in her hands. He licks her and nuzzles her. I twist and contort my mouth, the tears choking me.

'You're so great with him,' I finally choke out, rolling my eyes once again as she checks to see how I'm doing. Not well. The 'ferrying these little unconditionally loving creatures' speech was a cheap shot.

'He's a sweet boy,' Jenny says, standing.

'So, what happens now?' I ask, looking out back. The thundering herd.

'I'm going to take him back outside and see how we do. You will stay in here. I've set out some tea and biscuits. So, help yourself,' Jenny says, motioning to her dining-room table, which is filled with breakfast goodies. She takes John Henry's leash and tells him to come on. He obeys. He looks back at me and . . . that's it. His melty blue eyes are questioning what's happening, where he's going and what am I going to do to protect him. I lunge after them.

'Okay . . . that . . . ummm,' I say. Jenny keeps walking out to the backyard. I'm thinking she's had experience with people like me. I take a bite of a biscuit, mechanically chewing it and trying not to look out back. The back door opens and Jenny strides inside. No John Henry. I crane my neck and . . .

'Where's John Henry?' I blurt, biscuit shooting out of my mouth.

'He's out back,' Jenny says, casually pointing to the backyard. She looks from me to the biscuit. 'Good, huh?'

I nod. 'I'm having a small heart attack over here,' I say, my arms outstretched, my voice cracking. Jenny just laughs.

'Why don't you take a look for yourself?' Jenny says, motioning to the backyard. My steps are heavy and I cross my arms in front of my chest, my breath quickening. I turn the corner and look out back.

John Henry is running around the backyard, throwing a Frisbee into the air and catching it himself. A black Lab trots beside him, stops, and then they run again. They tussle and play and the Frisbee is up in the air again. I clap my hand over my mouth and just let the tears fall. I look back at Jenny and she just nods.

'He's doing great,' I say, my voice cracking, ridiculously emotional. John Henry trots over to the water bowl, laps and laps and laps. The black Lab comes over, shoves his face aside, and they both continue drinking. The other dogs swirl around the backyard, completely unaware of John Henry, doing their own thing and minding their own business.

'I told you,' Jenny says, offering me another biscuit.

'You did,' I say, walking away from the back door and into the dining room.

'You okay?' Jenny asks, studying me.

'Gonna be,' I say with a smile.

15

She's a Little Runaway

No nightmare. Mainly because I didn't sleep. Between analyzing my little run-in with Sam at the hospital and watching John Henry sleep all night, it was a lost cause. His every breath. His every twitch. His every yelp. In the crate. Should I open the crate? Is it cruel to put him in that little crate? No, dogs like to feel like they're in a den. But what if I set up a little bed on the couch? The bathroom floor? What about on my bed? In the end, John Henry slept in his crate, while I lay curled up in my sleeping bag next to him. Yes, it was a bit much. I just . . . my thinking was, either I do it that way or I hang off my bed and listen to him breathe from afar.

I put some dog food in John Henry's new bowl. He low-walks over to it. Smells it. No. Uninterested. He has to eat something. I look in my pantry. Peanut butter. Dogs like peanut butter. I put a little peanut butter on a piece of wheat bread and drop it in his bowl. I leave the kitchen thinking that I'm the offending factor in his breakfast equation. John Henry follows me.

'Eat your breakfast, sweetie. Come on, now,' I say, walking back into the kitchen. Pointing to his bowl. He looks at my hand. Pointing to his bowl. He looks at my hand. I squat down next to his bowl and point to the bowl. He looks at my face.

Sigh.

'The thing is, she lied,' Lisa says as we walk around the Rose Bowl later that morning. Throngs of runners, walkers, cyclists, strollers and leash-pulling dogs circle Pasadena's venerable New Year's Day attraction. Southern California's year-round opportunity for outdoor living is a blessing and a curse. Most days it fills me with guilt for staying inside and working all the time. John Henry is in dog heaven. He happily trots alongside Jill, Lisa and me.

'Not necessarily,' Jill says.

'Not necessarily?!' Lisa asks. Walking these three miles around the Rose Bowl is something I hope will jog us all back into some kind of routine.

'He could have lost his job. He could have discovered her cheating,' Jill says, her thick red hair up in a ponytail.

'Are you saying she deserved it? That there's some rational explanation for shooting your wife?' I ask, guiding John Henry past a lusty French bulldog.

'Internet down?' Lisa sighs, squeezing past a harried mother, an overzealous yellow Lab and a squirming toddler who's trying to get out of his overpriced name-brand stroller. Even the strollers here have high standards.

'Of course not,' Jill says.

'It just doesn't make sense,' I say.

Lisa says, 'She obviously made it all up. You're telling

me that between jet-setting all over the world and spouting meaningful yet under-appreciated poetry to each other—'

'Sure, the evidence points to some kind of breaking point,' I say, cutting in. 'Something was obviously wrong. Very wrong. Brutality like that always has some kind of trigger.'

'No pun intended,' Jill says. A swarm of cyclists pass us on the left as they scream, '*On the left! On the left!*'

I feel more than a little conflicted. I *know* in my gut there was a trigger. All evidence points to my conversation with Emma about Harry Sprague and Sean Stone, as well as the conversation we had at the mixer about painting and her reconnecting with Clara. But the catalyst? Could it have been the Harry Sprague situation? Did something about seeing bullying from a position of authority change the dynamics of Emma's marriage and push Jamie to the cowardly brink? Her own words haunt me now: *A bully wouldn't pick on someone who spoke up, now, would they, Ms Reid?* As if she'd finally found her voice. As if she'd decided that she was no longer comfortable with walking on eggshells. Could it have been the final straw? I shake my head. *Crack. Crack. Crack. Crack.*

'It's just sad,' I say with a sigh.

'That bastard almost took everything from us,' Lisa says.

'I know.'

'I'm not ready to be sad yet,' Lisa says.

'I know.'

'And she brought him in there, invited him to the party – knowing that he had some bullshit violent streak like that? I mean, be blind and whatever in your own life, but . . . really? You're going to just let him loose on people . . . on kids?' Lisa is gesticulating wildly.

'I don't think she had much say in the matter,' I say. Maybe she thought she could control him?

'Yeah, I'm getting that,' Lisa says.

'We'll never know what really happened,' I say.

'Somebody has got to know something,' Jill says, her eyes darting wildly.

'I'm telling you, no one knows anything. When her sister came to the school after the fund-raiser, it was clear that there was no one. She came to me thinking I had answers,' I say.

'Well, she wouldn't have said anything to the people at work,' Jill says.

'But *no one* knew her,' I say.

'That's not exactly right, though. Is it? We only knew *what she wanted us to know,*' Lisa says.

'And where did that get her?' I say. This last bit of gossip is right out of a Shakespearean tragedy. Emma Dunham was a sham. Little Miss Perfect had a dark side. More than a dark side. Little Miss Perfect was haunted. A shadow. A shell. But she wasn't. That's the thing. That's the thing that makes me want to scream. She was in there. There was a human being in there, who made jokes about Justin Timberlake, wanted to be a painter, had a younger sister who idolized her and was so impressive that she became the first female head of school at Markham. And she was magnificent. But . . . like a cancer, her secrets took her over. Put her down. The dark overtook the light. But maybe this doesn't have to be the end of Emma's story.

There's a legacy here. A sliver of something. *John Henry*. Emma's legacy can heal. Be something for Clara and those girls. I can at least try to save the part of her that she loved the most. The part of her that held the most dangerous thing in the world: hope.

'There must have been something else going on,' Jill says.

'Something else? How?' I ask. Jill shrugs and looks off into the distance. I'm just about to repeat myself when Lisa jumps in. John Henry trots along, taking in the general splendor. He's happy. Tail-wagging happy.

'Bottom line, Emma was Emma. She would rather die than let anyone know what was *really* going on in her life.' Lisa's tone is final.

'We'll never know what actually happened, but I'm sure it's not as simple as you're making it out to be,' I say, not wanting to talk about it anymore. Would knowing *why* it happened lessen the horror?

'Not all marriages are like that,' Jill says.

Lisa and I share a quick look.

Jill continues. 'Speaking of happy marriages, when are we going to get down to the business of the backyard barbecue wedding?'

Lisa is quiet.

'What about your family?' I ask.

'What about 'em?' Lisa says, her voice offhand yet annoyed, more commonly known as 'the tone you talk about your family in.'

'What about them?' Jill asks.

'Have you told your parents yet?' I ask pointedly.

'No, I haven't told them.'

'*What?!*' Jill and I say in unison.

'Look, I'm just waiting for the right time. That's all,' Lisa says.

'Have you told them about Wednesday? Jamie?' I ask, stopping her now. A group of joggers becomes annoyed with us, tutting and clicking their disapproval as they trot past. Lisa looks annoyed.

'You haven't told them about the shooting?!' Jill asks.

'Have you?' I ask, looking at Jill.

'Of course,' Jill says; she has her parents on speed dial.

'I don't want to make any proclamations here,' I say.

'But?' Lisa says, prompting me.

'But if you don't share this with your parents, you're going to have to write it off. It's getting to be too late. You're going to have to think of a lie and then roll with it. Forever. I mean, I don't want to sound fatalistic, but . . . it's getting to that point,' I say. I watch as Lisa runs through all the possible excuses; she shakes her head and is about to say something and then she doesn't and then . . . I continue. 'You know I'm right. And why you're questioning telling your parents when you helped save the lives of everybody in that room – I don't know. I would think they would want to know that.'

'I didn't save the life of—'

'Yes, you did,' I say, touching her shoulder, my face soft.

'Sam . . .'

'You started it,' I say.

Lisa is quiet.

'You know them better than I do, so maybe it's about

telling them and then deciding how to work the wedding . . . I don't know,' I say.

'It's your day,' Jill says, cocking her head like an errant teenager.

'Easy, girl,' I say.

'I'm just sayin'. I had to invite all these bullshit people and I've regretted it ever since,' Jill says, sitting on a curb now. Lisa and I sit down beside her, pulling our water bottles out. I take out a little dog bowl I bought at the pet store and fill it with water. John Henry laps it up. Laps it up. Looks around. Spills the water everywhere. Nuzzles my (now wet) knee. Lisa offers me a fun-size bag of M&M's; I put out my hand and she drops in a few. Two red, one yellow. We watch as the stream of runners hurry by, sharing M&M's and sipping water. We're clearly missing the point. John Henry lays down in between Jill and me. We absently pet him.

'No, you're right. It's the bride's day,' I say, making a face at Lisa. *Cuckoo. Cuckoo.*

'What are your parents doing right now?' Jill asks, yawning.

'I don't know . . . they're at home,' Lisa says.

Jill and I look at her. Lisa looks . . . stunned.

'You got a cell phone, right?' I ask finally.

'Yeah.'

'Well . . .'

'What . . . *now*?'

'I mean, you can go over there, but yeah,' Jill says, motioning to a more secluded area. Lisa looks at the small plot of land, covered in wood chips and leading up into the Linda Vista neighborhood of Pasadena.

'Now is as good a time as any,' I say.

'We'll be right here,' Jill says, tilting her head back. Getting some sun.

Lisa just sits there shaking her head.

'Go on,' I say.

'But leave the M&M's,' Jill says, extending her hand, her head still tilting back, eyes closed.

'You bitches are unbelievable.' Lisa slaps the M&M's bag into Jill's hand and marches over into the secluded area, pulling her cell phone from her pocket.

Jill and I are quiet. Jill brings her head up and opens her eyes. We watch as Lisa dials. Hangs up. Dials. Hangs up. Curses and gives us the finger. We both give her a thumbs-up and a *woot woot!* She's now telling us to get lost. Jill offers me the last of the M&M's with a yawn. I hold out my hand and thank her. Lisa dials . . . she's talking . . . pacing and talking.

'Do you think we overstepped?' I ask, petting John Henry's ears. He bends into me, leans into my touch. What a lovey. What a sweet boy.

'Nah,' Jill says.

'Nah?'

'What?'

'I saw Sam in the hospital the other day,' I say.

'And you're just telling me this now? I just . . . I think we really need to revisit a couple of the foundations of our friendship.' Jill pulls her sunglasses down the bridge of her nose; her blue eyes bore into me, her eyebrows raised.

'You have to give me time,' I say, making a face at John Henry. His floppy ears cock to one side.

'And?'

'It was good. I told him that he wasn't allowed to act like the other night never happened anymore. It felt good.'

'Good for you.'

Jill is quiet. Pensive. I pet John Henry.

'What are we talking? He's packing, like, what – ten? Ten inches?' Jill asks, her hands moving in front of her, measuring what she hopes to be the length of Sam's penis. Joggers, children and babies in strollers stride past. She looks from her hands to me.

I slap her hands down. 'Unbelievable.'

Long. Weary. Sigh.

Jill pops the last M&M in her mouth and looks off into the distance.

'I know this isn't what you want to hear, but all of this isn't necessarily a bad thing, you know? I mean, look at you. Just last week we were talking about Ryan this and Jeremy that and now? You're telling Sam what you want and deserve. I mean, that's got to count for something,' Jill says.

'I'm terrified I'm going to have to go back,' I say, my voice catching.

'It's not about going back. Because the girl who told Sam off in that hallway is the same girl I can't live without,' Jill says, bending into me. Tears pool in my eyes as I tug her close.

'Youuuu . . .'

'It's true. I don't want there to be a time when I . . . you're irreplaceable to me, Frannie. You've finally allowed yourself to be the girl I love with a man. And that's not something that wears off,' Jill says. Lisa flips her cell phone closed and walks back toward us. Jill and I straighten up and await the verdict. Jill raises her hands as if to ask Lisa to help her with standing. At first Lisa rolls her eyes, but then she grabs Jill's hands and hoists her up. Jill brushes the dirt from her pants as I stand. John Henry is ready to go. Smelling the wood chips, looking at the passersby.

'Well, my mom was crying, but she does that. She prides herself on it actually. Dad just wanted to know all about Grady. But I think . . . I think I got through to them. I think Mom just may let my wedding day be about me,' Lisa says as we start around the Rose Bowl once more.

'Oh, it'll be about you, all right,' Jill says.

'What did they say about Grady?' I ask.

'I told them just a little about him and said you really have to meet him. He just . . . he just wins people over,' Lisa says, getting choked up. 'That's happening a lot. You guys have that happen?' she says, pointing to her throat like she's got some kind of phlegm problem.

'Yeah, we were just talking about that,' I say.

'Crying for no reason, feeling all shitty for having it good,' Lisa says.

'Yeah, that's exactly what we were saying,' I say.

'Frannie here even told Sam off in the hospital the other day. Told him that he couldn't act like the other night didn't happen,' Jill says – tattles, really.

Lisa is quiet.

'What? What . . . what's going on over there?' Jill asks.

'You have to . . . I know something,' Lisa says.

My stomach drops.

Lisa continues. 'Grady was talking to Sam on the phone the other day. I heard something about a "lady friend." I asked what they were talking about, but Grady wouldn't tell me.'

'I . . . I thought . . .' I stutter. I can't form a thought. I can't make words. I can't . . . *I can't believe this is happening again.*

'*Lady friend* can mean a lot of things,' Lisa argues.

'Can we ask why he's even using that word to begin with? What is he, ninety?' Jill asks.

'A lady friend,' I repeat.

'Was I wrong to tell you?' Lisa asks.

'No,' I say, giving her a forced smile. Lisa looks mortified. 'I thought we . . . I thought we had something. There were babies and bathwaters. I wasn't going to . . . I wasn't going to throw it out, you know?' I say, spiraling.

'If it's any consolation, he's not doing well. This whole shooting has done something to him and it's not good,' Lisa says.

'I got that,' I say, remembering our talk in the hallway.

'Doing well enough to have a new lady friend though,' Jill says, squirting water into her mouth.

'I thought that he was talking about you. That Frannie was the lady friend in question,' Lisa says.

'Nope. Pass. We're not doing this. We're not going to run through the usual tired exercise of trying to fit our "facts" into some kind of fantasy scenario. Enough. He knows I'm here. He knows. He also knows that it's shitty to walk out on a girl with no explanation after having sex with her. What happened to us in that teachers' lounge sucked. Sucked. For him . . . I can't imagine. But it's time to stop running from us, from those gunshots, from everything. I don't think he's ready to stop running. And I can't blame him,' I say.

Lisa and Jill are nodding. A little scared of me, sure. But nodding.

We're all quiet as we make the final turn into the parking lot and start beelining to our cars. My cell phone rings. I know Jill secretly thinks it will be Sam. I don't recognize the number. Jill and Lisa stand by their cars, petting John Henry, talking about the wedding, talking about Sam. Jill is trying to get more information out of Lisa. We're all making our own arguments as to what 'lady friend' means.

'Hello?'

'Frannie?'

'Yes.'

'It's Clara.'

'Oh, hey!' I wave Jill and Lisa down. *It's Clara,* I mouth. *It's Clara*. They both perk up.

'I wanted to know if you wanted to come over for dinner on Thursday.'

'Sure, that sounds lovely.' I look at John Henry.

'How does seven sound? Do you have a pencil?' Clara asks. I give Jill John Henry's leash, race over to my car, beep it unlocked and pull a pen out of the cup holder. I find an envelope and write down Clara's address and home phone. John Henry watches me. My every move.

'Okay, so I'll see you on Thursd—'

'The girls are dying to meet John Henry,' Clara blurts. I breathe. Deeply and fully.

'Really?' I ask, my voice cracking. 'Meet him to keep him?' I'm not bringing this boy over to that house just so he can get his heart broken.

'Yes, Frannie. We'd love to have him. I'd love . . . I'd love to have him,' Clara says, her voice quiet.

'You're going to love him. He's . . . he's just the best,' I say, unable to take my eyes away from him. I did it. I did something. I did something.

Clara and I sign off and I quickly tell Lisa and Jill the news. We're all over the moon. Something about this orphaned dog finding a proper home in all of this has given us something. A glimmer of hope.

'Before we . . . before you guys . . . I actually wanted to ask you guys. My oldest sister just agreed to be my maid of honor – wait, matron of honor, right? She's married?' Lisa asks.

'Matron,' Jill says, on familiar ground again.

'I was wondering if you two would be bridesmaids, as well,' Lisa says.

'Oh my god!' Jill says, lunging at Lisa.

Breaking from Jill, Lisa says, 'Okay . . . Jesus, we're all just—'

'Yes!' Jill yells, her arm reaching out for me. I grasp her hand as she pulls me in close.

'I'd be honored,' I say, smiling.

'Yes! Yes! Are you kidding? Yes!' Jill says, pulling me into the group hug.

'With Maria Teresa as the matron of honor and my other four sisters as bridesmaids, that's about—'

'Ten thousand?' I say, interrupting. Lisa laughs.

'I thought you two could plan the bachelorette party. My sisters are a little out of touch with that stuff and they're all back in New Jersey. This way we can have something tasteful and small, you know?' Lisa says, giving Jill a quick wink.

'Strippers,' Jill says, pulling out her cell phone.

'Do you have them on speed dial?' I ask. Is she calling one right now?

'No! What – well actually yes, but I'm not calling them right now,' Jill says, tapping something into the calendar in her BlackBerry.

'Okay . . . well, we'll see you tomorrow then?' Lisa says.

'You heading back to the hospital?' I ask.

'Yeah, they finally brought a cot into Grady's room. Now, I can just sleep in my own bed,' Lisa says.

'How'd you work that?' Jill asks.

'I was just persistent,' Lisa says. I think back to the EMT who decided to let Lisa ride in the ambulance rather than experience bodily harm. Persistence, Jersey style, I imagine.

'You're getting married,' Jill says to Lisa.

'I know,' Lisa says, giving me a look of concern. She starts up her car. Her radio blasts: '*Ooooooh, she's a little runaway* . . .'

'Who is . . . is that Bon Jovi?' I ask, beeping my car unlocked in the distance. My shoulders are lowering. My breath is deepening. Finding a proper home for John Henry has almost taken my mind off of . . . ugh. The lady friend.

'Uh, yeah. Jerz all the way,' Lisa says, turning it up, her head bopping in time, her entire arm extended and pointing to what I imagine is a sea of adoring fans.

'See you guys tomorrow. Congratulations, sweetie,' I say, giving Lisa a quick squeeze on her shoulder. She looks up and thanks me. Thanks me and . . . *Oooooooh, she's a little runaway.* I laugh and walk to my car with Jill.

'Love you,' Jill says as I load John Henry into my car. He's now sitting in the front seat. I've taken it on as my duty to completely untrain him by the time he goes to Clara's.

'Love you, too,' I say, pulling her in close.

'We're going to figure out this lady friend business,' Jill says.

'Okay, sweetie,' I say, climbing in my car.

'See you tomorrow,' she says, walking toward her car. I watch her walk away. Watch her climb into her car, chewing on her fingernails and spinning her BlackBerry around in the other hand. Always doing eight things at once. She gives me a big wave and drives away.

16

Hero

The dream goes like this: I'm driving a bus. It's filled with kids. Cool kids. I know this in my heart. As I drive the bus filled with cool kids, I know it's an honor. That I'm not one of them. We're driving through a fancy Swiss village that I have no business being in. I make a turn and drive through what I think is a puddle. It's not. It's a river. And we're drowning. I've killed the cool kids. But they're being rescued. They're finding another bus. I'm trying to save all of their cool belongings, but I can't lift them. Spiders. Everywhere. The bus sinks. Deeper and deeper. No one comes back for me as I am drowning.

'*No!*' I jolt awake. John Henry lifts his head up from where he sleeps: in a little ball where my legs curl. I may have fallen asleep in that position, thought it was adorable that he leapt up and snuggled in tight, rather than sleeping in his crate. However, at four A.M. when my entire body was cramping in that position, his little snores were far less endearing. Did I move? Of course not. My time with him is limited. Our walks around my neighborhood, sitting on the couch with my arm lazing over his body, the occasional 'What do you think of that show, John Henry?' I know I'll cry like a baby when I walk away from Clara's

Thursday night without him, but I honestly don't think I'll be sad. I'll miss him, but every fiber of my being can't wait to give him the one thing Emma really wanted for him.

Between Jenny and me, I don't know who's going to miss the pup more. But every morning when I drop him off at her house, both of us always talk about how great it's going to be. How perfect it is. How much he'll love having a proper . . . a *loving* home. Something Emma wanted more than anything. Something she never had. Something she died for.

'Good to see you again, Frannie,' Pamela says, sitting down behind what was once Emma's desk. Monday morning. Back to school. Life goes on. The Tonka trucks are back to work, the kids are back to running in the halls and Emma is still gone. I can't even say the word. Just . . . gone.

The headmistress's office now smells of balsam and freshly mown grass. It's tastefully decorated and the light seems more diffused in here, calmer, if that's possible. With the Agatha Christie-inspired wingback chairs gone, I sink into the woolly heather-gray couch and curl one leg under my body.

Round two.

Pamela continues. 'So, how have the last few days been?'

'I feel like all I've been doing is talking about how the last few days have been,' I say, my voice clipped and annoyed.

'I see,' Pamela says, easing back in her chair.

'I don't mean to be—'

'Frannie, you don't have to be or say anything for me,' Pamela says.

'I'm crazy now, aren't I?'

'You may feel a bit crazy, but I can't say for sure. I mean, we're all a bit crazy,' Pamela says, taking a sip of tea.

'Yeah, but you're saying it in sort of an "I make dream catchers in Taos" kind of way. I mean, I'm saying it in, like, a "rocking in a corner of the room and barking" kind of way.'

'Ah, yes. But you get that crazy people don't ask themselves whether they're crazy, right?'

'No, I honestly didn't think of that.'

'Right. Because they're crazy.'

'Right.'

'So . . .'

'What if I said it was more about feeling like – undefined. Lost. Without meaning – not meaning . . . it's more without understanding. I thought I knew who I was. I thought I knew who everyone was and something about this has made everything I knew seem false. It's just . . . not how I thought it was,' I say, piecing it together.

'That makes sense.'

'It makes sense in a nonsensical way?'

'Yeah.'

'Am I going to go back?'

'Do you want to go back?'

'No! Noooo.' And I lose it. I heave forward and bury my face in my hands, sobbing.

'Frannie,' Pamela says gently. I look up, scrubbing my

face and wiping my cheeks, and take the tissue Pamela is offering me.

'I think I got her killed,' I say in a whisper. Saying it out loud for the first time.

'Why do you think that?'

'We talked about bullying and then we talked about reconnecting with her sister. Painting. She was . . . *resolved*.'

'How does that equal getting her killed?'

'We got to talking about her family and then the day of . . . she talked to her sister after years of estrangement and it probably set Jamie off. Like he was losing control or something. So, if she was in an abusive relationship, a shift like that? It would have . . . it could have changed things.'

'Changed how?'

'He was so small. Remember?' Pamela nods yes. I continue. 'He was so physically small. It was pretty clear, I mean, hindsight being twenty/twenty, that the only real control he had over her was mental. He was just . . . weak looking.'

'I agree.'

'He looked like a little boy with a big toy gun.'

'That sounds about right, too.'

'He couldn't even control it, you know? He couldn't hit anything that was moving. When Sam was going for the gun, Jamie missed him by a mile. His arm jerked back. He just . . . Emma. Just stood there.'

'And then . . .' Pamela trails off. I'm nodding. Trying not to lose it again and nodding. My mouth is twisted shut and my eyes are clenched closed.

'I was trying to see if she was . . . if she could be saved,' I say.

'And could she?' Pamela asks, her voice soft.

I am quiet. I open my eyes.

Pamela asks me again, 'Frannie? Could Emma be saved?'

'No,' I say. I let out a long exhale.

'So, you blame yourself for getting her killed, and then you blame yourself for not being able to save her. Is that correct?'

'I'm also blaming myself that Sam . . . that he had to . . .'

'I see.'

'He's not fine. He says he's fine, but . . .'

'I know. He killed someone. Yes, he is a hero and saved dozens of lives – yours included – but he's also a good man. And that's going to . . . that's going to affect him for some time,' Pamela says, almost to herself.

I am quiet.

'She lied about everything.'

'She had to.'

'I didn't even like her. In the beginning? I thought she was smug, too perfect.'

'You didn't know her.'

'I should have seen something.'

'She's been hiding the truth for a lot longer than she's known you. She was good at it.'

'I know.'

'You couldn't do anything. There was nothing to see. This was a brutal murder. How do you expect yourself to see that coming?'

'I don't know.'

'Frannie,' Pamela says, reaching across and taking my hand. Her eyes are kind and concerned. She curls her fingers around mine. The touch of her hand is . . . tearing something. Breaking something down.

Pamela continues. 'Some people are beyond saving – in fact, don't want to be saved.'

'She was starting, you know? It's . . . it's just . . . so . . . sad,' I say, holding tightly to her hands.

'I know. It's sad, but it's also not your fault. It's not your fault. It's not Sam's fault. Jamie pulled that trigger. Jamie is to blame. I need you to understand that.'

'Soon.'

'I'll take that.'

We are quiet.

'Did Clara call you? About John Henry?'

I smile. It burns my throat as I swallow my tears.

'She did. She's going to take him,' I say, beaming.

'You're still trying to save her,' Pamela says, her eyes concerned.

'Maybe.'

'Give John Henry the chance Emma never had?'

'Possibly.'

'What happens when you realize that you've become attached to him?'

'I don't . . . I don't understand.'

'What happens when you realize that you've become attached to him?'

'I don't know.'

'That's probably a question you want to know the answer to before you head over to Clara's.'

'I will.'

'You don't have to be Joan of Arc, Frannie. You don't have to sacrifice your own happiness. I think what you're doing with John Henry is right and amazing, but you never even factored in that you have a proper home and that Emma would have loved for you to have him. That sometimes you do get to keep the puppy.'

'Not this time though.'

'But keep your eyes open.'

I walk out of Pamela's office in a daze. I never even thought about my home as worthy of John Henry. Why didn't that even occur to me?

'*He ruined everything! He ruined everything!*' Harry Sprague. I look up and down the hallway and take off at a run toward the little boy's cracking yells. I come around a corner and find Sean Stone cowering in a corner right outside of the art room. I turn to see Harry Sprague being held back by Sam. He's still kicking and hitting.

'*He ruined everything! He killed her, Ms Reid! He killed her!*' Harry's voice breaks as the sobs take over. I look at Sam.

'I found them fighting. He was . . . he just keeps saying that he killed her,' Sam says.

'Let him go. Let him go,' I say to Sam, my eyes soft. Sam lets Harry go and I step in between him and Sean.

'Sweetie, sweetie . . . look at me. Look at me! Harry . . . Harry?' I say, kneeling in front of him, his face in my hands. Sam shoos Sean Stone away. He skitters down the hall.

'I did this, Ms Reid. I did this,' Harry says, crumpling

into my arms. His sobs are wild while he's simultaneously hugging me and clutching at me. My own tears come fast as I look up at Sam. His jaw is tight, his arms at his sides.

'Sweetie, I need you to look at me. Harry, honey . . . I need you to look at me,' I say, standing his little rail of body in front of me. His face is blotchy and red, his eyes pooled with tears, his mouth contorted in pain.

I continue. 'Baby, how long have you been walking around with this? You didn't do this, my sweet boy. You didn't do this.' I smooth his hair. Wipe his tears. Sam sniffles a little. Looks away. His jaw tight.

'I got in a fight. She told me I made her think different. She said I was brave and that she was going to be brave like me. And now . . . look! *Look what I did!*' Harry crumples again in my arms.

'Jesus Christ,' Sam says, wiping at his eyes. I see Pamela approach our little trio in the corner. She's about to step in but waits. Harry has to hear this from me.

'Okay . . . I need you to hear me, honey. I need you to really hear me. Can you make me that promise?' I feel Harry nod as he hugs me. I continue. 'Sweetie, no one could do anything to save her. It's sad, but it's also not your fault. It's not your fault. It's not Headmistress Dunham's fault. That man pulled the trigger. That man is to blame. I need you to understand that.' Harry's arms loosen around my body as he stands in front of me. His entire face is contorted in pain, confusion – way beyond anything a boy this young should be dealing with.

'Is that man going to come back?' Harry asks.

'No, sweetie. He's never coming back.'

'Someone got him?' Harry asks, his breath easing.

'Yes, baby. Someone got him,' I say, looking from Harry to Sam.

'Who . . . who got him?' Harry asks, wiping his nose on his school blazer.

I look to Sam. It's not my place to tell Harry. I wait. Sam drops his head with a heavy sigh. Pamela watches Sam. He kneels down as I motion for Harry to turn around. Harry looks up into Sam's eyes as I watch Sam's face twist with memory.

'I did, son. I got him,' Sam says. Harry leaps into Sam's arms, his tiny body hanging around Sam's neck like an elaborate medal.

'Thank you . . . thank you . . .' Harry sobs. Sam wraps his arms around the little boy, dropping his head to tuck into the boy's neck.

'You're welcome,' Sam says. Once.

This time he means it.

'Come on, honey. Why don't you come talk to me for a while,' Pamela says, taking Harry down to her office. I give him a smile as he walks down the hall. Sam stands.

'I can't believe he thought it was his fault,' I say.

'It seems to be a popular point of view,' Sam says, unable to look at me.

We are quiet.

Sam continues. 'You're great with him.'

'Thanks.'

Sam clears his throat.

'My daddy is sick,' Sam says, not looking at me.

'What?'

'Daddy is sick.'

'I'm so sorry,' I say, my voice soft. My hands reach out to him, yet . . . stall in midair.

Sam is quiet. He watches my hands as they stall out.

'Have I done that? Have I made you . . .' Sam motions to my hands, now at my sides.

'It didn't take much, I assure you,' I say honestly.

'Ha,' Sam says, smiling.

'I kinda always think that people don't want what I'm selling,' I say, laughing.

'Hm,' Sam says, watching me. Finally looking at me.

'I miss you,' I say. I look right at him. Chin up. Shoulders back. No mask.

'I didn't even know I needed you, so . . .' Sam says, looking away. He clears his throat again.

'Sam, I—'

'I'd better get going. I came in to get a drink of water and I've been gone for half an hour,' Sam says, giving me a quick wave and heading on down the hall. As he's walking out the double doors to the outside . . . he looks back. A smile. A shake of the head and out into the sunlight.

'What was that all about?' Jill asks, coming around the corner.

'How long have you been there?'

'The whole time,' Jill says, biting into a bagel.

'The whole time?' I say, walking up the stairs to our office.

'Well, not in the beginning, but right after you walked up. Sure,' Jill says.

'Unbelievable,' I say, my mind still cloudy and overwhelmed.

'He didn't even know he needed you,' Jill repeats as we walk into our office.

'Out of all that . . .'

'Oh, the Harry Sprague stuff was heartbreaking. Why is it that all of us want to take the blame for what some psycho did? I mean, what's wrong with us?'

'Are you . . . are you talking about your feelings right now?'

'You're not really creating a supportive environment.'

'Have you been to see Pamela?'

'Maybe.'

'Good for you,' I say, beaming.

'I'm going to talk about my feelings, Frannie.'

'Yes, you are,' I say, as if she just brought me back a tennis ball. Good girl!

Jill is quiet. Slumped in her office chair.

'It's unnerving how much I need you right now. Need you and Lisa. Martin. I'm just a ball of need. This is not a comfortable place for me, Frannie.' She doesn't look at me. 'I'm by myself for ten minutes and I'm checking behind doors to see if there's a bogeyman behind them.' She scrubs at her face again, rubbing her eyes, hiding the furrowed brow and pools of tears just below.

'What you're not factoring into your "ball of need" theory is that you're not the only one,' I say.

'"Ball of need" theory?'

'It has a ring to it,' I say with the slightest smile. 'All of us went through something that day and none of us have really been comfortable with who we are these past few days.'

'All of us?'

'Hm.' I let the littlest defiant laugh go. Jill looks away for the briefest second. I watch her.

She continues. 'I never really talked about anything. And then . . . Emma. I never thought about why I'm so competitive. If you don't want my life then there's something wrong with me. I just . . . I don't know when I started thinking like that, I just did. I'm not making any sense.'

'No, it makes sense,' I say.

'It's funny, but knowing you need me right now . . . it makes it better,' Jill says.

'So, you're codependent. That's comforting,' I say, laughing just a bit.

'Ha!' Jill laughs and then . . . it breaks, into a million pieces. The deeply lined furrow of her brow and the twisting mouth that looks as if it's holding back a tsunami.

I ask, 'What?' I take her hands in mine, gripping tighter and tighter.

'I thought I lost you and I did . . . I thought I lost everything,' Jill says, her voice catching as she pulls me into her, holding me, tight . . . tight . . . tight. My breath catches as I grip her, feel her shake in my arms. This is what it feels like to love someone. The fear that they could be harmed and you'd be helpless keeps you up at night. It's a rift in your logic. It turns you from sensible into someone who's inside out. A shirt worn backward.

'It seems you're not the only ball of need on the premises,' I say, quiet and in her ear.

'Balls of need unite,' Jill says, smiling. Laughing.

'You just couldn't help yourself,' I say, holding her tighter.

'I'm pregnant,' Jill says in my ear.

'*What!?*' I say, breaking from the hug. I don't wait for her answer. 'Oh my god, congratulations!' I say, hugging her again.

'You're hurting me,' Jill yelps from beneath my squeezing.

'Oh my god,' I say, pulling back.

'Are you crying?' Jill asks, wiping away a tear that's traveled down my dampening cheek.

'Yeah, I guess, I didn't even . . .' I say, slightly embarrassed. 'How far along? How long have you—'

'My doctor says I'm almost six weeks along,' Jill says.

'How long have you known?' I ask.

'Since last Wednesday,' Jill says.

A chill.

She continues. 'Exactly.'

'Light from dark!' I say, pulling her into me again. She's limp in my arms. I break from the hug.

'Is something wrong, I mean . . . with the baby?' I ask.

Jill is quiet.

'Honey?' I ask gently.

'No, the baby is healthy.'

'Have you told Martin?' I ask.

'He couldn't be happier,' Jill says, rolling her eyes.

'This is good, right? This is a new life. This is a baby. This is—'

'The end of my marriage.'

'What?' I ask.

'We can say good-bye to ever putting whipped cream on each other. Who's going to want to put whipped cream on aaaall this?' Jill motions to her perfect figure with disgust.

'I don't want to trivialize what you're feeling right now, or really want to know where you heard about this whipped cream business, but—'

'But nothing!' Jill looks terrified. Fighting back tears, her face reddening.

'Okay . . . I understand that this seems very real to you, but, honey, Martin is crazy about you,' I say.

'Yeah, *now*.'

'You get that people only do the whipped cream thing as a means to an end. Women want Whipped Cream Dude to marry them and maybe . . . father a child with them? A little happily-ever-after that, you know, starts with a really gross form of objectification,' I say.

'You're only saying that because I won't ever be objectified again,' Jill sniffles.

'Shit, I'll put a dollop of whipped cream on you right now,' I say.

'You would?' Jill asks. I pull her in for a tight hug and she crumples in deep, heavy sobs.

'Okay . . . it's going to be okay . . . shhhh,' I say, smoothing her long, red hair.

'I'm . . . terrified. What if I'm not good at it?' Jill says as she pulls away.

'You don't have to know how you're going to be at this. You don't have to put on any act about how you feel. But for you to think that you're not one of a kind, someone utterly remarkable . . . That's . . . that's a lie,' I say. Jill reacts to every word. Softening. Tears streaming down her face as I say *remarkable*. She grips my hand.

'I don't know what kind of mother I'm going to be,' she finally manages to say.

'None of us do.'

'I need to be perfect.'

'No, you don't.'

'I don't know how to . . . I . . .'

'You'll learn.'

'What if . . . what if . . .'

'All you can do is love this baby with everything you got. All the rest is gravy,' I say, wiping her tears.

'I love gravy.'

'I know you do, sweetheart.'

'We need to go somewhere where there's gravy.'

'We will.'

Jill hugs me again, her body still shaking as she cries.

It's not even nine A.M.

17

A Proper Home

'Frannie, so good of you to come,' Clara says, opening her front door that Thursday night. John Henry peeks his head around the door; his head cocks to one side as he looks up at me. I give him a smile and we walk into Clara's home.

The house is a classic Los Angeles Spanish-style home in the hills just below the Greek Theater. A large archway leads into the great room with dark hardwood floors underfoot. The barrel ceiling boasts rich, almost black beams. Paintings and sculpture abound. Tapestries hang on the walls; there are gilt-framed portraits of long-ago royalty next to a piece of modern art that resembles some kind of balloon animal. Clara watches me take it in, my hand tight around John Henry's leash.

'The girls are out back,' Clara says, walking through the great room. John Henry and I follow, taking in the rest of the house. We walk through the busy kitchen, pots boiling, tables set with place mats and the good china. For someone with a black-sheep past, she's certainly turned into quite the hostess. At the other end of the kitchen are a pair of French doors that lead out into the backyard.

I can hear the girls before I see them. Bursts of laughter,

shrieks of delight and the occasional toneless singing. I can hear a man's voice guiding them, easing them . . . parenting them. Bliss. Utter bliss. Clara gives me a quick smile, I give John Henry a gentle pet and we're through the French doors.

'Girls? Honey? Frannie's here,' Clara says, walking out onto the patio.

'*And John Henry?!*' they shriek. John Henry braces himself. Sits. His eyes dart from me to the herd of pigtails and pink clothes coming at us right now.

'Girls, you need to take it down a notch. You're going to scare him,' Clara says, a smile just under her words. 'This is my husband, Bruce, and these are the girls: Maude, Gertie and . . . *Emma*,' Clara says, pointing to three little matryoshka-doll girls.

'Nice to meet you,' I say, shaking hands with Bruce, a slight man with dark cocoa skin and salt-and-pepper dreadlocks. His entire demeanor radiates a melty calm. His voice is silken and his handshake is gentle but firm. He smiles and tells me it's nice to meet me. I just nod. I'm already getting choked up. This is going to be a long night.

I continue. 'And nice meeting you guys.' I look from one girl to the next. They couldn't be less interested in me. They're all staring at John Henry.

'*He's so cute!*' Gertie blurts, her hands extended as if she's already squishing his face.

'*He looks like mercury!*' Maude says. I don't even know what that means.

'She's really into science. It's his coat. The silver,' Clara says. I nod. Smiling. Smiling.

'Dogs have blue eyes,' Emma says. I find myself just staring at her. Delicate features. The set of the jaw. The mannerisms. Clara notices.

'I know. She just . . . well, I just had to name her Emma,' Clara says, clearing her throat and looking away.

'I imagine there's a bunch of dog stuff that needs to be transported?' Bruce says, setting down his mug of tea.

'Oh, yes please. It's in the back of my car,' I say, passing him my keys. The girls never take their eyes off John Henry.

'Now, if Frannie takes John Henry off his leash, can you guys promise me something?' Clara asks.

'*Yes!*' the girls shriek in unison.

'You need to let him be for a bit. He has to smell everything and maybe pee somewhere and you have to promise me that you will let him come up to you. You guys can't do your thundering horde thing, okay?'

'Yes, Mama,' they say as one. Clara gives me the nod. I can see the girls vibrating with excitement from here. This is killllllling them.

'*I want him to sleep in my room!*' Maude 'whispers.'

'*He's going to be my dolly!*' Gertie says.

'*I looooooooooove him!*' Emma blurts.

'Girls?' Clara says gently.

I let John Henry off the leash and he doesn't go anywhere. He sits next to me.

'I saw on *Sesame Street* that you have to get down at their level,' Maude says, pushing her glasses farther up her nose. A girl after my own heart. The girls sit. Immediately. On the brick patio. Putting their hands out to John Henry.

Gertie sings, 'Get *down* at his level . . . get *down* at his level,' as she flicks her hands in rhythm.

John Henry inches over to the girls, sniffing and smelling. The girls giggle and squirm as he inspects them. His tail begins to wag. Just the tiniest bit, but there it is. Clara and I both notice.

'Sit, John Henry,' I say. He obliges. Right next to an extremely excited Maude. Her entire face lights up as the dog settles in next to her.

'What are you going to doooooooooo?' Emma whispers.

'I. Don't. Know,' Maude says, not moving her mouth.

'Have they ever had a dog before?' I ask.

'Obviously not,' Clara answers with a smile. She says to Maude, 'Honey, why don't you try petting him?' Maude lifts her tiny hand up and pets John Henry on the side of his body. John Henry turns and watches her. And then smells her face. Sniff. Sniff. And then a biiiiiiig lick.

'*Hahahahahahahahahah!*' Gertie and Emma are in hysterics. Maude hops up onto her knees and pets John Henry with confidence. His ears. His neck.

'What a good boy, John Henry,' Maude says soothingly. John Henry leans into her, his eyes closed, his tail wagging. I'm officially crying. It's fine. We were all ready for this.

'*My turn!*' Gertie says, inching over closer to John Henry. She pets him and talks to him and tells him that she loves him and that he's her dolly and that she has tea parties every morning and that he's invited, but that he can't eat any of the cookies because they're not real, that

Mama says they're not real even though they look real, but he's a good boy. Clara and I are fighting to keep a straight face during her passionate monologue. John Henry licks Gertie and wags his tail and lets her pet him. Leans into her tiny touch. And then it's Emma's turn. Because she's so tiny, she walks over to the silvery dog and holds her hand out. He nuzzles into the palm of her hand. Now we're both crying. Clara passes me a tissue.

And then they're off. The thundering horde. Running around the backyard, playing, chasing, falling over into a pile of tiny pink clothes and silvery limbs. John Henry is the happiest I've ever seen him. He's alive and . . . in a proper home.

'How long did you think you were going to have that dog?' Bruce says, handing me my keys.

'I know, I went a little overboard,' I say, smiling.

'I see things have taken a turn for the worse out here,' Bruce says, picking up his mug of tea and taking a long sip.

'Yes, as you can see they hate each other,' Clara says, giving him a snuggle. He kisses the top of her head and tugs her closer.

'Oh, clearly,' Bruce says.

'Hon, can you watch them while I show Frannie some of Emma's paintings?' Clara asks, resting her hand on his arm.

'Sure,' he says with a quick check-in. Is she okay? Emma's paintings. Clara gives him a soothing smile and a quick peck on the cheek and motions for me to follow her through the French doors and back into the house.

'Thank you,' Clara says as we wind through the majestic archways of the Spanish house.

'For what?' I ask, following Clara down a narrow staircase.

'John Henry. I actually . . . I don't think you can know what he means to us,' Clara says, not looking back. I run my hand along the cold plaster wall of the staircase as I bite back emotion. So much emotion. How long have I been tamping this stuff down? Is there an end to it?

Clara and I turn a sharp corner and she flicks on a light. And at once I'm in another land. The majestic Spanish arches continue in this lower floor, but instead of being chopped up into smaller rooms, this is one large room worthy of a gothic novel.

'No natural light. It helps with the paintings,' Clara says, walking farther into the room. I look up: The same vaulted ceilings and dark wood beams. But, on the walls . . .

'Holy shit,' I say. Taking it all in. I can't . . . the tears roll down my cheeks as my mouth hangs open.

'Emma played with the idea of the "Grand Style." You see it in all of the English portraits of the eighteenth century that you'd find in the National Gallery,' Clara says, moving through the room. Huge gilt frames around masterpieces, but . . .

'They're different,' I say, stopping in front of one.

'It was an entire style based on the idea that you should not paint the subject as they are physically, but more as they are historically. So, short men became tall and mean men became handsome simply because they were in positions of power. What Emma did was, well—'

'She pulled the mask off,' I say.

'Exactly.'

The portrait is of a couple. Exactly as Clara described. Eighteenth century, right out of the National Gallery. The pastoral backdrop and the young wealthy couple on a stroll. But what Emma did was paint the moments before the couple thinks they're being watched. The woman is uninterested, looking elsewhere, her entire body bored and limp. The man is fussing with his clothes. Trying to suck in his gut, with a quick glance at his wife. She clearly wants nothing to do with him. He manages to look disdainful yet snubbed and insecure at the same time. And Emma captured it all.

'It's brilliant,' I say, walking to the next painting.

'This one is actually a play on real painting. *Miss Bowles* was by Sir Joshua Reynolds; it was one of the masterpieces of the Grand Style. The original is of the little girl sitting in the woods and she's clutching the dog, like around the neck. It's one of his most famous . . .' Clara says, trailing off as I get lost in the painting. In Emma's version, the little girl is standing, a very prominent stain on the front of her dress. You can see the portrait painter in the background, the easel, the paints. He's annoyed the little girl had the audacity to be a kid and stain her dress. Her mother is red-faced as she disciplines the little girl, with just the littlest glint in the mother's eye that shows she's aware that someone is watching. That she's holding back and playing to a crowd. The little dog is walking past, not part of the portrait at all. The mother sees an opportunity to move on with the portrait and save face. Thus, as Emma painted it, the little girl clutching the dog in the original masterpiece is now given a darker backstory.

'When did she do these?' I ask, walking around the room from one brilliant painting to the next.

'In college. This was when she was in her late teens and early twenties,' Clara says, shaking her head.

'Unbelievable,' I say, my voice a whisper.

'It's hard not to wonder what kind of painter she would have become,' Clara says through gritted teeth.

'I know,' I say, the hardwood floors creaking beneath my feet. The joyous bursts of laughter coming from upstairs waft down the staircase and into this magnificent gallery.

'I've decided to go to her memorial service,' Clara says, stopping in front of yet another one of Emma's masterpieces.

'Good.'

'I talked to the country club and I've decided to donate one of Emma's paintings to them. They're going to unveil it at the service,' Clara says, looking back up at the painting looming over us. The painting is of a trussed-up young woman, taking a moment in between modeling sessions to flirt with the painter. It's bawdy, wry and utterly dazzling.

'I love that.'

'Her work should hang where people can appreciate it. Know her. Know what she wanted to say,' Clara says, her voice distant.

'I couldn't agree more.'

'Are you going?'

'Yes. Me and a couple of other women from the school.

I'm originally from Mill Valley, so we'll be staying with my parents,' I say.

'That'll be nice,' Clara says, still distant.

'Thank you,' I say.

'It's my turn to ask for what.'

'For this,' I say, motioning around the room.

'Don't thank me,' Clara says.

I nod.

Clara continues. 'It's not right. She should've . . . it's not right.'

'I know.'

We're quiet. Another burst of laughter from upstairs seems to jerk Clara out of whatever dark memory she's lapsed into.

'Shall we?' she asks, motioning for me to head upstairs.

'Absolutely,' I say.

Dinner is a circus. The girls comically 'sneak' food under the table to John Henry. He's being spoiled within an inch of his life. I can't stop smiling. We languish over a banquet of saffron rice, roasted chicken and fresh green beans. The girls drink milk and Clara pours me red wine. We talk about politics, art and life. The night is beautiful, but before long it's time for me to go. To say good-bye to John Henry.

'Please let me help clean up,' I say, milling around the kitchen after Bruce has taken the girls up to bed.

'Not a chance,' Clara says, clearing the table of sippy cups, plastic plates and her best china.

'You know I'm stalling, right?'

'Oh, yeah.'

I nod. A heavy sigh. John Henry lies, splayed and exhausted, under the kitchen table. I don't want to wake him. I . . . I don't want to say good-bye.

'Okay . . . thank you again,' I say, gathering my purse and giving Clara a big hug. She squeezes tight and pats my back.

'Thank you,' she says. I nod.

'Okay,' I say again. She smiles. I walk over to John Henry and squat down next to his snoring body. 'Good-bye, sweet boy.' I look up at Clara. Good, she's crying, too. I look back down at John Henry as he twitches in his deep sleep and whisper, 'Your mom loved you.' Smiling. Sobbing. Smiling. Sniffling. Sighing. I want to touch him. Pet him. But I don't want to wake him.

He looks so peaceful.

Finally.

I'm a wreck as I drive home. Tears roll down my cheeks. The paintings. Those girls. John Henry. All of it. It's too much. I don't know how much more of this I can take. I pull down my street. Sam's Ferrari is out in front of my building. Sam's Ferrari.

Sam.

I pull into my driveway as the security gate moans and whines along the ground. I roll down my window as Sam unfolds out of his driver's-side door. He walks over to me, his hands stuffed in his jeans pockets.

'What are you doing here?' I ask, my stomach flipping.

'Can I come in?' Sam asks, motioning to my apartment.

'Sure, let me park the car and I'll meet you at my door,' I say as the security gate opens. Sam nods as I drive my car into the garage. What exactly is happening here? I haven't talked to him all week. I've seen him a few times, but he's been distant and preoccupied. I just thought this was how it was. Or maybe I hoped one night I'd come home and he'd be waiting for me out in front of my apartment in that Ferrari of his. Am I finally having my Jake Ryan moment? I beep my car locked, gather my purse and walk toward my front door. My heart is in my throat; my mind is racing. I climb the stairs. Sam is waiting at the top, leaning against the railing.

'How long have you been here?' I say, fumbling with my keys.

'A while,' Sam says.

'Oh,' I say, opening up my door. I set my purse on the couch and close the door behind Sam. Here we are again. 'Do you want something to drink?'

'No, thank you.'

'I've had a really rough night, so if this is going to be about you moodily answering simple questions, I think I'll take a rain check,' I say, not knowing where to put my hands. Jake Ryan moment. *Come on.*

'I'm going back to Tennessee,' Sam says, not looking at me.

'What?'

'Daddy's sick and not getting better. This is it.'

'I'm so sorry.'

'I know.'

Quiet.

'Why did you come here?'

'I leave tomorrow morning. I didn't want you to worry.'

I nod. 'How long are you going to be gone?'

'I don't know.'

'And Grady's wedding?'

'I don't know.'

I nod again. 'Your business?'

'It's taken care of.'

Quiet. Sam. His face creased and furrowed. His mouth tight, his entire demeanor changed. This is not the same man I knew.

'What's happening to you?'

'What?'

'What's happening to you? Where'd you go?'

'I don't know what you're talking about.'

'You've just . . . you're a black hole.'

'A what?'

'You're folding in on yourself. Disappearing.'

Sam itches his neck. Looks away.

'Sam?'

'What?'

'What's happening to you?'

'Nothing. This is who I am. We didn't really know each other well enough to have you—'

'Bullshit.'

'What?'

'I know you. I know you, Sam.'

'No, you don't.'

'What happened to us was terrible and—'

'You can't know what I'm going through!'

'Make me understand then!'

'I can't.'

'Jesus, talk to me.'

'Why?'

'It helps.'

'It helps you. Not everyone grieves and mourns the same way. You want to talk about things and go to memorial services and . . . that just sounds like bullshit to me.'

'I can understand that.'

'Good.'

'But you have to talk to someone about what happened to you.'

'What happened *to* me? Nothing happened to me. I killed someone. I. Killed. Someone. I happened to him. You've got it all wrong.'

'You saved us. You're a hero.'

'I may have been a hero after one shot, but four? What does four bullets into someone mean? Is that a hero, Frannie? Or was I just as bad as Jamie?'

'What are you talking about?'

'Your eyes were closed, right?'

'Yes.' Remembering.

'You don't know what happened. What *really* happened.'

'I heard . . . I know what kind of man you are, Sam. I know—'

'No, you don't. I do.'

'Then tell me.'

Sam is quiet. Twitching and shaking.

'Sam?'

'I wasn't any better than him. I was someone my daddy would be proud of. And that . . . that just doesn't sit right with me. Four bullets. He went down with the first. Why did I fire three more shots?'

'Because there was a lunatic with a gun pointed at a group of innocent people and you knew he wasn't going to stop. He'd just shot at you, thankfully missing, and you had one opportunity to take him out. You shot four times because you had to make sure he wasn't going to get back up. You're not a bully, Sam. You're not your father.'

'You can say that as much as you like, but when the chips were down I handled my shit just like an Earley. All these years running from my name and there it is bubbling up like sewage. I can't run from it. I just . . . I just need to admit that that's who I am, but . . . that's not the man you want, Frannie.'

'You need to let me decide about that,' I say, finally stepping closer. He lets me. He watches me. Close.

'You met someone else before, Frannie. This . . . *this* is the real me. You can take the boy out of Shelby Forest, but . . .' Sam turns his face away from me, his eyes down. I step closer and reach my hand out to touch his face. He lets me. I turn his face so he'll look at me.

'I need you to hear me. There was nothing you could have done. I know. It's sad, but it's not your fault.' Sam smiles as he recognizes the speech I gave to Harry Sprague in that hallway not four days ago. I smile back and continue. 'It's not your fault. It's not your fault, Sam. That man pulled the trigger. That man is to blame. I need you to understand that.' My eyes are fixed on his. I wait. Held breath.

Sam takes my hand from his cheek and holds it tight.

He licks his bottom lip and I smile. His eyes crinkle as a smile takes over his face. He leans down and kisses me. Warm, soft and far too long in the making. Sam breaks from our kiss, his hand still gripping mine, his eyes downcast. I wait.

'I don't think I can be the kind of man you need,' he says, kissing the palm of my hand and letting it fall.

'You're the best man I've ever known,' I say, trying to get him to look at me.

Sam looks up, those cinnamon-spoked brown eyes now red-rimmed and desperate.

'I love you, darlin'. Which is why I know you deserve better than me,' Sam says. And he's out the door, rumbling down the stairs. I can hear the Ferrari start up in the distance, tugging on my aortic valve. I'm standing in exactly the same spot, my hand frozen in thin air.

'I love you, too, Sam.'

18

Privilege

It really is an art. The sparkling water and the Teddy Grahams work as an enchanting combination that fuels both driver and navigator toward their destination,' Jill says, sitting in the passenger seat of my SUV the next day as she, Lisa and I zoom toward San Francisco.

'My concern isn't the alchemy of your chosen foods, my concern is your insistence on stopping every half hour,' I say, making an allusion to Jill's love of all things interstate highway bathroom related.

'The gas stations along the 5 are some of the best in the world!' Jill exclaims, finger pointing, hand held aloft.

'I'm sure they are, I'm just wondering why we need to see so many of them,' Lisa says from the backseat.

'I hope you guys are proud of yourselves, ganging up on a pregnant lady,' Jill says.

'You'd like that, wouldn't you?' Lisa jokes, giving Jill a little wink.

'Hot,' Jill says, tossing a few Teddy Grahams in her mouth. Lisa laughs and gives Jill an affectionate nudge. Jill laughs.

'So, we're crossing the Bay Bridge?' I ask, motioning to the approaching signs.

'Yep, then through San Francisco, across the Golden Gate,' Jill says, taking a long, quenching drink of her sparkling water.

'I thought your enchanting combination of ingredients was supposed to help with your navigation capabilities,' I say.

'Isn't this where you're from?' Lisa asks.

'I'm terrible with directions,' I say.

'Well, that's obvious, ma'am,' Jill says. And then catches herself.

'It's okay. It really is,' I say, now crossing the Bay Bridge. We are focused as we weave through the streets of San Francisco and happy to finally see the Golden Gate Bridge ahead of us. The abundant and green surroundings of Northern California begin to infuse into my every pore. The deep green of the trees, the dark blue of the sky – it's just . . . it's just *better* up here. It's exactly what I need right now.

'He did say he loved you,' Jill says.

'Right before he left, yes,' I say.

'But he did say it,' Jill says.

'Right before he left.'

'But he did say it.'

'Enough,' Lisa says.

Jill whispers, '*But he did say it.*'

We are quiet.

I'm trying to keep everything in check while being grateful that Emma's memorial is here, of all places. *Home.* Hoping this place will help bring closure to something that has left me inside out. That the safety of my hometown, where I feel the most authentic, is nothing short of divine. Being here is forcing me to stay the course, stand up and be who I really am.

We end where we began.

Jill guides me across the Golden Gate Bridge and toward Mill Valley. We're almost home.

'It really is beautiful up here,' Jill says, watching the lush landscape whiz by.

'Isn't it?'

'It's a shame we're coming up here under such *unusual* circumstances,' Lisa says, giving me a quick look.

'I know,' I say honestly.

'We'll have to plan another trip,' Jill says. I get off the freeway and find Miller Avenue. We slow down as we drive through the heart of Mill Valley. I take a deep breath. Taking it in. The dark wood shingles of the storefronts, the luxurious yet environmentally friendly vehicles parked diagonally as the citizens of Mill Valley stroll and chat down the streets.

'That'd be amazing,' I say. All will be well. We're in Mill Valley, for crissakes.

'Right here, see? The Two A.M. Club? Huey Lewis and the News got their start there,' I say, pointing.

Lisa and Jill just look at me.

'What? They're . . . oh, never mind,' I say, driving up the winding road that leads up to my parents' house.

'This is beautiful,' Lisa says.

'I'm going to throw up,' Jill says, rolling down her window.

'We're almost there,' I say, smiling over at Jill.

'Okay, Castle Rock is . . . right . . . right there. Do you see it? Right there on the left?' I say, pointing to a tiny street most people drive right by on their way to Mount Tamalpais. Lisa nods and Jill just moans a little. I put on my indicator and make the left down my street. I park in the driveway right behind my mom and dad's cars and turn the engine off.

I continue. 'You guys ready?'

'We were born ready!' Jill says.

'This is going to be a long coupla days,' Lisa says with a yawn, gathering her stuff up in the backseat.

Knockknockknockknock.

'*Frannie?!*'

'Holy shit!' Lisa and Jill are terrified.

Oh. My. God.

My mom, in all her glory, excitedly waving just outside my window. By the time I reach to unclip my seat belt, Jill is out of the car as Lisa is just closing her door.

'Sweetie!' my mom says, pulling me in for a tight hug. Her smell, her . . . everything. It's good to be home. For a lot of reasons. I . . . need this. I breathe her in and just let myself be swept away to the land where moms are magic and they make everything better with a glass of milk and an apple.

Mom pulls back from the hug and focuses on Jill and Lisa. 'Now, who's this, sweetheart?'

'Mom, this is Jill Fleming and Lisa Campanari. Lisa and Jill, this is my mom, Polly Reid.' Lisa and Jill extend their hands and excitedly greet my mom. The drive up was fine, Mrs Reid. No, we don't need to use the bathroom, Mrs Reid. We'd love a little nosh, Mrs Reid.

'Well, aren't you something?' Mom asks, looking from Jill and Lisa to me and back to Jill and Lisa.

'Mom,' I say, hoping I can move things along.

I hear the creaking of the stairs leading up to the house. Big, heavy footfalls descending the staircase. One by one by one.

'Oh, Hank!' Mom says.

'I see the girls, Polly. Frannie, sweetheart, why don't you introduce us?' Dad gives me a quick hug and kiss on the cheek before introductions.

'Dad, this is Jill Fleming and Lisa Campanari. Jill and Lisa, this is my dad.'

'Hank Reid,' Dad says, extending his hand to Jill and Lisa.

Hands are shaken. The drive was good, Mr Reid. No, we didn't have trouble with the roads, Mr Reid. The weather held up great, thank you, Mr Reid.

'Why don't you come on up then?' Dad finally says. Lisa and Jill scamper up the steps to my house, leaving my mom and me alone.

'How are you doing, sweetheart?' Mom asks, lacing her arm through mine. All you can see from my parents' house is trees upon trees upon trees. Mount Tamalpais, with its verdant, green landscape, was the backdrop to my childhood. There's nothing like it in the world. This view is exactly the elixir I needed.

'I'm doing better now. Happy to be home,' I say, following Dad, Jill and Lisa across the deck, through the large glass front door and into the house. I can see Jill craning her neck to get a long look at the view. It is neck-craning worthy. Mom closes the door behind us and the classical music that was a constant soundtrack to my life wafts through the house. As it always has. I breathe it all in and my shoulders lower, my heartbeat slows and a smile spreads across my face. For a millisecond. And then what sounds like a herd of the world's tiniest dogs bounds into the living room.

'Winston! FDR!' Mom says, as if this would do anything. Then they're all in a ball, rolling around the living-room floor in a tangle.

'Jill? Lisa? Before we sit down to dinner let me show you to your rooms. It's the Jungle Room for you, bride-to-be!' Mom says, guiding Lisa back into the main house. In the distance I hear her offer the Floral Suite to the mom-to-be.

'So, when does this memorial service start?' Dad asks, sitting down on the couch.

'Tomorrow. Ten A.M. And it's not a memorial service, it's a *celebration,*' I say, my voice dripping with sarcasm.

'A celebration? Of what?'

'That's what was on the announcement.'

'Hippies.'

'I don't think they're hippies, Dad.'

'Well, they're something.'

'I think they're a couple of people who are doing the best they can with a really shitty situation.'

'Watch your language around your mother.'

'She's not here.' Dad motions for me to look behind me.

'Lisa's all set up in the Jungle Room and Jill's perfectly settled in the Floral Suite,' Mom says, walking into the kitchen.

'Take me to your dinner,' Dad says in that robot voice he thinks sounds like a 1950s-era alien saying, 'Take me to your leader.' He's been doing the voice for years. 'Take me to your teacher' at Back-to-School Nights. 'Take me to your bleeder' when a little girl in the neighborhood fell off her bicycle and skinned her knee. And his favorite and mine, 'Take me to your weeder' when Mom first introduced him to the poor guy she'd hired to tend the garden.

'It's almost time, Hank,' Mom says, shooing him off with a quick pat to the bum. She slides her hands into a set of oven mitts fashioned after a pair of roosters and opens the oven door, pulling a cherry pie from its depths. The perfume of pure, unadulterated Americana wafts throughout the entire house. The intricately latticed pastry on top gives way to little bubbling red volcanoes of napalm cherries. Jill and Lisa emerge from their quarters, perking up immediately. Mom sets the pie on the counter. She whips off the rooster oven mitts and quickly checks under the tinfoil of the resting roast beef. Halved roasting potatoes are still whistling with doneness in the roasting pan's bottom. I can see Lisa and Jill trying to see . . . smell . . . get closer. Mom walks over to the counter with a head of iceberg lettuce. Cuts it into fourths and sets it on the dining-room table with homemade thousand island dressing.

We are in awe. Mouths open. Watering.

'Can you get the popovers, sweetheart?' Mom asks me, pulling out the place mats, dishes and cutlery. She walks back over into the kitchen, takes the potatoes out of the roasting pan and puts them onto a large Depression Glass platter. I grab the gingham-lined basket filled with homemade popovers and wind through the now bustling kitchen.

Mom continues. 'Jill, sweetheart? Can you finish setting the table?' Jill looks from me to my mom. I motion that she should probably get on that. Lisa smiles.

'Yes, Mrs Reid.' Jill snaps out of her haze and begins to set the table, moving around the chairs with place mats, plates and an unabashed idolatry of the real deal. My mother is everything Jill fancies herself to be. Wants to be.

After carving the roast beef and placing it on a platter, Dad brings it over to the table. He sets it in the center and awaits further instructions.

'You can sit, Hank,' Mom says, bringing the potatoes over to the table. He waits. Mom finally sits. Dad holds her chair for her and then he sits, as well.

'Lisa? Please,' Mom says, motioning for her to sit. I set the popovers on the table and tuck myself in, and Lisa and Jill sit down across from me.

'What a treat this is,' Mom says, flipping her napkin into her lap.

'Mrs Reid, this meal is . . . I don't think I've eaten this well since . . . well, since the last time I saw my mom,' Jill says, her voice cracking just a bit. Looking at this spread, I can't help but think of Sam. He would have loved this meal. Whether he believes he deserves it is a whole other conversation apparently.

'Oh, well . . . it's my pleasure, sweetheart,' Mom says, grabbing her hand with a tight squeeze. I see Jill fight back emotion as she settles her napkin in her lap. She looks at me with an apologetic shrug. I smile. And smile . . . until later that night when I realize that my mom has set out a pair of pajamas that she bought for me at a local boutique. Thought they'd be perfect for me. As I stand at my bathroom sink and gaze at myself in head-to-toe garden gnomes I wish I could crawl in a hole. But I can't. I have to walk down the hallway that chronicles my questionable fashion sense through the ages, walk past the Jungle Room and Floral Suite and into my teenage bedroom with its twin bed, *Tiger Beat* magazines and giant poster of Parker Stevenson.

I can only shake my head.

'Are those garden gnomes?' Lisa asks, coming up behind me in the tiny bathroom with her bag of toiletries.

'Don't say a word,' I say, taking out my contact lenses and putting on my glasses. All I need is my dental night guard and I'd better lock my door!

'Oh, I won't,' Lisa says, starting to brush her teeth.

'Are those garden gnomes?' Jill asks, walking into the now crowded bathroom.

'Don't say a word,' I say. Lisa spits.

'I haven't eaten like that in years. I'm just going to own this thing, you know? Gain a thousand pounds, the whole nine,' Jill says, pulling up her shirt to expose her still-flat belly.

'You go, girl,' Lisa says.

'I'm going to buy a muumuu for your wedding, Lis. In your colors, of course,' Jill says, looking at herself from the side. From the front. From the side.

'And what might my colors be?'

'Harvest colors. Persimmon, chocolate brown . . . you know,' Jill says, finally tearing her gaze away from the mirror.

'Say good night to Polly before you turn in, girls,' Dad says.

'Yes, Mr Reid.'

'Frannie? You do the same.'

'Okay, Dad,' I say, slinking behind Jill and Lisa to Mom and Dad's bedroom.

'Good night, Mrs Reid,' we all say in unison.

'Good night, girls,' my parents say.

No nightmares. No buses, no dusty campsites. Just the deepest sleep I've had in weeks. I think about Sam and what he's dealing with right now. I hope . . . I hope I see him again. I think about Clara and Emma's paintings. I can't wait to see the one she's chosen to donate. I know it's going to be spectacular.

And then I think of Emma. Beautiful Emma. A woman I barely knew but knew best of all. It's time to say goodbye. And thank you.

Breakfast and coffee is on the deck overlooking Sausalito, Tiburon, the San Francisco Bay and San Francisco in the distance. Jill questions my mom about various items in our home and Lisa talks sports with my dad. However blissful the morning is, we all slowly begin to come down to earth as ten A.M. looms. Jill walks out of the Jungle Room in a navy blue shirtdress cinched at the waist. Lisa is wearing a black pencil skirt, a navy blue silk shirt and a black cardigan. I join them on the deck in my pressed black sheath and beaded forest-green sweater.

As we drive to the Marin County Country Club, we are quiet. My hand rests on the gearshift. Lisa looks out the passenger-side window, her hair blowing in the wind. Jill is biting her nails. Gnawing and chewing as we go. There's nothing to say. It's all been said. Now it's just about showing up and paying our last respects.

We pull up to what looks like a large, traditional mansion set up on a hill. Valets rush around in red vests, taking keys, handing out parking slips and speeding off to places unknown.

'I've never been to a memorial service with a valet,' Lisa says, waiting in line.

'This is a country club. I've actually never been to anything here. Heard about it though,' I say, watching the lines of mourners hike up the steep hill to the country club's main house.

I step out of the car, handing the keys to the valet and receiving a ticket in return. Jill and Lisa step out of the car. Not a word. We join the rest of the mourners in the migration up to the main house.

This place is big. Beyond big. If I were to blur my vision for a moment I could mistake it for the White House. The columns, the white official-looking exterior, the sweeping driveway. So out of place in this woodsy, casual setting. As we get closer, no one makes eye contact with anyone else. What do you say? Emma didn't die of old age or a terrible disease or even in a car accident. Emma Dunham was murdered. By her husband. Whom everyone here knew. None of us know how to unpack that.

The crowd at today's 'celebration' offers no surprises. All white, all moneyed and all completely at a loss for words. We climb the steps up to the vast porch and finally into the club itself. I look up and take in the coffered ceilings, the sweeping staircases with marble floors . . . the sheer expanse of just this first room. I feel like I'm on some museum tour and in line to see Michelangelo's David.

A quartet plays tasteful chamber music in the corner as tuxedoed staff with trays filled with appetizers wend and snake their way through the mournful crowd. Flower arrangements are abundant, set atop any available surface, the smell of stargazer lilies thick in the air. I begin to search the crowd for Clara.

'Hey there.' From behind me. I turn. As do Jill and Lisa.

Ryan.

'What . . . what are you doing here?' I ask as he leans in for a hug. Jill and Lisa are quiet. Seething, yet quiet.

'I've come to pay my last respects,' Ryan says.

'You didn't even know Emma,' I say, feeling protective of her.

'I knew her as well as you did.'

'I'm not going to . . . you have every right to be here. Godspeed,' I say, lifting my hand in a wave.

'Frannie, I—'

I stop. Wait.

'Can we have a second?' Ryan says to Jill and Lisa.

Jill leans in close and whispers so just Ryan can hear her, 'I hear that's *all* you need.' A quick wink. Ryan clears his throat as Jill and Lisa make their way over to the bar.

It's just Ryan and me. We move into a more private corner. I'm already annoyed.

'What do you want?' I ask, scanning the room again

for Clara. I don't see her, but I do see a large painting swathed in white silk. That must be Emma's. Clara is here.

'I thought we could be there for each other. You know? To get through this?'

'I've already slogged through quite enough without you, but thanks anyway.'

'I'm here for you now, Frannie.'

'What's happening here? Do you want to get back together with me? Is that what's happening here? At a funeral . . . I'm sorry, a memorial celebration?'

'What?'

'What exactly do you want?' I remember what Pamela said about not going back if I didn't want to. And I don't want to. It's up to me to make sure I never do. Going back means going back with Ryan. This can't happen. I won't let it.

'I want to be there for you.'

'What does that mean? What does "being there for me" look like for you?'

'You know . . .'

'No, I don't. I know that I thought being in a committed relationship meant that you didn't sleep with other girls, but apparently our definitions were different.'

'I want to make this work.'

'What does that mean?'

'Why are you so caught up on what things mean?'

'Because I don't know what you're talking about. Like, what you're actually saying. Do you even know anymore? "Be there for you." "Make this work." These words are meaningless, Ryan.'

'It took a lot for me to come up here.'

'What does that mean? "Took a lot"? How so?'

'I took a chance.'

'There's no chance. You knew I'd be here. We know each other. Of course I'm going to talk to you.'

'Why are you doing this?!' Ryan's voice is sharp and angry. It cuts through the room. Jill and Lisa look over from the bar. I wave them off.

'Doing what? *Be. Specific.*'

'Twisting my words around. This.'

'I still don't know what you're talking about.'

'Nothing has changed. Still so intense.'

'No, Ryan. I'm clear. I say what I mean and mean what I say. So, when I tell you that we're through, reeeeeeally through, you'd better listen.'

'It took a lot for me to come up here,' Ryan says again, turning to leave.

'*I still don't know what that means.*' He doesn't turn back around, but I can see from here that the curl in his lip is disdainful yet snubbed and insecure. God, that felt good. After years of filling in all the holes of his verbal ambiguities, all it took was pushing him to be clear about what he actually meant that finally shooed him away. The terrifying prospect of specificity ran Ryan off.

'Good riddance,' Lisa says, handing me a sparkling water.

'What was he thinking?' I say, taking a long sip.

'That he could swoop in as you grieved,' Jill says.

'That felt good,' I say.

'For all of us,' Jill says.

'I don't care if Sam ever comes back, I'm never going back with Ryan,' I say, turning around once again and searching the crowd.

Lisa and Jill just smile.

'What?'

'Our girl's all grown up,' Jill says, wrapping her arm around Lisa.

'I have to go to the ladies',' I say.

'Okay, we'll be right here,' Lisa says.

'You'll be right here?'

'Yep,' Jill says, nodding.

I walk through the crowd of people – no one makes eye contact with me – and wait behind a trio of women for the bathroom. They're speaking in hushed tones. No one can believe it, they say. She was such a pretty girl, they say. He seemed like such a nice man, they say. A woman in a tasteful black Chanel suit steps out of the bathroom. The trio of women immediately goes to her, surrounds her and steadies her.

'Jane, honey? Do you need anything?' one of the women says. It's her. The woman from the graduation picture in Emma's bathroom. Jane Stanforth. Emma's mother. She looks exactly like Emma, just a few decades older. Her blond hair is curled just at her shoulders; her high cheekbones and bright blue eyes are effortlessly aristocratic. Her smooth forehead, no longer capable of furrowing, is cast down; she doesn't want to make eye contact with anyone.

'Please, let me get you something,' Jane Stanforth finally says, holding out an extended hand to one of the women.

'Jane?!' the women say in unison.

'It helps to be busy. Let me get you something,' Jane Stanforth says, again now using one of the women to stabilize her. To hold her up.

'Mrs Stanforth?' I ask, stepping forward. The trio of women take my measure, are unimpressed and are just about to tell me to leave Mrs Stanforth alone, when . . .

'Yes, dear,' Jane Stanforth says, her pool-like blue eyes falling on me.

'I worked with Emma,' I say, each word a triumph.

'Oh . . .' Jane Stanforth says, her head bowing.

'At Markham . . .' I say, trailing off. Looking at her. Hoping that she understands the significance.

'At *Markham,*' Jane Stanforth repeats, looking directly at me. Through me.

'Emma was a remarkable head of school. Truly a master,' I say, the emotion bubbling up at the truth to these words.

'You . . . you were there,' Jane Stanforth says, reaching out to me. The trio of women crowd around us.

'Yes, ma'am,' I say gently.

'You were *there,*' Jane Stanforth says again.

I nod. Yes. Yes, I was there.

'You . . .' Jane Stanforth can't finish her sentence. She doesn't want to know, but I can see her trying to read me. Trying to pull answers from just under my words, my skin, behind my eyes. It's all there. The nightmares. The horror movie slide show. The blood. *Crack. Crack. Crack. Crack.* She can see it in my eyes.

'I'm so sorry,' I say, looking away.

'What's your name?' Jane Stanforth asks. The trio of women stand sentry. I can see Jill and Lisa out of the corner of my eye. They're watching. Now they're setting their glasses of water down and walking toward me. Quickly.

'Frances Reid, ma'am,' I say. Lisa and Jill are now standing in the archway of the hall. Watching, craning to see what's going on. Another step forward.

'Frances Reid,' Jane Stanforth repeats in a daze.

'Yes, ma'am,' I say.

'You knew my daughter,' she says, wobbly on her feet.

'I did,' I say.

'You knew my daughter,' she says again.

'Yes, ma'am. She was one of the most admirable women I've ever known,' I say, my throat closing. Was.

'Jane?' A small man in a perfectly tailored suit strides over to our little group. His face is . . . unruffled. *Blank*. His skin is pale and transparent. His long, white fingers curl around the stem of a wineglass. My stomach drops and I feel instantly sick. I look from him to Jill and Lisa. It's as if my nightmares are real. Again. They're . . . it's happening again. It's happening again. I panic. I can't breathe. My eyes are darting wildly, my legs are unsteady and I can't—

'Nigel, honey, this is Frances Reid, she—'

'Jane, I need you to ask someone to check in the cellar for some more of those Spanish reds. We're out,' Nigel Stanforth says, his eyes bored and inconvenienced. I purse my lips together as tears pool behind my eyes. The trio of women have disappeared.

'Mr and Mrs Stanforth, I'm so sorry for your loss,' Lisa says, extending one hand to Nigel and pulling me in close with the other. Nigel languidly extends his hand to Lisa, thanking her for coming today. Jane is wobbly and can't stop staring at me. Her eyes are glassy and unfocused.

'She knew our girl, Nigel,' Jane Stanforth says, looking at me.

'Everyone here knew Emma, that's how memorial services work, Jane,' Nigel says.

'We have to go,' I say suddenly, blinking back the tears and trying to steady my breathing. I have a primal need to get out of here. A gut feeling. This place is bad. Nothing good ever happened here. I gulp back the tears as Lisa extends her hand once again to Nigel and then to Jane Stanforth, trying to take the focus off me. I'm in a daze as we head toward the front door.

How stupid. I thought it was my conversation about Harry Sprague that changed things. As we walk back out into the main room I know with everything in my being that . . . that Emma never had a chance. She just never had a chance.

'He was Jamie. I mean, he *was* Jamie,' I say, my voice a whisper.

'I know,' Jill says, picking up three water glasses from a passing tray.

'She married her father,' I say.

'I know,' Jill says, her jaw tight.

'And her mom . . . I mean . . .' I say.

'I know,' Jill says, her voice elsewhere.

We are quiet.

'How many people do you think knew?' I ask.

'About what?'

'About it all! The parents, Emma. Jamie! I mean,

everyone knew and just signed off on it. Why? Because they're wealthy and they have a big house?'

'People know how to hide things, Frannie. We didn't know about Emma and Jamie until . . . well, until it was too late,' Lisa says.

I can't stop shaking my head.

'Frannie?' I look up to see Clara. I take a deep breath.

'Hey,' I say, giving her a big hug. I continue once we've broken apart. 'Oh, I'm sorry. Clara Grey, this is Jill Fleming and Lisa Campanari. We all work – *worked* with Emma.' Jill and Lisa offer Clara condolences and respect. Clara nods and thanks them. Bruce comes up behind Clara with two glasses of wine.

'Oh, hey, babe. Bruce, you remember Frannie. And these are her friends . . . I'm sorry . . . I've already forgotten your names. I'm . . . this is all a bit much for me. I'm so sorry,' Clara stammers, taking a glass of wine from Bruce.

'Bruce Grey,' he says, extending his hand to Jill and Lisa as they introduce themselves. He pulls Clara in close, soothing her. Easing her.

'I see the painting is all ready to go,' I say.

'Oh, yes. It's ready to go,' Clara says, eyeing the swathed gilt frame that hangs over today's proceedings. Bruce rubs her back.

Minutes pass. We are quiet. Clara and Bruce share a few glances as Jane and Nigel Stanforth make their rounds. The resemblance to Jamie is uncanny. I can't wrap my head around it.

'So, you were the black sheep because—'

'I didn't play by the Stanforth rules. So many rules,' Clara says. I flick a quick glance to Jill. She looks away.

'Have you talked to your parents?' Jill asks.

'No. I'm sure they'll send over one of their cronies when it's time for the unveiling,' Clara says.

'They haven't seen it?' Lisa asks.

'Not yet,' Clara says, her eyes flicking from the painting to her parents. And just like clockwork a fragile-looking doyenne approaches our little circle by the bar.

'Clara, dear. It's time,' she says with nary a glance our way.

'I'll be right here,' Bruce says, giving Clara a final squeeze.

'I can't . . . I'm—' Clara looks like she's going to faint.

'For Emma,' Bruce says. His eyes bore into her. 'For Emma, baby.'

Clara nods. Curt. Once.

Clara walks toward the swathed painting and stands to the side of a podium that's surrounded with more flowers than I've ever seen. The woman who fetched Clara begins speaking.

'Hello. Hello.' The crowd quiets down as we all turn to face the woman; the painting hangs just above. 'We've all gathered today to celebrate the life of our beautiful girl Emma Jane Stanforth. Emma was a beloved daughter to Nigel and Jane—' Emma's mom stifles a sob as Nigel holds her close. 'A treasured aunt and a patient sister.' Clara shakes her head. *Patient*. The woman continues. 'On top of being the first female head of school at the prestigious Markham School in Pasadena, California, Emma was a world-class painter. We all mourn a life that could have been. Clara?'

The woman steps to the side, placing her hand on a tassel that's connected to a silken rope, which in turn is connected to the white swath of silky fabric covering Emma's painting just above. The woman motions for Clara to approach the podium. Clara's face drains of color. She doesn't look at the painting as she walks up to the podium. The microphone thumps and creaks as Clara fidgets. Bruce shifts his weight; his entire body is tense. I look from Jill to Lisa. We're all a wreck. Confused and scared. Emotional and ready to go home to weddings and babies and get as far away from this lifeless Stanforth tractor beam as possible.

As I watch Nigel Stanforth grimace and sneer at his only living daughter while his wife sobs and sways with inconsolable grief, I just keep thinking, There's more good than bad, there's more good than bad.

'Knowing Emma was a privilege. Being Emma's sister was a blessing. Don't take the people you love for granted. Don't ever be scared to love someone with your whole heart. Be transparent. This is Emma's last painting. It's called *Daddy's Little Girl.*' Clara's voice is barely a whisper. She turns around and nods to the woman. The woman pulls the tassel and brings down the swath of white silky fabric like a cloud.

The entire room gasps.

As Clara walks away from the podium, tears streaming down her face, she takes Bruce's hand, gives me a quick nod and exits the country club, never to return; the rest of us take in Emma's last gasp.

Just as her other paintings, this one is in the Grand Style, like a portrait you'd find in a noble castle. But with a twist.

In the forefront of the portrait is a little girl in a brocade dress with blond ringlet curls hiding behind a luxurious chaise. Her face is unmistakably Emma's. There's a bruise on her tiny forearm in the shape of a hand. Clutching. Tightening. Grabbing. The little girl is surrounded by fashionable dolls, obvious wealth and everything a little girl could possibly want, yet she looks terrified. For, in the not-so-blurry background, a man strides past a powerless and ineffective mother toward the little girl. She can feel him coming; we can see it in her eyes. The man: dark hair, beakish nose, slight frame, wielding a belt. Nigel Stanforth.

Daddy's Little Girl.

The crowd erupts. It's a fake! Clara – where's Clara?! – brought that up here to get back at her parents! This is a travesty! Jane Stanforth crumples into a nearby chair as Nigel Stanforth barks orders to take it down! Take it down! *Take. It. Down!*

But some people in attendance just stare at the painting as Jill, Lisa and I do. Taking it in. Listening to Emma's last painting as if Emma herself were speaking. We look from it to Nigel and then back at the portrait. Shaking our heads, lamenting – 'What a waste' and 'That poor girl.' And then we leave. One by one.

Even those who remain will start the whispers anyway: they always suspected, they'll say with a sneer as they do yoga in the morning. They knew something was wrong with that family, they tell their friends over fair-trade coffee. They just had a bad feeling about that father, they whisper on the links.

But for Emma?

She finally found her voice after all.

19

They're Playing Our Song

'Look, I warned you about using too much glitter last night. You knew your bridesmaid dress was strapless, now just make it work for you,' Jill says, slamming the door on one of Lisa's sisters as she comes out of the bathroom on the morning of Lisa's wedding one month later. The entire wedding party is huddled in Jill's master bedroom and now there's apparently a glitter emergency.

'Is she all right?' I ask, braiding one of the flower girls' hair.

'She'll be fine. She went nuts with the glitter last night at the strip club. What did she think was going to happen?' Jill says, pulling up the top of her dress. 'I think my boobs are getting bigger.' I hurry and finish the braiding, pat the little flower girl on the bum and send her along on her way. For her own good. Jill continues. 'Frannie, can you grab us some water?' Jill is knee-deep in Campanari sisters, not to mention Cleopatra Campanari is afoot. In a turban.

'Sure,' I say, happy to get out of that little room. I smooth my orange strapless dress down, hoping the wrinkles will work themselves out. The little chocolate-brown belt is tightening around my waist. This is definitely one of those standing-up dresses.

I walk out into Jill's house. It's alive with bustling waiters, florists darting here and there with this centerpiece and that. As I weave through the lively pre-wedding scene, I can't help but marvel at how we got here. It seems like yesterday that I was sitting in that library at back-to-school orientation. How small my life seemed then. How little I wanted for myself. How little I expected of myself and those who claimed to love me. I walk into Jill's kitchen and pull as many bottles of water from the fridge as I can carry – Lisa's got a lot of thirsty sisters. As I close the fridge, I run my fingers over the picture of Jill's ultrasound proudly displayed front and center. I make my way back to the master bedroom, my arms freezing as they cradle all the waters. Clara e-mails me pictures of the girls with John Henry now and again. Not only is he usually in some ridiculous outfit, but more often than not he's seated at an elaborate tea party. But I find myself smiling, not because of the outfits and the tea parties, but because Emma would love that he's with Clara now. Would love that he's being spoiled and petted beyond anything that is reasonable. Emma would love that her beautiful boy found his true home.

'Here you go,' I say, closing the door behind me. I distribute the bottled waters among the Campanari women.

'For such a little house, Jill, you certainly have decorated with taste and class,' Cleopatra says with a sigh from her completely posed languid position on Jill's bed.

'Thank you, Mrs Campanari,' Jill says, gritting her teeth.

As the hours pass and I inhale more Aqua Net than is

healthy for one human being, I begin to hear the guests arrive.

'Come on out, my love,' Cleopatra says to the chronically closed bathroom door. None of us have seen Lisa in her dress. Except Jill. Let's not get crazy.

'I look stupid, Ma,' Lisa yells from the other side of the door.

'You look beautiful,' Jill says.

'When are you due, sweetheart?' Cleopatra asks Jill.

'The summer,' Jill answers with an ear to the bathroom door.

'You're getting big,' Cleopatra says, eyeing Jill's still-flat stomach.

'Happy chicken, happy egg,' Jill says, rubbing her belly.

'I'm not coming out!' Lisa yells from behind the closed door.

'I will come in there after you, young lady. I swear to god. I have a key. I'll bust this door down, I don't care.' Jill is opening and closing drawers looking for a key. 'I know how—'

Lisa opens the bathroom door.

She is breathtaking. Her dark hair is swept up in front and falls in an effortless tangle around her shoulders. Her veil drapes down her back, falling and floating as she moves. Her dress is traditional. Way more traditional than I ever would've guessed. It hugs her curves perfectly.

'Oh, Lisa,' I say.

'What do you think?' Lisa asks, her face hopeful.

'You look stunning,' I say, reaching out to her.

'I look like a meringue.'

'You look like a bride!' Cleopatra rises from her languid resting position and floats across the bedroom floor to praise her daughter. 'You look just like me on my wedding day!' High praise indeed.

'You're beautiful,' Jill says, beaming.

'Thank you. For all this,' Lisa says, hugging Jill.

'I loved every minute of it,' Jill whispers in her ear.

'We ready to do this thing?' Lisa asks, raising her bouquet of harvest-colored flowers aloft. Jill shrugs and gives a small eye roll, and we're being ferried out into the living room. Lined up, paired off with our male counterparts.

'Grady said Sam couldn't be here. His father didn't make it,' Lisa says, gripping my hand.

'I figured,' I say, trying to smile.

'I'm sorry, honey,' Lisa says as Jill straightens her train. Straightens her train. Straightens her train.

'I really thought he'd come,' I say, unable to look at her.

'We all did,' Lisa says, giving me a quick squeeze before heeding Jill's final warning.

'Knock 'em dead,' I say. One of Grady's flag football buddies extends his elbow and I lace my arm through his. He smiles. We're next.

Flag Football and I make our way down the aisle. I finally see Grady. His entire right side is trussed up in slings and casts. Jill has put some kind of black fabric over as much of it as she could. He gives me a quick wink, but his gaze quickly jumps to just behind me. As I take my place with the other bridesmaids, Lisa begins her walk down the aisle on the arm of her father. I watch Grady.

He just watches her. With everything he's got. His mouth is tight as he holds back all the emotion that brought us here today. What we survived. What he survived. He resituates his arm and I see him wince. But nothing, not even the pain of his shoulder, can take his eyes from Lisa. Her eyes are on Grady. Only. She's shaking her head as if to say she doesn't want to cry. She's not going to cry. As she gets closer, I see tears already rolling down her cheeks. Grady pulls a handkerchief from his pocket and hands it to her.

'Thank you, baby,' Lisa says, wiping her tears.

Grady and Lisa turn to face one another, hands tightly held.

'Ladies and gentlemen, we are gathered here today . . .'

'Another glass of champagne, please,' I say to the bartender as the reception begins less than an hour later. He hands the glass to me and I thank him. The music kicks in and people gather on the dance floor. I scan the room and find Grady and Lisa, nuzzling and kissing at the head table. They haven't been apart from each other since Grady got out of the hospital. I can't help but smile. There is more good than bad. Life and love win if you let them. If you believe in them.

'Flag Football asked about you,' Jill says, sidling up to me.

'Nice guy,' I say, forgetting my champagne as Jill leads me away from the bar.

'But he's not Sam,' Jill says, finishing my thought.

'No, he's not,' I say.

'I've got the fever, Frannie. The wedding planning fever. All this could be yours,' Jill says, motioning around to the beautiful wedding that is all her doing. Cleopatra Campanari is holding court on the dance floor. Her turban is a bit askew and she's telling everyone, 'I'm shaking my groove thing . . . shaking my groove thing!'

'It's truly beautiful,' I say as we walk over to our table and finally sit down.

'I'm totally looking into the turban thing,' Jill says, taking a sip of her water.

'May I?' Martin extends his hand to Jill. She takes it.

'You've already knocked me up,' Jill says, giving me a quick wink.

'That's right I did,' Martin says, pulling her up.

'Hot,' Jill yelps as he leads her to the dance floor.

I stand and head back over to the bar in search of my lost champagne.

'One champagne please,' I say. The bartender pops open a new bottle. I watch the general splendor as he pours.

'Frannie?' I turn my head.

Sam.

I just . . . crumble. Tears stream down my face. I can't stop the wave of emotion that erupts from so deep.

'I-I knew you'd come,' I stammer.

'Frannie, I'm so sorry,' Sam says, reaching out to me. I take his hand, gripping him, tears rolling down my cheeks. 'I shouldn't have left that morning. I didn't want to feel and that night . . . you were right. I didn't know that. I . . . I went home and watched someone stare down those last few moments of life the same way he lived it: bitter, closed off and determined not to let anyone love him. Not even a little bit. I don't want to live like that. I know I might not be him, but I am of him. And I can live with that. But I can't live without you. I want to be that man who's worthy of you. I want to be the man you see.' Sam steps closer. His head tilts as the tears continue to stream down my cheeks. I smile. And reach up to him just as he licks his bottom lip.

'I love you, too,' I say, just before he kisses me. I pull him close . . . close . . . closer.

The opening chords of 'SexyBack' by Justin Timberlake thump and ripple through Jill's backyard. The entire wedding erupts in hoots and hollers as everyone races to the dance floor. I can feel Sam smiling. He pulls away just a few millimeters.

'They're playing our song.'

I close my eyes. And smile.

'The fates have spoken,' he says. Sam extends his hand to me. 'Shall we?' He eyes the dance floor.

'You've got to be kidding me,' I say, taking his hand. Sam leads me out onto the dance floor, my stomach flipping and my heart in my throat. Jill sees me and then Sam. A cartoonish double take ensues. Sam just smiles.

As I ready for a fast-dancing fiasco instead of a heartfelt reunion, it seems Sam has other plans. He pulls me in tight, swaying slow as everyone else bounces and hops around us. I tuck in close, laying my head on his chest, listening to his heartbeat and wrapping my arms as tightly around him as I can. Sam looks down at me.

'You okay?' Sam asks.

'Gonna be,' I say.

Read on for extra material from Liza Palmer . . .

Liza Palmer's Breakup Mix for Frannie Reid

Frannie's made enough mixes. It's my turn to ferry Frannie away from the Ryan Ferrells of this world and into the arms of more men like Sam Earley.

A well-crafted breakup mix should accomplish three things:

1. It should make the listener feel she is not alone in her grief. Other women have felt and survived exactly what she's going through.

2. While there should be a few songs that tap into The Sad, in the end the mix should be about empowerment. You really are better off without him and it was settling and, yes, someday you're going to feel okay again.

3. This mix will serve as an alternative from just going back and forth between "The Rose" by Bette Midler and "Liar" by Henry Rollins. (Although both songs are spectacular, they should be used in moderation during these fragile times.)

THE FRANNIE REID BREAKUP MIX

1. **"Last Year" —Akron/Family**
   A beautiful amuse-bouche to open things up. Simple, gorgeous and hopeful.

2. **"Reason Why" —Rachael Yamagata**
   Embracing The Sad, but cutting it with the truth with lyrics like, "It's not that I don't understand you, it's not that I don't want to be with you, but you only wanted me the way you wanted me."

3. **"Torch" —Alanis Morissette**
   This is where we remember what was good. Sink deep into The Sad. Ugly cry. Sob. Really admit how hard it is to get over someone you once loved with a mindset of: the only way out is through. (And maybe think about Ryan Reynolds a bit as that's who the song is actually about, hello.)

4. **"More Like Her" —Miranda Lambert**
   "You took a chance on a bruised and beaten heart and then realized you wanted what you had."

   This song is to all the Jesssssicas of this world.

5. **"Rolling in the Deep" —Adele**
   And we're done wallowing. This will be your anthem. Turn it up as loud as you can and sing along until your voice is hoarse.

6. **"Take a Bow" —Rihanna**
   Continuing on with anthems, this song is perfect for when one gets in touch with one's anger. Ahem. (The Glee *version is also acceptable . . .)*

7. **"Dear John" —Taylor Swift**
   That's right. TAYLOR. *EFFING. SWIFT. Breakups make us all feel fifteen again. And no one does anthems for fifteen-year-olds better than Taylor Swift. Ergo, we find ourselves here. Just let yourself sink into it, own your fifteen-ness and sing along.*

8. **"There there" —Radiohead**
   The driving rhythms of this song are what we're after—it fuels something: the crawl out maybe, the desire to return to living. And with lyrics like, "Just because you feel it doesn't mean it's there," it also lets us get in touch with why we allowed blurry lines in past relationships.

9. **"Orbiting" —The Weepies**
   Maybe we're better off alone; and as this song so beautifully says, maybe we were alone the whole time—despite being in a relationship.

10. **"Incomplete and Insecure" —The Avett Brothers**
This is our wake up call. "Will I ever know silence without mental violence . . ." Why is it so hard to be kind to ourselves? Let's live differently from now on . . .

11. **"This Year's Love" —David Gray**
Presented without comment. (Just listen . . .)

12. **"Near to You" —A Fine Frenzy**
A new love. A true and real love. And we're scared. "I'm battle-scarred, I am working oh so hard to get back to who I used to be . . . "

13. **"Be Here Now" —Ray LaMontagne**
His reply to "Near to You."

14. **"Day Too Soon" —Sia**
TIMING. IS. EVERYTHING. Listen to this song over and over.

15. **"The Means to Attain a Happy Life" —Henry Howard, Earl of Surrey**
In the TV series, The Tudors *(Season Four, Episode Four), Howard, played by David O'Hara, lets Charles Brandon, The Duke of Suffolk (played by Henry Cavill, ahem) read this poem aloud. Find it. Record it. And listen to it. (This poem is then read by David O'Hara later, but I won't tell you when or why so as not to spoil things.)*

Liza Palmer

Edwin Santiago

LIZA PALMER is the internationally bestselling author of *Conversations with the Fat Girl*. *Conversations with the Fat Girl* became an international bestseller its first week in publication, as well as hitting number one on the Fiction Heatseekers chart in the UK the week before the book debuted. *Conversations with the Fat Girl* has been optioned for a series by the producers of *Rome*, *Band of Brothers*, and *Generation Kill*.

Palmer's second novel was *Seeing Me Naked*, of which *Publishers Weekly* said: "Consider it haute chick lit; Palmer's prose is sharp, her characters are solid and her narrative is laced with moments of graceful sentiment."

Palmer's third novel, *A Field Guide to Burying Your Parents*, which *Entertainment Weekly* called a "*splendid novel*" and *Real Simple* said "has heart and humor", was released in January 2010.

Palmer currently lives in Los Angeles and is hard at work on her next novel as well as writing for the VH1 Classic show *Pop Up Video*. She now knows far too much about Fergie.

LIZA PALMER

Conversations with the Fat Girl

Taunted for being 'the fat girls' at school, Maggie and Olivia swore to be best friends forever. But now they're grown-up is their friendship big enough to survive?

Maggie's dreams remain unfulfilled. She works in a coffee shop, has never shifted the pounds, and harbours a painfully unrequited crush on her colleague. Worse still, she's agreed to be bridesmaid for the now size 6 (after surgery) Olivia, who has found her Mr Perfect as well as lots of new, more fashionable friends.

As emotions run high in the tension-filled lead-up to Olivia's wedding, both girls are forced to look squarely in the mirror and confront some harsh home-truths about themselves and each other . . .

LIZA PALMER

Seeing Me Naked

Her father is a cult novelist and living legend. Her mother is a fashionable socialite. And her brother is the rising star of the LA literary scene. It's no wonder Elisabeth Page feels intimidated.

It wouldn't be so bad if her own life wasn't frozen in time. Romantically, she's still involved with her childhood sweetheart – a journalist who she barely sees anymore, let alone trusts. And despite working for one of LA's hottest restaurants, her five-year plan to run her own patisserie has morphed into an eleven-year plan to nowhere.

But then she meets Daniel, who finally gives her a taste of how incredible her future really could be – if only she could drop everything and let him see her as she really is . . .

But can Daniel ever be more than just flavour of the month? Elisabeth is about to find out in this delicious story about love, insecurity, family and finding out who you really are.